D0448399

Mayhem in B-Flat

Mayhem in B-Flat

A HOMER EVANS MURDER MYSTERY

by Elliot Paul

DOVER PUBLICATIONS, INC.
New York

Published in Canada by General Publishing Company,
Ltd., 30 Lesmill Road, Don Mills, Toronto, Ontario.
Published in the United Kingdom by Constable and
Company, Ltd.

This Dover edition, first published in 1988, is an unabridged, unaltered republication of the work originally
published by Random House, New York, 1940.

Manufactured in the United States of America
Dover Publications, Inc.
31 East 2nd Street
Mineola, N.Y. 11501

Library of Congress Cataloging-in-Publication Data

Paul, Elliot, 1891–1958.
  Mayhem in B-flat.

  I. Title.
PS3531.A852M3 1988   813'.52   87-27566
  ISBN 0-486-25621-9 (pbk.)

To Saxe Commins

Dear Reader:

After many years, during which we have been a little stand-offish to one another, we seem to be getting together, according to recent statements received from my publisher, and it cheers me no end.

However, some of the reviewers have squawked because in The Mysterious Mickey Finn *and* Hugger-Mugger in the Louvre *there were so few references to sex. Consequently, in this volume,* Mayhem in B-Flat, *I have tried to fill that reasonable requirement. I cannot follow the excellent rule adopted by so many of my contemporaries, that is, to put nothing in my book of which my grandmother would not approve, for my maternal grandmother, the late Sarah Greenleaf Douset, was the most rugged member of my family and used to hide her well-thumbed Rabelais in green covers labeled "Hiawatha" so that none of us children would stumble on it inadvertently.*

The sex motif in Mayhem *reaches its climax in Chapter Nine, so if the readers who do not like sex wish to skip that chapter, it is O.K. with me.*

The next Homer Evans story, Fracas in the Foothills, *brings our group all the way from Paris to the badlands of Montana, where men love horses, and thus the reader who is weary of the European scene will be able to enjoy a good whiff of sage and whatever else there is lying around on the prairies.*

Elliot Paul

[The inclusion of this letter is for the sake of completeness and is not meant to guarantee that Dover will republish *Fracas in the Foothills*. As with previous volumes in this series, however, such republication may occur if there is sufficient demand for it. *The Mysterious Mickey Finn* and *Hugger-Mugger in the Louvre* are currently available as Dover reprints, nos. 24751-1 and 25185-3, respectively.]

Contents

Mayhem in B-Flat

I

Which Gets into the News Because a Dog Nearly Bites a Guarnerius

BECAUSE he was one of those rare souls who could visit Rouen without mooning over Joan of Arc, Homer Evans found that busy river port both colorful and alluring. It is true that he had dutifully signed his name in the guest book at the Restaurant des Deux Couronnes, that he had gazed at practically every stone in the famous Tour de Beurre, and had missed at least one train because of the inaccuracy of the historic old clock in the rue de l'Horloge. But what he liked best was sitting by the river on the *terrasse* of the Hotel d'Angleterre and watching the barges and freighters come and go.

Homer liked the Normans, who can live hard and still be gay, and who can drink and eat like the men of old without beefing about their arteries and inner organs. In fact, although Evans never mentioned it even to his intimates, he himself was aware that one of his ancestors, the Baron de Vans, known as Claude l'Original, had been William the Conqueror's boon and bottle companion and had lifted an important siege of the old walled town of Calvados by smuggling to the invaders a stoneboat loaded with applejack that had been doctored with powdered quartz from the ancient curbstones. It had not been the Baron's military ingenuity that had won him the Conqueror's highest favor, but the fact that Claude had retired to an inner room of the castle and brooded because it had been necessary to ruin the applejack, even for the purpose of destroying Protestant enemies.

So, as he sat in the spring sunshine, Homer had been thinking about Claude, his lusty forebear, and the fragrant slopes of Normandy, on which apples still grow. And as he mused and basked, he had been watching also the deft movements of a group of men loading heavy casks into a scow.

"Good men," Evans murmured. "The ancient cold blue eyes and square shoulders, the same thirst and energy . . . And a tougher world to buck, a continent grown weary, a system collapsing around their ears. But look at them! Still on the water front, still doing footwork around barrels that would crush them, if they hadn't retained their incredible alertness. I suppose half of them have blood the same as mine, more than half, if one can believe what was written of the old Baron . . ."

"What Baron?" asked Miriam, but Evans, in his preoccupation with the stevedores at work, had let it slip his mind that she was there beside him.

The season was early spring, so that the fruit trees in blossom and the chalklike deposits on the faces of distant cliffs brought into brilliant relief the stark chimneys, derrick masts and spars along the river banks before them. Gay-colored clothes fluttered from clotheslines strung along the barges, happy dogs rolled over in the sun, and all along the quais the freighters, large and small, some dingy, others freshly painted, were receiving or discharging their loads. One year had passed since the spectacular conclusion of the Louvre murder case,* those unforgettable few days when Miriam had been shaken with terror because she had maneuvered Homer into the case. That terrible suspense, and the reaction following its happy termination, had left no mark upon her brow, perhaps, and had not caused her to be less careful or successful in the choice of her clothes, but the searing experience had left a little buzzer in her mind that sounded off sharply whenever she had an impulse to interfere in Homer's placid life or to complicate his serene existence. She was about to repeat her innocent question, "What Baron?" but she thought better of it and simply was content to sit by the Seine, warmed by soft spring sunshine, and to wonder mildly why Homer, who seldom left Montparnasse, had suddenly been impelled to take her away from Paris to visit Normandy.

There is no telling what else might have entered her mind, if she had not, just at that moment, noticed a look of horror cross Homer's expressive face and seen him grip the arms of his chair until fibres of straw and cane were strained from their moorings. As her glance followed swiftly the direction of his, she made a grab where her holster should be, and was chagrined to find that she had left it, gun and all, in her room upstairs, beneath a pillow.

All Miriam observed as she gazed at the group of stevedores, was a huge iron-hooped cask up-ending as it wobbled down a chute, causing two of the men to leap

* *Hugger-Mugger in the Louvre,* Random House, January, 1940.

5

frantically out of its erratic course, one landing prone on a grimy deck, the other splashing into the Seine. Evans had risen, with relief on his face, and from somewhere in the hold of the scow appeared the head and shoulders, then the powerful body of a man who was strangely familiar.

"The Singe," gasped Miriam.

"I was hoping we should see him before we went back to Paris," Homer said, and calmly sat down again, reaching for his cool vermouth cassis.

"Don't tell me, Homer Evans, that you knew the Singe was aboard that old scow," she said, indignantly.

"Oh, no. Not at all . . . But first let's see what happens," Evans said. He indicated the deck of the scow with an easy gesture, and Miriam turned toward it again just in time to see a terrified man, with the Singe in hot pursuit, leap to a near-by barge, lunge in desperation at a swinging hook suspended by a cable from a derrick mast, and be drawn upward into space above the deep gaping hold of the freighter. The Singe, reaching vainly for the dangling man, gave a sharp signal to the engineer and the hook, with its clinging human appendage, stopped rising and began to twirl. The mast ceased swinging, the pulley ropes came to rest and pitiful shouts began to leak downward from the victim, who had thrown one leg over the huge derrick hook but could not, because of the grease on the cables, get astride.

"But why?" asked Miriam, trembling with apprehension. "Why won't he let the man go up or come down? He's sure to fall." For the Singe, after repeating some terse instructions to the derrick engineer who left his post, turned his back on his unfortunate quarry, washed his hands and arms in a near-by bucket, and started across the gangplank to the quai. There were several hundred men working in the neighborhood, and at least six policemen on duty within call. The *terrasses* of the Hotel d'Angleterre and the Café de Rouen next door contained dozens of clients at their ease. Still no one made a move to interfere. The man aloft bawled, pleaded and dangled, the derrick mast and boom remained motionless, the Singe crossed to the foot of the *terrasse* as if nothing had happened, the stevedores whose mishap had ushered in such an odd string of events went fearfully back to their work.

"You met Miss Leonard once in Paris, I believe," said Homer, rising. The Singe glanced up in surprise and smiled.

"I'm in working clothes," he said. "Do you mind if I go upstairs a moment to change? I'm glad to see you again."

"But . . . monsieur . . ." Miriam said, unable to restrain her dismay. "That chap you chased up the rope . . . Won't he fall?"

"That's up to him, mademoiselle," the Singe said. Evans, aware of Miriam's agitation, smiled in his most charming way.

"Perhaps you wouldn't mind if I suggested to the firemen that they spread a net below, to catch the chap when he falls," Evans said. "I brought Miss Leonard here from Paris to show her the town, and it would spoil her trip if there should be bloodshed. Of course, the fellow richly deserves whatever might happen. I saw what he did . . ."

"So did I," said the Singe, "and I got to protect my boys. But just as a favor to Miss Leonard, I'll put up no

7

kick if the firemen catch him, just so long as I never get sight of him around this river again."

"Not much chance of that," said Evans, smiling once more.

"Not any chance at all," agreed the Singe, and grinned.

Miriam sat nervously at the table, trying to keep her eyes away from the dangling man whose cries grew more feeble and abusive as he clung to the hook in mid-air. She sipped her drink, but it tasted flat, tried to comfort herself with the assurance that if Evans made no objection, the cruel and unusual punishment must be all right. A few drinkers left the various *terrasses* and stood in an uneasy group around the quai, demanding that someone do something. The derrick engineer and his fireman, however, were nowhere to be seen.

After having had a short chat with a policeman, who went off in search of a member of the fire department, Homer rejoined Miriam and, seeing how uneasy she was, suggested that they go inside and have their talk with the Singe in the lobby.

"I shall not move from here until that man gets down," she said, with unusual vehemence. The crowd by the riverside had reached larger proportions, and gradually work stopped along the water front. Stevedores and sailors began chatting in droves. Contractors and shippers moved uneasily, like hens. Waiters stood, napkin in hand, in front of the cafés. The Singe, with great unconcern, reappeared at the main entrance of the Hotel d'Angleterre. On his way to Evans' table, he noticed with a scowl of disapproval that large numbers of people were interesting themselves in his affairs and beckoned once to a stevedore who was lounging within range.

"Tell 'em I said to get back to work," said the Singe, and then he, too, observed that Miriam was on the verge of panic. No doubt the thought crossed his mind that this tender-hearted girl, who could not bear the thought of seeing Godo the Whack (for it was he on the hook) fall thirty or forty meters into a hold strewn with bilge-soaked paving blocks, was the selfsame young woman who had bumped off six of his gangsters, on various occasions, up river and down, without a quaver. "Sorry, miss," the Singe said. "If I'd known you were in Rouen on a pleasure trip, I'd have settled this matter in private and out of sight. I should have done that anyway, as a matter of fact. But I lost my temper . . ." The gang leader glanced at Evans for justification. "You saw what Godo did?" the Singe asked.

"Yes, I saw," Evans said.

The fact that neither Homer nor the Singe seemed inclined to enlighten her about Godo's misdemeanor exasperated Miriam still further. She was on the point of rushing into the hotel and shutting herself in her room, when the two-voiced horn of the fire truck echoed down the near-by rue Jeanne d'Arc. The crowd at the quai backed and filled to clear a passage for the firemen in bright brass helmets and red-striped trousers.

"*Alors*," said the fire chief, looking up at Godo and down into the hold. "Where's the derrick engineer? It would have been simpler merely to find him and have him let down the hook."

"No one seems to know where the engineer went," a bystander volunteered.

"But surely there are other engineers?" the chief persisted.

Miriam bit her lip to suppress a scream, for Godo, in trying to pull himself astride the hook, had slipped and narrowly saved himself.

The firemen, by that time, had lifted the net from the truck and were examining it thoughtfully. One of them measured it, then measured the hold. "The hold's too big," he said. "We can't stand on the four sides and hold the net. We'd all be carried downward by the force of the falling body. The momentum, *monsieur le chef*, increases in proportion to the velocity. This unfortunate man, who weighs at least seventy kilos, will fall sixteen feet during the first second, thirty-two the next, and so on."

"*Vos gueules*," shouted Godo, which is one of the strongest phrases of invective a Frenchman can shout.

"Respect yourself," said the chief, looking upward. "You should not have called my department, but an engineer. The hold is so wide that my men can't support the net from the sides."

"It's nearly time for our train," Evans said. Then he added, to the Singe: "Why not walk to the station with us? We'll send our baggage by the hotel truck. There's a boat train due at four fifty-five."

"I shall not leave this chair until Godo is safe," repeated Miriam, firmly.

"He's not likely to be safe again as long as he lives," the Singe said.

"At least, until he gets down from that frightful hook," said Miriam. "After that, I don't care what happens. I can't stand heights. Makes me dizzy to think of them."

"I'm slipping," yelled Godo. "Do something, you fat-heads. Take the net down into the hold, and catch me there."

"If your suggestion had been framed in a more courteous style, I might have considered it," the chief retorted. "I must remind you that I am in no way responsible for your safety, since this barge is not on fire."

"Set it on fire, then, you sap," said Godo. "Cripes! What service!"

Four firemen descended by ladder into the deep hold, the chief stationed himself on deck to give the signal. "I'm really sorry," the Singe repeated. "I didn't intend to make a public circus out of this affair. I was going to wring Godo's neck and let it go at that. He's been troublesome before, and I gave him fair warning."

"Can't be trusted," Evans said.

"It isn't easy getting first-class gangsters," said the Singe.

Not only Miriam, but hundreds of other onlookers screamed, gasped, and wound up with an "ah" that was almost prayerful when the chief signaled to the crowd that Godo had landed safely. Godo himself appeared on deck for a brief instant, then dived into the crowd and was not sighted again until he had reached the hill road leading to one of the suburbs up-river.

"Now perhaps," Miriam said severely, "you won't mind telling me what he did to deserve such treatment."

"He displaced a wedge with his foot, so that the heavy cask of applejack would leap the skids," Homer said. "I assume he had a grudge against one or both of the men whose lives would have been lost if they had not been so alert."

"Some row about a fiddle," said the Singe. "Godo

pinched a G string, the other guy called him, they had a fight. I never got it straight what the trouble was."

"Let's go to the station," Miriam said. The incident had broken the charm of the river for her, and she was annoyed with herself for having been squeamish. Since the Hugo Weiss case * and the murder of the Marquis de la Rose d'Antan, she had been conversant with the rigid gang discipline of the St. Julien Rollers, having seen not only the Singe in action but his famous predecessor whom Evans had been instrumental in sending to Devil's Island, the unscrupulous Barnabé Vieuxchamp himself. Now that the nerve-racking incident on the quai was closed, Miriam found herself more and more impressed with the force of character of the Singe, who had held the entire Rouen waterfront in a grip of terror before her eyes. Not a man or woman had dared voice an objection to his edict. No one among the rugged hard-drinking company of hoisting engineers from one end of the quais to the other had thought of volunteering to give the necessary turn to the lever in order to rescue the man who had incurred the Singe's displeasure. And still, as he sat there conversing easily with Evans, Miriam could find nothing criminal in his face, no marks of the beast, no coarseness. More and more she saw how alike were the Singe and Evans, with the same blue eyes, broad forehead, open smile, strong hands and a poise that excluded all unnecessary nervous movements. Her mind harked back to Homer's absent-minded reference to the "Baron," and the Baron's numerous progeny, all related to him. What could it mean? Did the man she worshipped above all others, and the most relentless outlaw in France

* *The Mysterious Mickey Finn*, Modern Age Books, 1939.

have a common ancestor? Were the promptings of their blood essentially the same? Had their separate cultures, so different on the surface, a common denominator? Surely they liked each other. Even more surely, neither one would voluntarily give way, if it came to a clash. Miriam hoped the conflict would never come, and still a dread possessed her. She wanted to get out of Rouen and safely back to Paris. As eagerly as she had desired that Evans get into action the eventful spring before, she was more determined to keep him safely out of it now.

Why was she shaken by sudden premonition? Was the dread inspired by the Singe contagious? She had felt it sweep over the *terrasse* as he had approached, had seen it spread from deck to deck when his head had suddenly appeared out of the hold of the scow. The men and women around her on the quais and in the cafés and houses and factories and warehouses were Normans, with the celebrated *sang froid* of their conquering race, nevertheless they all gave the Singe a clear berth and let him have his way. She sighed, as they arose and started walking toward the rue Jeanne d'Arc. Evans was right. A life of quiet and contemplation, a conservation of one's talents was the thing. Perhaps, after all, she should try to get Homer to visit the distant Montana ranch with her, so they could ride side by side among the foothills at dusk and listen to the cattle grazing and the moan of the prairie wind. France, she felt, was decadent and dangerous, at least for the time being.

"By the way, how's Chief Frémont?" asked the Singe. "I haven't seen him in quite a while . . . You know, I like Frémont. He's not like those lousy politicians who shove him around whenever they're in trouble."

"Things have been quiet in the department," Evans said.

"Let's hope they stay quiet," Miriam exclaimed so fervently that both men glanced at her in surprise.

"Nothing doing down this way. Just routine business," said the Singe, to comfort her.

"Ah, damn it. He's considerate, too," said Miriam to herself. The Singe's chivalrous attempt to reassure her, paradoxically, had sent a colder chill down her spine. Seeing the railroad station safely reposing at the end of the street, in such superb ugliness as to match the beauty of the cathedral, she lost a part, at least, of her anxiety and tried to join the talk. The truck arrived with their baggage, the boat train with its magnificent new engine slid neatly into the station, the Singe shook hands with her and with Homer, then stood on the platform as they found their seats in a café car with a comfortable table between them.

"Homer," Miriam said, in a tone unusually subdued, "you're not keeping anything back from me?"

"Why, no, dear. Of course not. What do you mean?" he replied, with the utmost candor.

"The Singe? Your meeting him like this? It doesn't mean that there's trouble?" she continued. Casting a glance through the car window, she saw that the Singe was still standing on the platform. The train stopped seven minutes in Rouen.

Evans, following her glance, waved cheerily at the Singe, who responded.

"I was hoping we would see him before we left Normandy," Evans said. "Old times' sake, you know. The

Singe seems like a part of Normandy, really. Have you noticed . . ."

"I have noticed that he looks very much like you, and acts the way you act sometimes, when you're not enveloped in your celebrated calm . . ."

"Er? What's that? Looks like me?" asked Evans, as if struck with an idea. He glanced toward the Singe again, just as the train gave a lurch to start and both he and Miriam were surprised to see that the Singe was trying to attract their attention, to give a signal of alarm or, at least, of caution. As they were staring at him, Evans trying to convey without moving that he had caught the suggestion, the big Norman turned abruptly and walked swiftly toward the rear of the moving train.

Miriam was pale and trembling. She had thought to be rid of the Singe, to have Homer safely separated from him, and now, by giving that strange signal, the gang leader had linked himself with them once more. What did it mean? Evans, of course, was busily sizing up the other passengers. Near the rear end of the car was a party of five, two men and three women, obviously tourists and quite as obviously, from their accent, Philadelphians. Homer, after a cursory glance, decided that they had nothing in common with the St. Julien Rollers. But in front and to the left, he saw on the baggage rack, most carefully placed, two expensive violin cases in black leather. And in the seat below, with his slender expressive back and shoulders toward Homer, was Anton Diluvio.

"That's Diluvio, the violinist," Evans whispered to Miriam, hoping to allay her unusual nervousness by turning her mind toward music. "Have you heard him play?"

"Three years ago," she said. The train was well out of the station and was heading through the verdant Norman countryside, so she was able to breathe more freely.

The two other occupants of the car sat facing one another, with picturesque indifference and hostility, across a table next to that occupied by Diluvio. The woman, who was in her late thirties, was dressed quietly and well, but the set of her shoulders and the look of determination on her face offered a striking contrast to her shapely legs and slender ankles. If ever a woman had something urgent on her mind, it was she, but she was not talking about it. Her companion, if such a word may be used to describe a man who showed such refined disapproval of her being there, was tall, with a red face and stiff white hair brushed back in the style of the nineties.

"Brother and sister," murmured Evans, to Miriam. "An interesting and promising pair."

As the train clicked over the smooth roadbed, Homer tried to study the pair, and his observations netted him little in the way of information. The man was about fifty years old, full-blooded and energetic, with shrewd gray eyes which he kept half closed when he appeared to be thinking. The ruddiness of his complexion had not been acquired on the moors or the sea, Evans thought, but in taverns. Still, the man was well preserved, and surely the only one in Car D of that particular boat train who could have produced such a marked effect on the Singe.

When tea was served, both brother and sister asked for whiskey and soda.

"Boston," said Evans to himself. "Mount Vernon or

16

Pinckney Street, by God. Now how in the name of heaven could the Singe have been mixed up with Beacon Hill society?"

Miriam sat silent, and was pleased to find that her former agitation was slipping away. If there was to be a case, and Homer's life was to be endangered again, at least it seemed that he and the Singe would be working on the same side of the fence, and would not fight one another. That comforted Miriam no end, and she felt in her handbag for her automatic, touching its reassuring corrugated surface almost affectionately. At least, this time she would not be to blame if anything went wrong, and her confidence in Evans had grown day by day since they had first set out to find Hugo Weiss.

The red-faced stranger across the aisle took down a small grip to get out a magazine, the *Atlantic Monthly,* and in doing so exposed the initials L.B.

"Not a Cabot," murmured Evans. "Oh, well. Lots of good families have B for an initial." Then it occurred to him that he might have misinterpreted the Singe's signal entirely. Godo the Whack, who had tried to crush a couple of his pals with a barrel of Calvados, had certainly intended that to be his last act in Rouen. Had not the Singe warned him before, and known about the quarrel over the stolen G string? Most likely the Singe, having seen the luxurious express standing in the station, had quickly decided to board it himself and to be waiting at the hangout in the rue Cardinal Lemoine, the Bal des Vêtements Brulés, when Godo came slinking in. That Godo would promptly breathe his last, Evans felt sure, and was equally sure that it was none of his affair. When the Singe did a job, he did it well and thoroughly. There were no loose ends to dangle in the face of stray police, no unnecessary trouble for Frémont's already over-worked department.

So plausible did the foregoing theory seem, in explanation of the Singe's actions, that Evans almost accepted it and relaxed his vigilance over the unknown red-faced Bostonian whose initials were perhaps L.B., and his sister, who detested him. Familiar suburbs of Paris began to whisk past the windows, tall gawky buildings were interspersed with low plaster houses.

"We're almost there," said Miriam, always thrilled when approaching Paris. "It seems to me as if we'd been away a long, long time."

"Three days is relatively a long time," Homer said, but his mind was not on what Miriam was saying. For he had seen an almost imperceptible movement of the left hand of the ruddy Bostonian, L.B., and a second later had noticed, in the gloom beneath L.B.'s table, the form of a huge dog that had lain there silently and motionlessly all the way from Havre to Paris. At first Homer thought it was a Dane, then decided it must be a Boxer.

The train entered the gare St. Lazare. Anton Diluvio, the violinist, rose deliberately and with great care reached for his renowned Guarnerius. At precisely that moment, Evans saw the red-faced man snap his fingers softly and the huge dog, with a fierce admonitory scowl on its fore-head, leaped out from beneath the table toward Diluvio. The violinist, startled and terrified, let go the black leather case in his upstretched arms and had not Evans, with incredible swiftness, thrown himself between the dog and Diluvio and caught the violin in mid-air, the precious instrument would have crashed to the floor.

The tableau that followed would have been ludicrous had anyone except the Philadelphians been present to witness it.

L.B., the Bostonian, was apologizing profusely in his best Harvard manner. Diluvio was struggling to calm himself. Evans, with the violin case under one arm, was petting the Boxer and assuring the musician that the beast was not only harmless but superbly trained. Miriam, who had drawn her automatic in the first flush of excitement, sheepishly slipped it back into her handbag, glad no one had observed her action. The Bostonian's sister stood raptly in the aisle, unmindful of violins or dogs, her eyes fixed upon Diluvio, who seemed unaware of her worshipful gaze.

At the insistence of L.B., whose face was redder than ever, Diluvio placed the violin case on the table, opened it carefully, and laid aside the silk cloth.

"Oh," gasped Miriam, for the Guarnerius, in all its sturdy loveliness, lay unharmed on its green velvet casing, and when Diluvio touched the "A," a bell-like sound arose that seemed to speak out from an age of perfection itself.

"I can't tell you how relieved I am," the Bostonian said.

Diluvio, now that he had got over his first shock at seeing the Boxer appear from nowhere, was graciousness personified.

"I assure you that I keep as far in the background as possible what is known as the artistic temperament," he said. "I am fond of animals, and admire your dog, who certainly may be pardoned for having been glad to stretch his legs after a three-hour ride. And you, sir," Diluvio continued, turning to Evans. "Had it not been for your presence of mind and amazing agility, I might have been seriously handicapped in preparing for my recital here tomorrow. My violin is well made and strong, but delicate beyond belief. It would take quite a lot to break it, but almost nothing to put it out of adjustment. The sounding post, you know, if misplaced the least fraction of a millimeter, has to be reset by an expert, and even Rebec, the best in Paris, is often unable to get a perfect result within two or three days."

The Bostonian, during Diluvio's remarks, seemed to lose a little of his self-satisfaction. "By Jove, you *were* quite a distance away, you know, for a catch like that," he said, almost disapprovingly, to Evans.

Homer smiled so warmly that Miriam at once suspected an ulterior purpose. "I'd been admiring your dog for some time," he said. "So, naturally, when you beckoned him to come out, and I noticed Mr. Diluvio had his violin in his hands, I saw the possibilities of disaster."

"Oh, quite," said L.B., coldly, and busied himself with his baggage.

The sister was still lingering tensely in the aisle when Diluvio reached up for the second violin, turned his shapely back to them all and made his way to the door.

2

Of the Light That Lies in Woman's Eyes, and Other Pertinent Matters

HOMER EVANS, unless the circumstances were exceptional, never joined the bustle of uneasy people who crowd the exits of public conveyances. He simply sat quietly and waited until all was clear, then walked out peacefully. Miriam had learned to do the same. The group of Philadelphians, with suitcases, grips, handbags, steamer rugs, golf bags, and God knows what, squirmed and wriggled their way to the station platform and were bumped by porters, laden and unladen, and with varying tempers, vocabularies, and degrees of articulateness. The gare St. Lazare at its best is smoky and dingy, but a modicum of the spring sunlight came slanting through from the west and filtered downward on the crowd of tourists, some of whom were seeing Paris for the first time and were somewhat dismayed.

Miriam saw that Evans was listening intently for something. Anton Diluvio, after renewing his thanks, left the car, violins in hand, and directed his porter politely until there came on the scene a tall thin woman with prominent cheekbones and a sort of open mouth, like that of a bluefish. She was dressed in dark tailored clothes, had a cigarette stuck on her lower lip, and with jerky movements of elbows and skinny fingers, she took charge of the violinist, the violins, the porter, the baggage and whatever showed signs of impeding their progress to the exit.

"That's Hattie Ham," said Miriam, smiling.

Miss Baxter, the chic *Bostonienne,* when Hattie Ham arrived, got out of sight as fast as her medium heels could carry her, followed precariously by a couple of bewildered and indignant porters, both laden almost to the breaking point. The red-faced white-haired brother was still in the car.

"Don't blame the handsome sister for going to a separate hotel," Evans said to himself. "Ah, these fine old families. They fight like cats and dogs until menaced from without. But if one member is threatened, all the rest start digging for their securities and offering their assets, rudely, of course, to cover their emotions. But why is this imperious woman so eager to avoid Hattie Ham?" Then Homer remembered that Hattie, also, was from Boston. With a sigh of satisfaction, he turned to Miriam, who, aware that his mind was occupied elsewhere, had been sitting patiently beside him.

"There's much that intrigues me in this Boston delegation, and it's interesting, too, how Hattie Ham and Diluvio got together. That I'll tell you about some time," Homer said.

Finally, the red-faced brother, L.B., with a grunt of farewell to Evans, snapped a leash to the dog's breast harness and led the Boxer to the doorway, much to the consternation of a porter who was about to enter. The Boxer wrinkled his forehead at the terrified little man in blue denims and passed majestically on without even sniffing.

"Blast it," said Evans. "I was hoping the old boy would call the dog by name. Well! I'll have to resort to the cable. Do you mind if we stop in the boulevard des Capucines on the way over? I crave a bit of information, a lot of information, in fact. Just by luck, you know, Tom Jackson's in Boston, on the *Transcript.*"

"No," said Miriam, compassionately. "You mean he won't be in Paris this summer?"

"Not until later," Evans said.

He gave directions to the chauffeur and within a few minutes they pulled up, baggage and all, in front of the Commercial Cable office. Evans and Miriam mounted the stairs, where Evans greeted the manager pleasantly, then wrote the following message which he handed to Miriam to read:

TOM JACKSON
TRANSCRIPT
BOSTON
SEND COMPLETE INFORMATION CONCERNING OWNER OF BOXER DOG BOSTON LICENSE NUMBER 132 INITIALS PROBABLY ELL BEE STOP MIRIAM SENDS REGARDS
HOMER EVANS

"Well," Miriam said, "I'm in the fog, as usual. When you care to pierce it, I shall be more than ready."

"We've put in a fascinating afternoon, it seems to me," Evans said.

"A trifle hard on the nerves at times, but intriguing,"

Miriam admitted. "Still, I hope you won't forget your time-tested principle of *laissez faire*. A life of action, you have often said, is not for you. You are not beguiled by the prospect of achievement."

"I can't explain why I'm so curious about the train of events we've just witnessed," Evans said. "First I find the Singe engaged in what seems to be manual labor and legitimate enterprise, then he shows signs of more than a passing acquaintance with a red-faced and stuffy Bostonian, one L.B., owner of one of the most remarkable dogs I have ever seen. The Bostonian then sets the dog, who has hidden himself for three hours without twitching even an ear, on a famous concert violinist, at the moment when such a maneuver is most likely to frighten the latter into dropping a priceless Guarnerius. There was a time in my life when I should have passed up such a fascinating series of incidents, but you, my dear, by forcing me on occasion to use my powers and perceptions, have increased the former and sharpened the latter."

"Oh," said Miriam, overcome with awe. "Then I've really been good for you . . . In every way?"

Homer reached for her hand and stroked it gently. "I am undoubtedly more alive than I was before, and you are the only explanation . . . There, dear. Don't take it so hard. We're going to have a good time, if things go on happening, as I believe they will. Also, if we have luck, we may save some very nice people from disaster. Why not? It's spring! We breathe the air of Paris! Life lies before us!"

"I've never heard you talk that way before," said Miriam, astonished, "but I shall learn eventually, perhaps, that your capacity for experience has no limit and your conduct no fixed rules. But tell me, Homer, did you really know that dog was hidden there and that he'd frighten Diluvio?"

"I knew the dog was there, but not for what purpose," Evans said. "Well! We've an evening before us in Montparnasse. What shall it be? Dinner at the Coupole, and a round of the cafés to size up the new tourists? Then a dance, perhaps, at the Coq d'Or, where there is a pianist from Harlem and a saxophone. After midnight we'll drop in to hear the Flamencos at the Catalan place in the rue Henri Martin. Have to cross the river, of course, but what's the difference . . ."

Miriam stopped short on the sidewalk and stared at Evans almost fearfully. "What *is* the matter? What has changed you so? Not the fear that I've been bored . . . ?"

"That never occurred to me," Evans said. "Perhaps I've been thinking too much about the Baron . . . Ah, the Baron, my dynamic and troublesome ancestor. Tonight, after dinner, I'll tell you what I know about him, and later we'll go to Normandy and dig up all the records. Work, again. But we'll enjoy it. And how my publisher will be delighted, if I turn out another book, this time a biography."

"But the case? The Bostonian with the dog? The Guarnerius? A moment ago you were filled with concern for them," she said.

"Until the recital opens tomorrow night, we've nothing to do but amuse ourselves," Evans said.

And they did amuse themselves royally, as only Evans could when a rare mood prompted him to vie with his energetic acquaintances and squeeze each moment dry.

Miriam had spent many a week in the saddle during spring and fall roundups in Montana but never had she been more thoroughly and pleasantly exhausted than when she closed her eyes and sank to sleep at seven the next morning, with echoes of Montparnasse and Montmartre still ringing in her ears. The story of Claude l'Original, Baron de Vans, marauding companion of William the Conqueror, was strangely mingled in her dreams with that of Hattie Ham, the bleak Boston spinster who, feeling she was useless in the world, had attached herself to Anton Diluvio, the violinist, in order to protect him from the horde of adoring women who were threatening his career and the peace of mind she believed was due a promising young virtuoso. And among the strangely assorted characters who passed back and forth across her reveries stalked the ominous and arresting figure of the Singe, sometimes a menace, again a bulwark of protection and beneficence.

Had she but known it, Evans, who had exhausted her and their friends that night in a ceaseless round of pleasure, was not reposing but, in fact, was fully occupied. She had been so sleepy, when entering the apartment, that she had not noticed on a brass tray on a small table near the entrance a folded cablegram that Homer had hastily slipped into his pocket. She was to meet him on the *terrasse* of the Café du Dôme on awakening, and that, for the moment, was enough for her to know.

Evans, having breakfasted at Pharamond's on a delicious grilled mackerel with browned potatoes and a half bottle of Macon to wash it down, was ushered into the apartment of Jacques Maritan, the junior partner of the firm which controlled the Salle Gaveau, at ten o'clock.

"I'm calling at a barbarous hour," Evans said, apologetically.

"Which accentuates the honor and the pleasure," Maritan replied, with cordiality. He had known of Evans' keen interest in the *Société des Instruments Anciens* and assumed that Homer's visit had to do with an approaching rehearsal of old French music. Instead, Evans asked his permission to inspect the Salle Gaveau, and to borrow from Maritan's private library whatever books he had about that remarkable instrument maker, the lusty Joseph del Gesu, now known to the musical world as Guarnerius. Both requests were granted, and as soon as Maritan had had time to dress he piloted Homer through the dressing rooms and corridors backstage in the famous old concert hall. The two men had been friends many years, so Maritan was only mildly surprised when Evans walked to the footlights of the stage, jumped experimentally across the wide orchestra pit, and back again. That accomplished, Homer asked to exchange his two season tickets, in the tenth row just left of the center where he invariably sat, for four tickets in the second row on the left-center aisle.

"You're coming to the Diluvio recital, then?" Maritan asked.

"I am," said Homer, "and I venture to hope you will be somewhere in the offing. Also, you might hint to the critics and reporters, who are likely to pass up Diluvio because he is only an American, that if they condescend to be present, they may be repaid in terms of news."

"Mysterious as ever," Maritan said. "However, I'll do as you suggest."

The next stop for Evans was the Hotel Murphy et du

Danube Bleu in the Place de la Contrescarpe, and there his errand was a more delicate one. He wanted to find out if the Singe, whom he had last seen streaking it down the platform at Rouen, had come to Paris. Since their first casual meeting, in connection with the famous mummy murder, Bridgette Murphy, proprietress of the hotel, and the taciturn leader of the St. Julien Rollers, had become fast friends. Evans knew that if he asked Bridgette directly if her Norman admirer had spent the night in the Murphy et du Danube Bleu he would place her in an embarrassing position, for Bridgette was deeply indebted to Evans and liked him wholeheartedly. Still, she could not be expected to disclose the whereabouts of the Singe without the latter's permission. So Evans merely looked into Bridgette's dark Franco-Irish eyes. They were bright and sparkling as usual but he thought he detected in them that enigmatic and satisfied look with which an affectionate woman is likely to betray the recent presence of the man she has set aside for her warmest devotion. The look was there, all right, and when Bridgette brought out a bottle of her favorite Irish whiskey the eager way in which she drained her first and second glass confirmed Homer's conclusion. As soon as possible, he excused himself without seeming too abrupt, and made his way around the corner to the Bal des Vêtements Brulés, which at that mid-morning hour was being scrubbed out by the waiters, under the sharp eyes of the proprietor, Monsieur Trouvaille.

"Has Godo the Whack been here?" Evans asked, coming straight to the point.

Monsieur Trouvaille was uneasy and evasive. "Not lately," he said.

"No use to stall. I want him and I want him without delay . . . Not officially, you understand. A friendly call," said Homer.

"I'll pass the word around to the boys," said Trouvaille. "On the level, I can't tell you where he is just now."

"Then how about his fiddle? Has he left it here?" asked Evans. The proprietor's protestations in the negative would have convinced a judge and jury.

"The sooner he sees me, the better for him," Evans said, and started down the hill, across the boulevard St. Germain and the pont du Louvre, and into the prefecture.

Chief of Detectives Frémont was in his office, elbow-deep in documents, which he was signing assiduously and shoving into baskets marked, from left to right: "Urgent," "Important," "Routine," and "For Future Reference." On seeing Evans he rose cordially, scattering originals, duplicates and triplicates in all directions and making havoc of a tray of rubber stamps, some of which were wet and others dry.

"My friend," said the Chief, wringing Homer's hand. "What brings you here today?" Then a shade of apprehension crossed his broad honest face. "I trust we're not to be involved in one of those complicated problems which only you are capable of solving. I had promised Hydrangea . . ."

"No cause for worry," said Evans, suavely. "I merely thought you were working too hard, that you needed relaxation. So I've taken the liberty of buying for you a ticket to a violin recital tomorrow evening. An acquaintance and countryman of mine is playing a program at the Salle Gaveau and I shouldn't like to have you miss it . . ."

"But, Monsieur Evans," objected Frémont, nonplussed. "You know I can't tell one note from another. And particularly I detest the violin. It chatters like a monkey, then yowls like a cat from hell. And the freaks who choose to play it . . . I beg of you, excuse me . . ." Then he caught a look at Evans' face which was all earnestness, and subsided. "Forgive me. I know you are most serious when you seem to be trifling," he said. "At what hour does this ordeal begin, and am I to attend alone or . . ."

"Bring Hydrangea, if you like, and station some good men at each exit and entrance," said Homer. "Preferably, good men who cannot be spotted as officers at a distance of a hundred yards."

"As you say," the Chief agreed. "Last year and year before you steered me through the labyrinths of the decadent world of art and I came out unscathed, thanks only to you. But if musicians are about to do their worst, I shall be exposed and disgraced as an ignoramus."

"It may well be that more glory will be thrust upon you, and then again, my forebodings may prove to be unfounded and I shall have to apologize for disturbing you," said Evans, and his final words were drowned by the Chief's heartfelt sigh.

"I can see that I'm in for something frightful," Frémont said, and jabbed despairingly left and right with a rubber stamp.

"Just two more requests, and I'll leave you to your work, a large part of which you should delegate to your subordinates," Evans continued. "You remember, in connection with the Louvre murder case, an unsavory party, a member of the St. Julien Rollers, yclept Godo the Whack?"

"Unhappily," groaned Frémont, mopping his damp brow.

"I'd like to talk with him, dead or alive," Evans said. The Chief scrawled a note.

"Also," continued Homer, consulting the cablegram from Jackson in his hand, "I'd like to have you find, in some ultra-stuffy and respectable hotel, probably the Chestwick, or the Wilton in the rue Jean-Jacques Rousseau, a tall red-faced American . . ."

At the word American, Frémont's forehead was dewed with perspiration again. "Ah, God. I might have known there'd be an American," he muttered.

"A tall red-faced American with a prominent nose and stiff white hair who comes from Boston, bringing with him a magnificent dog of the race known as Boxer. His name, if he uses it on the register, will probably be Leffingwell Baxter . . . L for Lucille, E for Eugène, a couple of FF's for as many François . . ."

"Take pity and print it out, in block letters. These foreign names!" begged the Chief. Evans complied, smiling.

"I want this tall Bostonian shadowed, and particularly I want your men to observe the behavior of the Boxer dog, whose name is Moritz . . ."

"Maurice," wrote Frémont on his pad. "And what, may I ask, does this dog do that other dogs do not? Tell fortunes, read newspapers, smoke pipes?"

"You may say that he's dignified and that he won't bite unless instructed to do so by his master," said Evans.

Frémont straightened up reproachfully. "I'm only the Chief of Detectives of Paris, successor as you have said, to the glories of Egypt, Rome and Athens. Nevertheless, I might work more intelligently if you would give me a hint as to what to expect from this hideous miscellany of fiddlers, foreigners, pedigreed brutes and distasteful thugs."

"I assure you, friend Frémont, that I shall keep you abreast of developments, that I will share with you whatever information I pick up, today and henceforth. Just now I am more in the dark than you are . . ."

"Impossible," said the Chief, and reluctantly said good-bye as Evans left the prefecture.

Miriam, meanwhile, had slept the sleep of youth, not exactly untroubled but decidedly refreshing. At four she awoke, bathed, and selected a fetching summer ensemble of burgundy chiffon, flowered with Mediterranean blue and white. Her sleek automatic she transferred from the leather handbag she had carried the day before to a bag of colored straw, and before leaving the apartment to keep her appointment with Evans at the Dôme she whisked out the gun, experimentally, three or four times, to make sure the braided straw handles would not interfere with her lightning-like draw. Satisfied on that score, she patted her hair, straightened her girdle, looked down her smooth silk stockings at her stylish leather shoes, and stepped into the hallway.

The corridor was empty, but she proceeded with the caution she had learned to exercise whenever Homer Evans was involved in any sort of inquiry. At the doorway, downstairs, she started walking briskly in the wrong direction, wheeled quickly to see if she was being followed, then went on to the Dôme. Evans, as always punctual, was in his place, a copy of the New York *Herald* spread on the table in front of him. He rose with the welcoming smile that never failed to thrill her to the tips of her toes, said "Good afternoon," and handed her the paper.

"There's the program for this evening," he said, indicating a column headed "Diluvio at the Gaveau." Eagerly she read the following list:

1. Sonate for Violin and Piano, Opus 13
                                        Sauvequipeut
2. Variations on an Air by Monteverdi   *Vivaldi*
3. Concerto Serioso   *Tienemiedo*
        Allegro
        Largo
        Presto
4. Elegie plus ou moins in Ut   *Philidor*

"Not at all banal," she said. "But look at the second part."

"The first half's for musicians," Evans said. "The rest for those who pay."

The second half of the program read as follows:

5. Narcissus   *Nevin-Diluvio*
6. Star of the Sea   *Anonymous* (Old American)
7. Prelude in C-sharp Minor   *Rachmaninoff-Diluvio*
        (arranged for Violin, alone)
8. Course au Chariot de Ben Hur   *Paull-Diluvio*

"I don't see why Hattie lets him play such stuff," said Miriam. "She should take better care of him, if she undertakes the job at all."

"Love is deaf as well as blind," Evans said, and beckoned the waiter, who was hovering near.

Montparnasse, all around them, was approaching one of its most enticing hours, with tourists and habitués gathered in the four principal cafés for aperitifs. Along the sidewalks, beneath the plane trees, strolled the happy-go-lucky throngs, seemingly without purpose and yet in search of relaxation, the heat of the day already modified, rounds of shopping and sightseeing safely accomplished, an evening ahead in which care would have no part. It may be that in other cities the sun also rises and sinks again into oblivion, and all, when the check is presented, turns out to be vanity and vexation of spirit. In Montparnasse, in those unforgettable days, much more than that was in the air. The quarter afforded refuge for the weary, stimulation for the jaded, an armistice for the oppressed. Yielding to the prevailing mood, Evans and Miriam relaxed and sipped their drinks, simply placing whatever might be in store for them in the neat wire baskets marked "For Future Reference" with which clear brains in youthful bodies should invariably be equipped. Before they rose to go to dinner, however, Evans drew from his pocket the cablegram from Jackson and handed it to Miriam, who read:

EVANS
43 RUE CAMPAGNE PREMIÉRE
PARIS
DOG OWNER IS LEFFINGWELL BAXTER BOSTON BRAHMIN SECRETARY BUNKER HILL ASSOCIATES STOP BOXER IS MORITZ BY MAX OUT OF LENI STOP BAXTER FORTUNE CALUMET AND HECLA ROYALTIES FROM MOODY AND

SANKEY HYMNBOOK STOP SILENT PARTNER STILLWATER
AND TIEF MUSICAL INSTRUMENT DEALERS STOP CRIPES
WHAT A TOWN DE PROFUNDIS

"I don't see that Jackson's message gets you any
further," said Miriam. "But it wrings my heart."

3

In Which an Audience Gets More
Than Its Money's Worth

At quarter to nine o'clock the Salle Gaveau was the scene of brilliant activity. In front of the entrance in the rue la Boëtie, taxis and limousines were discharging guests in evening clothes, the women with gaily colored light wraps, the men in the conventional black with gleaming white shirt fronts. There were others less elaborately dressed, and long lines of students moving inch by inch toward the ticket windows, for Diluvio had a following not only among the elite of society but also among those music lovers whose means permitted them to enjoy the sounds but would not admit of all the trappings. The auditorium and the balconies were already dotted with archipelagos of early comers, ushers led groups and pairs down the aisles and chirped their thanks for the tips, which on a balmy spring night, with an artist who brought to the hall a generous sprinkling of Americans, were well above the average.

Backstage, leaning against a pillar and estimating the house with satisfaction, was Jacques Maritan, the young proprietor, and near by, in a large dressing room from which sounds of unsubdued conversation leaked out, were a dozen critics and reporters, who were being served assorted liqueurs. The talk was not entirely respectful to Diluvio, because of the program. The first part contained several little-known selections from the music of past ages, which would necessitate the critics writing something out of their heads instead of looking up what they had last said about the self-same piece. And the second half consisted principally of popular tunes which those blasé gentlemen could not contemplate without loathing. Still, they had been tipped off by Maritan that something was in the wind, and that shrewd impresario had never before let them down. Also, the liquor was unlimited and free.

A murmur from the crowd outside betrayed the fact that Diluvio had arrived at the stage entrance and in a moment the tall good-looking young man, followed by Hattie Ham on whose lanky form was flapping a sort of tuxedo, passed through the corridor and entered the dressing room reserved for the principal artist. Diluvio was carrying his famous Guarnerius tucked under his left arm, and his shirt front was protected by a dark silk scarf that he whipped off impatiently as soon as he was indoors. Hattie was empty handed. She scorned handbags, as feminine frivolities, and had no need for a music case since she invariably played Diluvio's accompaniments from memory. Whatever comments were made in public or private about Hattie Ham's eccentricities of behavior, everyone granted her first-rate musicianship.

Homer Evans and his party were ushered to their seats, in the second row, left center, at five minutes to nine, when the hall was already filled. They formed a striking quartette, Miriam in her jade-green peppered organdie, cut moderately in the back; Hydrangea, the former Blackbird from Harlem, in old-rose chiffon which exposed an impressive area of her rich dark skin. Homer, tall and elegant, walked behind them down the aisle, his arm in that of Chief of Detectives Frémont, whose stocky figure and candid reproachful face were eloquent with misgivings and dread.

"Will there be only violin playing . . . No juggling or anything?" Frémont asked.

"I think I can promise you a lively entertainment," said Evans, amused.

As soon as they were seated, Homer excused himself to go backstage. At the entrance to the corridor he was greeted by Maritan, who, because of the unusually good ticket sale, was gay.

"Can't you tell me what's up, in confidence?" the impresario asked. "The reporters are getting tight and the critics are beefing about the program. Not one of them ever heard of Sauvequipeut, but they won't admit it. You know everything about the musical graveyards. Why not drop in for a drink and give them a hand?"

"I'll do it later, gladly," Evans said. "But first I'd like a word with Diluvio."

"He never talks with anyone before a recital. Mademoiselle Ham wouldn't let him," said Maritan.

"I'll have a try," said Homer and passed on to the principal dressing room.

"Go away," was the response he received in a shrill female baritone when he tapped on the door.

"Excuse me, Miss Ham," Homer said. "I won't trouble you but a moment. It's important."

Hattie Ham, with an oath, pressed all the buttons she could find and several attendants appeared. "Throw this man out on his ear. He's disturbing Anton," she said.

Maritan hurried down the corridor before the attendants could make up their minds. "Miss Ham, your caller is Mr. Homer Evans . . ."

"Never heard of him," was the brusque reply.

"Mr. Diluvio will remember me," Evans said, calmly. "I had the good fortune to catch his violin on the boat train . . ."

"A thousand apologies," said Diluvio, cordially, and then to his protector and accompanist: "Be still, Hattie! It's you who are getting on my nerves."

The door opened. Maritan and the attendants, astonished, retired, and Homer entered the dressing room. "I'm so glad to see you," Diluvio said. "Miss Ham, Mr. Evans . . ." Hattie, who was draped grotesquely over a low armchair, shot Evans a venomous glance.

"Miss Ham's father and mine were old friends and classmates," Homer began.

"My father was a hopeless fat-head. I don't know about yours," snapped Hattie.

"Not a bad sort, but not exactly clever," said Homer.

"Get down to brass tacks. Never mind the genealogy," Hattie said, rising with a knee and elbow movement almost like that of a daddy longlegs. "What have you to say to Anton that couldn't be said tomorrow morning, or never, for that matter? We haven't got all night, you know."

39

"Hattie, you'd better leave us alone for a few minutes," Diluvio said severely.

To Evans' intense surprise, the gaunt woman in black stood up obediently, almost fearfully, and walked out without a word of protest.

"Sorry," said Diluvio.

"Quite all right," said Evans. "I didn't want to make Miss Ham nervous before the performance, but you both are in danger. You must keep your head, whatever happens this evening. I must leave you until after the performance. But by no means leave your dressing room once the recital is over, until I come for you. I am not a police officer, but I have with me, out in front, the Chief of Detectives, Frémont."

"Indeed," said Diluvio, calmly. "I assure you, Mr. Evans, that this comes as a complete surprise to me. I was not aware of any danger. What sort of danger?"

"I wish I could say," Evans answered.

"To tell the truth," Diluvio said, and his face was wistful in spite of his quiet smile, "I wouldn't mind a slight relief from the usual. It's hell, you know, getting up every day, having breakfast, practicing, lunching, practicing, taking some asinine form of exercise which doesn't involve the use of the hands . . . I'll do as you say, but, old man, let me in on any excitement you can."

Evans, touched and pleased, gave his promise.

Hattie, who had been pacing the corridor, stepped into the dressing room as Evans stepped out. Homer made his way to the side entrance and quietly took his seat in the auditorium just as the gong rang and the outer doors were closed.

The lights in the auditorium grew dim, a glow rose

from under the curtain as the stage lights went on. Programs rustled, nervous coughs sounded here and there in the audience, then the Salle Gaveau and its distinguished occupants settled down. The curtains parted, an attendant tiptoed across the stage and opened the piano and Hattie Ham appeared at the left stage door. She went straight to the piano and took her seat without fuss, and in spite of her somewhat grotesque physique and badly chosen attire, no one laughed or even giggled. She was so completely sure of what she was doing, so intent on losing her identity as an interpreter and aid to the artist, that she was impressive and equal to the occasion.

"Hot dog," whispered Hydrangea, tense with excitement.

Frémont looked at his dark sweetheart with sad reproachful eyes. At such moments, she eluded him. She was lifted into some strange realm of which he, conscientious police officer, knew nothing. Miriam, musician to the core, was equally moved. Her ivory skin, in the dim light, glowed and gained by contrast with Hydrangea's dusky back and shoulders. Evans, as always, when music was imminent, seemed to detach himself from his surroundings and sat, hands resting in his lap, without strain. Diluvio appeared on the stage, violin in hand, and bowed gravely as he was greeted with restrained applause. That was what he liked at the beginning. No hysteria, no wild demonstration. Merely willingness and readiness on the part of his hearers, and the hope that he would do his best.

Hattie struck a chord suggestive of the mode of the Grecian ages and Diluvio, raising his violin, asserted the

Monteverdi theme. It was a simple succession of notes, departing from the tonic, mounting, lingering on the platform of the dominant, descending to earth once more. The variations were not tricky, but inevitable, elaborations which held all the purity of the original theme. Frémont, affected perhaps by Hydrangea's rapt enjoyment, began to think that a fiddle was not so bad. He began to admire the tall young man who played without grimaces or gymnastics, who did not try to scratch the varnish from his violin. Miriam and Evans were listening intently, at one with the composer and his epoch, the patient instrument maker, the talented artist and the perfect accompaniment.

The applause, at the end of the first number, was by no means restrained, and Diluvio, smiling with pleasure, dashed into the lively movement of the sonata by Sauvequipeut. Hydrangea held herself in check until the rollicking finale, when she gasped: "Oh, man! Go to town!" The enthusiasm of the audience mounted, as the sonata was followed by the Vivaldi concerto and the ironic elegy by Philidor, who not only had been the king's first musician, in the days of Louis XIV, but had held the world's championship at chess, which he always contended was a silent exercise in musical form.

When the audience rose for the intermission, Frémont at first thought the show was over, and heaved a sigh of relief.

"I'm glad I came, my friend," he said to Evans, "although nothing has happened."

"Let's hope I was wrong," said Homer, and took the Chief out for a drink.

The audience, reassembled after the intermission and, having survived the serious part of the program, settled down for some harmless musical fun. Hattie Ham stepped onto the stage and this time was rewarded by a burst of applause from the discerning clients.

"Whatever will Diluvio do with Narcissus?" asked Miriam of Homer, and was surprised to note that he had not heard her speak. He was watching the violinist tensely and his hands were no longer lying idly in his lap but were braced against the sides of his chair.

Diluvio acknowledged the applause, bowing first to the right and then to the left, and raised the violin. Hattie played the short introduction, which pleased the audience by its familiarity, Diluvio's bow was posed and the first note sounded. The violinist turned deathly white, raised the bow, and Homer Evans leaped catlike across the orchestra pit and in an instant was beside him. Hattie abandoned the piano and strode to their side.

"This is not my violin," said Diluvio, and Evans took the instrument from his trembling hands.

Miriam clutched at her automatic, Frémont rose to his feet, as did a large portion of the audience. There was danger of a panic, for all the doors were tightly closed.

Evans was whispering in Diluvio's ear. "Pull yourself together. Don't tell anyone what has happened," he said, and to Hattie: "Go back to the piano." Then he faced the audience and held up his hand.

"*Mesdames et messieurs,*" he began in his faultless French. "There has been a slight mishap. Monsieur Diluvio inadvertently brought the wrong violin to the

43

stage, and if you will be patient a moment and remain in your seats, he will continue the program with another instrument."

He led the trembling violinist off stage to his dressing room where he placed his hands on his shoulders and said: "I promise you, Mr. Diluvio, that no instrument shall leave this building. Every door is guarded. You will help us, and most of all, yourself, if you carry this thing through." He handed to the violinist his second violin, a sound Cremona, touched his shoulder reassuringly, and could not suppress his admiration as Diluvio, dazed but unmistakably game, bowed politely and went back to the stage. As soon as the artist had left the dressing room, Evans took up the substitute violin, examined it carefully and sought out Maritan.

"Don't let this out of your sight, Jacques," he said, and went back to his seat in the audience.

The audience listened nervously to Narcissus and the Star of the Sea. When the prelude for violin alone was reached, Hattie Ham silently left the stage and then entered the dressing room, banging the door.

"What's happened?" demanded the reporters of Maritan.

"I'll give you the whole story later," the impresario said, for want of a better reply.

The reporters, however, were not to be put off. "Has Diluvio lost his Guarnerius?" one of them demanded, and Maritan's expressive face, not trained by American poker, was not equal to a deception.

"Take it easy, boys, and stick around," he said. "Someone in this place has the instrument. We'll get it, never fear."

There was a dash for telephone booths, as the lugubrious three notes of the prelude in C-sharp minor were heard faintly from the hall. The transcription, a musical curiosity, came quickly to an end and Diluvio waited for Hattie to reappear for the final number. Members of the audience began to cough and stir in their seats.

"Now, what the devil?" muttered Evans, to Miriam.

An attendant appeared on the stage and whispered something to Diluvio, who was obviously bewildered. Homer lost no time. He hurried backstage and found Maritan, the reporters and a squad of attendants scanning the corridors and dressing rooms for Miss Ham. She was nowhere to be found. Seeing Sergeant Bonnet of the prefecture in a group at the doorway, he beckoned the officer and asked him to take charge. Then he went back to Miriam and asked her to come with him to the stage. After a hurried explanation to Diluvio, Evans again addressed the audience.

"Miss Ham has been upset by the accident here tonight, and in her place, Miss Miriam Leonard will act as Mr. Diluvio's accompanist."

Miriam went to the piano, quaking, and pitched into Ben Hur with creditable gusto. Diluvio joined in and somehow, without rehearsal, they got along with the piece. First Ben was ahead, then the other chap! The chariots were rounding the turn when there was a loud altercation at a door in the rear and Sergeant Schlumberger, the Alsatian officer second in command to Frémont, burst in and lumbered down the aisle to where his chief was seated.

"What is it? Have you lost Leffingwell Baxter?" asked Frémont hoarsely.

"We have him, all right, but he's dead," was the guttural reply.

"And Maurice, the performing hound?"

"He won't let anyone go near the body," grunted Schlumberger, wiping his thick wet neck with a scarf.

4

Of Methods of Sounding the "A," the

Dog Who's Friend to Man, and the

Attributes of English Hotels

THE tension in the Salle Gaveau, by this time, had reached such a pitch that several women screamed and some even started yelling "Murder." In an instant, Homer Evans had leaped quickly to the stage, over a gap that only lacked six inches of the Olympic record.

"Silence," he called, and when he was seconded by Anton Diluvio, himself, the members of the audience pulled themselves together with creditable Franco-American responsiveness. Comparative quiet was restored. Miriam, panting from the exacting Ben Hur finale, sat expectantly at the piano.

"Ladies and gentlemen," Evans began. "It is true that a murder has been committed." Gasps from the crowd. "But," Homer continued, "the crime did not take place in this hall, and no one here has anything to fear. You have all listened with pleasure to the artist of the evening, Mr. Anton Diluvio, who has performed under strain and to the best of his ability." Evans paused for the scattered applause.

"Ladies and gentlemen, I am sure that each of you wishes to aid Mr. Diluvio in every possible way and with that in view I shall disclose that his priceless Guarnerius, one of the best which has come down to us from that master instrument maker, has been stolen. Furthermore, Miss Hattie Ham, the accompanist who seconded Mr. Diluvio's efforts so ably, has disappeared in an unaccountable way. Fortunately, we have with us tonight the Chief of Detectives, Monsieur Bertrand Frémont, whom I will ask to step up here with me to the stage."

"In the name of God," protested Frémont, sweating, but Hydrangea gave him a gentle shove.

"Go on, Chief! Do your stuff," she said, and reluctantly Frémont stepped up the ladder from the orchestra pit and stood miserably beside Evans, looking anything but determined. Evans and Frémont held a whispered consultation, then Homer started speaking again.

"What we have to ask of you, friends, is simply this: We must clear this building in an orderly way, so that the thieves and abductors may be apprehended. Chief Frémont—and you must not be deceived by his modest and unassuming manner—has already taken the precautions to have each exit guarded by trusted members of his force. Not even a pet cat could slink from one of these doors without being observed."

"Quick work," said someone in the audience, and the crowd murmured its approval.

"Will those of you who still have your ticket stubs please raise your hands?" Evans asked, and a large number of those present responded. "Good," he went on.

"Those with ticket stubs will please pass out first, show your stubs at the door, and retain them for identification, in case we need you."

A few began to file out, others followed, leaving perhaps a hundred persons standing in their places. "Those who have lost their stubs will be given slips of paper corresponding to the numbers of their seats," Homer said, and Maritan and his assistants quickly complied.

"Good night, and thank you for your co-operation," Evans said, as the last of the audience was passing through the aisles. "We shall now proceed with the investigation."

"If this is press-agent stuff, it's good. That's all I can say," said a reporter from a stage doorway. Diluvio turned to him, pained.

"I beg of you, sir," he said, for he disliked personal notoriety to such an extent that his various press agents had been at a loss as to how to keep his name properly before the public.

"You have my word that there is nothing phony," said Maritan.

"Then how did you know all this was coming off?" demanded the reporter, unconvinced.

"The Chief of Detectives will explain that, in due time," said Evans, and Frémont groaned.

"I'm cooked! This is my finish. Violins! Vanishing lady baritones! Performing dogs! Dead Bostonians!" he muttered, but Evans slapped him cheerfully on the shoulder.

"Buck up," he said. "The laurel wreath awaits. But now there's much to be done."

"Just where shall we begin?" asked Frémont.

49

Evans beckoned Miriam to join them, and an appreciative "ah" from the reporters greeted her progress across the stage.

"Who's the pippin?" asked one of the newspaper men, and Maritan shrugged his shoulders.

"And the spade in the auditorium?" the reporter persisted. "She's the only one sticking around." Hydrangea was, in fact, alone in the huge empty auditorium, regarding Frémont with admiring eyes. She had seen him in action only once before, in the Sanitorium Sens Unique, and was relishing the evening's excitement.

Evans took Miriam and Frémont aside, and asked Diluvio to join them. "The late Mr. Leffingwell Baxter from Boston is already dead and his faithful dog, Moritz, is showing his remarkable intelligence in keeping the police from gumming up the evidence, if any. Let us leave them in the Hotel Wilton, for the present."

Two of the reporters, who had overheard, set out on the run, but most of them decided to stick with Evans, for already he had inspired them with confidence.

"The violin which was substituted for Diluvio's Guarnerius is in the safe, and luckily the safe is a modern one," Evans continued. "Therefore, our course is clear. We must find Miss Hattie Ham."

"On the level, is that her right name?" a newspaperman asked.

"You will find it listed in the Blue Book," said Evans. "If you were familiar with Boston society . . ."

"I'm from Des Moines," the reporter said, "but let that pass."

The officers who had been guarding the various doors were summoned in turn and questioned by Evans and

Frémont. They knew Miss Ham by sight, having seen her once in her ludicrous tuxedo, and each and severally they swore that no such woman had passed their portals.

"Search the hall," Evans said, and nodded to Frémont. The latter, although laying no claim to brilliance, was thorough and systematic. He outlined his plan for the search and his men carried out his instructions with such assiduity that four large clothes hampers were required to contain the umbrellas, jewelry, watches, brass knuckles, handbags, lipsticks and miscellaneous articles discovered under the seats and in the corridors and dressing rooms. Among the articles found were a copy of *Science and Health with Key to the Scriptures;* several reefers; various sheets of music corresponding to numbers on the program; a pair of lumberman's rubbers; four packs of Kem cards; a ship-carpenter's awl; a rare scarab which attracted Evans' interest at once, he having recently taken up the study of Egyptology; three bank books; Frank Harris' *Life and Loves,* Vol. 1; and various addresses and telephone numbers scrawled hastily. One drunk was found asleep in the second balcony, but he was quickly identified by Maritan as a harmless chap who had once been a tenor at the Opéra Comique and had lost his grip because of despondency over what he believed to be the decline in the standards of that famous institution.

Of Miss Hattie Ham, however, no trace was found. Neither was there a Guarnerius, nor even an ocarina. The gentlemen of the press, discouraged, began to drift away in order to get their story into the morning editions. One by one the officers were dismissed, until there remained in the hall only Evans and Miriam, Hydrangea and the Chief, Sergeants Schlumberger and Bonnet, Jacques Maritan and Anton Diluvio.

"I wonder if I might trouble you for a brandy and soda?" asked Evans, calmly, of Maritan. With the cool glass in his hand, he excused himself from the group backstage and returned to his place in the auditorium. "Miriam," he said. "You remember the prelude in C-sharp minor? Would you mind playing it, rather slowly, at about the tempo Mr. Diluvio followed this evening?"

"Ah, God! America!" exclaimed Frémont, his eyes protruding from his head. "You don't mean to say we're going to stop for music, just now?"

"Only one selection," replied Evans, and Miriam began.

"Bang, bong, plumb," rang out from three bass strings of the grand piano, and Miriam glanced inquiringly at Diluvio, who nodded to indicate that the tempo was exact. In the middle of Rachmaninoff's gem, as everyone knows, there is a sort of free-for-all which may be interpreted with gusto, or not, according to the performer's mood. Miriam, keyed up by the evening's events, let go with all the strength she had developed busting broncos. Evans, meanwhile, had taken out his watch and was counting the seconds.

"Thank you," he said, at last, before the piece was finished, and turning to Frémont and the two sergeants, he said: "Please follow me."

Without further words he led the way to the fatal dressing room, paced the distance from the armchair to the door, then proceeded to the rear of the stage which all evening had been in darkness. There was stored an extra curtain, on which was a scene labeled "Venice," sawhorses, props of various kinds, and aloft an antedated mechanism by which, in former days, the curtain had been raised and the scenery shifted.

"A flashlight, please," said Homer, and the Chief handed him his powerful lamp. As Evans turned the strong beam skyward, each man gasped, for dangling several meters in the air was a black-clothed figure turning slowly to and fro.

A shout brought Maritan and the violinist to the scene, and the impresario, clutching at some ropes that were tied to large hasps on one side, tried to untangle them.

"Allow me," said Miriam, who could sling a pack-saddle of fishhooks over a mule's back while anyone who cared to said "Jack Robinson." Deftly she unskeined the clumsily tied ropes, tested one, then another, and slowly the black-draped figure began to descend. Diluvio, white as chalk, grasped the feet and the knees, while Evans caught the shoulders. Homer had whipped out his jack-knife. A large handkerchief had been used as a gag, and the senseless Hattie had been strapped up in a sort of acrobat's harness. As Evans unbound her he detected a faint odor of chloroform.

"Tell me she's not dead," moaned Diluvio, and Evans quickly reassured him, after listening to Hattie's heart. A moment later, the dazed accompanist opened her eyes and her lips began to form words which quickly were identified as "Whiskey." A tumbler of whiskey was brought, and after she quaffed it off, she looked straight at Evans with her sharp hazel eyes and smiled a brave but feeble smile.

"From now on, Mr. Homer Evans," she said, faintly, "you swing the baton. I got you wrong at first, and I

53

apologize. You are the Master's Voice, and that goes also for Diluvio." To which the relieved violinist bowed a swift assent.

"What happened?" asked Frémont, completely at sea.

"Don't ask me. I came off stage for a snifter and sat down in my easy chair, and from that time on your guess is as good as mine. But how about the violin?"

"No trace," said Anton, "but what does that matter?"

Until that moment, Diluvio had borne up well under the unusual strain, but his face was drawn and tired, and Evans, having in mind the corpse in the rue Jean-Jacques Rousseau, was getting increasingly anxious for a look at the defunct Bostonian. Also, he remembered the dog, Moritz. The Boxers, he knew, although they appear to be staid and deliberate, are a high-strung race with sensitive nerves. He did not want to leave the splendid animal too long at his task of fighting off flatfeet, newshawks and hotel attendants.

"Miriam," he said, gently. "Would you mind escorting Miss Ham and Mr. Diluvio to their hotel? You should stay there on guard until relieved by Sergeant Bonnet, then come at once to the Hotel Wilton."

Now Hattie Ham, having been drugged and dangled aloft a matter of some two hours, was very near the jitters. She knew she was in danger, and that Diluvio was in peril as well. When she saw that a handsome young American girl had been assigned as their only bodyguard, her teeth began to chatter. Homer, divining her uneasiness and its cause, took a tuning fork from a table and stood it up on the grand piano.

"Miss Ham is pardonably nervous. Will you please reassure her?" he said to Miriam, with an affectionate smile.

"Why, certainly," replied Miriam, and with that she drew her automatic with a motion quicker than the eye could follow. There was a sharp report and, although the tuning fork still stood precariously in its place, the sound of a clear unmistakable "A" was heard across the stage. She had grazed the tines just enough to set them in vibration.

"You see," Evans said, "you're in good hands." And Miriam, grasping an arm each of Hattie and the harassed violinist, led them unprotestingly away.

There was to be no performance at the Salle Gaveau the following day, so at Homer's request Maritan closed and locked the doors and Frémont assigned officers to guard them until a thorough examination could be made. Hydrangea, whose interest in the Chief's work did not extend to the viewing of corpses, consented to be taken home by Schlumberger, the Chief's colored chauffeur, Melchisadek Knockwoode, being temporarily disabled following an unusual run of luck at the races.

Thus it was that Evans and Frémont started off together for the rue Jean-Jacques Rousseau. Now it would seem that such a distinguished French philosopher, the father of so many of our modern ideas, would have an impressive street to perpetuate his name. Unhappily in Paris this is not so. The rue Jean-Jacques Rousseau juts off at an improbable angle, just across from the Magazin du Louvre and brings up in an ignominious little square in front of the Bourse. And it is not lined with fine buildings or beauteous monuments, but rather with soiled *bistrots,* unprosperous little stores and shops, and a few dingy dwellings. The dingiest of these is called the Hotel Wilton, and patronized mostly by English visitors who do not want to be entranced with anything on the east side of the channel, least of all in Paris. There is a gloomy lobby with stuffed chairs ranged around the sides, in which at tea time may be found a few guests imbibing warm liquid of a color and consistency best spared the reader, and munching dry biscuits as they talk about the way the world is going to pot. Early in the evening, the lights are dimmed, which at first glance would seem an impossible task, and the guests go upstairs to bed, complaining about the dust in the stair carpets and the fact that the *chef,* in spite of continual admonitions, insists on sprinkling nutmeg on Yorkshire pudding. Behind them, as they snore, the nightly miracle of Les Halles, or the central market, is taking place, with busy workers distributing the food supply and sidewalks piled high with fragrant mushrooms, strawberries and stacks of carrots and cauliflower in brilliant lamplight. Northward are the teeming boulevards, with cafés and restaurants whose gaiety are proverbial the world over. To the south lies enigmatic Montparnasse. But the guests of the Wilton know not of these things, and care less. They are occupied with being cautious and respectable, which takes practically all their energy and time.

The night watchman was standing stiffly at the door, as he had done man and boy, and when the Chief and Homer Evans entered he glared at them suspiciously and mumbled that no such thing had ever happened in his hotel before. At the desk inside, the clerk was doing crossword puzzles from the London *Times.*

"What French wine suggests room money?" he asked peevishly as Evans approached the desk.

"God, I suppose it's Chambertin," replied Homer, with a grimace.

"That fits, all right," mumbled the clerk, who had been racking his brains several hours.

Mr. Leffingwell Baxter of Boston, according to the clerk's statement, had registered at five in the afternoon, the day before, after an altercation with the management about the admission of Moritz, the dog. Only when Mr. Baxter had produced a worn Easter card from the elder Wilton, part owner of the establishment, had the manager, a Mr. Ferdinand Tredwell, given way. The late Mr. Baxter had then gone to his room, unpacked his baggage, and secured a large bone for Moritz, before he would consent to take his tea. After tea he had taken the dog for a walk around the Palais Royal and had dined on whiting with paperhanger's sauce, followed by a joint the remnants of which Moritz had ignored. That was topped off with orphan's caviar, or tapioca pudding.

"Perhaps it's a mercy that this Baxter died, after all," said Chief Frémont, at the end of the lugubrious recital, for the Chief was no mean trencherman and the mention of such victuals as had been consumed by the deceased prejudiced the good officer against him right from the start.

On entering the lobby they had not noticed that in a dim corner was slumbering a distinguished middle-aged Frenchman who turned out to be the medical examiner, Dr. Hyacinthe Toudoux. When awakened, the doctor greeted his associates and friends with a few remarks, the general trend of which was derogatory to Anglo-Saxons.

Then he picked up his kit of instruments and followed Evans and the Chief upstairs. Two police officers in uniform had their backs to the door, aware from time to time of sniffing and a suppressed growl that issued from the crack beneath the heavy wooden door.

"Don't try to enter, I beg of you. That beast is the most vicious I have seen in eighteen years' service in the department," the senior officer said.

"Please go away. He smells you," said Evans, and the officers bristled indignantly. "No offense," added Homer, and asked Frémont and the doctor also to withdraw until he had made his peace with Moritz. As soon as the others were out of nose-shot, Evans turned the handle of the door and said: "Moritz!" The Boxer, whose nerves were worn to a frazzle by his frantic vigil, made as if to spring and checked himself in mid-air when Evans made a certain almost imperceptible motion, that of snapping his thumb and third finger, soundlessly. When Frémont and the officers responded a moment later to Evans' call, they found him seated on a straight-backed horsehair chair in one corner, with the dog's large head on his knees.

"Quiet, old boy. These are our friends," said Evans, gently, making that snapping motion again near the dog's damp muzzle. As if to verify the statement, Moritz straightened himself gravely and, passing around the circle, looked up first at Dr. Hyacinthe Toudoux, then at Frémont and lastly at the pair of patrolmen. He made it plain that the last two were not his favorites but, after a philosophic sniff at their trousers legs, he looked back at Evans and returned to his side.

"This is the savage brute who has terrorized the Paris police department, lo these many hours," Homer said.

"It is strange that men trained so sternly in the performance of their duty could not understand that this good dog was offering them an object lesson they could ill afford to ignore. But never mind. Let's have a look at the remains."

"*Nom de Dieu,* can't we have some more light?" asked Dr. Hyacinthe Toudoux. "I might develop pictures here, on a pinch, but surely you don't expect me to ferret out a cause of death in such obscurity."

"The management of the Wilton doesn't hold with glaring modern lighting," said the clerk, who had followed them as far as the doorway.

"Call the manager," barked Toudoux, and the clerk complied grudgingly.

The manager, Ferdinand Tredwell, joined them a few minutes later. He was clad in an old-fashioned nightshirt and flannel slippers turned up grotesquely at the toes. "About the dog?" he said. "Am I to understand that his board will be paid, and that he is to occupy the room?"

"To the devil with board and room," answered Dr. Toudoux. "We want some proper light in here."

"Our guests have not complained about the lighting," Tredwell said.

"Send a man to the kitchen. There must be a large bulb or two there," suggested Evans, and soon the tiny light near the ceiling had been replaced by an extension and a sixty candle power tungsten.

"Now go away, all of you except the doctor and Mr. Evans," ordered Frémont.

"I think I should be present," objected Tredwell, and after a nod from Evans the Chief agreed.

The body of Mr. Leffingwell Baxter was seated in an armchair before a small table on which was an unfinished game of checkers. One elbow rested on the table, the other hand was on his knee. His eyes were half closed, as if he were thinking, and there was no sign of violence whatever. Opposite the corpse, another chair was placed, as if Baxter's opponent had risen without haste and left the table. The dead man was wearing a light-gray suit of tropical worsted, with a white shirt, stand-up collar and a bow tie somewhat like oatmeal in color and texture.

"Please touch nothing, just yet," said Evans, as with his magnifying glass he examined the surface of the table, the checkers and the thickly carpeted floor.

"I might have known," groaned Frémont. "No revolver, no blunt or sharp-pointed instruments, no bitter almond odor. Nothing tangible. Perhaps this duffer died of heart failure. I see no evidence of murder at all."

"In good time," said Homer. "First, I should like to have the photographer take some necessary shots, then the fingerprint man should go over most carefully the table surface, the checkers and the arms of both chairs. Thanks to the dog, nothing has been disturbed. And while the routine work is being done, I should like to talk with Schlumberger, who found the body and who, I understand, has watched Baxter's movements beginning yesterday at noon. Mr. Tredwell, I am sure, will put another room at our disposal."

"This situation, gentlemen, is without precedent," said the manager, but he led the way to a room across the hall and soon there was a muffled whine of the siren as Sergeant Schlumberger's roadster brought up at the hotel. The honest Alsatian came up the stairs, puffing not so much from exertion as dismay. With him was Officer Serré, who had helped with the shadowing of Baxter.

"I trust, Sergeant, that you and Serré did not murder this man yourselves," said Frémont, sarcastically.

"I can't understand," said Schlumberger. "I picked the fellow up, with his dog, when he left the hotel just after lunch today. He walked along the rue de Rivoli, crossed to the Tuileries and after proceeding briskly to the Orangerie and back to the Louvre, went under the archway, stopped a moment in a tobacco shop across from the Comédie Française, then entered the courtyard of the Palais Royal.

"There he looked at his watch and led the dog around all four sides of the square, sat on a bench and read a newspaper, smoked a cigar, the butt of which I have with me, gentlemen, and at two o'clock he entered a small shop called 'Aux Citoyens' and remained standing at the front counter, talking with the proprietor, Monsieur Rebec."

At this point, Evans interrupted with a question. "What sort of a shop is Aux Citoyens? I don't seem to remember."

"That's the strange part of it," said Schlumberger. "The shop contains ribbons, medals and decorations of all sorts, civil and military, and from all lands. One can buy there the rosettes and ribbons of the Legion of Honor, the Victoria Cross, the Croix de Guerre, with or without palms, the order of St. Idelfonso, the Iron Cross, anything at all. I have heard that Rebec has been careful

61

to sell only to authorized persons the various tokens of honor our own and foreign governments have bestowed."

"Did Baxter buy one or more of the decorations?" asked Evans.

"He did not," said Schlumberger. "But there is more to be said about the shop. You may well imagine that it would be hard to eke out a livelihood selling medals, even at fancy prices, for the things last practically a lifetime and one seldom sees an individual with more than fifteen or sixteen at a time. Under those circumstances it would be difficult to establish a regular clientele. M. Rebec also, in a workshop in the rear of the shop, repairs and sells old violins."

"Damnation," said Frémont. "If this case is to be linked with that infernal concert, we are up the spout."

"I think there's no doubt a connection," said Evans.

"And I suppose also that pimp and cutthroat called Godo the Whack . . ."

"Very possibly," said Evans.

Frémont writhed and groaned.

Light footsteps were heard in the hallway and a tap on the door quickly followed. "Come in," said Evans. "It's Miriam," he explained.

Miriam entered and looked around, surprised. "What? No body!" she said.

"It's in the room across the hall," Evans said. "The camera men and fingerprint experts are busy there now."

"Go on with your story," the Chief said to Schlumberger, after Miriam had sat down quietly in a corner. "How did you contrive to lose a six-foot Bostonian in a shop only three yards wide?"

"When Baxter and M. Rebec went into the back room,

I began to worry about a possible rear exit. I signaled an officer and sent for Serré, who relieved me in front of the shop. Then I went around to the rear of the building and found that there was a door leading from the workshop to the rue de Richelieu but the door was nailed up. The *conciérge* told me it had not been used for years. I had lunch, then rejoined Serré and we waited until nearly five o'clock. I assure you, gentlemen, that this afternoon was the only occasion in my long service when I wished I had possessed a decoration I might renew. But finally, I entered the shop without pretext, quietly. The front room was empty and I could have filched enough medals to stock a shop of my own, for neither the proprietor nor my quarry put in an appearance. At last I opened the door of the rear room and there I saw M. Rebec, with an odd-looking glass in his eye like jewelers wear, peering into the insides of something that looked like an old mandolin. He looked up, surprised but not startled, placed the instrument on his work bench and rose politely.

" 'Excuse me,' " I said. " 'I was looking for a Mr. Baxter.'

" 'Oh, Baxter,' " said the proprietor. " 'He was here a while ago. Merely called to say "How do you do." He must have slipped out while I was examining this excellent recorder, which dates from the time of Molière.' "

"To the devil with Molière," said Frémont.

"I thought it best, under the circumstances, not to betray my agitation," said the sergeant.

"Quite right," said Evans. "What then?"

"I found Serré, told him Baxter had got away, God knows how, left him to watch the shop and the proprietor, summoned two other plain-clothes men from the prefecture, and rushed back to this incredible hotel. Mr. Baxter, according to the clerk and Mr. Tredwell, here, had not returned. To be sure, I went up to his room and looked in. He was not there. I sat in the lobby until eight-thirty, and in came Baxter, his impressive dog, and another man I did not know. Apparently they had dined, for they went straight upstairs."

"Was either Mr. Baxter or his companion carrying anything?" asked Evans, eagerly.

"Yes," said Schlumberger, "the other man had under his arm a pasteboard box, such as tailors use for suits, perhaps a little larger."

"I'm beginning to catch a glimmer of light," said Evans, and sighed with contentment.

Frémont grunted. "Describe the man with the suitbox," he said.

"He was tall and wiry, with large hands and feet, dressed in dark-gray clothes not recently pressed. That's about all I can say," said Schlumberger, miserably.

"I didn't see him, if he's still in Baxter's room," said Frémont. "Did you manage to lose him, too?"

"Don't be severe," Evans said. "The sergeant took every reasonable precaution, I am sure."

"I waited until ten o'clock, ten-fifteen, to be exact, and grew increasingly nervous. I felt sure things were going wrong, and still one of my men was watching in the corridor with his eye on Baxter's door, another was stationed near the rear exit and I was guarding the lobby. At ten-fifteen the man with the suitbox descended. I signaled for him to be followed, then mounted the stairs and . . . Gentlemen, my anxiety had reached such a point that I resorted to the keyhole. Baxter was sitting at a table, facing me. Not a sound came from the room except the faint snoring of the dog, Moritz. I knocked. Once. Twice. I pushed against the door and it opened. You know the rest. The dog flew at my throat. I shouted. My assistant tried to help, and all through the racket the man sat without moving. It was clear that he was dead."

"Now this is a case worth while," said Evans. "Not at all banal, eh, Chief?"

"I shall lose my mind," said Frémont, and rose wearily to his feet.

The photographers had finished their work, and the fingerprint man, Sergeant Cidre, confronted them happily.

"For once I get a break," he said, and Evans nodded without surprise. "There are fingerprints everywhere. On the table, on the checkers, on the ashtrays, the arms of both chairs . . ."

"All Baxter's?" Evans asked.

"No, indeed, two other chaps' as well."

"Two others?" asked Schlumberger, indignantly. "Impossible."

"Oh, yes. There were two of them, all right. But the strange part of it is that Johnny No. 3's prints are only to be found on Baxter's starched cuffs," the expert said. "In a few hours, I'll have pictures for you that will do your hearts good."

The Chief turned to Dr. Toudoux. "Now, perhaps, Doctor, you can tell us when and how he died," he said.

Dr. Toudoux began his examination of the body with his customary caution and dexterity, but the longer he worked, the more baffled he became. Mr. Tredwell, the manager, sat stiffly in a chair near the doorway, the dog lay sleepily beside him until Miriam entered. Then he crossed to where she was standing and looked up, expectantly.

"Good Moritz," she said. "You've had a busy evening, and you want to go out."

The frown on the dog's forehead deepened appreciatively, his mouth sagged slightly, and he wagged his tail, left, right, left, right. Asking Evans' permission, Miriam led the dog down the carpeted stairs and out into the rue Jean-Jacques Rousseau. When she returned half an hour later, Dr. Toudoux was in one of his worst humors.

"I'll have to take this defunct Bostonian to the laboratory and go over him there. Evidently he grew rigid almost at the instant he died. I cannot even hazard a guess as to what killed him, but I shall track down the cause, never fear. One expects a medical examiner to take one look, then say 'Ah, yes. He kicked the bucket at 9.15 or 10.24.' Ah, science! And ah, my beautiful Eugénie, doubtless waiting anxiously at the window for my return! Friend Evans, how you can waste your best years without knowing the joys of a hearth and home, I cannot understand. Myself, I frittered away my life until the age of fifty-four, vaingloriously boasting of my bachelorhood. But you, Monsieur. You who have an intelligence that dwarfs those of all among us. How can you be so blind?"

Miriam had turned as red as a Montana sunset, and Frémont's face had assumed a rather purple hue. "No cause! No hour! My head is splitting open. No revolvers, darts, daggers, stilettos, gimlets, rat-tail files, ropes, razors, almonds, serpents, crossbows, time bombs. Not even an odor, except the musty smell of this incredible hotel. I have reached the end of my national highway, and before me lies only the muddy unpaved road to failure."

"Let's all go home for a little rest," said Evans, gently. "You, Doctor, to your charming Eugénie; you, Chief, to the jewel of the African hills. For my part, I shall think a while and drive with Miss Leonard around the lake in the Bois de Boulogne, and perhaps, since Moritz has adopted our fair scion of the prairies, he will deign to come along. It would not be good for his nerves to witness the removal of the body, so let us spare him."

They all started for the door, and the Chief beckoned the waiting orderlies with the stretcher.

"Come on, Mr. Tredwell. You may as well go back to bed," said Evans, for the hotel manager was sitting straight in his chair, apparently asleep. Receiving no response, Evans shook the man's shoulder. Then turning with an agonized cry, he clasped Miriam in his arms.

"Tell me, dear! Do you feel ill? Are you all right?" he asked, hoarsely.

"Why, yes," said Miriam, shaken with astonishment. She had never known Evans to be so distraught or terrified, and never, in public, to be the least bit demonstrative.

"Stand still, everyone! Don't move a step!" said Evans, in that tone of command he used rarely but was even more rarely disobeyed. He walked over to Moritz and, with both hands raised to the level of his chest, said calmly to the dog: "Sit down."

Wrinkling his forehead, the Boxer sat down, unhurriedly.

"Your sharpest scalpel," Evans demanded of the doctor, who handed him an instrument without a single lost motion.

Evans stooped, and slipping the sharp blade underneath the dog's breast harness, he cut it clear, then gently took Moritz by the scruff of the neck and lifted him a foot from the floor. Carrying the bewildered animal to the empty room across the hall, he dropped him there and closed the door.

What's wrong? What's all this about?" asked Frémont.

"Our unfortunate manager is dead, and has died in the same manner as Leffingwell Baxter," said Evans. "Please do not go near that dog harness. I wish to examine it here and now."

He reached into the doctor's case for a bandage, looped it around the harness without touching it and placed it on the bed table, which was covered with glass. With the strongest magnifying glass the doctor had in his kit, Homer went over the leather straps, one by one, and soon let out an exclamation of satisfaction.

"Look at this, Chief," he said, and focused the glass. "You will observe a small pointed object, like a phonograph needle. You will find somewhere on the bare legs of poor Tredwell a little scratch, no doubt, where the dog rubbed him in passing. And, if I am not mistaken, the late Baxter has a similar abrasion, probably on the palm of his left hand. We are opposed, my friends, to a killer who not only is willing to slaughter his victims in a fiendish and cowardly way but exposes innocent bystanders without number. That needle point has been dipped in deadly poison, of a kind we cannot hope to identify without intensive study . . . That will be the doctor's contribution."

Miriam felt her legs begin to weaken and sat down.

"My father told me it was not good for dogs to be continually petted," she said, faintly.

"I shall go to Montana and kiss him on both cheeks, the moment this case is over," Evans said, fervently . . . "Well, that's all for tonight."

5

In Which a Good Time Is Had,

But Decidedly Not by All

Now Anton Diluvio, although he came of good New England stock and had been christened Andrew Flood in the meeting house at Stow, Massachusetts, ranked high among the modern masters of the violin. It was true, as he-had stated to Evans in the course of the fateful ride in the boat train between Rouen and Paris, that he did not let his high temperament run away with him. And it was also true that he had had more than his share of trouble with fond women before he had been taken in hand by Hattie Ham. Hattie guarded him conscientiously from the onslaughts of admirers but, just lately, it seemed to him, she had gone about her task a bit too zealously. Likewise, Paris was Paris and through the half-open windows of his room in the Plaza-Athènée was drifting a breeze scented with new leaves and other aromas that disturb young violinists as much or more than ordinary men.

No sooner had he seen Hattie safely into her adjacent room and shaken hands with Sergeant Bonnet, who was to protect them both from harm, than Diluvio began to feel an urge to cruise around a bit on his own and try to forget, at least for a while, the loss of his rare Guarnerius. Conscience put up a struggle but the odds were too great. No sooner had he hit the pillow than he began to turn and twist, to think of the deluge of publicity that on the morrow was to engulf him, of how he should invest his large cut of the box office receipts; in short of nearly everything except his personal safety and his promise to Homer Evans to beware. Why Hattie had been trussed up and hoisted into the scenery, he could not venture to guess, but his confidence in Evans had already reached such proportions that he thought of questions and answers as being in Homer's department, and nothing he need stir his own brain about. His nature was artistic, not scientific, and after a stiff dose of squirming and pillow-thumping he rose quietly and dressed in the dark. Hattie, he believed, would be sleeping soundly. His immediate problem was Bonnet.

Sergeant Bonnet, it will be remembered, had in the course of the Louvre mummy case lost track of a slippery party named Xerxes, of the even slipperier firm of Lewson-Phipps and Xerxes, and the memory of what Chief Frémont had said to Bonnet still rankled. Since that unfortunate mishap, the sergeant had made leeches ashamed of themselves, so closely had he stuck to his assignments. The open window, however, gave Diluvio an idea. He glanced out and downward and found that beneath it was a balcony, not more than fifteen feet below the level of the sill. On the day before, upon his arrival in Paris, he had received gratis from a manufacturer a large supply of violin strings, so he braided several dozen of these together into a rope, knotted the lengths together skilfully, and just as the clocks began to strike one he attained the balcony in question and by a clever flip of his catgut rope detached the upper end, coiled it and slipped it into his pocket.

The windows leading inward from the balcony were closed but not securely locked and as the violinist stepped fearfully in, he was glad to find that the room was empty. From that point he gained the ground floor lobby and bribed the Russian doorman to say nothing of his absence.

"The Dôme," he murmured, as a nightfaring taxi edged over to the curb, in response to the doorman's whistle.

The Café du Dôme, at that hour, was going full blast, as were all the neighboring establishments. Streams of tourists flowed along the sidewalks, in indolent counter motion; the fire-eater sent sprays of lighted gasoline into the lower branches of the plane trees, waiters bustled to and fro on their augmented *terrasses,* Moroccans in burnooses and fezzes offered colored carpets for sale. Diluvio, thrilled by his guilty sense of freedom, reviewed the women of the demimonde who strolled along, and it seemed to him that all of them were beautiful. He followed happily the rhythm of their hips and shoulders as they passed, and reflected that none of them would be likely to recognize him, to burble about harmonics and overtones, or to know Bach from a last year's bird's nest. Fiddlers and non-fiddlers were all the same to them, he hoped, as he sat down with a sigh of satisfaction near the center of the *terrasse.*

Achilles, the venerable and sharp-tongued news dealer,

came shuffling along with a sheaf of wet New York *Heralds, Matins, Petit Journals,* etc., tucked under his arm and Diluvio bought a few at random, not to read, but to hold in front of his face if any music lovers loomed on his festive horizon. From the table on his right, a hearty voice boomed, "Come here, Achilles, you old crowbait, and let me read the headlines free of charge."

"If only you could learn to paint whiskers," the old man cackled, in response. "Last year you made them look like putty, now they frizzle like chickweed."

Turning to observe who was on the short end of the foregoing repartee, Diluvio saw a huge man with forearms tattooed and bare, wearing a blue cotton shirt, duck trousers, cloth sandals and no socks.

"That's Hjalmar Jansen, the painter," whispered a Topeka school teacher to another from Dallas, on her right.

Diluvio could not be sure of the school teachers. They might or might not have been present at his recital, so he grabbed up the *Herald* to shield his face and could not help seeing the headlines.

DILUVIO ROBBED IN SALLE GAVEAU
Accompanist Drugged and Assaulted
Guarnerius Worth $500,000
Whisked from Backstage
Virtuoso Near Collapse

To Diluvio's disgust, a two-column cut of his head and shoulders, taken by a photographer who thought that musicians should look like a cross between an *abbé* and an interior decorator, stared up from nearly every table on the acres of *terrasses* around him. Suddenly he felt conspicuous and insecure. He tried to busy himself with the rest of the news, after having ordered his second double bourbon and ginger ale, and came upon the following item:

BOSTON MAN MEETS DEATH
IN PARIS HOTEL

But the *Herald,* not daring to offend the Wilton management, whose advertising account netted the paper about $6.75 a season, or to risk a libel suit from Baxter's aristocratic family in case foul play was not proven beyond a doubt, passed over the story lightly. The article admitted that a chap had passed on, and that was about all there was to it.

Beside Hjalmar Jansen, and looking her blondest, sat Mathilde Dubonnet, the model he had acquired during the Louvre murder case and whose husband, although at first in despair, had become reconciled to the new arrangement when he saw what his former wife had to put up with from Hjalmar. Mathilde was complacent and pretty, but by no means a Portia or Minerva. She glanced at the photo on page one of the *Herald* and an instant later her eyes met those of Diluvio.

"Why, that's the man who lost the violin," she said, her voice shrill with the joy of discovery.

Diluvio was aghast, and had to act quickly. The big painter, whatever luck he might have representing whiskers, looked to Anton like a man who would rally round when a fellow artist was in distress. Acting on the spur of the moment, Diluvio shifted over to the vacant seat at Jansen's table and said, almost in a whisper:

"I say, old man. Don't give me away. I want a peaceful drink without being bothered."

74

"Why, sure," said Jansen with a grin. And in no un-certain terms he ordered Mathilde to be discreet and silent, under penalty of a No. 1 rap in the puss. Within a few minutes, the two men were chatting easily, and downing double whiskies at a rate that looked bad for Diluvio's *legato* in the near future. Without being crude, the violinist conveyed to the big painter his natural hankering for a woman of the looser sort, and it was agreed that Mathilde should be sent back to the studio to wash brushes while the two men set out for the Bal Tabarin.

"There's a kid at the Tabarin who goes haywire when-ever she sights Mathilde, so I like to spare her pain," ex-plained Hjalmar, as the model trudged obediently away.

"I understand," said Diluvio, which was by no means an overstatement.

The regular doorman at the Bal Tabarin was absent that night because of a broken jaw and sprained shoul-der, and the substitute, a huge freckled Finn named Gus, had been chosen for his bulk rather than his reasoning powers.

"You can't come in without shoes," grunted Gus, eying Hjalmar's well-worn sandals.

Hjalmar looked at Diluvio and grinned. With impres-sive team work, considering that they had never rioted together before, the violinist caught hold of Gus's broad sash, as Hjalmar jerked his feet from under him. While other attendants protested and milled around ineffec-tively, Hjalmar and Anton overpowered the Finn, lugged him around a convenient corner, and there they took his shoes away, leaving him Jansen's sandals. A few moments later they were seated comfortably at a table near the stage, and the manager was apologizing to Jansen and offering a round of champagne on the house. The painter was too gracious to refuse.

"Who's that baby fourth from the left?" asked Diluvio happily, as the girls came dancing in.

"That's Nicole, the one I told you about," Hjalmar said, and hearing her name, the dark curly-haired young dancer favored them both with a welcoming smile.

At another near-by table was sitting a distinguished-looking elderly man in evening clothes who followed the course of the smile from Nicole to Hjalmar and showed signs of anxiety.

"Why, it's Maître François Ronron," Jansen said, and soon he led Diluvio to the old man's table. In the course of the Louvre murder case, to which Maître Ronron contributed so brilliantly, the lawyer had met Nicole at Hjalmar's studio and had formed the habit of attending each performance at the Bal Tabarin, in order to protect the girl from the many temptations which beset young dancers.

Diluvio listened with interest to the reminiscences of the lawyer and Hjalmar, and was particularly pleased to learn how highly they rated the powers of Homer Evans, who had promised to retrieve his violin. His companions were so eulogistic, in fact, that their words, coupled with the soothing effect of the champagne, caused Anton to forget not only the $500,000 Guarnerius, but also Hattie Ham and Sergeant Bonnet. The show was a good one, not noisy but never dull. The lithe bodies of the dancers, their friendly glances and the holiday mood of the audience all contributed to Diluvio's peace of mind, and when he was asked by Maître Ronron if the career of a virtuoso was not an exacting one, he assured the amiable jurist that, if one were careful to relax now and then, concert fiddling was no tougher than any other kind of profitable exertion.

"Now a painter," Diluvio said, "has to worry about whiskers, whether to paint them one hair at a time, which is practically impossible, or to break them up into imaginary planes, which is frequently unconvincing."

"Old Achilles was right," said Hjalmar, for a moment despondent. "I'm going stale. I need a change."

By a strange coincidence, Maître François Ronron was in a similar state of mind. He had just made frightful hash of a tort case before the Court of Appeals, by inadvertently wearing a ring the Pope had given him on the day the referee chanced to be a freethinker. Until he had met his young friends, and was reminded that youth, too, has its adversities, the Maître had feared that he might be cracking up.

"Ah, well," he said, "a good bender, as you Americans say." And he ordered more and better champagne.

Nicole, who was having a well-earned respite during an Annamite juggling act, came over to the table, and after borrowing a handkerchief from the Maître, whom she addressed as "Coco," she spread it over the seat of a chair and sat down, a precaution made necessary by the fact that she was wearing no clothes and the straw of the chair was prickly. Nicole was a girl without guile, and her emotions, easily stirred, were reflected in her countenance. It was plain that she adored Hjalmar, respected "Coco" or Maître Ronron, and admired the handsome young Diluvio.

"How was I, Hjalmar?" she asked, eagerly. "Am I really learning to dance?"

"Not bad," the painter admitted. "If I could paint whiskers half as well as you do the Maxixe . . ."

"Why paint whiskers? There are plenty of smooth-faced men," said Nicole.

Before the exponents of the various arts and professions had time to deal with that eminently sensible suggestion, Hjalmar let out a cry of surprise and delight. For entering the doorway was Bridgette Murphy, proprietress of the Hotel Murphy et du Danube Bleu, in a stunning peacock-green evening gown, and, at her side, the Singe.

In an instant, Hjalmar was on his feet, and as he advanced across the dance floor to meet Bridgette and the gang chief, a sort of gasp of appreciation arose from the audience. For the two men were as nearly matched in physique and bearing as seemed to be possible. Alone, either one would have been impressive, but the sight of them together caused even the most stolid of the merry-makers to give pause, and reflect that after all, the man of today, at his best, does not suffer by comparison with the heroes of old. Someone in the hall, however, must have been occupied with thoughts of a different nature, for just as Hjalmar reached the Singe's side, a corked bottle, heavy with champagne, came hurtling through the air from the direction of the doorway, and had not the painter caught it in mid-air, it would have crashed against the Norman's head and felled him in his tracks, rugged as he was.

"Many thanks, monsieur," said the Singe, without turning to glance at his assailant.

"It was nothing," said Hjalmar, still clutching the bottle. "But the guy got away. That Finn at the door isn't worth a damn. You could drive a horse and buggy past him."

"Let me at him," said Bridgette, squaring off, but a glance from the Singe was sufficient to quiet her.

The manager drew near and offered apologies, but no one paid much attention. Hjalmar led Bridgette to the table where Maître Ronron, Diluvio and Nicole were awaiting them, and the Singe followed leisurely and was introduced as Monsieur Peret. Nicole kissed Bridgette on both cheeks, then tripped back to the dressing room, to prepare for the can-can which was the climax of the night's entertainment. The tort case, the Guarnerius, painted whiskers and the untoward incident of the champagne-throwing were all forgotten as the party, which now occupied two tables placed together, settled down to a period of peaceful drinking, of sprightly conversation and keen enjoyment of the show. As the orchestra launched itself into the compelling rhythm of the can-can, the clocks outside, although no one inside heard them, struck the hour of four.

At precisely that hour, while Homer Evans and Miriam were circling the lake in the Bois de Boulogne in a slow-moving open taxi, Hattie Ham, in her commodious bed in the Plaza Athenée, stirred, then awakened. It may have been that a linnet chirped on her windowsill, or a scavenger may have overturned an ash can. In any event, she stretched her long thin limbs, opened her eyes and was aware of a slight headache due to the chloroform. She got up, covered her flapping pajamas with a bathrobe, stuck her feet into square-toed leather slippers, and

79

then discovered that, what with one thing and another, she had neglected to supply herself with cigarettes. Her brand was Sweet Caporal, but at that hour, and following such a harrowing experience, even French cigarettes would be better than nothing, she thought. Remembering that Sergeant Bonnet had been left on guard in the hallway, she opened her door cautiously and in an instant was faced by the anxious sergeant.

"Could you spare a cigarette, Sergeant?" Hattie asked.

"But certainly, madame," said Bonnet, whisking out a packet of Nadias. His vigil had been a tiresome one, and he was glad to have company for a while. They strolled up and down the corridor, smoking, and talking in whispers so as not to awaken Diluvio.

"Has he slept well?" Hattie asked.

"Like a top. I haven't heard a sound," the sergeant said. "If all the men I have to shadow, in the exercise of my hazardous profession, were of his type, police work would not be what it is."

At half past four, Hattie went back to bed, having in mind that she would have a busy day with the clippings, and slept soundly until eight o'clock. At that hour, it was her practice to order Diluvio's breakfast, arrange it the way he liked it, then serve it to him without a word. As he ate, she would take out his violin, set up the music rack, place whatever music he needed for his morning practice on a convenient table, then go back to her room until summoned for an accompaniment. Diluvio usually practiced alone until eleven or later, after which he needed the piano.

When the waiter knocked at her door, in response to her ring, she not only ordered what was needed for Diluvio and herself, but ascertained from Sergeant Bonnet that he was addicted to onion soup in the morning, and asked the waiter to set up a table for the sergeant in the hallway. With the tray balanced on one hand, a trick she had learned when serving with the Y.M.C.A. in the days of the A.E.F., she tapped lightly on Diluvio's door.

There was no response.

She tapped again, *mezzo-forte*. "Poor dear. He's tired," she said to the sergeant. Nevertheless, she knew that Anton let nothing interfere with his daily practice, and knocked a third time, loudly. Then she turned the door-knob and screamed, as the laden tray crashed to the floor.

"He's not here," she said, and started screaming again.

"Impossible," said the sergeant, but a quick search proved that she was right. The bed had been slept in, the window was open, but there were no knotted sheets or ropes to indicate that the violinist had made his exit by means of the balcony, which in broad daylight looked more difficult to attain than it had in starlight to Diluvio.

"Do something," shrieked Hattie. "Don't stand there like a numbskull. Call the Chief! Send word to Mr. Evans! Inform the management!"

But Bonnet was too stunned for immediate action. "This is the end for me," he said. "I might have been forgiven for losing a man in a subway crowd or a department store. But a bedroom, with one door and a sheer drop of four stories to the ground! What will Frémont say? I shall be drummed out of the force, held up to ridicule. I swear to you, madame, that I have not closed my eyes this night, that not for one instant have I deserted my post at this doorway."

"Good morning," said a familiar voice in the corridor.

"I'm sorry to trouble you at this hour, but I must have a few words with Monsieur Diluvio." The newcomer was Chief Frémont who, after a few hours of sleep, was itching for action. What he said, when informed that Diluvio had vanished, would, if related, prove detrimental to the interests of the reader, since it would result in the suppression of this story in practically any country in the world. Sergeant Bonnet, completely crushed, sat miserably in a corner, and with a pair of scissors from the dressing table began snipping at the stitches of his sergeant's chevrons.

"Spare your abuse for those who are better able to bear it," he begged. "I only know that I did my duty, as I saw it, and it has, as usual, landed me squarely in the soup."

"His clothes? Are any of them missing? See! Here are his pajamas, just where he stepped out of them," Frémont said, having been somewhat calmed by the violence of his outburst.

"Evans! Where is Evans?" shouted Hattie. "He's the only one among you with brains enough to pound sand in a rat hole." Nevertheless, she got enough control of herself to check up on Diluvio's wardrobe and told the Chief that the absent fiddler must be wearing a blue serge suit, wheat-colored shirt and a cream-colored felt of a pattern much in vogue.

The Chief, at that, sat down beside Bonnet and mopped his forehead. "Blue serge! Great God! Blue serge! Three-quarters of the men on the streets of Paris wear blue serge, and those devilish pale hats. Why can't a violinist show a little originality in his dress, or at least let his hair grow long behind? This fellow will look like all the tourists put together. And what about that balcony? Was he timid about heights, madame? Was he, perchance, an acrobat as well as a musician?"

Hattie looked down from the window and shuddered.

"He is athletic, but always reasonably cautious," she said, and sobbed.

The clerk and attendants were interviewed and the Russian night doorman was rousted out of bed, following which he swore, with his hand on the hundred-franc note Diluvio had given him, that no tall young men in blue serge had left the hotel after one o'clock that morning. Seeing Hattie, who never was handsome and surely was not at her best in the early hours, the Russian concluded that the violinist was entitled to a night out, if he wanted it and, furthermore, that it would probably do him a world of good.

"Bonnet, stop sniveling and set the dragnet," said Frémont, disgustedly. "Haul in all blue-serge types with normal haircuts who can't produce their papers," he said. Then he turned to Hattie and added: "We'll go to Evans' apartment, since nothing else will placate you. Likely as not Evans would be at home, and, if he is, he'll be annoyed. He starts his day about eleven in the morning, no matter who is abducted or murdered . . ."

"Murdered!" repeated Hattie, and underwent an astonishing change. Her eyes protruded, then rolled inward until the pupils disappeared, her hands and arms began to twitch, her teeth chattered, and after swaying on her tiptoes she fell senseless to the floor.

"Your choice of words is most unfortunate," muttered Bonnet to the Chief as he started away in pursuance of his sweeping orders.

83

6

Certain Unorthodox Means of Repairing the Raveled Sleeve of Care, with Sidelights on Criminal Psychology

THERE were no clocks to strike four on the rim of the lake in the Bois de Boulogne, but had there been, and had they struck, Homer Evans probably would not have heard them, so deep in thought was he. Miriam stood near by, on a rustic bridge leading to one of the small islands, and was watching the effect of the passage of a couple of ducks across a placid water surface which, between lily pads, reflected some of the rosiest work of the Goddess Aurora. Moritz was crashing happily through what would have been underbrush had not some public employee cut it zealously and stacked it beneath the stately moss-green trees.

For knitting up the raveled sleeve of care, sleep, of course, comes first on the list of specifics, but not far down from the top will be found the Boulogne woods outside of Paris on a hushed spring morning.

Evans was responding to nature's matutinal spell. The look of perplexity that had rested on his face as he had thought over in silence the events of the past two days and nights was giving way to one of interest, in fact, of determination. When he spoke, it was not of priceless violins, suspended spinsters, immobilized Bostonians, or mystery men with suspicious suitboxes who appeared and disappeared at will. He was preoccupied with the strange behavior of Godo the Whack. As usual, after a bout of intense thinking, Homer resumed his speculations aloud, to Miriam, in the hope that her responsive young brain would see an angle he had missed or, by an intuitive association of ideas, would give him a valuable lead.

"Aristotle," he began, "laid down some valuable laws on the unities of time and space. Had he been involved in modern criminology, undoubtedly he would have added to those a few on the unity of psychology. Men who wish to live outside the pale of our fundamental code betray themselves in two ways: first, by acting naturally, according to the pattern of conduct indicated by their previous behavior; secondly, by acting in a way that, viewed in the light of their habits and temperament, is obviously unnatural. We get them going and coming, as it were.

"I am thinking of that blot on the 5th *arrondissement* of Paris and the docks of Rouen, known as Godo the Whack. Luckily, he is no stranger to us, having crossed our paths in the Tout-or-Nada affair. He has shown himself to be cautious and cowardly, lacking in initiative. Above all, he has been in terror of his leader, the Singe."

"After what I saw at Rouen, I can understand that,"

said Miriam, shuddering as she remembered Godo's dangling form, held aloft above a gaping hold on a derrick hook.

"Godo did not know the Singe was in the neighborhood when he tried to wipe out a couple of his fellow workers in the vineyard of evil. But, as I have already said, he intended the murder of those two members of the Rollers to be his last act in Rouen as long as the Singe was alive. The Whack understood also that he would never again be safe in Paris. I can only explain Godo's bravado in one way." He paused hopefully.

"Perhaps someone put him up to it," said Miriam.

"Good girl," said Evans, pleased. "Someone is behind him, and someone who thinks he can buck the Singe and get away with it. There has been dissension of late among the St. Julien Rollers because of an edict of the Singe, namely, that each member of the gang must have his papers in order, and possess a permit to work. In the past, under the leadership of Barnabé Vieuxchamp, now on Devil's Island, the Rollers were constantly being put to inconvenience because the police would pick up stray gangsters and hold them in quod on the charge of having failed to secure documents of identity. That is why the Singe, who otherwise has been careful not to mix legitimate enterprise with his chosen field of endeavor, organized his export business which sends into a thirsty outside world an excellent supply of applejack. His gangsters, when ordered to perform actual labor long enough so they could obtain work cards to protect them from police raffles, were unwise enough to grumble and the Singe in many cases had to resort to physical persuasion."

"He ought to be good at that," said Miriam.

"None better," said Evans. "Of course, I can't ask the Singe about these matters, outright. He's as ethical as Maître Ronron or Dr. Hyacinthe Toudoux, according to his lights. But I am of the opinion that someone, within the gang, is attempting to consolidate and exploit the resentment against the Singe, to form an organized opposition which is trying to depose our Norman friend in favor of a rival. That hypothesis contains one flaw. I cannot think of a single crook in Paris who would dare tackle such a job or, if he dared, would think it possible to pull it off. Perhaps some brilliant new comet is about to streak across the sky of our underworld; but if that is so, surely some of us would have heard about it. Bonnet and Schlumberger, while not brilliant men, are patient and efficient and have worked out a system under which it is scarcely possible for a gangster in Paris to have his shoes shined without knowledge of that minor extravagance reaching headquarters.

"Well! Enough for Godo, at present. Let us assume that he has an unwise backer and has performed his rash acts according to instructions and under promise of protection. Let us review our fascinating ride on the boat train. You will remember that when the Singe was standing on the station platform, politely waiting for our train to depart, I thought he made a signal to me. Then he walked rapidly away toward the rear of the train, and I have reasons for thinking he may have boarded another car and reached Paris when we did, a sudden change of plan. Assuming, perhaps incorrectly, that the Singe's abrupt action had to do with someone in our car, I tried to decide who it might be. Of course, I recognized Diluvio and thought about his valuable violin, which was on the baggage rack. The crowd of Philadelphians I counted out, since it was their first visit to France and the Singe had never been in America. That left the late Leffingwell Baxter, of Boston, and his charming sister. It was some time before I discovered Moritz, lying quietly under the table, but after I was aware of the presence of the dog, I noticed that his master quieted him now and then by moving his third finger quietly over his thumb. When Diluvio reached for his violin, however, Baxter struck the palm of his hand rather sharply with all four fingers. Would you care to see a demonstration?"

Miriam nodded. Moritz was watching a brushpile into which a chipmunk had disappeared. Evans spoke to him quietly, then slapped his left palm with the fingers of the same hand. It was hardly audible to Miriam, but the sound reached the cropped ears of the Boxer and the transformation of a gentle creature into one hundred pounds of compact fury was startling, indeed. Bounding toward them on the bridge, teeth bared, head low, and growling ominously, the dog skidded on all fours and turned this way and that, in search of an invisible foe.

"There, old boy," said Evans, soothingly, and giving the all-quiet signal hereinbefore described. "I was only showing you off to your mistress, just in case . . ."

"Oh, Moritz," gasped Miriam, squatting and reaching for the dog's head. He was trembling and his forehead was deeply wrinkled with perplexity. From that moment he did no more hunting but stayed close to Evans and Miriam on the rustic bridge, as if he were a part of a group of sculptured figures that henceforth would be inseparable.

"My temptation," Evans went on, "was to jump at the

conclusion that the Singe had known Baxter and was suspicious of him, just because Baxter showed later that he had designs on Diluvio. We must not forget, however, that alongside the boat train, on the next track at Rouen, was a local third-class carriage crowded with men and women, mostly peasants or workmen. It is possible, and I think most likely, that the Singe saw someone in that other train, by looking through the windows of our car, and that his gesture, which I mistook for a signal, was involuntary."

"I don't think the Singe would make involuntary motions," said Miriam.

"That's the point. He got a real jolt. You know, as people do who see ghosts . . ." He paused because Miriam had clutched his arm.

"Forgive me, Homer, but the strangest idea crossed my mind. Are you *sure* that Barnabé is still on Devil's Island?" she asked.

Evans straightened himself so suddenly that Moritz grew rigid also. "By Jove," he said, and began pacing the bridge with the dog walking solemnly behind him. "My dear," he added at last, "again you have saved me from blundering. Your theory fits the facts. Barnabé would have a following among the Rollers he formerly ruled. He would try to displace the Singe. And if anyone could do it, it would be Barnabé, who is ruthless and clever, with none of the Singe's finer instincts. Of course, if the Singe had caught sight of Barnabé, who might have been in Rouen if he had got back into France, he might have been surprised out of his usual self-possession for an instant, before he got going. I must talk with the Singe, somehow, to see what I can pick up, indirectly.

And Frémont will cable French Guiana this very morning about Barnabé. Of course, the Chief will be all tangled up in the murders of Baxter and Tredwell—I hope no more have occurred—and the theft of the Guarnerius. And we'll have to pry discreetly into Diluvio's love affairs, to say nothing of the secret yearnings of Miss Baxter. A busy morning, what?"

"You must sleep a little while," said Miriam, gently.

"And you must register your dog," Homer said, and led the way back to the taxi.

In the meantime, while Aurora had had fair success in beautifying with her morning hues other roofs and steeples of the world capital of arts and letters, she had had comparatively little luck with the Bal Tabarin, which was ablaze with electric light. There, as the reader knows, at four o'clock an expectant hush occurred as the orchestra struck up the tune for the can-can. The choice quartette of dancers, of which the dark-eyed Nicole was number four, sidled on stage from right to left in perfect step with the music. Four sleek legs, in black silk stockings, were hopping sidewise inch by inch, and their four perfect mates were raised at the hips, bent at the knees, and were describing provocative rotations. The girls looked taller and more impressive in their can-can costumes, with starched white ruffles and enticing old-fashioned drawers. They were as completely covered for the can-can as they had been naked in the preceding act and, somehow, the allure was more compelling. Maître François Ronron could not remain seated, but rose and applauded vigorously. Diluvio, in trying to compare the merits of numbers two and three, front row, had forgotten that violins existed. Hjalmar slapped the Singe on the knee. If anyone in the gathering eyed the proceedings somewhat coldly, it was Bridgette Murphy, who had switched to Irish whiskey from champagne and was planning a series of rather brutal maneuvers in case any one of the dancers should get too much attention from the cold blue eyes of her escort. The exigencies of the Singe's profession had left him little time for recreation, so the evening's entertainment, together with the wit of the company in which he found himself, had caused him to think more highly of the pleasures of a frivolous world. He had been an enemy to society, according to the press, but just then he was struck with the fact that society had its points, without doubt.

When the show was over and a sad moment of reality overtook the others in the hall, Hjalmar Jansen suddenly thought of the *Presque Sans Souci,* a barge which had been confiscated by the State in the Hugo Weiss kidnapping and T.N.T. plot, and since that time had been moored near the Pont Royal, as if the State, having acquired the craft, had not known exactly what to do with it.

"How about a little cruise down the Seine?" asked Hjalmar, for whom, when he was in action, technicalities of ownership seemed unimportant.

"Capital, indeed," said Maître François Ronron. "We must ask the girls to go along. It will do them a world of good."

The Singe, sensing that Bridgette was uneasy, smiled at her reassuringly, so she replaced the empty bottle she had grabbed from a near-by bucket and took his arm, possessively. Dimly she recalled that somewhere behind the Panthéon was a hotel she formerly had believed would go to pot if she left it even for half an hour, but as a girl she had pulled up lobster traps with her Irish father and the thought of an excursion on the water, with or without can-can dancers, struck a responsive chord in her heart. Diluvio, who had been wondering how he was going to get back into the Plaza Athènée, welcomed the delay Hjalmar's project afforded and, flipping a quarter he had handy, he perceived that tails had come upward in favor of dancer No. 3, a red-headed girl whose hair, he knew, had not been dyed and whose lines did not bring to mind his lost Guarnerius, as did those of dancer No. 2. The red-head's name was Yvonne and her chum, No. 2, called Nadia, was taken in hand by Hjalmar, who did not want to spoil Maître Ronron's morning by preempting Nicole.

The party set out in a small fleet of taxis and while Hjalmar, assisted by the Singe and Diluvio, got the decks cleared and the motor running aboard the *Presque Sans Souci,* Maître Ronron entertained the women with recitations from French classical poets and dramatists in the Café Delafon, just across the narrow quai.

Since Diluvio knew little or nothing about motors or rigging, he gladly accepted the task of swabbing the spacious deck of the *Presque Sans Souci,* to which he devoted himself with gusto, humming happily the strains of the difficult Mendelssohn concerto in E-minor. He was not only stimulated by the early morning exercise but happy to be able to take liberties with the tempo and dynamics of the music without looking forward to peevish paragraphs in the press next day. All in all, he was so preoccupied that he did not observe, coming toward the Pont Royal along the quai, a solitary figure wearing a

Philomele *toque* in navy blue, a neatly tailored suit in which harsh lines had been subdued, and smooth silk stockings of the ravishing tint known as Persian smoke. The figure, and the face that went with it, belonged to none other than Beatrice Baxter.

It seems that at two o'clock in the morning, Sergeant Schlumberger regretfully had tapped on the door of Miss Baxter's room in the Plaza Athènée and had informed her that her brother had died from undetermined causes in the Hotel Wilton, and that murder was suspected.

"Can you think of anyone who would want to kill him?" the sergeant had asked.

"Practically anyone in the Boston telephone directory," Beatrice had replied. And when asked if she wished to view the remains, she had replied that, since they had not been mutilated, she had a fair idea of what they would look like.

The honest sergeant had left her, pondering on the ways of American women abroad and of family life in foreign parts, generally. But for Beatrice, sleep had been impossible. The Baxter millions, which had come to the Baxters from Calumet and Hecla copper and Moody and Sankey hymn books, would now be entirely in her control. Formerly she had been under Leffingwell's thumb. With all taxes and executors' fees deducted, her fortune would soar above the half billion mark. Somewhat bitterly she rose from the bed, smoothed her sheer silk nightgown, and studied herself in the long mirror of her closet door. She saw reflected there the figure of a handsome woman, in the Indian summer of her physical charm, her face as yet unblemished with wrinkles, her eyes, if anything, improved by the crow's-feet at the outer corners. As the trend of her thoughts shifted, the eyes were in turn scornful, wistful, almost fearfully tender, then determined.

Stepping resolutely to the wardrobe she slipped on a negligee embroidered with Cape Cod trailing arbutus, and moleskin slippers to match. Then she pushed a button, not rudely, but in a way that looked bad for anyone who might fail to answer the summons. A maid appeared, quite promptly.

"Send up the doorman, please," said Beatrice.

Now the maids in the Plaza Athènée are not unfamiliar with the ways of the world, and particularly their experience with American visitors in gay Paris has been wide and rich. Nevertheless it would be uncandid to say that Cleo did not blink. But once she had thought it over, the maid admired rather than censured what she took to be the rich American's directness.

"Bien, madame," she said, and tripped down the stairs.

A moment later the doorman appeared. "Grigori Hippolitovitch Lidin. Madame sent for me?" he said.

"I have just been left about three hundred and fifty million dollars," Beatrice Baxter said.

The effect on the exiled Russian was devastating. He stood erect at attention, eyes front, hands at his sides, fingertips touching the braid of his trouser legs. His jaws were clenched tight, so that only his face muscles moved as he tried to focus his gaze on a distant point and repeat Russian prayers. Grigori Hippolitovitch had been a captain in the army of the Tsar and his struggles to maintain himself in France had toughened rather than sapped his natural resistance. But gradually he began to sway, there was a roaring in his ears like that of an approaching train, and the next thing he knew he was stretched on a divan, and a fragrant woman in filmy gray, whom he mistook first for an angel and later for a nun, was pouring Scotch whiskey between his half-opened lips.

"Sorry, madame," he said, and tried to rise.

"My fault," Beatrice said, contritely. "I've always been rich, and although I try to remember what money means to those who don't have it, its real significance keeps slipping from my mind. I sent for you, not to taunt you with my miserable wealth, but to ask you to help me. I'm unhappy. What I really want, I cannot have."

"Madame, there's nothing you can't have for . . ." Grigori turned pale again and clutched the bottle of Scotch. "For half the sum you mentioned."

"That's what I'm going to find out. All my life it's been dinned into my ears that everything and everyone has a price. Do you think so, Grigori?"

"As far as I know," Grigori said.

"I want a man," said Beatrice simply, then hastily: "Not you, Grigori. There's nothing wrong with you, as far as I can see, but I have set my mind on someone else. I want you to help me, and I shall pay you well."

"A woman as refreshingly frank as you are is entitled to the services of any gentleman—free of charge. And, pardon me, madame. You are beautiful, too. Frequently rich women are lovely and alluring, madame, but their accursed money makes them suspicious even of their own charms. What man is it whom you have honored with your longings? Is he at present in this hotel?" the doorman asked.

"He is, and I want you to inform me about his movements, each time he goes out and the moment he comes in."

"His name?"

"Anton Diluvio."

The Russian rose from the divan and started pacing the floor. He had already received one hundred francs from Anton, and quickly he decided that no bargain he could make with Miss Baxter could be retroactive.

"Beginning tomorrow morning," the doorman said.

"And one thing more," said Beatrice. "There's a woman named Hattie Ham, who dresses like a Lesbian and keeps Diluvio under her thumb. Watch her, too, and keep me posted." With that she reached into a platinum mesh handbag and pulled out a hundred-dollar bill. "Please accept this, on account, and don't envy me, Grigori," she said. "Thus far, true happiness has eluded me, but now that my brother is dead, and can't hold me back, I'm going to have it. Do you understand?"

"I am utterly at your service. I honor your directness and your courage. Permit me, as a former officer, to kiss your hand," Grigori said and, suiting the action to the word, he brushed her hand with his lips and left the room.

Directly he had gone, Beatrice Baxter dressed herself in the manner already described and started out for an early morning walk to clear her mind and still her pulses. It was thus that she approached the Pont Royal and, nearing the *Presque Sans Souci,* she saw Diluvio in his shirt sleeves swabbing the decks.

She paused a moment, heart beating furiously, then, when his back was turned, she hurried up the gangplank and down the ladder into the hold where there was still a quantity of hay left over from the Huge Weiss case.*

About five-thirty, the barge was ready, the party was assembled amidships, with M. Delafon and his chef and a large supply of food and liquor. As the sun's rays were gilding freely the river surface, the barge, which formerly had been used for smuggling by the St. Julien Rollers, nosed out into the current, with Hjalmar at the helm, and the early morning stragglers along the river were regaled with the sound of a hearty chorus, the words of which were as follows:

> *Chère Adeline, mon Adeline,†*
> *Les nuits sans toi*
> *Sont vides pour moi.*
> *Parmi mes rêves*
> *Ton corps se leve.*
> *Soit le fleur*
> *De tout mon coeur*
> *Chère Adeline.*

Above the other voices could be heard the pleasing baritone of Maître Ronron, Hjalmar carried the bass, Diluvio a tenor *obligato,* and the girls from the Bal Tabarin, supported by Bridgette Murphy, M. Delafon and the chef, did a stirring job with the air. From the doorway of the deserted café, Mme. Delafon, who had made it a lifelong rule to put business before pleasure, was weeping into her apron and declaring to the single remaining waiter that if there were any justice, the *Presque Sans Souci* and its licentious passengers would

---

* *The Mysterious Mickey Finn.*
† *Sweet Adeline, My Adeline,* etc.

sink in midstream, through the instrumentality of an avenging God. Through it all the Singe stood wistfully, not being able to carry a tune, but he was enjoying thoroughly the way in which Hjalmar handled the boat and was puzzling about why a first-class seaman with a master's ticket should give a damn whether whiskers were painted or not. A modest man, the Singe acknowledged that he had much to learn about life and he felt a surge of gratitude toward his Franco-Irish sweetheart who, although she had an obsession about making him respectable, had brought him into contact with such charming and versatile friends.

By the time Hattie Ham had keeled over at Frémont's mention of murder, and the dragnet had extended its meshes to the empty Bal Tabarin, the *Presque Sans Souci* had skirted St. Germain and all hands had been served with a fragrant ham omelet.

The carefree scene aboard the barge contrasted sharply with what was taking place in the laboratory of Dr. Hyacinthe Toudoux. The stroke of four, on the famous but inaccurate clock on the corner of the quai de l'Horloge opposite the prefecture, accompanied the medical examiner's determined gestures as he thrust his arms into a sort of white Mother Hubbard he wore while dissecting corpses. As he had foreseen, his wife, Eugénie, the former Marquise de la Rose d'Antan, was waiting up for him when he got home at two. But before his venture into wedlock, Dr. Toudoux had been in the toils of a mistress more exacting than any wife could be, namely, science. So, in bed, after Eugénie had turned her back to him with the grace which characterized all her movements, the doctor had perversely started thinking about poisons, and from that time on, sleep shunned his side of the bed. Cautiously he slipped from under the covers, dressed in an adjacent room, took up his kit and crossed the Place Dauphine to the prefecture.

There lay the bodies of Leffingwell Baxter and Ferdinand Tredwell, the former of which, because of his height, required an out-size slab called "Patron" in the trade. As Evans had predicted, a slight scratch had been found on the palm of Baxter's left hand, which could have been incurred if he had stooped to pat the dog. The lethal phonograph needle was sealed in an air-tight transparent case, and as Toudoux paced to and fro between the corpses, he racked his brains and twiddled his thumbs, trying to decide how such a minute sample of poison as was contained on the needle point could be tested for arsenic, strychnine, Prussic acid, henbane, hemlock, Paris green and cyanide of potassium, to say nothing of the long list of oriental snake poisons on which the doctor had written a brilliant monograph some years before, and since then had dismissed from his mind.

In a snake cage in the corner were several living specimens of the American prairie rattlesnake, *crotalus confluentus,* but the stiffs before him showed none of the signs of rattlesnake bite or any other symptoms of disorders he could identify.

"Damnation," he said. "I shall have to start from scratch." But the more he tested, the worse things went. Beakers of liquids which should have turned green, burst into bright vermilion, or else sulked and coagulated without changing color at all. Litmus paper was equally recalcitrant. In the lobby of the Hotel Wilton, while waiting for Evans and the Chief to appear, the doctor had inhaled so much dust that he could not have smelled a bitter almond tree if he had had one in a pot in his laboratory.

The doctor's months of bliss with Eugénie had moderated to some extent his hasty temper, but had not subdued it. It was not long before Toudoux was cursing and breaking glasses and other small items of public property like a Lithuanian on the second day of a wedding party.

Sergeant Schlumberger looked in from time to time, for he had been left on guard in Frémont's office, and at Evans' suggestion had undertaken to dig out the facts regarding thefts of important violins which had occurred in Paris since the inception of the Third Republic. The *dossier* of Monsieur Rebec, who kept the shop called Aux Citoyens, was as near a blank as a record can be. Rebec had been born in the rue de l'Arbre Sec and at an early age had been apprenticed to a viol maker who had died at the turn of the century. The medal and decorations shop had come to him through an uncle, about whom nothing else was known. Rebec had never married, had never been arrested and during the Great War had been exempted from military service because his establishment had been the only one in which high officers of the army and navy and civil dignitaries could purchase the various badges they had to wear on public occasions.

"I can see how it would be possible for a man to evade me," Schlumberger said forlornly, "but this chap" (indicating Baxter resentfully) "was leading on a leash a dog the size and like of which is not often seen in Paris. Wherever he went, passers-by lined up and stared at the beast. It was like the progress of a motion-picture star up and down the streets and avenues. Will you tell me, Doctor, how a man can take such an animal into a small shop with one front door, the back exit having been nailed up several years ago, and simply vanish?"

"I can only assure you that he will never do the trick again," said Toudoux. "Also that poisons should cause convulsions, which in turn would bust up checker games and scatter the checkers all over the floor. This big duffer simply died with his elbow on the table, as if such an important change of state were not worth noticing. Ah, well! I have never lived in Boston. Do men in those parts give up the ghost less reluctantly than others?"

"The hotel manager, Tredwell, died right in front of your nose," the sergeant said. "Not even Monsieur Evans was aware of his passing. This case, Doctor, is starting out badly for all of us, and if you take the trouble to read the morning papers you will see that the editors have no intentions of letting us down easily. 'Foreigner Slain While Police Mill Around Hotel' is one of the milder headlines."

The doctor and Sergeant Schlumberger were joined at this point by Sergeant Cidre, the fingerprint expert, who was so exultant that he was spinning almost like a top, in an effort to show them both a huge diagram on which had been pasted the photographs of so many assorted fingerprints that it looked like a futuristic engraving.

"I haven't had such a picnic since the Versailles conference," Sergeant Cidre said. "Look at this. The prints made by No. 1, that's the tall chap from Boston, are in gray. Those of No. 2, the Johnny with the suitbox, are in red; and No. 3, who touched the cuffs of No. 1, is shown in green. I have even restored each checker to its exact place on the board."

Dr. Toudoux's suggestion as to what his colleague might do with any checkers that chanced to be left over caused the fingerprint expert to leave the laboratory in high dudgeon, and thus brought the conversation to an end.

7

Of Luck, Which, While Possibly Blind,
Is Not Invisible

It was not yet nine o'clock in the morning when Evans
was awakened by the sound of an altercation just outside
the door of his apartment in the rue Campagne Premiére.
The voices he heard, as he rubbed his eyes and yawned,
were those of his *concierge*, Chief of Detectives Frémont
and Hattie Ham.

"I don't care if all the fiddlers this side of hell have
been skun alive," the *concierge* was saying. "Mr. Evans
is not to be disturbed."

"I've already been disturbed. Let them in," said Evans,
slipping on a bathrobe which had been woven from the
undyed wool of black sheep of Avilla and embroidered
with a quaint pictoral history of the life of Jonah.

"Anton's gone! He's been kidnapped, perhaps murdered," wailed Hattie.

"Calm yourself, Miss Ham," said Evans, severely, "and
tell me your story. It is highly improbable that Diluvio
has come to bodily harm, unless by accident. Of course,
Chief Frémont has already checked up the hospitals."

Frémont looked guilty and stammered. "This woman got me rattled," he said. "If you'll permit me, I'll use your phone."

The mention of hospitals caused Hattie to gurgle, quake, clutch at her blouse with frantic fingers, gasp for air, and knock her knees together, but she fought off another swoon by a very close decision and sank into an armchair. "That chowder-head of a sergeant let him get away," she said. Then, prompted by Homer, she gave him a fairly orderly recital of the events that had occurred at the Plaza Athènée. Frémont, meanwhile, had ascertained that no one answering Diluvio's description had been taken to any of the public hospitals: also, that while the dragnet had already ensnared forty-three Americans in blue serge and without papers, among whom were two amateur pianists and three men who admitted to having played the alto saxophone, none of the suspects, according to the fingerprint expert, Sergeant Cidre, had calloused finger tips on his left hand, as a confirmed violinist must have.

"Sergeant Bonnet is a trustworthy man," Evans said. "If he was guarding the door, Diluvio must have gone out through the window. And, since he would not have gone without a struggle if he had been kidnapped, the chances are one hundred to one that he slipped out voluntarily. What would be more natural, on a spring night, after such a harrowing evening? Diluvio is high strung. He would be restless. He is a man who would shun the garish attractions of Montmartre in favor of the impersonal gaiety of Montparnasse. If you will go to number 22 rue Montparnasse and inquire of my friend Hjalmar Jansen, who should be painting there in his studio, most likely he can give you news about Anton. Hjalmar spends his nights in the principal cafés, knows everybody, and is always ready to lend a hand. Since I shall be busy this morning, you might ask Jansen, if he has no definite information, to go the rounds of the cafés with you and make inquiries.

"If that fails to disclose a reassuring clue, I suggest that you seek out Grigori, the Russian doorman at the Plaza Athènée, tell him you are a friend of Colonel Lvov Kvek, his old commander in the army of the late Tsar, and offer him one hundred and ten francs if he will tell you anything he might know about Diluvio, on condition that you will never disclose the source of your information. Diluvio, if he escaped by the window to the room below, must have passed the doorman on his way out of the lobby downstairs and would certainly have bribed him. He would have been feeling in an expansive mood, anticipating a few hours of liberty, and would have handed out a hundred francs, rather than fifty."

"But Anton could have told me if he had wanted to go out," objected Hattie. "I don't try to hold him prisoner, against his will."

"In case he had informed you, Bonnet would also have known and would have been obliged to follow," said Evans. "Diluvio didn't want to be shadowed, quite naturally. Now, Miss Ham, last evening you said that you had confidence in me and would follow my suggestions. I was to 'swing the baton,' was the way you put it . . ."

"All right," said Hattie, gamely. "I'll behave. But, so help me Jesus, I don't terrorize Diluvio. He needs the protection I give him. No one outside could understand."

A moment later, after Hattie had started on her errand,

Frémont sighed and said: "I don't know how you do it, my friend. Not five minutes ago, that woman was screaming and tearing her hair. Now she eats out of your hand. I hope you appreciate the fact, Monsieur Evans, that the rest of us do not find the other sex as tractable as you do. Had I suggested to Miss Ham that her lover had risked his life and limb in order to give her the slip and romp in Montparnasse with other women, she would have clapperclawed me pink. Ah, well! There is an old French proverb which says that fortune is blind, but not invisible. Make the best of your luck, young man, and accept the homage of one who, if tactless and unendowed with genius, does not stint his admiration or his gratitude."

"Your worth is not diminished by your modesty, my friend," Evans said. "There is much more in this affair than as yet meets the eye. First of all, I want you to get in touch with the most trustworthy official on Devil's Island . . ."

"The Government of France," the Chief said, gravely, "is many times inept, and seems, now and then, unjust. But it would never be foolish enough to send a trustworthy officer to Devil's Island. To deal with such a gang of cutthroats as one finds in French Guiana, other cutthroats plus arms and authority must be called upon. But what in God's name has Devil's Island to do with million-dollar fiddles, poisoned dog collars, and hysterical women with stiff shirt fronts and, no doubt, if one looks closely enough, suspenders?"

"I want you to dispatch a cable to the penal authorities in Guiana, nevertheless, with the authority of the Minister of Justice behind you, and instruct the officer in charge of the colony to send you a complete set of fresh fingerprints of Barnabé Vieuxchamp, impressed on the margin of the most recent newspaper available," Evans said.

"But why fingerprints of Barnabé? We have hundreds on file. And why on the margin of a newspaper?" the Chief asked. "The Minister of Justice will think I've gone off my rocker."

Evans smiled and walked to the window, where he released by pressing a button a small American flag, the folds of which fluttered in the morning breeze. It was the signal to his barber, Henri Duplessis, whose shop was just across the street.

"I want to be sure that Barnabé is still on Devil's, or more likely, St. Joseph's Island. If he has escaped, with connivance of one or more of your cutthroats plus arms and authority, the fresh fingerprints on a dated newspaper could not be produced. Otherwise, they could," Evans said. "Now, to strike nearer home, let's go to the prefecture and have a look at Cidre's fingerprint exhibit; also interview Toudoux, who'll be in one of his famous rages; and see what Schlumberger has learned about the thefts of expensive violins. Later, we'll have a talk with M. Rebec, who sells decorations and tinkers with musical instruments of the epoch of Molière and Amati. When Schlumberger told us about his interview with the proprietor of Aux Citoyens, I smelled any number of rats. Did you?"

"I'm going over that rear exit as carefully as Toudoux examines his revolting corpses," Frémont said. "If necessary, I shall dismantle the building. Were Houdini still alive, I should cable for his fingerprints on today's New York *Times*. Men from Boston do not go into shops, leading conspicuous dogs, and make their next appearance in a hotel half a kilometer distant, some hours later. And however I may bullyrag Schlumberger and Bonnet to their faces, for the good of their morale and the discipline of the force, I do not think they are chumps or that they are deaf, dumb and blind."

Miriam, meanwhile, had suffered a slight departure from her morning routine in the rue Vavin. It was her practice to have her coffee delivered when the hotel clock said "Nine." After that she practiced an hour on the harpsichord, walked in the Luxembourg Gardens and at eleven o'clock entered Homer's apartment softly and started playing Czerny on his grand piano, so that his awakening might be accomplished to the tune of the finger exercises whose repetitions and variations he relished in preparation for a day to come. The Czerny School of Velocity, he believed, was a form of aesthetic exercise that increased the listener's powers of appreciation and lulled dangerous tendencies toward dynamic activity. There was something of Shakespeare's "tomorrow and tomorrow and tomorrow," of the profundity of Hebrews, 13:8, in the restrained measures of Czerny—a kind of illustration in terms of sound of the Gallic *sens de mesur* which makes for an abundant civilization without hurry and nerve strain beyond man's natural capacity.

The coffee ceremony in the Hotel Vavin was simplicity itself. The cook prepared the coffee, placed it on a tray, near a small plate on which reposed two fresh golden-brown crescent rolls, then called out: "Sten*ka!*" Stenka, formerly of Zagreb, was a husky lass with broad shoulders and a wide forehead who, although she could carry heavy trunks up and down eight flights of narrow stairs, had a softer side to her nature which, according to the cook, kept her lingering too long in gentlemen's rooms.

On the morning in question, the cook repeated "Sten*ka*" four times, with a marked crescendo, so marked, in fact, that the fourth "Stenka" brought down a package of pepper, two nutmegs and a bottle of olive oil from the shelf above the sink and so stirred the cook's resentment of unnecessary waste that she promised all within hearing to take the value of the articles, with interest, out of Stenka's commodious hide.

"Here I am," said Stenka, perspiring good-naturedly as she stepped in from the courtyard, and not, as the cook had expected, from the door leading in from the stairway. "The gent in 15 sent me out for some sand."

"You're crazy," said the cook. "No one sends out for sand. What does he want it for?"

"He said he wanted sand, that's all, and he gave me two francs," the Serb girl said.

"No doubt the sand is thrown in," said the cook, who, because of her duties and her physique, was seldom exposed to men's advances.

"I'll take up Mademoiselle Leonard's coffee if it's ready," Stenka said. To do this, the girl had to pass Room 15, where she was to deliver the paper bag she had filled with sand. When she did so, she found the occupant of Room 15 sitting fully dressed, with scarf and cap, on the bed and holding an extra sock in his hand. This struck her as bizarre but, as has been explained, she was not of an inquiring nature.

"Whose breakfast is that?" asked Godo the Whack, for it was he. "Is it for the American chippy?"

"She's not a chippy. She only has one friend," Stenka
said.

"He's going to miss her," Godo said, pouring sand into
the sock. "Now look here, kid. You're going to do what
I tell you, understand?"

"You're not going to hurt Mademoiselle Leonard?"
asked Stenka, frightened and bewildered, for Godo, when
he had entered the hotel at five that morning, had seemed
gentle and understanding.

"Never mind what I'm going to do," said Godo, fixing
her pale wide eyes with his sharp dark ones narrowed
almost to slits. "Here's what *you're* going to do. You're
going to lead me to her room and open the door. I'll be
standing behind you. See? After that, you fade away. Get
your clothes and beat it from here. I can use a big strong
heifer like you, and otherwise I'd have to cut your throat.
Get me? You go straight to the Place de la Contrescarpe,
Bal des Vêtements Brulés, and wait there till I come for
you. Or would you like to be slit up like a rabbit, and not
breathe any more?"

"You won't hurt Mademoiselle Leonard?" asked
Stenka again.

"Nix. I'm not going to hurt her. I'm going to give her
some news about her boy friend. We've met before. So get
going," Godo said.

Stenka picked up the tray and stepped into the hall.
Once or twice she thought of screaming, but visions of
slit rabbits passed before her eyes like targets in a shooting gallery. "Glub," she said once, and felt Godo's jack-
knife in an area which he referred to more fondly at one
time than another, it seemed. Miriam, Stenka knew,
would be sitting up in bed, in a becoming negligee, with

her back toward the doorway, looking out into the courtyard where the foliage of a single plane tree underwent
its morning changes in the sun. Stenka wanted to cry, but
did not dare. She liked the plane tree and the hotel, in
spite of the cook. Also, Miriam had always been kind to
her.

"Come in," Miriam said, when Stenka tapped fearfully
on the door. Moritz, however, looked inquiringly at his
new mistress, and the short stiff hair began to rise at the
back of his competent neck. The ensuing events were so
unexpected to all concerned, and followed one another
so precipitously, that it is difficult to record them in a way
that does justice to their qualities and effect. The Boxer,
in the absence of instructions, went in for some direct
action on his own responsibility. He sprang, not at
Stenka, who was screaming and dropping the tray with
all its contents, but leftward, to Miriam's bed, in such a
way that he was between Godo and Miriam when a sack
filled with sand crashed down. The blow stunned Moritz,
but he had planned in advance a couple of moves after
the first one, so a clear mind was not essential just then.
He did not try for Godo's throat, because of the tightly
wound scarf, but with a crunching sound he brought his
jaws together on the Whack's forearm before Godo could
withdraw it and was dragged into the hallway. Miriam,
although she had drawn her automatic from beneath the
pillow, had the presence of mind not to use it while
Stenka and Moritz were weaving back and forth in the
line of fire. But that extra split second gave her time to
slip on the silencer.

In the hallway there were mingled snarls and curses
and Miriam got to the door just in time to see the flash

of a jackknife and a trembling of the Boxer's taut body as in spite of one stab and another he refused to relinquish his hold. Miriam shot the knife from Godo's upraised hand, then picked up the sandbag. For a man who would try to kill her dog, her beloved automatic was too good. She had heard that one must not strike too hard with a soft blunt instrument, so she tried, as she brought the sandbag down on Godo's head, to stun him without crushing his skull. In spite of her lack of practice, she was successful. Then she called off Moritz and roused Stenka, whom she ordered to drag the unconscious Godo back into her room.

"He said he wouldn't hurt you. He promised . . ." wailed the Serb girl.

"He's his own worst enemy, never fear," said Miriam as she closed the door. Moritz was clasped in her arms, breathing hard and bleeding profusely, while she was staunching his wounds with all the skill she had learned on the range. At first glance, she thought they were deep but not serious, his bulging shoulder muscles and loose skin around his throat having protected him, as nature had intended. Stenka, who was overjoyed because she would not have to leave the hotel and work for Godo, was quickly reassured and promised to carry out Miriam's instructions to the letter, night and day, as long as they both should live. As the Serb girl passed the kitchen, where the cook was yelling for her, she told the latter that she had to find a horse doctor to look after a dog, at which the cook decided that Stenka was harmlessly insane, and thus a special ward of God, and not to be mauled or fired.

In accordance with a lifelong habit, Miriam kept a

lariat coiled neatly in the top tray of her perfumed wardrobe trunk. With this she tied up Godo in what is known as the Laramee style, for lone prisoners; washed the wounds on his forearm and cauterized them with a curling iron, none too gently; felt of his skull and was pleased to find it intact; then gagged him with the sock, sand and all. She was thinking that, as soon as Stenka returned, she must send word for Homer, but her association with Evans had sharpened her initiative. First, Godo's room should be searched. She must determine, if possible, whether Godo had entered the hotel alone, or had confederates.

Unfortunately, Stenka, who had a literal mind, had struck a snag in her first attempt to carry out Miriam's instructions. There were no veterinarians in Montparnasse, and although several second- and two first-class pharmacists volunteered to rally around, Stenka would accept no substitutes. Mademoiselle had said a horse doctor, and that was that. Finally, a policeman told her he knew of a good vet in Montmorency, not twenty minutes from the Gare du Nord by train. Having no money, and having been accustomed to long treks across the Serbian steppes in her girlhood, Stenka set out on foot, hoping the cook and others whom it might concern would understand.

After waiting a reasonable time, Miriam decided to leave Moritz on guard over Godo, who was beginning to mutter and stir. The sandbag was already in use as a gag, so she reached into the second bureau drawer where, among lavender-scented articles of clothing too intimate to be paraded before the reader, lay the braided buckskin quirt that had been given her by the eldest son of Shot-on-

Both-Sides. With that she was more at home than with city weapons, for she had found it necessary to knock many a mustang cold after gentler means of persuasion had failed. She stroked the quirt lovingly, inhaling its healthy odor of leather, reversed it and as Godo opened his eyes and was forming an indecent expletive he could not get past the gag, she brought the butt down on his skull with just the right emphasis. In fact, as she was performing this stern but necessary act, a half-forgotten admonition contained in her music lessons from the Seek and Ye Shall Find Correspondence School flashed through her mind.

"*Forte* (f) is by no means *fortissimo* (fff)."

Moritz, stirred from his well-earned nap by the scent of buckskin and the restrained thud of the blow received by Godo, opened his near eye, rose, stretched and walked slowly over to where the Whack was lying. The dog's forehead wrinkles deepened, and he turned his head upward and looked at Miriam.

"Watch him, Moritz, old fellow. I've got to leave you for a while," Miriam said, and the dog, as if to show he understood, stepped over Godo and seated himself on his haunches between the prostrate gangster and the door.

The hotel was quiet at that hour in the morning and as she entered the corridor Miriam was pleased to see that none of the other guests had been aroused by the unusual occurrences. The door of No. 15, Godo's room, was locked, but her own key, from No. 85, although it fitted somewhat loosely, moved the latch and Miriam, automatic in hand, stepped in. The bed was in disarray, but at first glance there seemed to be no one in the room, and no baggage. Putting up her gun, she looked behind the curtains of what, in the absence of an accurate term, might be called a wardrobe. Then she glanced under the bed, ripped open the mattress and dumped out the excelsior. No result. That the drawer of the night table had no false bottom was evident, since it had practically no bottom of any kind. She was about to return to her room, disappointed, when she noticed that, above the so-called wardrobe, there was a space between the top and the ceiling. Balancing herself lightly on the only chair she reached in and was thrilled to find a large suitbox, so light that at first she thought it was empty.

Not wishing to be caught in Godo's room, she carried the suitbox hurriedly to her own and untied the cord. Then she raised the lid of the suitbox and gasped, for lying there on the dull gray cardboard, right-side-up and with bridge and strings intact, was a marvelous violin.

"The Guarnerius," she said, in awe.

8

Which Indicates That a Herring Has Been Drawn Across a Checkerboard

AT JUST that moment Homer Evans, accompanied by Chief of Detectives Frémont, was crossing the square in front of Notre Dame. The face of the great cathedral was still in shadow but strong sunshine illuminated the spires, the gargoyles and the roof, green with age. Happy children and their nursemaids were playing in the graveled paths of the churchyard, and across the *place,* in front of the huge Hotel Dieu, or city hospital, a few convalescents in rags were basking in the sun on wooden benches, dreading the day when food and bed should be denied them once again.

Beyond, in the Marché aux Fleurs, as if by mocking contrast, cut flowers and plants and shrubs in pots were ranged in profusion.

There was so much of history, of suffering, of childish gaiety and riotous colors mingled with the city's gray that it was almost with relief that Evans, oversensitive to all those things, stepped into the neat laboratory of the fingerprint department, just off the Avenue de la Justice. Frémont was close behind him, and both were greeted heartily by Sergeant Cidre, who had a huge chart in his hand.

"There has never been a case like this since the days of Bertillon," said Sergeant Cidre, extending the chart on a table and waving his free hand. "It's almost vulgar, having so many fingerprints at the scene of the crime. But just to add spice and variety, there is No. 3, the phantom occupant of the room, with only the thumb and forefinger, and those on the cuff of the deceased, nowhere else to be found. Nos. 1 and 2 have at least two dozen apiece, each one of which I could enter in the international concourse and expect to win a prize."

Evans was gazing at the chart, on which the table top and chair arms from Baxter's room, and even the checkers and checkerboard had been sketched with accuracy, and which was dotted and daubed with the fingerprints of Leffingwell Baxter (No. 1) in gray, of the mystery man with the suitbox (No. 2) in red, and the miserly No. 3 in green. Frémont was watching Homer's face, for it was there he had learned to look for light, and not directly at exhibits. Finally Evans relaxed and smiled.

"Well. What's wrong with the picture?" he asked.

Sergeant Cidre's eager face showed signs of pain. "I assure you, Monsieur Evans . . ." he began. "I exercised every possible precaution."

"Your work is superb. In fact, most enlightening. Tell me, Chief, just what does this chart reveal?" Evans continued.

"Well, after all," said Frémont, "there's no mystery. The man with the suitbox got Baxter into a checker game, fixed the poisoned needle on the dog's harness, then made his getaway when the victim dropped dead. No. 3 is no doubt a careless laundry man or a *garçon* at the hotel."

Homer shook his head. "Sergeant Cidre, are you a devotee of the game of checkers, or draughts?" he asked.

"I am not," said Sergeant Cidre. "But I am a thorough and conscientious officer and leave no stones unturned. I consulted our files, with the help of our archivist, and found that these men had been playing what is known as the English game, with twelve checkers apiece, and a board with eight squares on a side, alternately black and red. The draughts or checkers were black and white, respectively, each player using one color consistently. After studying the position of the checkers on the board, and counting the number at the sides that had been removed, I found that eight moves had been made by each player. Since it is the custom for the black to move first, the opposite of the rule in chess, I assumed that No. 2, or Mr. Suitbox, let us call him, used the white checkers and consequently moved last."

"After his opponent had dropped dead?" asked Evans.

"My poor head," said Frémont, pacing the room.

Cidre was crestfallen. "I should appreciate it, Monsieur Evans, if you would point out my error, or errors."

"You are a credit to the department, Monsieur Cidre," Evans said. "With unerring patience, you have given us our only valid clue. Let us not lose sight of it. Mr. Suitbox did move last, and after his opponent had died. For us, in this case, that is Axiom One."

"Perhaps he didn't notice that Baxter had died," said Frémont.

"Mr. Suitbox gives promise of being an observant man. I think we can safely say he would notice it, if his checker companion passed on. But like all clever crooks, he becomes the victim of his own cleverness. He not only gilds the lily but uses the best gold leaf, which may be traced. Our Mr. Suitbox will doubtless make the same reflection on the morning he is guillotined."

At the mention of the guillotine, both Frémont and Cidre brightened perceptibly.

"You will understand, Monsieur Evans, that the routine work of checking the prints of No. 2 is a work of hours. If we have luck, I shall report to you today, either giving you Mr. Suitbox's name, or assuring you that he has never been fingerprinted in France or elsewhere," Cidre said.

"You will find his prints," said Evans. "Never fear. But the chap I want to identify is the one you call No. 3 —the possible laundry man or valet. He is a chap who does not overdo the thing, it seems. Also he is invisible, and either O.K.'d by Leffingwell Baxter or well known to Moritz, the dog."

The conference was interrupted by a commotion at the doorway of the laboratory, where three or four attendants were improvising a sort of inexpert defensive formation and were unable to prevent a five-yard gain, between guard and tackle, by a woman all elbows and knees, with black, flapping, masculine clothes. This woman, who could be none other than Hattie Ham, was dragging behind her a blonde who was as chic and reluctant as Hattie was dowdy and insistent. Both Homer and Frémont recognized the latter as Hjalmar's faithful model, Mathilde Dubonnet.

"Diluvio's been shanghaied," Hattie said, distractedly, brushing away a couple of police officers who still had the idea she should not have crashed the gate.

"Shanghaied?" repeated Homer.

"A bunch of drunks have lured him out to sea," insisted Hattie, and Cidre, alarmed for his chart, got it safely out of the way.

Finally, after Homer had succeeded in calming her with well-chosen words and a drop of the prefectorial brandy, Miss Ham told her story and was favored with strict attention. She had gone to Hjalmar's studio and there found Mathilde in tears because Jansen, with Diluvio, had lit out for the Bal Tabarin the night before. At the Bal Tabarin, Hattie had been given the name and address of one of the taxi drivers who had taken Diluvio and some of the show girls to the Pont Royal. There Hattie and the tearful Mathilde had come upon Madame Delafon, proprietress of the café across the quai from where the *Presque Sans Souci* had been moored, and had been told how the party of merrymakers had sailed down the river in the barge, singing "Sweet Adeline."

"An innocent prank. Ah, spring!" Evans said, but Frémont was inclined to take a sterner view of the situation. The *Presque Sans Souci* was Government property, and Anton Diluvio was the owner of a fiddle of fabulous price that had been stolen from under Frémont's nose. For a man who had just lost an article valued at 20,000,000 francs blithely to go on river trips with show girls, indicated to the Chief a lightness of character amounting almost to criminal irresponsibility. Also, Frémont knew that wherever Hjalmar Jansen went, chaos followed close behind.

Evans, who seemed to be in excellent spirits, tried to reassure the women. "You see, Miss Ham, I was right. Diluvio, naturally a bit overwrought after last evening's experience, went out for a quiet drink."

"By descending a sheer wall twenty-five meters high," muttered the Chief.

"He had the good luck to run into Hjalmar Jansen," continued Evans, smiling, "and Hjalmar, seeing that Anton needed distraction, unselfishly put aside his personal affairs and set out to entertain him. Go back to the hotel and rest, Miss Ham, or busy yourself with the clippings from the press. Diluvio will return, in good condition, the better for his holiday."

"Hjalmar's with Nicole," wailed Mathilde and started breaking whatever items of office equipment fell within her reach, merely to emphasize her insistence that something be done. Frémont, meanwhile, looked helplessly at Homer while Sergeant Cidre, on his knees, tried to gather up fragments of date stamps, paper weights, T-squares, pots of graphite, tubes of mucilage, pencil sharpeners and other articles tossed helter skelter by the frantic Mathilde. Had not Evans promised the women that if they would be quiet and go to their respective lodgings he would start down river that very morning to head off the *Presque Sans Souci*, there is no telling what might have happened. But eventually a semblance of order was restored, an officer was detailed to escort Mathilde to Hjalmar's studio, and Homer, accompanied by Frémont and the distracted Hattie, set out for the Plaza Athènée.

"I long for a few words with the charming Miss Baxter before we start for Rouen," Evans said. "It must not be overlooked that the death of the late brother Leffingwell means to her three hundred and fifty millions in cash and the control of the two hundred millions she had previously owned but could not spend without her brother's consent."

"You mean she bumped off Baxter?" asked Frémont, nonplussed.

"She does not look to me like a Borgia, but one never knows," answered Homer.

A moment later they inquired at the desk of the Plaza Athènée whether Miss Beatrice Baxter was in her room. The clerk tried to phone, and received no answer. The maid was summoned from the fourth floor and, frightened, asserted that Miss Baxter had not breakfasted. Before Cleo had finished speaking, Frémont and Evans were in the elevator. They rushed down the corridor, turned the knob of the door of room 417 and found it locked. The Chief's sturdy shoulder crashed against the panel, the wood gave way, as did also the lock, the threshold and a part of the door frame, which dragged along some laths and plaster.

The room, of course, was empty. Evans approached the bed, and motioned Frémont to stand aside.

"Ah," he said. "The fair Beatrice slept fitfully, indeed. That such a sightly woman, rich beyond the dreams of avarice, should be chronically restless is a rebuke to the entire male population of Boston. But I see no evidence of foul play."

The maid, still trembling, informed them that Miss Baxter's blue toque and suit to match were missing, but by her manner Frémont suspected at once she was holding something back.

"Mademoiselle," the Chief said, sharply. "Our inquiry involves at least two murders . . ."

Cleo began to scream and chew her handkerchief, until Evans laid his hand gently on her shoulder. "Stop badgering this girl. She is innocent, and anxious to tell us all she can," he said, and Cleo began to nod and control her sobs.

"Miss Baxter rang in the middle of the night and asked for the doorman. Poor woman. She was lonesome. She meant no harm," Cleo said.

"Send up the doorman," said Frémont gruffly, then to Evans: "She's made a clean get-away. That's plain. She had access to the dog and must have stuck the needle in his harness."

"Patience. Here's the doorman," Homer said, smiling indulgently.

The tall Russian, having been awakened from sleep, stood before them in the doorway. Frémont walked straight up to him and said: "You were in this room last night! Confess!"

"You are mistaken, sir," Grigori said.

The Chief turned to Cleo, who began to shudder and bawl and ran to Evans for protection. "Did you summon this man at two o'clock or not?" the Chief demanded of the girl.

"Waaaaaah," replied the maid, gasping for breath, and shaking her head affirmatively.

Frémont wheeled and faced Grigori again, who was standing at attention. "I shall stand no nonsense," the Chief said. "Either you tell me what you did in this room, and where Miss Baxter is hiding, or you shall be questioned at the prefecture and then deported."

For answer the Russian stood even more erect, clicked his heels and bowed. "I have never been in this room, and I would not know Miss Baxter if I saw her. This girl (indicating Cleo) is mistaken. She had too much work to do, like the rest of us, and her memory is confused."

The Chief went to the window and blew his whistle, and a few seconds later two patrolmen appeared. "Take this man to the prefecture and lock him in the Goldfish Bowl," Frémont said. Then he grasped the telephone, almost pulling it out by the roots, and got Schlumberger on the wire. "The dragnet," said the Chief.

"All available men are shagging that fiddler," the Alsatian replied.

"Tell them 'To hell with the fiddler.' It's a woman we want. Beatrice Baxter, American, thirty-eight years of age, well made, with blue hat, suit and Persian stockings . . . Yes, Persian . . ."

"Persian smoke," blubbered Cleo, but the Chief had already hung up the receiver.

The shriek of a siren on an approaching auto caused Grigori to stiffen another degree, the maid to collapse on the bed, and even Evans to raise his eyebrows in surprise. The car brought up, with a squealing of brakes, before the main entrance of the Plaza Athènée and soon afterward Sergeant Cidre, chart in hand, came panting into the room.

"I've found our party. I've identified No. 2. We've got the criminal dead to rights," said Cidre, excitedly.

"Miss Baxter?" asked Frémont, eagerly.

"Gentlemen," said Evans. "This is getting out of hand. First one jumps at a conclusion, then another. Please let us keep our facts in order, and examine them calmly.

The prints of No. 2, if I am not mistaken, are those of Jean Peret, known otherwise as 'the Singe.' Am I right?"

Sergeant Cidre was crestfallen, and definitely annoyed.

"My dear sir," he said to Evans. "If you knew all along who committed this atrocity, why did you permit me to work all night, with my assistants drawing overtime pay? It is true that the fingerprints of No. 2 correspond exactly with those of Peret, or 'the Singe.' If you are playing some American practical joke, I can only say that it seems to me to be in execrable taste."

Frémont had the phone in a stranglehold again and was jiggling the hook furiously. Homer begged him to desist.

"But the Singe! He'll get away! He may be as far as Esthonia by now," said the Chief.

Homer's face grew stern. "Gentlemen," he said. "I have spent a large part of this morning dealing with women who are emotionally unstable. Must I devote the rest of the day to nursing hysterical men? Although you have not invited me formally to interest myself in this case, I have assumed up to date that you wanted my assistance. That I gladly will give you, but only on condition that you exercise a modicum of forbearance and common sense.

"Now before making any more false moves or futile gestures, do you care to listen to what I have to say?"

"But the Singe? The Baxter woman?" objected Frémont.

"If it will comfort you, I will give you my word that neither one of them has killed Leffingwell Baxter or Ferdinand Tredwell or any other person in whom we have the slightest interest. Do I make myself clear?"

"The fingerprints. I cannot be mistaken," said Cidre.

Not impatiently, but less deliberately than usual, Homer strode to Cidre's side and relieved him of the chart, which he spread on the rumpled bed, which smelled enticingly of Forvil's excellent "Coral." Then he turned to Grigori.

"Grigori Hippolitovitch," he said. "You served under my good friend and companion, Colonel Lvov Kvek, did you not?"

"I had that honor, in happier days," replied Grigori.

"You have no intention of running away, while this inquiry is in progress, I take it?"

"Most certainly not."

"Then will you please go downstairs and bring me a checker board and some checkers—English, French, Spanish, any kind? The various games are fundamentally the same."

The doorman bowed and left the room, eyed uneasily by Frémont. Once the board and draughts had been procured, Evans invited the Chief to sit across from him at a near-by table, and asked Cidre to look on. The checkers were dusty and showed fingerprints quite plainly. Frémont, a fair player, helped set up the men, choosing black at Evans' suggestion. The Chief moved, Evans riposted, black moved again, white offered a jump which black was obliged to accept. After eight moves, Homer stopped the game and glanced expectantly at the two perspiring officers. Grigori stood by.

"Now, gentlemen. Let us examine that chart again. I trust I shall not have to dot the 'i,' " said Homer.

The Chief's broad brow was wrinkled with perplexity.

"I'm not myself today," he said.

Homer turned to Cidre. "And you, sir? Do you observe the Mene Mene Tekel scrawled all over your excellent handiwork?"

The expert shook his head.

"Is it possible that none of you noticed that when the Chief jumped one of my white checkers, he picked it up from the board himself, and I, in turn, picked up the black checkers over which I jumped?"

"Merciful God," exclaimed Frémont, and Cidre, blushing fiery red, clasped his forehead in his hands.

"In your chart, all the white checkers have fingerprints of No. 2, or the Singe, and all the black ones are smeared with those of the late Leffingwell Baxter, although both players must have jumped at least two of his opponent's men. Ergo: the game was arranged after Baxter's death, and the fingerprints were planted. That narrows our field no end, for what is clearer than that the murderer of Baxter also is out to get the Singe by throwing the blame on him?"

"But the Singe must have been present, or how else could his fingerprints appear in such profusion?" asked Sergeant Cidre.

"It is precisely that intriguing question that I propose to clear up," Evans said. "The rest of the case should be child's play."

9

In Which Hayseeds Serve as Cupid's Darts, and Jolly Well, at That

MEANWHILE, although perplexity was rife in the Plaza Athènée, and Miriam was increasingly uneasy in the Hotel Vavin, the *Presque Sans Souci* rolled merrily down the Seine toward Rouen and presented the rustics on either bank with a picture of abandon and frolic. Monsieur Delafon had set up his bar amidships and was ably assisted by the waiter he had brought aboard. Near Mantes an accordion player had been borrowed from the bosom of his protesting family on another barge.

Refreshed by the country air and warmed by the spring sunshine, Nicole and her comrades from the Bal Tabarin shed their sophistication and world-weariness and were playing children's dancing games, to the delight of Maître Ronron who paused now and then, between sips from his well-chilled glass, to wipe a tear from his eye as he reflected how youth, beset by the exigencies of a ruthless world, too often is misguided. The girls had placed wild flowers in their hair and had removed the outer layers of the can-can costumes, and as they cavorted, limbs bare, in their worn but neatly laundered chemises, it would have been a stony heart, indeed, that was not touched by the innocent scene.

Hjalmar, spinning gleefully the wheel as he steered the barge through the tortuous channels, or turned it into the tangents of the placid canals, was roaring a seamen's chanty the lilt of which was quickly caught by the accordionist.

> *Whiskey killed my brother John*
> *Whiskey! Johnny!*
> *So I drink whiskey all day long*
> *Whiskey for my Johnny.*

But of all that glad company, the one who seemed most to enjoy the morning's excursion was Jean Peret, known as the Singe. Leaning against the stern rail, his pale-blue eyes fixed dreamily on some distant point in the landscape, he stood silently, his feet well set upon the deck, his broad shoulders thrown back as he breathed deeply of the fragrance of the fields and marshes.

The fact that he had chosen a station at some distance from the girls from the Tabarin might have been due to his innate delicacy, so often a characteristic of strong, silent men—a feeling that since in the exercise of their profession the young dancers had men's eyes trained on them continually they should be given a real holiday aboard ship. Again, the Singe's decision to remain aft might have been made out of consideration for his sweetheart, Bridgette Murphy, who stood close at his side, her expressive Irish eyelids drooping as she watched the calm reflections of trees and houses in the Seine. Unschooled as he was in emotional niceties, the Singe had observed that whenever he looked at another woman, and especially if she were unclothed, Bridgette showed signs of extreme agitation, sometimes going so far as to snatch up breakable or unbreakable articles and to lay about her with small regard for life and limb. On one occasion, the recollection of which still brought a blush of embarrassment to the Singe's tanned brow, he had been obliged to resort to corporal punishment in order to curb Bridgette's impulsive demonstrations, and the reconciliation that had followed, lasting three and one half calendar days, had caused him to lose a cargo of brass knuckles he had been intending to smuggle into Wales.

Still musing on the foregoing incident, the Singe reached for Bridgette's small white hands with one of his huge ones and smiled as the final stanza of Hjalmar's chanty came to his ears.

> *Whiskey is the curse of man*
> *Whiskey! Johnny!*
> *So I destroy it when I can*
> *Whiskey for my Johnny.*

To introduce, even momentarily, a note of pathos into this gay chapter, is a task that costs the author much, nevertheless the reader, after sharing the sun-swept deck of the *Presque Sans Souci* with its care-free voyagers, should steel himself to glance into the hold, where, in a rather musty aroma of timothy hay, stood Beatrice Baxter. Once or twice she had mustered courage to ascend the ladder, from which she could hear snatches of sprightly conversation, sharp strains of the accordion, deep masculine mirth and high-pitched girlish laughter. But, of course, she did not dare join the party, in the hope that she would not be noticed. In fact, her pale and wistful face already had been seen by Delafon's hard-working *garçon* who immediately attributed the alluring vision to the unusual amount of red wine he had been drinking and had doused his head in a bucket of river water he was barely able to haul up the side.

In a life which had had its share of frustration, Beatrice Baxter had never felt more helpless before. She was a stowaway, bound she knew not whither. She had boarded the barge on an impulse, to be near the man she loved. What should she do? Much of the determination she had shown in the Plaza Athènée seemed to have slipped away, and as she gazed, from her ladder, on Anton Diluvio, seated on a camp stool in the bow, he seemed more remote and unapproachable than ever.

The violinist was in his shirt sleeves, and in the hand that was world-renowned for its skill with the bow reposed a cool double whiskey. Anton was reveling in his new-found sense of freedom and irresponsibility. Banished from his mind were thoughts of crowded concert halls, the mighty measures of the great composers, the profit and the loss. He had forgotten the Plaza Athènée, the Salle Gaveau, Bach, Beethoven, Haydn, even Joseph del Gesu, otherwise known as Guarnerius, who, in one of his periods out of jail, had fashioned the instrument Anton should have been worrying about. Unjust as it may seem, Diluvio had also forgotten Hattie Ham and her frantic solicitude.

However, the continuity of the night's entertainment and the sprightliness of the morning had not stilled in Anton the small voice or whatever it was that had prompted him to steal out of bed and roam the night before. He looked yearningly at the show girls, whose skins were turning an appetizing pink from the sun; but he, too, was aware of the change that had come over them because of the transplantation from the white lights of the Tabarin to the verdant Norman countryside. Yvonne, the red-head, once or twice, had stopped romping for a moment to sit on the deck at his feet, but when he offered her his whiskey, as a sort of preface to a bolder suggestion, she refused with a cute little *moue* and expressed a longing for some buttermilk, such as she had tasted at her grandmother's farm in 1917. Diluvio, always the gentleman, sighed and sent her back to her playmates. As the barge was passing Sartrouville, and, unknown to him, the gaze of Beatrice Baxter was enveloping him with tenderness and longing, Diluvio noticed that he was getting drowsy and decided to take a turn around the deck. Having done so, he still was conscious of an urge to take a nap, and, unobserved by the others, he walked toward the long ladder leading to the hold, which was quickly vacated by Beatrice in a state of excitement almost approaching collapse. She barely had time to hide behind a bale of hay when Anton reached the hatchway and started to descend. That he did not hear the beating of her heart was due to the fact that he had resigned himself not to think of such matters until safely ashore. His coat, vest, collar and necktie he had removed at dawn, preparatory to swabbing the deck. So he proceeded to strip off his trousers and shoes, and after shaping an impromptu bed out of loose timothy, he lay down full length and gazed upward at the staunch beams overhead. The beams, after an admonitory wriggle, straightened themselves into parallels and were fairly steady.

What followed was scarcely understood, even by the principals themselves. Almost at the borderline between sleeping and waking, Anton was aware of a subtle perfume which seemed to mingle with the timothy smell. He could not identify it as Forvil's mysterious "Coral," never having inhaled it before. Was he dreaming, or did he feel a hand in his, soft arms stealing around his neck? By the time he tasted eager tears and caught the rhythm of the sobs that shook his frail companion, he was by no means asleep. He was aware that a kindred mind shared a single thought, with a voltage that made his own seem feeble indeed. In fact, he soon decided that concert fiddling was a sheltered existence and had kept him from understanding the facts of life at all. However, natural pride and a manly sense of duty prompted him to try to be equal to the occasion, and his sense of musical form stood him in excellent stead. Had it not been for the sound of the accordion, the sighs, gasps, grunts and prayerful endearments of the happy pair might have reached the deck above, and set off the entire company.

In the dimness of the hold, Diluvio tried to catch a glimpse of the face of his mysterious partner, but her eyes were closed and the scent of Forvil's "Coral" obscured his senses until he scarcely could tell one from another. It would be an abuse of the author's privilege to describe this incident in detail, but it will do no harm to assure the reader that had Miss Baxter had her half billion dollars in gold aboard she probably would have chucked them overboard along with everything else. Also, it would not be amiss to pause to pay tribute to those ancient pioneers of music whose wisdom has sent down to us through the ages the *allegro, andante,* and *presto,* in the order named, as the ideal form of aesthetic expression.

Eventually, Diluvio slept, in fact he was in the soundest sleep of his career within forty-five seconds after the tense moment when Homer Evans, in the Paris prefecture, had torn open a cablegram from French Guiana.

"The devil," Homer said, as he handed the message to Frémont. "This knocks my conjectures into at least a dozen cocked hats."

FRÉMONT. CHIEF OF DETECTIVES, PARIS
BARNABÉ VIEUXCHAMP NUMBER 36475 DIED CHARVEIN
CAMP MARCH TWENTY-SIX TARANTULA BITE

DELEUZE

The foregoing is the text of the message.

"Checkers or none, I'm going to arrest the Singe," said Frémont, doggedly. He had been on that theme since he and Evans had left the Plaza Athènée.

"As you like," said Homer, "but I warn you against it."

"At least, if the Singe is innocent, he can establish an alibi, or give a clue," Frémont persisted.

"Chief, you are not in form today," Evans retorted. "If someone is trying to frame the Singe, he will know who it is and all the racks and thumbscrews in the Carnavalet would not induce him to say a word. You must know the gangsters' code by now. Feuds are settled out of court."

"His fingerprints are all over the checkers," said Frémont, "and I'm going to haul him in. Good God! We haven't a single suspect. We can't even tell the press about the poison, and Toudoux is getting in deeper every minute. No cause of death! No motive! Nothing! Have you seen the papers today? And have you seen the memoranda I've received from the prefect, Monsieur de la Chemise Farcie?"

The Chief clawed into a drawer like a mastiff among rose bushes and brought out a handful of papers. "Here. Read this. 'Would appreciate prompt solution as I had planned yachting trip early next week.' Or this one. 'Give you free hand. Will not interfere. Expect brilliant results.' That's the line he takes when he thinks I'm going to make the bloomer of the century. And I am, I suppose. If I pinch the Singe, you'll think of nothing else but getting him off."

"You would not suggest that I stand by and see him framed," Evans said.

"He's done enough to be guillotined forty times, and we've never laid hands on him," said Frémont.

"The purpose of the law," Evans said, "is not to wipe out lawlessness completely. That would be both foolish and impracticable. Our best jurists, from time immemorial, have simply set the stakes so high that only bold and clever men can stay in the game."

"You can talk me deaf, dumb and blind, I know," said the Chief. "But you can't explain away the fact that the Singe left his fingerprints in that room, all over the place. Suppose he didn't pick up the right checkers. Assume that he arranged the game after Baxter had been poisoned. Does that let him out? You are being stubborn, Monsieur Evans. You are letting your sympathies run away with you. I shall put your friend the Singe in the Goldfish Bowl and if he won't talk, he'll stay there during my incumbence in office, which, I fear, will be short. Ah, fame! Ah, public ingratitude! On the first of each month there will not be the comforting check on the Bank of France. And beggary will be doubly bitter, after the heights."

In writing of heights and depths, to which he is much addicted, an Americo-English poet once penned a poignant stanza which, although it has no bearing on the Paris prefecture, will take the reader back to the hold of the *Presque Sans Souci,* enough time having elapsed to make that change of locale discreet and feasible.

> *When lovely woman stoops to folly and*
> *Paces about her room again, alone,*
> *She smooths her hair with automatic hand,*
> *And puts a record on the gramophone.*

Now T. S. Eliot has spent much of his time in London and has had, perhaps, no occasion to consider the above situation with reference to the hold of a barge strewn with timothy hay. It is true that Beatrice smoothed her hair as best she could, and reached down elbow deep into the timothy to retrieve the *chic* blue toque that formerly had helped hold it in place. There was no gramophone handy, and if there had been she would not have played it, for the blood was coursing happily through her veins, and instead of thinking of what had occurred as folly, she was convinced that it was the most salutary act she had performed in her lifetime. The half billion, in gold, bills or even securities, no longer was oppressive to her, in her exalted mood, but she was aware that almost as many hayseeds as she had dollars had lodged themselves in her skirt and had torn into ribbons her stockings of the tint known as Persian smoke. With fond glances at the sleeping Diluvio, she set about tidying herself as best she could, and as she plucked hayseeds, her mind, never dull, worked fast.

What she had desired had come to her in the most unexpected way, but how could she consolidate her gain? What would Diluvio do or say on awakening? Would he find her disappointing, in her disheveled state? Would he remember?

That last doubt she put away. He surely would remember. Rapidly, a plan formed in her mind. If he had been profoundly moved, as she had, would it not be better if he were kept in suspense, if the element of mystery surrounding their meeting were deepened? She must leave the *Presque Sans Souci* while he was still asleep, keep out of his way until she could be sure he was longing for her, then make a reappearance at a chosen moment and throw herself at his feet.

After plucking out more hayseed with trembling fingers she set her shoulders in a determined way and mounted the ladder. The drinking and the music had been proceeding without stint since Diluvio had gone below, so to her intense relief she was able to walk across the deck, dive over the side, and strike for the shore with her graceful Back Bay crawl, without being observed by anyone except the self-same waiter who thought he had glimpsed her before. This time, the fellow not only soaked his head but drank a full bottle of vinegar, to the accompaniment of fervent prayers and resolutions.

IO

The Sinner Without Malice

WHEN for the fourth time Godo the Whack showed signs of returning consciousness and Miriam was obliged to quiet him with the butt end of the quirt again, her uneasiness caused her to bite her lips and pace the floor. The only telephone in the Hotel Vavin was in the hallway on the ground floor, within easy earshot of the kitchen, and the transmitter was so cracked and battered that in order to get words through it, the speaker had to raise his or her voice so that it could be heard all over the hotel. Furthermore, Miriam knew that Homer Evans had a switch at the head of his bed by means of which he could disconnect the telephone bell, so that it would not sound before one o'clock, the hour of his rising. The thought that she might call Chief Frémont, without disclosing the nature of her appeal, crossed Miriam's mind, but the capture of Godo with the rare violin was so important that she did not want to disclose it to anyone until Evans had questioned the Whack and examined the instrument.

Moritz, still sitting on his haunches between Godo and

the door, was aware of Miriam's anxiety and shifted his weight from shoulder to shoulder, sighing deeply and wrinkling his forehead, with ears erect, in an effort to divine the cause of his mistress's perturbation. His wounds, because of Miriam's skilful first aid, pained him little if at all, but he had shown distinct disappointment on each occasion when Miriam had gonked the trussed-up gangster. He had been hoping, in his philosophical way, that Godo would regain enough strength to warrant a thorough going over in which a capable dog could take part.

Seeing the faithful animal sitting at his post so patiently, Miriam, between bouts of worrying as to how many times a man can be cracked over the head without causing him permanent harm, was reminded of the immortal lines of Walt Whitman:

> *O to be self-balanced for contingencies*
> *To confront night, storms, hunger, ridicule,*
> *   accidents, rebuffs,*
> *As the trees and animals do.*

"Good Moritz," she said. "I don't know how I ever got along without you."

The answer was a deep sigh, as the dog relinquished his sitting position and stretched himself at full length on the floor, his head toward Godo and his paws, although relaxed, well set for instant action. As the minutes wore on, and Stenka showed no signs of returning, Miriam could endure the *status quo* no longer. Hastily she scribbled a note to Homer saying simply "Come at once" and calling Moritz to her, she tucked it into his new harness. Immediately after their drive in the Bois de Boulogne, on the night Leffingwell Baxter had been murdered, Homer and Miriam had gone directly to Evans' apartment in the rue Campagne Premiére. Would the dog remember, and could she make him understand? He was a stranger in Paris, never having been on the streets, unleashed.

The dog, at first, had assumed he was to go out for exercise and that Miriam would go with him, but when she stopped at the doorway, caressed his soft muzzle and murmured endearing words in which his name and that of Homer Evans recurred on several accented beats, Moritz looked appealingly at his mistress for guidance. She pointed down the hallway and, with a gesture toward the left, tried to convey that he must find Homer in his apartment, and let him know that his presence was needed in Miriam's room.

Moritz caught a glimmer, trotted to the end of the hall-way with only a slight limp to mar his easy shoulder motion, and there he paused, turned, and looked at Miriam again.

"Go on! Out of doors! Find Homer, please," implored Miriam.

The dog made an experimental start down the stairs, then glanced back for approval. Approval was written all over Miriam's face and confirmed by her eloquent posture.

Alone at the outer door of the hotel, Moritz looked upward at all the windows and at last accepted the fact, reluctantly, that he was on his own. A Pekingese, escaping from a passer-by, came yapping up with a ludicrous challenge, but Moritz, preoccupied, merely brushed him away with the back of one huge paw. Now why should his mistress have tucked paper into his harness? And why, with a man in the room who obviously needed shaking like a rat, would she send him out of doors?

The reader, no doubt, has often paused by the side of a shaded pool in the dimness of the woods in summer and, gazing into the limpid waters, has believed at first that they were empty. How thrilling, then, to see, rising from the depths, a trout, moving oh so effortlessly and swimming into vision, to link his own fantastic silent world with that of the reader. It was something like that, in Moritz's receptive mind, the way the awareness of what he was to do first stirred, then drifted to the surface of his consciousness. Suffice it to say that the morning clients of the Select, and those across the boulevard at the Coupole, were mildly surprised to see a sleek, faun-colored Boxer, strange to the Quarter, trotting purpose-fully in the direction of the rue Campagne Premiére, intent on his errand, undissuaded by admiring words or glances from pedestrians, ignoring a bullying police dog who never knew how near he had been to disaster, paus-ing only when opposite Homer's street. There the dog sat down on the sidewalk, the better to look upward in search of a traffic light. Finding none, Moritz checked up again, to be sure, shook his head at the laxness of for-eign customs, then picked his way between careening taxis, increased his pace as he neared the familiar door-way, and hurried up four flights of stairs.

An experimental bark brought no results. A louder one proved equally unproductive. A third, in which the Boxer made use of his deep chest tones, brought the con-ciérge, using language which, a moment later when she spied the note and read it, brought tears of remorse to the good woman's eyes.

"Come at once." No signature, no explanation. It was the hour when Miriam should have been starting out with Czerny at the grand piano, and there was no sound. Evans had departed with the Chief of Detectives Frémont. The concièrge was not long in deciding what to do, and thus it was that Homer, sitting perplexedly in the prefecture with the cablegram from French Guiana in his hand, heard his name called, went to the phone and an instant later was speeding toward the rue Vavin in Frémont's cheese-colored roadster at a rate that evoked curses and prayers, respectively, from the sinners and the righteous all along the way.

Moritz, the while, halted at the doorway of the apartment building to weigh the question as to whether he would be justified in taking a whirl out of that police dog before reporting back to Miriam for duty. He decided in the negative, but not without a sigh, and trotted back to the rue Vavin, arriving at the hotel just as Evans in the roadster pulled up to the curb. The sight of Homer reassured him, and Evans' words of praise brought joy to the dog's honest heart. He had done some hard and painful thinking, crossed unexplored precincts, and all had turned out for the best.

Miriam, keeping watch over Godo in room 85, felt that admonitory faintness that caught at her heart whenever Evans was approaching, then heard his familiar footsteps in the hallway, accompanied by the rhythmic pat pat of the Boxer's callused paws. She hurried to the door and paused a moment fearfully, until she was sure of Homer's approbation. That it was heartfelt and unreserved she soon had no cause to doubt, and a second later she was pouring out her thanks to Moritz, not with caresses to soften his sterling character, nor sweetmeats to ruin his digestion, merely in a torrent of words to which the dog responded by wagging his stump of a tail, left, right, left, right.

Standing tensely before the bed was Homer Evans, his eyes on the rare violin. For a moment all else was swept from his mind as he glanced first at the rich red glow of the varnish, lost secret of old Cremona, through which showed the faultless grain of Dalmatian pine, the telltale tiny feet of the bridge, the pointed chin of the sturdy scroll, the angular sound holes no other master-maker than old Joseph del Gesu would dare to carve. Miriam, motionless, her hand raised anxiously to the level of her breasts, was waiting for the final word.

"Is it . . . ?" she tried to ask, but the words would not come.

Homer looked at his hands, palms upward, then reverently he raised the instrument from its suitbox shelter and gasped as he turned the back to the light. The circular spot of wear at the center served to intensify the effect of the varnish. The wood was unmistakably maple, the pattern of the grain displaying a natural beauty no art could enhance. Evans turned the violin sidewise, to examine the purfling, peered into the sound holes, cautiously plucked the second string and listened to "A."

"My dear," he said at last, to Miriam. "You have retrieved our friend's Guarnerius, the second in importance that was left us by that master who died in oblivion and even now is not given his due. This violin, companion piece to Paganini's famous 'Devil' now kept under glass in Genoa, was named by old Joseph 'The Sinner without Malice' and was made as a sort of monument to human frailty. The master had been visiting a friend, quite a famous violinist, and in a moment when his scruples had been mellowed with Piedmont wine, had thoughtlessly seduced the twelve-year-old daughter of his host. Repentant of his abuse of hospitality, old Joseph set to work to fashion a violin the tone of which would be bold and seductive, hoping that its use would provide the irate father with so many illustrations of how easy it is to fall from grace that eventually he would forgive Guarnerius."

"And did he?" asked Miriam, eagerly.

"I am glad to say he did," replied Homer. "But since that day every violinist who has come into possession of 'The Sinner' has had a very stormy time. The last one before Diluvio, the renowned Belgian, Bossere, met his death in Flint, Michigan, not ten years ago, when the wife of one of the city officials, stirred to action by Bossere's rendition of 'Les Plaisirs d'Amour,' dived at him from behind, on a narrow stairway, causing him to break his neck. You already know that Anton, before Hattie took charge of him, was in continual turmoil. Of course, the great Paganini had his troubles but he was clever enough to build up the legend that he was the Devil, in earthly disguise, and thus he frightened off all except the most intrepid and worth while of his admirers. Besides, Paganini's great fiddle was designed to terrify, or should I say *epater,* rather than to break down moral or conventional barriers."

"There is something to be said for pianos, after all," sighed Miriam. At that point, Godo stirred and started choking on a few stray grains of sand. From force of habit, Miriam reached for the quirt. Then she looked questioningly at Evans, thankful that he was on hand to guide her.

"I've quieted him four times already," she said. "Another wallop won't unfit him for questioning—or anything, will it?"

Distastefully Homer felt over Godo's cranium, then went to the sink to wash his hands. "Let him have it once more, now you've got the knack," he said. "I've plans for the Whack that I don't wish to discuss while he's conscious . . . And don't mention to anyone, not even Frémont, that you've retrieved the priceless violin."

A restrained thud, as Evans was reaching for a towel, let him know that Miriam had carried out his suggestion about the Whack. After listening to her story as to what had happened to bring Godo and the fiddle into her bedchamber, he loaded the limber Whack into the rumble seat of the cheese-colored roadster with Moritz to guard and discourage him in case he should come out of the fog, and, inviting Miriam to hop into the seat beside him, set out for the prefecture. It was the hour when Frémont was obliged to receive the gentlemen of the press, so Homer drove around to the entrance of Dr. Toudoux's laboratory on the west side of the squat gray group of buildings in which the business of protecting the public from itself went continually on. The doctor, his white uniform bedraggled and his brow moist with sweat, was seated in a corner with his head in his hands, so distraught that when one of his laboratory rattlesnakes (crotalus confluentus) stuck his head through a knothole in his wooden cage, Toudoux batted him back most peevishly and promised the astonished snake the next turn in the snake-oil refining machine. Seeing Evans, however, the discouraged medical examiner shed some of his gloom and rose hastily. On the large slab of the size known as *patron* was stretched the body of Leffing-well Baxter, and beside the principal corpse was that of the accidental victim, Ferdinand Tredwell, ex-manager of the Wilton hotel.

"In the name of that dear woman * who, after tribulations enough to break down any saint, has entrusted herself to me, I appeal to you for help, Monsieur Evans," the doctor began. "What is this strange poison that turns off life like a light switch, without symptoms or after-trace? I have turned these unfortunate victims practically inside out, tested their organs, nerves, glands, veins, arteries and tissues. I have even analyzed the marrow of their bones. What need is there to look for ordinary poisons, may I ask, when the effect of the one we seek resembles nothing known to science? I have studied poisonous drugs, reptiles, insects, trees and plants. And now, as I ransack my memory, no case like this comes to mind. No clue! No precedent! The only sample of unused poison I have is so tiny that it rests on the point of a gramophone needle. I am overwhelmed, not at the prospect of failure and disgrace for myself, but to think that at the moment when life is crowned with domestic happiness I shall be publicly proclaimed a nitwit and be forced to resign."

With sympathetic interest, Evans listened to the doctor's long plea and dissertation. "I assure you, Doctor," Homer said, "that we shall solve this problem. And why

* Eugénie DeSault, former Marquise de la Rose d'Antan, see *Hugger-Mugger in the Louvre*, Random House, 1940.

should a man of your capacity complain because a case is without precedent and outside the humdrum routine? On the contrary, you should rejoice that so soon after chance has favored you in love, fate lays at your feet a challenge worthy of your scientific skill. The criminal to whom we are opposed is clever, indeed, but not invulnerable. I had thought, up to the moment I received this accursed cablegram from French Guiana that I detected the hand of Barnabé Vieuxchamp in the doings at the Hotel Wilton but now, like you, I am without clues or even ideas."

Absent-mindedly he handed out the message for Toudoux to read, and when the latter had done so the change that came over him was nothing short of amazing. The medical examiner, prancing and cavorting around the room, began to scoop large books into his arms and, seating himself on a stool, started opening them at random and snorting.

"Who is this upstart Deleuze, the signer of your impudent message?" the doctor asked angrily.

"What's impudent about it?" Evans asked, surprised.

For answer, Dr. Toudoux held out a volume entitled *Les insects venomeux de la France et dehors,** signed simply "Toudoux."

"Pages 10 to 43," the doctor said, his indignation mounting as he marked reference after reference with any scraps of paper he could lay his hands on. "Chapter entitled '*Lycosa narbonnensis.*' Tarantula, indeed! I shall challenge this Deleuze, even if I have to travel to his detestable pesthole half way across the world. You will see that I have written, beneath my signature, what

* *Poisonous Insects of France and Other Lands.*

has remained unquestioned for twenty-six years. 'The *Lycosa,* vulgarly called the black-bellied tarantula, is not dangerous to man but, because she destroys other pestiferous insects, should be protected and not harried from pillar to post by hysterical or superstitious laymen. Not one authenticated case of a human death by spider poisoning, and particularly following the bite of a *Lycosa* is on record.' "

The doctor paused. "Is there, perchance, in the detestable convict camp in question, which in itself is a blot on the fair name of France, a man who calls himself a physician? Are death certificates of Frenchmen, however depraved, signed by nincompoops and knaves?" he continued. In his excitement, Toudoux grabbed the pair of foils that were fastened to the wall and made a pass that missed cutting off the big toe of the late Leffingwell Baxter by a small fraction of a millimeter.

Homer Evans, although in much better control of himself, was visibly impressed. "Tarantula not fatal, you say?" he asked.

"Bring me a cartload of them! There are plenty in Southern France. I will feed them from my hand. I will dandle them on my head. What I want now is to know who signed that death certificate, and send him my seconds. He must have read my treatise, in order to get his degree. The affront must have been intentional." The doctor raved on but Evans was not listening. Standing tensely, one hand resting lightly on each of the marble slabs, he was lost in thought. Miriam was anxious because a crowd had gathered around the roadster and, having been attracted by Moritz, were getting curious about the unconscious Godo the Whack. Still, she could not bring herself to interrupt Homer's cogitations. It was Frémont, bursting in from the main prefecture, who brought him down to earth again.

"That pesky woman who wears suspenders is on the phone again. She wants news of the fiddler, insists you promised to find him before noon," the Chief said. "And all my assistants, after hours of bustle, can't even find Godo the Whack."

Homer smiled. "Oh, Godo. I brought him along. Miss Leonard was thoughtful enough to catch him and tie him up for us. If you'll bung Godo into a good safe cell, so we can let our dog relax, I'll dictate a statement for the press. Then you and I will make a dash down river to make sure that Diluvio is all right and suggest that he report to Miss Ham, just to save her from losing her mind."

"To blazes with all fiddlers and their keepers, male or female," said Frémont. "I want the Singe under lock and key, if I have to burn Rouen and sift the ashes. And that Baxter woman who hypnotizes doormen and turns herself on and off like a light. Where is she? I have already confirmed from Boston that she benefits enormously under the terms of Baxter's will. She has the motive for murder. She ducks out of sight before her miserable brother is fairly cold. I've no doubt she and the Singe are in cahoots, and are now in some distant country, together, alternating fits of lecherous indulgence with gales of laughter at the expense of the Paris police."

"One quest at a time," urged Evans. "Perhaps a jaunt in the country will give you an opportunity to reflect and change your mind before it's too late. The Singe is one of the victims, not the perpetrator, of the murder, and

Miss Baxter, if I'm not mistaken, is not concerned with multiplying millions. Furthermore, she was not present when her brother died. She was, in fact, sitting four seats to your right, in the same row, across the aisle, at the Diluvio recital when the deed was done. And if you knew more about the Guarnerius called 'The Sinner' you would be in a better position to interpret her subsequent behavior."

"And if you will bring me a dozen black-bellied tarantulas, I'll put them in my hat and clap it on my head," said Dr. Toudoux, still steaming with rage.

The Chief's eyes began to roll inward, his face assumed a color somewhat like Danish cabbage and he might have had a stroke had Miriam not taken him by the arm and led him gently to the sidewalk.

"*Adieu,* reality!" Frémont murmured, as the outdoor air cooled his brow. "You have been harsh and unyielding! Perhaps it's better to go mad."

II

A Day in June Runs Ahead of Form,

as Far as Rareness Goes

AMIDSHIPS of the *Presque Sans Souci* the show girls had tired of playing "Drop the Handkerchief" and were seated in a circle on the warm deck boards, pink as tender young shrimps, and laughing gaily at the quips and sallies of Maître François Ronron, whom they respected as much for his erudition as his extravagance. The veteran lawyer was fond of quoting from the works of the writers who have their niche in all true Frenchmen's hearts, but of all those the Maître preferred Rabelais.

So it happened that when Anton Diluvio awoke, refreshed from sleep, the accordion was silent, as was the tramp of feet; and the steady flow of Maître Ronron's voice was accompanied only by the murmur of waters along the sides of the barge and occasional bursts of applause. Now it must be admitted that Anton, in the past, had awakened all too frequently in an aroma of strange perfume, but never before had his arm been flung out so eagerly to clasp a form that was not there. Ordinarily, in fact, he would have glanced to one side and the other through narrowed eyelids, furtively, and wondered (a) how deep he had got himself in jeopardy, and (b) what prospects there were for an unobserved get-away. It was not so in the hay-strewn hold of the *Presque Sans Souci*. Unaccustomed to being denied what he wanted when he wanted it, Anton's first reaction was one of indignation, followed quickly by a feeling of misgiving, then of panic and acute anxiety. His agitation was not soothed when he heard the text of Maître Ronron's recitation, which was from the discourse of Panurge, expounding the verses of the Sybil of Panzoust.

"Why so? I prithee tell," was the rhetorical beginning.

"Because," responded the old lawyer with evident relish, "when the feat of the loosecoat skirmish happeneth to be done underhand and privily, and in covert, behind a suit of hangings, or close hid and trussed upon a haymow . . ."

At that point Diluvio, still doubting if he were thoroughly awake, tried to duck behind a stanchion. From where he stood, he could see the entire deck of the barge and nowhere aboard was any woman remotely resembling the one who had brought him peace and rapture, only to snatch them as suddenly away.

Maître Ronron, observing Anton's return to the company, smiled cordially and repeated the opening of the quotation.

"When the feat of the loosecoat skirmish happeneth to be done underhand and privily, and in covert . . ." ("Ah, *ça!*" sighed Yvonne) "behind a suit of hangings, or close hid and trussed upon a haymow, it is more pleasing to the Cyprian goddess . . ."

"Who is she?" piped up Nicole, snuggling closer to Maître Ronron's shins.

"Your special protector, Aphrodite, my dear," the Maître said. "Now hear me out to the end."

". . . it is more pleasing to the Cyprian goddess" ("Aphrodite," Nicole murmured) "than to perform that culbusting art, after the Cynic manner, in the view of the clear sunshine; or in a rich tent, under a precious stately canopy, within a glorious and sublime pavilion; or yet on a soft couch, betwixt rich curtains of cloth of gold, without affrightment, at long intermediate respites . . ." ("Ah, no," objected Nadia) "enjoying of pleasures and delights a belly-full, all at great ease, with a huge fly-flap fan of crimson satin, and a bunch of feathers of some East-India ostrich, serving to give chase unt） the flies all around about; whilst, in the interim, the female picks her teeth with a stiffstraw, plucked even then from out of the bottom of the bed she lies on."

Diluvio could bear no more. Perhaps, in some nook or corner he had not examined, the woman whose lips were so eager and so sweet, and whose spell so mysterious, was waiting for him to find her. Blindly he stumbled from bow to stern, without results, until finally Bridgette Murphy, still standing aft with the Singe, noticed Anton was acting strangely and asked what was the matter.

The question took Anton completely by surprise and he might have answered indiscreetly had not he been swept from his feet and floored by the strong left arm of the Singe, while Bridgette herself was upset and laid low beside him by the other arm. Before either could get his or her breath, a shot rang out and the Singe ducked down below the rail to join them. Hjalmar, grasping instinctively that something was unstuck, spun the wheel so hard a-lee that Maître Ronron slid off his soap box into the lap of Nicole.

The barge was passing the town of Luneville, where in a deserted blacksmith's shop and near-by hideout the Singe's gang had carried out minor operations in the past, and because the channel was narrow and close to the shore, Hjalmar had come up alongside a squat brickred tugboat that was anchored there.

"Shall I heave to?" yelled Hjalmar, ready with the wheel again.

"Keep right on going," said the Singe. By that time they were safely downstream from the tug, and the Singe, leaving Bridgette and Diluvio, still bewildered, on the deck, walked over to Hjalmar's side for a consultation.

"Who were they shooting at, and why?" the Norwegian asked. "And don't we go back after 'em?"

"They'll follow us, all right," said the Singe. "Can't you hear the anchor chain creaking?"

"Let 'em come," Hjalmar said, happily. "I'll swing out broadside, make 'em bump us, then we'll board and scuttle her with all hands."

"Sorry. This is my affair," said the Singe.

"Aw, don't be a hog," said Hjalmar. "I don't get a good workout very often these days."

"You couldn't take orders," the Singe said.

"As long as I liked 'em, I could," said Hjalmar. "Besides, I'm running this ship and don't you forget it. If any outsider thinks he can take a potshot at my passengers and get away with it, I got to disabuse him. See?"

"They probably have an arsenal aboard," said the Singe.

"She's headed after us," Hjalmar said, looking back to where the tug was getting under way. "Can she catch us?"

"Sure! She can make fifteen knots. We're good for only six. And the women. We've got to get them ashore. We've got to get everybody ashore except you and me."

"Have a heart," said Diluvio who had overheard. "I want to be in on what's going."

The Singe looked from one to another. Since childhood he had been in many tough spots, but always he had known who was running the show. Either he had been the boss, or someone else. Hjalmar, quick to size up situations that promised violent action, squared his shoulders and stepped up to the Singe, his right hand touching his forehead in a snappy salute.

"I like you, see," he said. "I don't ask questions, understand. I'm skipper of this old tub, but from now on I take orders from you. What you say goes, and if anyone gets in your hair when you're busy, just slip me the word . . . But this guy, Diluvio, the fiddler. He needs a change and some exercise. I'll vouch for him. See! He's O.K."

The Singe, now in full control of himself, was touched. The brick-red tug was gaining. They were on a secluded stretch of river. Something had to be done.

"Diluvio," he said. "Send all the passengers below, then haul up the ladder." Overjoyed, the violinist led the protesting Bridgette to the hold, then started explaining to Maître Ronron that there would probably be gunfire and the girls would be nervous unless he went below to protect them.

From upstream drifted the ominous huh-huh-huh-huh-huh of a machine gun and the plop of spent bullets could be seen, a hundred yards astern.

"Come, duckies," the lawyer said. "We'll play hide and seek in the hay until this blows over."

The girls, nothing loath, clambered down into the hold, followed by the Maître, the accordion player, the *garçon* and M. Delafon, with a tub of iced champagne.

"Shall I swing around and ram 'em?" Hjalmar asked, at the helm.

"We haven't got guns," the Singe said. "We've got nothing at all."

The machine gun stuttered again, this time nearer. Hjalmar, grinning, started roaring a favorite song:

> *So give me a drink, bartender,*
> *And then I'll be on my way . . .*

From amidships, where now all was snug, the bottles of liquor from the bar having been let down out of harm's way, Anton Diluvio walked calmly astern.

"What's next, sir?" he asked, saluting the Singe.

The stalwart Norman shook his head wistfully. "You don't know how hard it is to get good men in a gang," he said.

A salvo of machine-gun bullets caused all three to take cover under the stern rail, which was built of rough-hewn timbers six inches thick. From there, Hjalmar crawled cautiously back to the rudder post, where he rigged up the wheel with a couple of ropes so he could control the course of the *Presque Sans Souci* without exposing himself to the gunfire from the tug.

"What the hell," the big Norwegian said. "They can't board us, and this old wagon is thick and bulletproof. Why can't we just sit tight and cruise downstream? They'll have to lay off with their artillery when we get near Rouen."

"They'll think of something," said the Singe. "You don't know the mob we're up against."

"It's their move, anyway," said Diluvio.

As they rounded another bend, and the view ahead, through a sheltered porthole, disclosed another long stretch of open marshy country, the red barge picked up steam and nosed alongside. Hjalmar knew the channel, and steered the *Presque Sans Souci* gently to starboard, crowding the tug toward shallow water. The skipper of the tug, swearing in a way that brought a chuckle of appreciation to Hjalmar's lips, rang for full speed astern to avoid being pushed aground.

"We're heavier than they are," Hjalmar said. "We can run 'em off the river if they get too gay."

The tug, just a few yards astern, veered over to port but Hjalmar was too quick for them. Inch by inch, the *Presque Sans Souci* edged toward the other bank, until the tug had to drop back again to keep clear of the muddy bottom. Yells and threats went up from the cabin of the brick-red tug and some of the blood-thirsty crew began to show themselves on deck. The Singe, at a porthole, observed them grimly, without saying a word. What he did not see was that the mate, known as Dental Jake because of his deft use of a dentist's drill on victims who would not talk, had inserted the suction hose of an old-fashioned force pump into a drum of kerosene. After a whispered consultation with Jake, the skipper of the tug eased his bow right up under the overhanging stern of the *Presque Sans Souci* and kept it glued there. Hjalmar, not knowing what was afoot, grinned and took another drink of brandy.

"O.K. with me," he said to the Singe. "They'll push us into Rouen all the faster."

Below deck, however, the dark-eyed, curly-haired Nicole, favorite of Maître Ronron, had dropped back to the stern in search of what she modestly termed "The lady's room." She did not find what she sought but she did observe the nozzle of a hose inserting itself into one of the stern portholes and was horrified to see, trickling into the timothy hay, a thin stream of liquid that smelled like kerosene.

In Paris, once Godo the Whack had been unloaded from the roadster and hustled into the Goldfish Bowl at the prefecture, Homer Evans, true to his promise to Hattie Ham, set out, with Miriam and the protesting Frémont, in search of the *Presque Sans Souci*. Noticing that Frémont's condition verged on grogginess, Homer asked Miriam to drive straight to Luneville, with the Chief in the front seat at her right.

"I'll sit in the rumble seat with Moritz," Homer said. "I've got to think."

The dog, content because someone was on hand to do the thinking, fitted himself into the available seat room by curving his back, inclining his neck and tucking in his paws. Only when Miriam, driving skilfully through the maze of traffic, made an important change of direction did the Boxer raise himself on his haunches, sniff, then settle down to doze again.

Directly in front, through the window, Homer could see Frémont shake his head, somewhat after the manner of Henry Irving when Banquo's ghost had begun to fade away. "Poor Chief," Evans said to himself. "If only he knew it, my head is ringing, too. That suitbox makes it more than probable that one and the same person directed the murder of Baxter, the theft of 'The Sinner without Malice' and the hoisting of La Ham. Most certainly that person was not Godo the Whack. Not by any means. Nevertheless, Godo has become a problem. Did he, having been handed the violin for safekeeping, stumble by chance into Miriam's hotel, or had he instructions to kidnap her?"

That Godo would crack, under official persuasion at the prefecture, and give the name of the master mind in question, was not likely, Homer thought. In the first place, Chief Frémont would not resort to physical torture, and secondly, Godo was not the type that would squeal. He was vindictive, brutal, slippery as an eel, but he had never been known to talk too much.

Leaving the Whack, for the moment, in one of the neat compartments of his mind marked "For Future Reference," Evans focused his attention on certain details of the Baxter murder. The intentions of the murderer had included a frame-up of the Singe, of that Homer was convinced. But that did not explain the choice of Leffingwell Baxter as the man to die. Had another French gang leader merely wanted to land the Singe on the steps of the guillotine, he would not have killed a well-connected and wealthy foreigner in an English hotel. Baxter's possession of Calumet and Hecla stock did not seem to link him with the Paris underworld, and neither did the Moody and Sankey hymn-books or the Bunker Hill Associates.

"I must learn more about Baxter," Homer promised himself, and then he wondered why Miss Beatrice Baxter had disappeared. He had seen her look hungrily upon Diluvio in the boat-train and dive unceremoniously into the crowd on the station platform to avoid being seen by Hattie Ham. He had observed that she did not get along with her brother and that they had set off without words for separate hotels. He had watched her at the recital, under the spell of 'The Sinner without Malice' and had not been surprised that she had yelled for doormen or taken a walk at dawn thereafter. But had she walked the streets of Paris, keeping to that section of the right bank where Boston women usually go, the dragnet would have snared her within five minutes after Frémont had sent out his S.O.S.

In the front seat, Frémont stirred again, uncomfort-ably. Perhaps, through the unbreakable glass window and in spite of the speed with which Miriam was driving down the straight country road, he felt the force of Evans' cerebration and it pricked his conscience. For just before he had appeared in the laboratory of Dr. Hyacinthe Toudoux, the Chief had made up his mind about the Singe and had broadcast orders for his arrest, on the charge of murder.

Suddenly Evans rose from his seat, and nearly lost his balance as Miriam swerved sharply to avoid a peasant's cart that was being backed into the roadway by a protest-ing stallion.

"My sainted aunt!" he said. "The suitbox! Siècle Frères! That was the label."

In an instant, he saw in his mind's eye the southern façade of the courtyard of the Palais Royal, the little shop Aux Citoyens where M. Rebec carried on his dual enterprises, and next door, to the west, the somewhat stuffy window of Siècle Frères, the tailors. Now the tailoring of Siècle Frères was set apart somewhat from that of other Paris tailors because the old firm in the Palais Royal had never succumbed to American influence. They still turned out suits, capes and overcoats in the style of the nineties, with tight-fitting backs, trousers almost up to the chin, fancy vests (but never too fancy) and shoulders that simply begged for shrugging. Fervently Evans wished he had followed his first impulse, that he had let Hattie Ham worry and Diluvio prance until after he had interviewed M. Rebec and inspected the medal and decoration shop. Was it a coincidence that the suitbox, probably the one lugged into the death chamber and surely the one in which the Guarnerius had been hidden, bore the stamp of the shop next door to that of Rebec? At least, it was a lead.

The roadster came to a stop, not too abrupt but none too gentle, either. "Which way from here?" asked Miriam, for they had reached the main square of Luneville-sur-Seine.

Reluctantly Evans tore himself away from his thoughts. Moritz, preparatory to descending to the ground, shook himself and stretched and Evans, mentally, did almost the same. From the man of thought he transformed himself into the man of action.

"Frémont," he said, tersely. "If you will be kind enough to make inquiries along the river front as to whether the *Presque Sans Souci* has passed, I'll do a bit of investigating on my own and meet you here in fifteen minutes. And Miriam, please see that Moritz is properly exercised and have the car filled up with gas."

The Chief was already half way down the lane, intent on his mission, when Evans turned into a pathway leading across a stretch of comparatively high and rocky ground, where the soil was thin and crisp and the weeds and grasses sparse. On the slope of this rise, not far from the marshy ground by the river, stood the deserted blacksmith shop formerly used by the St. Julien Rollers. The door was not locked, and windows were covered with dust and soot, and a quick examination by Evans disclosed nothing strange except a large cigar box, with holes punched in the cover, that had been placed on the large brick hearth, so far back beneath the chimney that it almost passed unnoticed.

At first Homer attached no importance to the box. In fact, he had decided to have a look at the shop only on the off-chance that something inside it might give him a clue, as to whether the Rollers had split, or were about to split, into two opposing factions, as he suspected. However, it being an invariable rule with him, when he was on a case, to examine all bizarre objects or situations, he picked up the cigar box and heard, within, a few feeble chirps and the rattle of light objects. Removing the elastic that held the lid closed, he raised it and a cricket crawled briskly out, while others, all of a size and model, hopped this way and that. There were about three dozen in all.

"The devil," Evans said, disappointed. The confused patterns forming in his mind were varied and troublesome, but in none of them was a place for a cigar box loaded with crickets. He replaced the elastic, after easing the most enterprising of the captives back to their prison, and was about to set down the box when a boy about ten years old entered the shop, one hand cupped over another. Seeing Evans, the boy let drop what he had in his hands and started to run. Homer, pursuing him with reassuring words, saw two more large crickets on the dirt floor. It did not take many seconds to convince the boy, agile as he was, that he could not get away from the well-dressed stranger who sprinted like Nurmi and promised not only immunity from harm but unlimited spending money as he ran.

"All right, you win," said the kid, stopping sulkily. "What do you want?"

"You like to catch crickets?" Evans asked, handing out a ten-franc note.

"No," replied the boy.

"Perhaps you do it for money?"

"Well. What if I do? They don't belong to anybody," the boy said.

"Who wants to buy them?" Evans asked.

"Some city guy. I don't know him," the boy replied, but with noticeable hesitation.

"He told you not to tell?" Homer suggested.

The boy's expression showed that Evans had hit upon the truth.

"You're right not to tell," Evans said. "I'm glad you're on the level. But maybe you could let me know what he does with 'em."

"He thinks they're good for bait," the boy said, disgustedly. "You couldn't catch a crayfish, even, with one of those things, especially when they're big and tough.

But what do I care? The sap buys 'em, so I sell 'em."

Evans was about to thank the boy and go back to the square to rejoin Frémont when he noticed, near the edge of the marsh, part of a mushroom, evidently freshly broken off, pure white on a bed of green moss. Absent-mindedly he picked it up, then stiffened. Forgetting the boy and all that had passed, he started along the edge of the marsh, stooping here and there, gasping with dismay, gathering broken stems of mushrooms and wrapping them into his handkerchief.

"Come on, kid," he said, and started on the run for the public square. Moritz, delighted, came bounding toward him, skidded, then looked hurt when he found himself completely ignored. Miriam, watching from the driver's seat of the roadster, turned pale, clutched her automatic and leaped from the car. Homer entered the commissariat and without preliminary greeting, spread his kerchief of mushroom stems on the desk in front of the astonished Commissaire Queré.

"Call all available men here at once," Evans said, and Queré, without question, started jabbing at buttons. "These mushrooms I have here are the deadly *Amanita verna,* the 'Destroying Angel.' They mean sure death in agony to anyone who eats one. Someone in this town has just been picking them. You should send a man to every house without a telephone near by, and notify by phone whoever you can. Seize all mushrooms in shops and restaurants. Forbid their use until each one is examined by an expert."

Homer turned to the boy. "This is serious, kid," he said. "If some kid in this town has been picking these for fun, and should take a bite, he'd die. And if someone took one home, to help feed the family, the family would die and the town would be so sad you couldn't stand it. Kids would try not to look at each other in school, and no one would yell or play games. There'd be priests and doctors stumbling around, and women bawling into their aprons each time the church bell tolled. You wouldn't want that to happen, would you, kid?"

Tears were streaming down the boy's face. "Honest to God, I didn't see no one pick those mushrooms. I was down by the shop three times this morning, with crickets to put in the box. I didn't see a soul. If I did, you can stuff every one of them things down my throat."

"All right, kid. I believe you," Evans said, as a dozen men came running from the shops in the square and the church bells started clanging. Frémont, approaching the *place,* came in on the hot-foot.

"What's up?" he asked.

Succinctly Evans explained. Then he inquired about the *Presque Sans Souci.*

"She passed here, all right, and a red tug set out after her. There's something queer about it all, because no one on the water front will talk," the Chief said. "I don't like the way things are shaping up. Can't we leave this toadstool hunt to Queré and go on down river?"

"How long ago did the barge go by?"

"Not long, if you can believe the natives. They're all scared sick, but I didn't have time to pump them," the Chief answered.

Homer snatched a map from the pocket of the roadster and called Miriam to the counter. Rapidly he pointed out a small network of roads, by means of which, if they had luck, the barge could be intercepted before it reached

Rouen. Miriam was nervous. Disaster seemed to permeate the hazy summer atmosphere and cast a lurid glow over the otherwise fair landscape. Trembling, she started to take the driver's seat, but Evans, always sensitive to her state of mind, took her gently by the arm.

"Let me drive. I think I can remember the road," he said, and Moritz, sitting on his haunches in the rumble seat, let out a suppressed squeal of approval that he tried to nullify with an aspect of extreme gravity immediately afterward.

"Make room, *mon vieux*," said Frémont, climbing over the side to the rumble seat, and the dog moved to the left.

Coincidently, aboard the *Presque San Souci*, Nicole was screaming for "Coco," as she called Maître François Ronron in moments of extreme agitation. The lawyer came aft with alacrity and when he saw the nozzle spraying kerosene he beckoned Monsieur Delafon, the now sober waiter, and the accordion player to hurry to his assistance.

"The law of October 16, 1804, as amended by the statute of June 3, 1893, provides a heavy penalty for arson, and section 17 makes a very fine distinction between criminal incendiarism on land and the setting of unauthorized fires on rivers, in harbors or in territorial waters of France. Our opponents, wily as they may be, this time have overstepped themselves," Maître Ronron said, and rubbed his hands with satisfaction.

"Monsieur Delafon," the lawyer continued. "I shall take your deposition first. You will make a convincing witness."

"But, your honor," said the accordion player, who was

showing signs of nervousness. "We have no ladder. Just how do we get out of here?"

Monsieur Delafon turned on the musician sharply, drawing himself up to his full height. "Remember there are ladies present, and that you are a Frenchman," the restaurant proprietor said.

"Sure, cap, no offense," the accordion player said, "but maybe we ought to try to move the hay."

"An excellent idea," said Maître Ronron. "The removal of the bulk of the hay beyond reach of the inflammable fluid will in no way diminish either the guilt or the civil liability incurred by those blunderers aboard the tug. *O tempora! O mores!* What crudities one has to face in practice these degenerate days. No finesse. No play of wit. Crude oil through a spout, and on a navigable river . . . By all means, let us move the hay."

Delafon, who had already tried to do so, vetoed the plan. There were so many heavy bales to be shifted before the oil-soaked ones could be reached that it would have taken a gang of stevedores at least an hour to clear them away.

Bridgette Murphy began to curse. The girls from the Bal Tabarin huddled together and crossed themselves. None of them except Nicole could swim a stroke, and neither could the waiter or the accordion player. Maître Ronron, who by maintaining the calm that had placed him in the front rank of his profession did much to keep his terrified companions from panic, suggested that they gather beneath the open hatchway and shout in unison for help. This they did, but without result, since Hjalmar, the Singe and Diluvio were far astern and could hear nothing above the barking of the barge's unmuffled exhaust. Finally the old lawyer gave the signal for silence, and just at that moment the hose pipe was withdrawn from the stern porthole and a handful of flaming waste was tossed in.

"That constitutes arson, under the act," Maître Ron-ron said. The acrid smoke of burning timothy arose and, half choked by fumes of kerosene, the accordion player, with a nervous glance toward Delafon, repeated the question he had asked some moments before.

"How can we get out? We'll be grilled like mackerel," he said.

Yvonne and Nadia, in their neat chemises, stood hand in hand, their large eyes wide with fear and bewilderment. The waiter began regretting, aloud, that he had led a somewhat profligate life. It was Nicole who made the first move.

"I can swim," she said. "Perhaps I could warn Mr. Jansen, or attract his attention as he drifted by."

"Were only my life at stake, I should not expose you to the slightest danger, but for the sake of our comrades . . . If you wish . . ." the lawyer said, and wiped his smarting eyes.

"Capital," said Delafon. "Had I chosen a less exigent profession than *restaurateur,* I might have learned natation, but alas, when other lads were at the swimming hole or romping in attics with midinettes, I was bent over the cooking range, or dodging the ready boot of a chef whose jealousy had been aroused by my aptitude for making sauces. Ah, well! One cannot, as the Americans say, play every instrument in the band. Come this way, my pigeon . . ." And he shoved a bale of hay toward a high

168

porthole, upended it, and boosted Nicole to the top. In spite of the smoke in their eyes and lungs and the imminence of a fate so horrible that it has been singled out from all others as a consequence of sin, Maître Ronron, Delafon and even the accordion player and the waiter, gasped their admiration as the girl wormed her way through the porthole, head first, and disappeared.

Unaware of the terror beneath him in the smoky hold, Hjalmar Jansen was prone on the deck, manipulating the wheel by means of ropes he had rigged and singing a rollicking song. Now and then he caused the *Presque Sans Souci* to veer from side to side but because the tug was faster and had more power, her nose stayed tight against the barge's stern. The Singe was squatting near a stern porthole, trying to identify the members of the tugboat's crew and to figure out what their game was. Anton Diluvio, on the starboard side, was gazing happily at the sky and whistling the middle movement from Beethoven's sonata in E-flat, for violin and piano, in a manner designed to double-cross the most alert accompanist.

"I am not Paganini," Anton was saying to himself, "but the old masters didn't have to contend with a public like that of today, crammed with classics. If the old boys let their minds wander and muffed a repeat sign, they could *ad lib* a bit until they got their bearings . . . Hello! What's that?" The sight of Nicole struggling in the water brought him to his feet, and caused bullets from the tug to buzz like angry hornets around his head. Without a moment's hesitation, he dived over the high rail.

169

"Hey, what the hell?" yelled Hjalmar.

The Singe, whose eyes were fixed on the tug, at the same time shouted:

"They're backing away."

Then, as the tug receded, the Singe caught sight of the force pump and the kerosene drum that previously had been hidden by the overhanging stern of the *Presque Sans Souci*. "Run her nose into the bank," he yelled. "They've doused us with oil and set the hold afire."

Hjalmar, at the same time, saw the mate of the tug, Dental Jake, make a grab for a pair of boat hooks, one in each hand. Simultaneously he was aware that Nicole and Diluvio were in the water, and that the girl was in distress. Dental Jake, from the deck of the tug, made two skilful jabs and caught the clothes of both swimmers, one with the right boat hook, the other with the left. The Singe and Hjalmar, watching helplessly, saw both victims dragged aboard the tug.

It was the work of an instant for the Singe to replace the ladder in the hatchway but by that time the smoke was so thick he could not see below. He slid down the ladder, fireman style, and found himself, choking and spluttering, in the midst of the half-suffocated group in the hold. Instinctively he lifted Bridgette from her feet but was halted by her struggles.

"Children first," she said.

Without a word, the Singe dropped her to the deck and picked up Yvonne and Nadia, one under each arm. His muscles bulged and ached and the veins stood out on his forehead as he mounted, rung by rung. In an instant he was down again.

"Can you make it?" he asked Bridgette.

"That I can," she said, and staggered up the ladder. Maître Ronron and Delafon were arguing, feebly. The former was a commander in the Legion of Honor while Delafon was only a chevalier. That, according to the lawyer, gave him, as senior, the right to claim the honor of remaining, while the restaurant man contended that Maître Ronron's higher rank obliged him to go first. The Singe, impressed, slung one on each shoulder and again made the laborious ascent.

"These blokes have got more guts than sense, but I like to hear 'em talk, so help me, I do," said the accordion player.

"A fine generation. Not like us tramps," said the waiter. "Just the same, it's a hell of a mess they made of the war and the budget and all that. You must admit they let the country go to hell."

"You said it, brother. Go on up the ladder," the musician said.

"No. You go first. When gents like that set an example, it's up to us to follow it. Get me?" the waiter said. Eventually both of them reached the deck.

At the wheel, Hjalmar was thinking fast. Two hundred yards downstream, the channel skirted the east bank of the river and there was an ideal landing place. If he could hold the barge to the bank while the Singe made a hawser fast to a tree, all hands could get off by means of the ladder before the heat overcame them. The deck was hot beneath his feet and the sweat rolled off his rugged face and tattooed forearms. It was not his own safety he was thinking of, but how he could get a crack at those thugs, on anything like even terms. Also, how to rescue Nicole and Diluvio?

171

The Singe, having emptied the hold of its terrified passengers and left them in an impromptu shelter behind the bar, hurried aft in reckless disregard of the sharpshooters on the enemy craft.

"Who's steering that bloody wagon?" asked Hjalmar, with a nod toward the tug. "Whoever he is, he's no slouch."

"That's Nosepaint. I gave him his start," said the Singe, sadly.

Hjalmar grinned. "Then he's your own creation. You can do what you like with him," he said.

The stern face of the Singe relaxed. "You make me feel better," he said. Then his figure grew tense. "They're heading for shore, too," he whispered. "They're going to make a quick landing and be there waiting when we try to get off."

"Maybe we can use a smoke screen. That's all we've got," Hjalmar said.

Together, they watched the tug neatly shoulder the bank, saw the hawser made fast, and Dental Jake, with the machine gun on his shoulder, leap for the shore and run downstream toward the landing Hjalmar had selected. Flames were bursting like crocuses through the smoking deck between the stern and the shelter amidships.

"We've got to land, machine gun or no," Hjalmar said. He gave the wheel a final twirl, braced himself for the shock and raced over the hot deck with the Singe for the bow. Both men grabbed a hawser and each succeeded in looping the heavy rope over a stump. Then they crawled back amidships to reassure their bewildered companions. The stern was ablaze, and the wind, unluckily for them, was carrying the smoke down river and afforded no cover at all. It was clear to Hjalmar that they could not stay amidships more than a few minutes, so he motioned the Singe and they picked up the heavy bar, one at each end, and walked with it to the bow just before the deck was sprayed by the first salvo of machine-gun bullets.

On shore, Dental Jake, Nosepaint and four members of the tug's crew were waiting with clubs and revolvers. The machine gun was trained on the deck. For anyone to descend a ladder in the face of such odds was suicide, and to remain on the burning barge was suicide, too.

"My poor faithful wife," sighed Delafon. "How she will deplore the hasty things she said . . . and use inferior butter in my restaurant!"

Maître François Ronron smiled encouragingly at Bridgette and the two almost swooning girls. "According to Plato," he began, "Socrates said: 'The fear of death is indeed the pretense of wisdom, and not real wisdom, being a pretense of knowing the unknown; and no one knows whether death, which men in their fear apprehend to be the greatest evil, may not be the greatest good.' "

"You are thoughtful to say so," said the trembling Yvonne.

"*Nous sommes tous mortels, et chacun est pour soi,*" quoted the waiter, and he added in an undertone to the accordion player: "Molière, *L'École des Femmes.*"

"*De mortuis nil nisi bonum,* my eye," said the Singe.

12

In Which Temptation Suffers
a Series of Upsets

THE reader will remember that Stenka, the chambermaid, started out from the Hotel Vavin some hours before the occurrence of the events described in the preceding chapter, for the purpose of calling a veterinarian to tend the knife wounds of Moritz, the dog. Unfortunately, the husky Serbian girl had a poorly developed sense of direction, so instead of starting for the Gare du Nord, as recommended by the Montparnasse policeman, she wandered off toward the Place de l'École Militaire, and in passing through that historic square received no fewer than eighty-four improper proposals from the soldiers on the spacious *terrasses* of the neighborhood cafés.

Now Stenka, as the reader already knows, was of a generous, yielding nature and disliked refusing anything that was asked of her, but her feeling of loyalty to Miriam impelled her to shake off her admirers and continue walking, in the hope that she would find a horse doctor. By the time Stenka had reached the river, she had outdistanced the last and most persistent of the *poilus*. She paused a moment at the Pont de l'Alma, looked this way and that, and decided that she would be most likely to find the man she sought downstream, in the country, rather than upstream, in the city. So she walked along the quai with her graceful sturdy stride, swinging her arms and whistling a tune the words of which had to do with a maiden who had been badly let down by a party named Mischa, after a summer episode which lingered unhealthily in the maiden's memory. The amateur fishermen along the way, with practically no exceptions, expressed desires similar to those the soldiers had felt but, having rods and tackle to take care of, were unable to follow Stenka as fast or as far as the infantrymen had. Again the girl was firm in her determination not to be diverted from her errand. When she reached the outskirts of Paris and was about to enter Passy she inquired of the customs men if they could direct her to the office of a horse doctor. There were three customs men on duty and after cutting a pack of cards they designated one of their number to go along with Stenka and act as her guide. He led her to a small hotel and, after a whispered consultation with the proprietor, ushered her into a room he insisted was the doctor's office, although it was furnished only with a bed, one chair and another object unsuitable for use by horses. The doctor, he said, would not return for twenty minutes or so. In the course of the scuffle that ensued, Stenka became convinced that the man was not being frank with her and was obliged to drop him out of the second-story window into a graveled courtyard in order to make her escape.

After walking several more miles, the girl saw a peasant's cart pulled up under the shade of a tree. It was drawn by a fine gray stallion and the owner-driver was snatching a nap while the horse was finishing his oats from a nosebag. Stenka, after making sure her clothes were securely fastened, aroused the peasant, who told her he was bound for St. Germain where one of his neighbors was a first-class vet.

"Does he live in a hotel?" Stenka asked, and on being reassured that the doctor occupied a farm house without running water she climbed up beside her new friend, who proved to be a tractable companion, and soon they were jogging along toward St. Germain. The peasant, it developed, was suffering from lumbago.

Meanwhile, Beatrice Baxter, having swum unobserved to the left bank of the Seine, had hidden herself in a thicket in order to remove her clothing and hang it in the sun to dry. She had no money, having left her handbag in the hold of the *Presque Sans Souci*. She did not know where she was, or how far from Paris or Boston. Nevertheless a strange new happiness possessed her. She rose from the moss, flicked off a couple of ants, and stretched her arms upward.

"Anton," she murmured. "Is it possible that I was dreaming?"

A slight twinge from a little-used set of muscles set her right on that point without delay. "Ah," she continued. "I have been blessed beyond my wildest imaginings. I tried to force my destiny, to wring from it what was mine, and almost instantly I succeeded. Should I have rebeled sooner, while still I had my youth? I think not. I am convinced no mere schoolgirl could have felt what I have felt this day. Henceforth there shall be no more uncertainty, no hesitation. I shall have Anton and nothing or nobody shall stand in my way."

Having spoken thus she stretched and shuddered rapturously once again, and felt of her skirt to ascertain if it was drying. In another half hour it was ready for use. Her sheer and fragrant combination and the slip were warm from the sun. Her toque, after further de-haying, was presentable. Her shoes, which she had filled with dried leaves, no longer were soggy. Only the stockings of the tint known as Persian smoke had to be discarded. First, she decided, she must get back to Paris and the Plaza Athènée, after which she would make the necessary funeral arrangements for her brother, go through with the requisite legal formalities, and then keep within striking distance of Anton until the moment she hoped for should arrive. Blithely Beatrice started walking in what she supposed to be the direction of Paris, accompanying her rose-tinted reveries with a refrain from the *Beggar's Opera:*

"What I did, you must have done."

Meanwhile, on a thickly wooded road downstream and across the river from Luneville, Homer Evans was gripping the steering wheel and had his eyes glued on the ruts, which jolted the roadster from side to side. Miriam, beside him, was keeping a sharp lookout ahead for signs of the river. In the rumble seat, Frémont was muttering and gripping his automatic, not because he scented danger but for want of anything more constructive to do. Moritz was sitting tensely on his haunches, head held high, sniffing the air and frowning with each slight change of direction. When the car came almost to a standstill, because of a hole or a boulder, he turned to lick his wounds perfunctorily, then resumed his statuesque attitude.

As they were rounding a curve obscured by a clump of birch trees, an involuntary grunt escaped Moritz's throat and he turned toward Frémont with an expression which would have betrayed to a keener student of domestic animals a pitiful anxiety to communicate something important. The dog's nostrils were working, his head was held high, his eyes were eloquent with appeal.

"Control yourself," snapped the irascible Chief of Detectives. "You had your chance when we were in Luneville."

Moritz, more tense than ever, turned disgustedly away. Slowly he raised his right front paw and tapped the glass behind Miriam. The first time she did not hear, so the dog repeated the operation, tapping with his claws on the window to make a sharper sound. When Miriam turned, he shifted his feet and barked from deep in his powerful lungs.

"Be still, brute from Boston," said Frémont, but Miriam was more impressed. She signaled to Evans, who stopped the car, and Moritz, leaping to the ground, stretched himself full length to put his paws on the window beside Homer.

"There's something in the wind," Evans said, and descended to the roadway, which was thick with ferns.

"I smell smoke," said Miriam, at which Moritz leaped eagerly in the air and bounded to and fro with joy. Someone had understood. He was not, then, cut off from his chosen mistress by that ghostly wall that kept him apart from most of humankind. She could smell, as well as see, hear and make noises. Before the dog had got far with his demonstration of satisfaction, Miriam was half way up a tree.

"Oh, Homer," she gasped, pointing upstream, and Evans leaped into the branches of another tree near by and ascended as skilfully as a spurred lineman mounts a pole. There, a quarter of a mile distant, was the *Presque Sans Souci,* in flames, smoke pouring from the stern and amidships. Also, there was visible the brick-red snub-nosed tug. By straining his eyes, Homer could see a group huddled in the bow of the burning barge, and another, less colorful, on the shore.

"What's wrong?" he asked, bewildered. "Why don't they get off? They'll be burned."

It was there that Miriam's keen eyesight, by means of which she had spotted so many stray steers on the distant foothills and plains, proved invaluable.

"Why," she said, "that's a strange gang of men on shore. They've got something set up there . . . A machine gun."

"Great God," said Homer, shinning down the tree with small regard for his well-tailored clothes or the palms of his hands. "There's not a moment to lose. Come, Frémont!"

And he started through the woods, with the amazed Chief not far behind him. Moritz, at first, started off through the bushes at full speed but a word from Homer brought him back.

"Stay close at my heels. I may need you, old man," he said, and the Boxer, without question, obeyed.

"I might have known," groaned Frémont, as a brier ripped off a generous strip from his britches. "Once that

Gonzo or Jansen gets loose, tranquillity dies. I shall deport him, once for all, when, if ever, this case is over. I shall ship him back to America where his antics will be less conspicuous. Government property! Incendiarism! Larceny! Bah!"

Miriam, whose neat sport suit had not been designed by Schiaparelli for climbing trees, or anything more strenuous than shuffleboard, took a few seconds longer than Homer in getting to earth again, but once there she made excellent time through the woods and soon was abreast of Frémont, whose reflections on the flora and rich dark soil of central France were becoming increasingly caustic. The Chief's shirt-tail, because of his exertion, was trailing in the breeze and any reader who has had experience with French shirt-tails knows that a man might as well try to make time across country dragging a full-size blimp as to run through alders and thorn bushes with yards of excess cotton in tow. Chief Frémont, it must be remembered, was a city man, through and through. He could have given a muskrat quite a handicap in a race through the Paris sewers, or outstripped an elk in traffic. The wildwood or bosky grove, however, was not his element. A wild grape vine snatched at his automatic just as a sassafras root gave him the leg and sent him sprawling. He saw a few white lights in shimmering clusters, was aware of a rank taste and marshy odor, the damp ground swelled and billowed, then revolved and as it came to rest he entered what he mistook for a long dark tunnel.

Neither Homer, well in the lead, nor Miriam, who was runner-up, nor Moritz noticed that Frémont had passed out. As they ran, the smell of smoke and burning pitch grew more acrid and their footing more uncertain on the swampy ground. A shot rang out, then another, then the sharp rat-tat-tat of a machine gun provoked angry echoes in the dell. Evans clutched a sapling and brought himself up short, catching Miriam and saving her from falling as she was about to pass. Moritz growled softly and the hair on the back of his neck began slowly to rise.

"That's right, Moritz! I know! There's bad medicine ahead," Evans said. "From now on, we'll have to proceed more cautiously. Follow me closely, Miriam, and you bring up the rear, old boy. We seem to have lost Frémont, but he'll turn up, no doubt."

Now Miriam, as a girl, had stalked the white-tail deer among the cottonwoods of the Lower Yellowstone with Rain-No-More, the son of Shot-on-Both-Sides, her father's lifelong friend. Nevertheless, she was astonished at the cunning with which Evans made his way through the brush without deranging a stray leaf or even frightening the linnets from their nests. The gunfire had ceased as abruptly as it had begun, the crackling of burning timbers sounded faintly. Otherwise, the silence of the afternoon was unbroken, until a piercing scream cut the air.

Evans wheeled. "Why! That was Bridgette Murphy," he whispered, puzzled.

Miriam, pale and disheveled, gasped. She was not thinking of Bridgette, but the Singe. Where Bridgette was, he might also be found. Was the struggle she had dreaded, between Homer and the stalwart Norman gang leader, about to take place? Suddenly she was sick and afraid.

"Please, Homer. You'll be careful . . ." she faltered.

The woman screamed again, and this time other female voices joined in.

"Down," said Evans, sharply, throwing himself flat on the ground and peering through the bushes. Moritz flattened himself close to the earth and Miriam, trembling, followed suit. She had drawn her automatic and was sighting experimentally along the barrel, her face chilled by a desperate resolve. Inch by inch they crept along until, concealed by the heavy undergrowth, they were not more than fifteen yards from the machine gun on the bank. There Dental Jake, with two of his cronies, were watching grimly the progress of the flames toward the bow of the barge and keeping the weapon trained on the only possible quarter from which the trapped occupants of the *Presque Sans Souci* could descend. From her point of vantage, Miriam saw with relief that the Singe was not among the gangsters on shore. In fact, to her astonishment, she caught a glimpse of his head for an instant above the rail of the barge, not two feet from Hjalmar Jansen. Hjalmar, in spite of the flames at his rear and the artillery in front of him, could not keep up a mere passive resistance. At the risk of being picked off by one of the enemy sharpshooters, he rose to throw an empty cognac bottle at the rival skipper, known as Nosepaint, who was hit full in the wind and collapsed, gasping frightful oaths and rolling on the sod in pain.

Out of sight, and sheltered from bullets by the heavy timbers of the barge's rail, Maître François Ronron, with Yvonne and Nadia close beside him, was sitting as comfortably as his years and the circumstances would permit, a paternal arm around the waist of each of the show girls. The heat from the blaze amidships was blistering.

Neither the Singe nor Hjalmar seemed to have a con-
certed plan of escape. Each time the blue-eyed Norman
had said he was going to give himself up, to save the
others, Bridgette Murphy had made such a wild demonstration that the Singe had hesitated, not so much on
account of her cries and lamentations, but because he
knew Dental Jake would slaughter the whole company,
anyway. "No witnesses" was Jake's motto and his savagery
was legendary, even among the hardened members of the
mob. Dental Jake and Nosepaint both had been kicked
out of the St. Julien Rollers when the Singe had taken
over, and both had boasted up river and down that they
would have his hide. The rest of the crew of the tugboat
were well known also to the Singe and had been passed
over by him, in setting up his organization, because they
were not amenable to discipline, and cared more for
violence than money.

"Jolly well struck," said Maître Ronron, when Hjalmar felled Nosepaint with the bottle. And to the girls, he
added: "Dry your eyes, my pigeons! Many is the time in
court when my adversaries had swamped me with facts
and arguments, I have waited for the jury to come in,
convinced that my client was done for, only to be surprised by a favorable verdict."

"The only time they had me up, things went just the
other way," said the accordion player, ruefully. He was
interrupted by an exultant yell. Disregarding all danger
from bullets, Hjalmar was on his feet, dancing and making hoarse exultant noises. Beside him the Singe straightened himself, also, less excitable but with a new glint of
hope in his steel-blue eyes. The show girls wept and
clung closer to Maître Ronron, who was shouting:

"Ah! *Merci, brave bête! Quel courage!*"

For through the portholes they all had seen a sleek brown Boxer come hurtling from a bush as if he had been shot off a catapult, and had heard the impact as he had crashed against the rear of Dental Jake and taken hold with his teeth. The thug pitched forward against his machine gun, tipping it over, tripod and all. Coincidently there were two shots and as many gangsters dropped, on either side of Jake.

Hjalmar, beside himself with joy, slapped the Singe on the back with his heavy hand, and pointed.

"There's Homer, by God. I might have known! There's Evans! Don't you see him?" For answer, the Singe vaulted clean over the side, just as Homer, leaving Jake for the moment to Moritz, dashed across the clearing to where Nosepaint was struggling to his feet. With a blow of his fist Homer knocked the skipper three feet into the air, from which altitude he descended heavily, a limp and insensible heap.

The Singe landed safely on his feet, like a cat, in spite of the twelve-foot drop, and Hjalmar hit the dirt a split second behind him. Four gangsters, who had been playing seven-up in the shade of a tree, waiting for the victims to be smoked off the barge and slaughtered, had risen, cards in hand. Hjalmar lit out in their direction. He got started so fast, for a big man, that the gangsters did not have a chance to run and soon they were a tangled mass of arms and legs and grunting sweating bodies, with Hjalmar punching and kneading them into a more or less compact mass that quickly showed evidence of his excellent sense of form and composition.

Miriam, now on the edge of the clearing, gun in hand,

184

was unable to make further use of the weapon. Moritz had tried to shift his grip and was all over Dental Jake, who was struggling to rise as the Singe started grimly toward him. Bracing himself on the tripod, Jake, one arm protecting his throat, got to his feet and dived into the woods, brushing Moritz off against a tree as he ran. Once free of the dog, he dodged from bush to bush, doubled back toward the tug and, skirting the clearing, got aboard and hauled up the gangplank. Moritz, meanwhile, was stunned and lay still where he had fallen, but the Singe, having lost sight of Jake when he had changed direction, was crashing through the woods like a moose, intent upon action. Maître Ronron, reassured by the turn of events, was helping Bridgette Murphy place the ladder from the barge to the shore. Half fainting, the show girls descended, clad in their now rumpled chemises, followed by Bridgette and the old lawyer, who was as calm and dignified in moments of good fortune as in adversity.

At the time Dental Jake had staggered up the gangplank of the tug, Miriam had been cut off from the sight by a thick clump of alders, and Homer had been engaged in restraining Hjalmar from swinging one of his antagonists like a club to knock down the others.

"Go easy, old man," Homer said. "Don't make more work for Toudoux. His time is invaluable, just now, and he mustn't be disturbed."

Hjalmar, looking around him for the first time since he had come ashore, saw that the tug was in motion.

"The tug! They're getting away! Diluvio's on board, so's Nicole," Hjalmar yelled. Side by side they made a dash for the tug but arrived at the bank too late. A trail of crimson disclosed that Jake had been bleeding profusely but the tugboat was under way and they were helpless to stop it.

"Never mind," said Maître Ronron, who approached them, beaming. "The law is patient, and our case against him is complete. Arson on a navigable river. Most unusual. In fact, almost unique, my friends."

It must not be forgotten that Chief of Detectives Frémont was left lying in the woods, unconscious from a fall, and thus had missed the rescue. He recovered, however, just in time to hear a heavy man come crashing toward him through the brush. As Frémont rose, the Singe, mistaking him for Dental Jake, made a dive at him. The terrain, as Frémont already had cause to know, was made difficult in that locale by a profusion of sassafras roots, one of which tripped the Singe, who sprawled at Frémont's feet and found himself looking upward, feeling rather silly, into the barrel of the Chief's spare automatic.

"Stick 'em up," the Chief said, curtly. He did not know by what miracle the criminal he sought had dropped into his lap, but he was not in the mood for reasoning why.

"I'll have to stand up first, or turn over on my back," the Singe said. "What's the idea?"

For answer the Chief, still keeping him covered, fished for the handcuffs. "I arrest you, in the name of the Third Republic, for the murder of one Baxter of Boston, and a British chap who formerly kept an atrocious hotel."

13

Mopping-up Operations

HATTIE HAM, whose life had contained a large share of disappointments, had a fair amount of poise and self-control under ordinary circumstances. But in matters concerning Andrew Flood, better known to the public as Anton Diluvio, she frequently showed signs of emotional instability and excitement. For half an hour after having been promised by Homer Evans and the officials at the prefecture that the violinist would be found and produced without delay, she sat tensely in a straight-backed chair, tearing into flakes the score of Lalo's Spanish concerto and a couple of embroidered handkerchiefs she had intended to send as a present to an aunt in Boston. Then she made a grab for the telephone. Unluckily the telephone girl downstairs was not at the switchboard, for reasons Hattie would have accepted in a calmer moment. That caused Hattie to press buttons, until the *valet de chambre,* the elevator man and two waiters from the restaurant came running to her room and hustled from there to the lobby to beseech the day clerk to answer the call.

At last a feeble connection was established with the prefecture. Hattie had a few words with Sergeant Schlumberger, and on being told by him that he had no news for her, she hauled the instrument out by the roots, to which clung considerable plaster, and chucked it through the open window into the alley four stories below, narrowly missing Mr. E. Berry Wall who was toddling in with his dog.

The evening before, Hattie had gained some confidence in Evans, but having seen him in the office of Dr. Hyacinthe Toudoux that morning, pottering with a couple of corpses, at a time when anything might have been happening to Anton Diluvio, her faith in Homer had been severely shaken. He was not, in her opinion, a man who could keep his eye on the ball. This, and other frantic thoughts, started her pacing the floor, with small regard for her squat square heels or the repeated shocks on her spine. She paced so vigorously, in fact, that a fidgety American state senator, who, in the room just below, was trying to take a French lesson from the chambermaid, found it impossible to make headway and, after the maid had escaped, he registered a complaint at the desk and quit the hotel in a huff.

At the same time, in Montparnasse, Mathilde Dubonnet, Hjalmar's beautiful model, was weeping all over the studio. She had learned a great deal of obedience and submission since Jansen had taken her in charge. She had resigned herself to posing in the nude during drafty winter months and in heavy stiff brocade period costumes in the stifling heat of summer. She had washed dishes and brushes until her fingers were worn almost to the bone, had lugged thousands of empty bottles back to the *bistrots* to exchange them for sous. It was only when she suspected that Hjalmar was with Nicole, of the Bal Tabarin, that Mathilde got out of hand, but when she did so she worked up a fury unusual in blondes.

First, Mathilde reduced to kindling wood and splinters the two wooden chairs, an adjustable easel and six stretchers. Then she started throwing tubes of paint here and there, to the discomfort of passers-by in the rue Montparnasse, pausing only when she noticed in her hand a tube of Cobalt blue (Rembrandt), the price of which she remembered was forty-odd francs.

"And to think that I fell for it," she moaned, wincing and grinding her perfect white teeth. "I didn't trust Hjalmar. It was the other man, that musician with his innocent brown eyes. I thought they were going to have a quiet talk, man to man, about things I didn't understand. Instead of that . . . the Bal Tabarin. Waaaah. Hehehe. Bou bou. Hu hu hu . . ."

Half-blinded by her tears she fished around for a palette knife, approached a stack of Hjalmar's paintings, and grabbed one at random with the intention of slicing it to ribbons. Then she sank shuddering to the army cot near by and buried her face where the pillow would have been, had Hjalmar held with such effete contrivances. The canvas she had hit upon was the portrait of herself that had won the prize in the Salon d'Automne, the one that had been compared to the *Maja Desnuda,* except for the color of the hair, by the shipping editor who was also second-string art critic on the *Daily Mail.* It had been painted in the heyday of her first infatuation, that unforgettable spring twelve months past when she had rejoiced day and night in having found a man who was her master. Mathilde bobbed up from the bed, dented some dishpans by banging them together, tossed a sheaf of art photographs into the yard of the convent next door, and started chewing clothespins to keep her teeth from chattering.

The telephone rang.

Mathilde, afraid for a moment to answer, hugged it to her breast to still the thumping of her heart. Alas, she knew she would forgive . . . But the voice was not that of Hjalmar, but Hattie's.

"Have those false alarms at the prefecture reported anything to you? I thought not. And how about Evans, that famous sleuth? Not a word."

"Waaaah. Bububu bu. Miaaa," responded Mathilde.

"We've got to act," said Hattie.

"Hehehehe. He's with Nicole. I feel it in my bones. Waaah. Bebebe. Bu bu," was Mathilde's contribution.

"I'm going down river myself, and kick up hell," said Hattie.

"Oh, please let me go, too," wailed Mathilde. "I'll go crazy if I stay here all alone."

"Get your hat on," snapped La Ham.

Grigori Hippolitovitch, night doorman of the Plaza Athènée, had been a light sleeper ever since the revolution, and his rest had been broken by the various summonses he had received that morning. Consequently he was in the lobby when Hattie came larruping out of the elevator demanding a touring car, alternately in Boston English and Back Bay French. The Russian had a cousin who drove for the secretary of the Ministry of Public Works, an official whose principal duty it was to tell all comers that the Minister had just stepped out. For that reason the car was seldom used during office hours. Grigori, of whom Hattie approved because of his aristocratic bearing, made swift arrangements and soon the commodious limousine was at the door. The doorman relieved his cousin, took the wheel, and promised to deliver the vehicle at a certain Russian embroidery shop before five-thirty that evening.

After a brief stop in the rue Montparnasse, where Mathilde was collected, they started down river at the highest speed consistent with safety, and at times from ten to fifteen miles an hour above that figure. In the army of the late Tsar, Grigori had been in the cavalry and had grown accustomed to charging from place to place as fast as his mount could travel. He was not a little impressed by Mathilde, who had removed the traces of tears from her face and was dressed in a manner that afforded a striking contrast with Hattie's dismal attire. The model's self-control, never her longest suit, did not stand up many minutes. Hattie, seeing her frail companion was coming unstuck, tried to start a soothing conversation.

"I don't mind Anton's tangling with a woman now and then," she said. "If only I could be sure he was safe . . ."

Mathilde's eyes grew round with fright and astonishment. "You don't mind other women!" she repeated. "Oh! I mind them terribly. I could stand it if Hjalmar were killed outright. You know . . . with no pain or blood or anything. But Nicole! That stringy little beast! That brazen trollop who shows her hide to all and sundry every night, with skin like a Chink or a Hindoo and great cow's eyes!"

With that Mathilde began to shudder and quake, and started yanking buttons out of the upholstery. The vase filled with artificial flowers, being easily detachable, she shied at a postman on a bicycle, and having wrenched loose the speaking tube, she shook it and stamped on it as if it were a snake. Her handbag fell to the floor and its contents spilled out, revealing a small pearl-handled revolver her former husband had given her after having found her struggling with a burglar in the bedroom the third successive night when he returned home from the Louvre.

Grigori Hippolitovitch, glancing ruefully at the damage to the appointments and the upholstery, sighed but voiced no objection. He understood the Russian soul, even when he came across it in a Frenchwoman. He had loved a Gypsy, once, through the long glamorous nights of old Moscow, and remembered all too vividly what he had suffered on account of a certain livery-stable attendant. He could recall, as he gripped the wheel until his fingers were white, how he had jerked out the fellow's beard, handful after handful, almost stifled by the fumes of manure. Ah, bygone days! Ah, passionate memories! Grigori jammed his foot down on the gas and missed a Thomas Cook and Sons bus by less than a millimeter as it rounded a curve outside St. Cloud. There and elsewhere along the route the folk by the wayside turned to stare and shake their heads as the limousine and its impulsive occupants streaked in and out between obstacles, courting death at every turn. The traffic police, however, took one look, saw plainly the Government seal on the car, and shrugged their shoulders, for it is a maxim in the Third Republic, and elsewhere, that an official who rates a large closed automobile is never wrong unless another official controlling two or more vehicles is involved.

"Grigori," Hattie asked, "if you had started from Paris on a barge ride with a boatload of floosies, what would have been your first stop?"

"Waaaah. Floosies," sobbed Mathilde.

The Russian's handsome face lit up and he squared his shoulders. Then, before he spoke, his countenance showed wistful regret.

"You understand, madame," he said, "that since the days of the Little Father, such indulgences have been denied me. Ah, boatloads of women! Floosies, I believe you called them. Miss Ham, your baffling language is richer than I had suspected. Floosies! What memories of the Volga you evoke. There is something completely satisfactory in having boatloads of women and frolicking at random."

"Waaaah. Miaaaa. Bou bou bou," shrieked Mathilde, fumbling on the floor for her lipstick and gun.

"To hell with the Volga," said Hattie. "We're dealing with the Seine, just now. If you had lit out with a raft of women, pie-eyed drunk . . ."

"Rouen, without a doubt, madame," said Grigori. "There is no other spot downstream from Paris where such a happy party could be properly received and entertained. Ah, the rue des Cordonniers! The colored glass, red plush, the vodka, or, at least, the applejack, which I am willing to admit is quite as good, although smoother. We shall find your virtuoso in Rouen, never fear."

"Step on it, then," said Hattie.

"Unhappily, we can go no faster," Grigori said. "My cousin's employer is only a secretary, remember, and probably had to accept this vehicle second hand. One reads constantly in the papers about Government economies. Still, I'll do the best I can."

Meanwhile, in the woods southwest of Luneville, what might be termed "mopping-up operations" were in progress. The charred hulk of the *Presque Sans Souci* lay smouldering by the shore and attracted the passing attention of stray tugs and barges headed upstream or down. But the skipper of a tug with a long line of barges in tow cannot heave to and watch a fire without endangering his craft and cargo, not to mention his job or his license. Miriam was engaged in roping up Captain Nosepaint and the four gangsters who had been pummeled by Hjalmar. The two dead thugs whom Miriam had been obliged to pick off while Moritz was gnawing at Dental Jake had been laid out in the shade and, in the absence of sheets, had been covered with ferns. Had any experienced buckaroo been handy, he would have been surprised to notice that in tying up the prisoners Miriam was using neither the Laramee nor the Deadwood style. She had had a whispered consultation with Homer, and he had decided, since it was impossible to transport the gangsters to Paris for questioning immediately, and furthermore, because they would be unlikely to spill anything no matter what pressure the police put upon them, that they should be given a chance to escape and that Homer and Miriam, with Moritz, should trail them.

In a near-by mossy nook, Maître Ronron was helping the scantily clad show girls fight off the mosquitoes, gnats and ants and explaining to them that if Nicole were molested or detained against her will on the tug by Dental Jake, the charges against him would be multiplied until it would be difficult to choose between them, and the penalties would total at least two hundred years. The old lawyer, in the presence of Yvonne and Nadia, kept up the pretense of light-heartedness but when he turned away, his refined old face was haggard indeed as he thought of his protégée in the hands of the ruffian he had just seen in action. In his fifty years of practice, Maître Ronron had come in contact with thousands of criminals and crooks, but most of them had been well dressed. Dental Jake was something new in his experience, which was just as well, since he was unable to visualize the full possibilities of the situation.

Standing near the ruin of the barge, and using to the utmost his gifts of reason and persuasion, was Homer Evans, his arm around the shaking shoulders of Bridgette Murphy. When she had learned that Frémont had arrested the Singe and accused him of murder she had picked up the machine gun, tripod and all, and, shrieking curses and maledictions, had started off with it in search of the Chief. Hjalmar had been obliged forcibly to detain her, although he was equally indignant that his new-found friend was in irons.

Moritz, the dog, whose head had cleared, first went to the river to lap up a drink and ease his parched throat, then set about chasing chipmunks and lizards with his customary zeal. The Boxer had sensed quickly that the principal business of the afternoon, as far as he was concerned, was over and would be followed by a lull, and it was a rather even thing as to whether Moritz enjoyed more the rest periods or those of violent action. He had not forgotten Dental Jake but his confidence in his master and mistress was such that he assumed off-hand they would arrange for a future meeting and until that moment came, the dog was content to let be. He glanced at the sun, concluded that his dinner hour was still distant in time, sighed, then started sniffing for minor diversions to pass the intervening hours.

Gradually, under the spell of Homer's words, Bridgette began to relax. The Singe, after his arrest, had sunk into a deep silence, not exactly sullen, but dense. He had enjoyed the gay companionship on the barge. The brush with the rival gangsters and its sudden dénouement had stirred his fighting blood. After that, the brisk contact with the law and officialdom had come suddenly, without warning, and had seemed to depress him beyond quick recovery. That he had been or would be framed, he had not the least doubt, but he had the presence of mind to keep mum until the police showed their hand.

"I know he's innocent," Homer was saying to Bridgette. "I'll prove it beyond a doubt. There are two ways you can help me. First, by keeping a level head and laying off Frémont, who'll eat out of the Singe's hand once he finds out what a boner he's made. Secondly, by telling me the exact truth and nothing but the truth, in connection with the Singe's movements. Now think carefully. Where was he between eight and eleven last night? If you don't know, say so frankly."

Bridgette blushed. "He was with me," she said. "So what?"

"Where?" Homer continued.

"In my room at the hotel," Bridgette answered.

"Any witnesses?"

Bridgette, whose cheeks were pink with embarrassment, turned crimson. "And what do you think I am, a peep show?" she asked, indignantly. "Of course there were no witnesses."

"Did anyone see him go in or come out?"

"Not that I know of. He doesn't go around with a brass band."

"And you're sure he was with you last evening, between eight and eleven," repeated Evans, smiling reassuringly.

" 'Tisn't likely I'd forget," said Bridgette. "And if he ever gets out of this scrape, I hope you'll try to get some sense in his head. He doesn't need money. I've been shoving it into the bank, day in, day out, these fourteen years. We could be married and live like other folks."

Homer repressed a shudder. "I should hardly like to suggest to the Singe that he live like other folks, but first let's get him out," he said. "Now listen carefully and do me and him another good turn. Don't tell Frémont or anyone about his alibi. As long as the police are clinging to a false theory, believing it to be true, we have all the advantage, don't you see?"

"Not a word will they drag out of me," said Bridgette. "Not even if one of them showed up here right now with a pint."

14

Which Takes the Reader into Sinful Territory, at a Moderate Cost, However

NICOLE and Diluvio, half suffocated with gags made of oily waste, blindfolded and bound hand and foot, had not been in a position to relish the stirring events of the afternoon. They had heard the oaths and tramp of feet when Nosepaint and Dental Jake had led the crew ashore, they had smelled the burning pitch and pungent wood smoke from the *Presque Sans Souci*. The shooting had caused Nicole's heart to skip accented beats and the violinist to writhe with disappointment because of his inability to join the fray. What had been the fate of their friends they could only guess. When Dental Jake returned on the run, and alone, the two prisoners felt a glimmer of hope that dwindled on the way downstream as Jake, at the wheel, let fall a string of promises as to what he intended to do with them. He had a different program for each of his helpless captives, needless to say, but it would be hard to decide which of the projects was the worse to contemplate.

It was dusk when the brick-red tug slid ominously to

the quai in Rouen, not two hundred yards downstream from the point where, centuries before, the ashes of Jeanne d'Arc had been cast into the Seine. The slap of the hawser sounded on the wharf and a strange voice asked of Jake:

"Who trimmed you?"

There was a scuffle, the same voice begged for mercy, and a moment later Nicole was unable to suppress a faint gurgle of fright when two strange longshoremen, in grimy overalls, entered the cabin carrying large gunny-sacks stained with coal dust. She had read of women in harems being sewn into sacks and drowned for the most trifling offenses.

Dental Jake, bloodstained and grinning, with a broken shovel-handle in one of his hairy hands, directed the operations, and from his remarks the trembling girl deduced that she was not to be chucked into the river at once, although possibly later.

The longshoremen laid hands first on Diluvio, and the first one, known as Duke, fingered Anton's blue-serge suit in a speculative way and asked to be kept in mind when its distribution was effected. The other man insisted that the matter be decided by cutting the cards. While they were talking, they picked up Diluvio and slid him into one of the sacks, afterward sewing up the open end with twine and a sail needle.

"If he tries any rough stuff, give him the boots," said Jake.

While Nicole was being stitched into the smaller sack, to the accompaniment of ribald comment and suggestions, Dental Jake told his accomplices to load the two captives into a truck and deliver them at a certain No. 27.

"I'll be waiting for you there, and make it snappy," Jake said.

Long ago, both Diluvio and Nicole had ceased to struggle. They simply tried to breathe deeply enough to keep themselves going, and to conserve what little strength they had left. They were lifted, lugged, dumped on the floor of a truck, then jolted barbarously over thousands of cobblestones. The burlap of their sacks was scorched as they were slid down a metal coal chute, then Jake's voice was heard again and they were thrown over the longshoremen's shoulders and carried up three flights of stairs. The porters dropped them unceremoniously to the floor which, from the sound and impact, they deduced was heavily carpeted. There they lay, bruised and apprehensive, while the stevedores were sent away. A muffled dialogue ensued in the adjoining hallway, involving a deep and rumbling female voice and that of Dental Jake.

After what seemed an interminable time the door opened again. Nicole was first to be removed from her sack. Bruised and smeared with coal dust, clad only in her soiled pink chemise, and with her dark hair awry, she presented such a pitiful figure that a grunt of compassion escaped the deep chest of the woman with the hearty voice. She was tall and plump, in an evening gown of dark-green velvet which showed to excellent advantage her voluptuous and commodious figure. A wealth of black hair was piled above her painted face and heavy eyebrows, and she was holding in her hand a tumbler of liquid which, in the dim light that sifted through the dark-red lamp shade, was a particularly offensive shade of linoleum green.

With an evil light in his eyes, Dental Jake advanced on Nicole, grinning and swaggering. As she tried to scream, he grabbed her, reached into her mouth with thumb and forefinger, and pulled out the gag. With his other hand he grasped her slender throat, choked her until her mouth sagged open wider, took the shaving brush from the statuesque landlady, dipped it in the green liquid and with gleeful brutality swabbed Nicole's mouth and throat. Then he released her and burst into harsh laughter as she gagged and tried to protest. Her voice had been reduced to the faintest croaking whisper, completely unintelligible.

"Come on, kid," said Jake. "Sing us a song."

"Let the poor thing be," said the big woman in her deepest baritone. "She's about all in."

"O.K.," said Jake, more pleased with himself than ever. "I'll attend to her boy friend now." He kept up a provocative banter as he unsacked Diluvio, who strained every nerve to keep his temper. Jake did not untie the violinist's bonds but he repeated the process with the shaving brush and vile green liquid, which tasted like osprey scrapings dissolved in lukewarm Moxie. As soon as the ordeal was over, Diluvio cast his eyes around the room. First, he beheld the landlady and a twinge of hope revived him. For the landlady was looking straight at him and he thought that he detected in her large and smouldering eyes that light which formerly had caused him many times to yell for Hattie Ham. The swift exchange of glances was not noticed by Dental Jake, who was leering meanwhile at Nicole and enjoying her terror and embarrassment. The room was about fifteen feet square, with a huge brass bed which had a strip of carpet about two feet wide across the bottom. The wall paper was bright heliotrope streaked with methylene blue, and sported vertical rows of blobs which might have been spanked babies or peonies. Large mirrors had been placed on the ceiling above the bed and on the adjacent walls. The lamps were draped in red, and the Three Graces, in imitation alabaster, stood on the mantelpiece.

The landlady, Horsecollar Phoebe, observed that Nicole was shivering. "Can't I get some clothes for the girl, a wrapper at least, and give her a bath?" Phoebe asked.

"I got a better idea," said Jake. "We'll strip bright boy, here, so he won't think about making his getaway." And pushing Anton over on the richly caparisoned bed, Jake pulled off the violinist's shoes without unlacing them, peeled off his coat, vest, pants and shirt; in fact, left him only his shorts. "Ain't he handsome?" Jake asked Phoebe. "Just too delicious. But don't you fall for him, Phoebe, or I'll fix his face so that he'll have to cut a hole in the seat of his pants and walk around on his hands. Eh, bright boy?"

"Aax coaaax," was all Diluvio was able to enunciate, in a ludicrous *sotto voce*. The taste of Jake's atrocious liquid silencer was still so sickening that Anton scarcely registered the studied abuse. Diluvio had one thing firmly in mind. He must keep cool, if he was to rescue Nicole and escape himself.

"Can I feed 'em?" rumbled Phoebe, whose mind seemed to dwell perpetually on physical comforts.

"Feed 'em good," snarled Jake. "They'll need to be strong for what's ahead of them."

"There'll be no rough stuff in my house," said Phoebe. "That was understood with Nosepaint."

"From now on, things'll have to be understood with me," Jake said. "Get going."

The rue des Cordonniers in Rouen begins just back of the water front, with an inconspicuous entrance from which street lamps have been withheld, and it ends at the top of a slope half a mile from the river, at the rue de l'Horloge. The street is narrow but not straight—is curved, no doubt, in order not to confuse the righteous. On both sides are doorways with panes of colored glass, mostly ruby red, and the numbers of the various houses are ingeniously displayed and illuminated. Tourists who stray there see placards above the ornate doorknobs with the inscription *"Entrez sans frapper,"* which means, "Come in without knocking." In fact, so hospitable are the denizens of that particular street that some of them sit for hours in windows, with warm smiles for passing strangers and inviting gestures which tend to dispel timidity and caution.

While Nicole and Diluvio, in No. 27, were being refreshed with *ragout* of spring lamb, spiced with thyme and rosemary, and tumblers of cider and applejack, Anton was further encouraged by learning that Phoebe spoke a sort of English, having run a house on the Gold Coast of San Francisco, and one of the few that did not close during the famous earthquake. At this moment a weary but determined group, already known to the reader, was entering without knocking the door of No. 1. The trio referred to consisted of Grigori Hippolitovitch Lidin, Hattie Ham and Mathilde Dubonnet.

They had been delayed by two blowouts, a collision

with a narrow-gauge switching engine, and the necessity of telephoning Grigori's cousin to warn him that the official limousine could not be returned on schedule time. It had been Grigori's idea that upon his arrival in Rouen he could park Miss Ham and Madame Dubonnet in some modest hotel like the Angleterre, while he combed the dives in search of Diluvio and Jansen. But in presenting his plan to Hattie, some over-eager glint in his eye had caused her to demur, and she had insisted on going along. So had Mathilde. The blonde model had been relieved of her pearl-handled revolver by Hattie, in whose skirt pocket it reposed, but she had lost none of her enmity toward Nicole.

In No. 1, they sat on plush benches around the rim of a dancing floor, sipping brandy and watching a few customers dance with the girls, who seemed somewhat despondent. The madame was a respectable-looking old woman with silver-gray hair, who passed away the dull hours knitting rompers for her little grandson. When Grigori inquired as to whether she had seen a bunch of Americans on the rampage, the question brought tears to the old lady's eyes. "Alas," she said. "Americans seldom stop in No. 1. They pass at least fifteen numbers before they can make up their minds."

That sounded so sensible to Hattie that she was for skipping Nos. 1 to 15, but Grigori was more thorough. Musicians and painters, he contended, were more impulsive and less inhibited than ordinary tourists and might dash into the first joint handy. At that Mathilde began to weep again, and to visualize Hjalmar's broad back weaving in and out of colored doorways all up and down the line.

No. 3 and No. 5 proved barren, as far as roisterers with foreign capital were concerned, although the brandy wasn't bad and in the last-named place Grigori had been overjoyed to find that the *sous-maitresse,* or hostess, was Russian and had been reduced to supervising a lupanar by the same political cataclysm that had jolted Grigori into a doorman's uniform. Before the third brandy had been served to Hattie and Grigori (Mathilde being temperate almost to the point of abstemiousness) Grigori and Anastasia Ivanovna were embracing and mingling their tears. That spectacle touched the heart of the proprietress, who avowed that Anastasia had been so lonely and friendless that her plight had wrung the hearts of the inmates and customers, who knew and respected a lady when they saw one. However, duty was duty, with Grigori, so he squared his shoulders and after an affectionate farewell to his countrywoman and many promises to write, he piloted his charges toward No. 7. Outdoors, he dropped back pensively, to give Hattie and Mathilde room to walk on the narrow sidewalk, humming a Caucasian song that is wild with nostalgia and longing:

> *"How can I make the panthers love me?*
> *Ah, faithless is his (or her) heart!"*

His musings were rudely interrupted. A roughly dressed giant who was approaching with a bundle under his arm, instead of making way for Mathilde and Hattie, barged into them and jostled them off the sidewalk. Grigori found himself squarely in front of Dental Jake, for it was he, and grabbed him by the sleeve.

"Is that the famous French politeness?" he asked, and

205

swung with his right, landing square on Jake's chin. Grigori had a very creditable right and formerly, when he had planted it on the button, antagonists had taken the count, or at least had been staggered. Jake only grunted, however, and with his free arm jabbed Grigori on the cheek bone, causing the Russian to see more stars than had swum before his eyes since he had passed out, face-up, in the foothills of the Caucasus years ago and his horse had stepped on him. Soon the two men were toe to toe, and engaged in a slugging match that fans would have gladly paid to witness. Jake's bundle dropped to the gutter and when he got to work with both hands, Grigori was clearly getting the worst of it. At that point Hattie got into action. With the small pearl-handled revolver she fired point-blank into Jake's broad rear and the bullets, peppering his thick hide in an area that had been thoroughly bitten by Moritz, caused the thug to howl with pain, grab up his bundle and hustle down the street and out of sight.

He had not been gone a moment when Hattie let out a yell. A blue-serge vest had been dropped from the bundle and in it was a fountain pen, of a distinctive pattern embossed with green and gold, that had been carried by Anton Diluvio.

"Help, murder, stop him! Follow that man!" she shrieked, causing heads to pop out of windows. As soon as she could control herself, she blurted out an explanation to Grigori. "It's Anton's! That's his pen! They've killed him. Please do something, quick."

Anastasia Ivanovna, who had been watching breathlessly from the window of No. 5, spoke earnestly to Grigori in Russian. "Be quiet," the latter said to Hattie.

"I have important information. The bruiser who just got away hangs out in No. 27. That's where we'll find Diluvio, but we've got to keep our heads."

He drew the two women into No. 5 again, where in Anastasia's room they held a council of war. Grigori, with a definite course of action in view, became as convincing and forceful as formerly he had seemed irresponsible.

"First of all," he said, "if your fiddler is held captive in No. 27, and his clothes have been taken away, he'll need a suit. Besides, in a joint like that they'll watch suspiciously any party that enters, if there's the least thing queer about it." In the end, he persuaded Hattie to remain at the window of No. 5, where she could see the doorway of No. 27, and let him go ahead, alone, to reconnoiter. Mathilde was sunk in deep despair. She felt sure that no one could strip Jansen as long as he was alive. Because a package would attract undue attention, Grigori borrowed a suit of clothes belonging to the landlady's son-in-law, who was away at the Sorbonne, and put it on underneath his own clothing. With two long French bayonets, one stuck in each sock, he started away and soon they heard his song "How can I make the panthers," ringing out between the narrow buildings at the other end of the street and saw him enter No. 27, rolling merrily to appear drunker than he was.

In Paris at the prefecture, another door was opening and closing as the Singe, still silent and contemptuous, was ushered into the cell known as the Goldfish Bowl, bereft of necktie, shoestrings, belt, and the contents of his pockets. Frémont, closeted with Schlumberger, was poring over the fingerprint diagram of the table and checkerboard from the fatal room in the Hotel Wilton.

In his laboratory, Dr. Hyacinthe Toudoux was pacing the floor, and intermittently smashing government beakers and test tubes. The two corpses, and especially that of Leffingwell Baxter, were showing increasing evidence of wear and tear. Had it not been for Madame Toudoux, the former Marquise de la Rose d'Antan, who telephoned hourly to whisper soft words of encouragement, the medical examiner might have lost his mind. As a matter of fact, he did get well over the borderline when a truckdriver and his assistant popped in to deliver two new stiffs from down river, at just the moment when a sample of spinal fluid was causing sesquisulphate of manganese to boil and bubble when it should have coagulated and turned pea green. The accompanying bill of lading from Frémont stated that the corpses had been potted standing, by Mademoiselle Montana.

"Shades of Pasteur, Koch, and Lister, sustain me now," the doctor muttered, jabbing his pencil clean through the receipt he was trying to sign. "Was ever a public official thus tormented? I have tested for every known poison, and even have invented three new ones, accidentally, in this cursed investigation. And I am deeper in the fog than I was when these two miserable corpses were as warm as Anglo-Saxons ever get. Were it not for Eugènie, I would remove the decorations from this troubled breast, pin them on the first Anamite peanut vendor who passed by, then jab myself with the accursed phonograph needle that has brought modern science to a standstill."

15

Of the Law and Ordinance of Nature

IT IS perhaps to the weather's credit that it pays scant attention to the good or evil deeds of man. The calm and beauty of the evening that descended on the woods southwest of Luneville after the burning of the *Presque Sans Souci* was an example. The sun set gently, not angrily, and pink fleecy clouds festooned a green-blue sky. Birds, quickly forgetful of the violent scenes they had been forced to witness, tucked their heads beneath their wings and started chalking off some good sound sleep, against an early rising. Crickets chirped, bats winged their zigzag flight in pursuit of mosquitoes, and the frogs added their treble and diapason above and below the chorus of their night-faring neighbors.

By arrangement with the Chief, who had stubbornly refused to release the Singe, Homer Evans had been given full charge of downstream operations while Frémont had returned to the capital to gather up loose ends and prod Sergeants Bonnet and Schlumberger in their routine investigations and check-ups. With the Chief had departed Delafon, the *restaurateur,* and his waiter; the accordion player had been generously paid and, after having been sworn to secrecy, had started up-river to rejoin his family. A police launch, summoned by telephone by Frémont, had been sent from Rouen and had conveyed back to that historic city Maître François Ronron, the two remaining show girls, Bridgette Murphy and Hjalmar Jansen. The old lawyer had promised to secure clothes for Yvonne and Nadia and rush them to the Bal Tabarin in time for the night's performance. Hjalmar had been instructed to prowl around the Rouen water front and find out what he could about the fugitive snub-nosed tug.

With their backs against stout trees, Captain Nosepaint and his four well-trundled outlaws were tied in a sitting position and were keeping a sullen silence as Homer, Miriam and Moritz approached them from the river. As soon as he was within earshot, Evans, for the benefit of his captives, said that he was hungry and thirsty and that he saw no reason for hanging around indefinitely, since the prisoners were securely tied. He walked around the captain as if the latter were a sack of meal, felt of the knots Miriam had skilfully left vulnerable, then suggested to her that they hike back to Luneville for a hearty dinner at the Restaurant Serieux and resume their vigil later. He even promised to bring back food and wine for the thugs, at which Nosepaint cocked his heavy eyebrows sardonically and spat, to indicate that, food or no food, he would have nothing to say.

Homer led the way over a narrow path a distance of two hundred yards, then back through the thickest of the woods to a point where they could watch the gangsters' movements and hear every word. As they crawled along, Miriam again was astounded at the ease with which Homer made his way in the most tangled thicket as silently as the jaguar in his jungle, and how unerringly he had surveyed the terrain. Her own training, with Rain-No-More and the Blackfeet of the Montana hills, stood her in excellent stead as she strained every nerve to avoid snapping twigs and succeeded in approximating Evans' smooth performance. The Boxer, quivering with eagerness, stepped softly behind them. He had taken the precaution of sniffing each thug, until he could have spotted them, blindfolded, in Molyneux's most fragrant salesroom, or the waste-heap outside a sardine factory.

Captain Nosepaint was a man of few words but of a restless disposition. As Homer had foreseen, the bandit skipper had begun tugging against his bonds and squirming like Houdini the moment his captors were out of sight. A grunt of satisfaction escaped him when he got one hand loose and it was not many minutes before he stood up, unsteadily, cursing softly, massaged his cramped limbs, felt his jaw tenderly at the point where Homer's fist had landed, then set to work on his companions. Miriam, in order to make the ruse more convincing, had trussed up the four subordinates quite thoroughly, but Nosepaint did not wait to untie knots. In the thin starlight, the watchers saw him get down on all fours and start gnawing through the ropes, and one by one the gangsters stood up, groaning.

Instead of setting out in the direction Homer had taken, Nosepaint and his battered crew lit out toward the river, so that Evans was obliged to skirt the clearing in order to keep them in sight. Two hundred yards upstream the fugitive skipper found a rowboat moored in front of an empty shack some Parisian used week-ends. Nosepaint hurried to the back of the shack, where there was a sort of go-down, ripped off some boards and came forth with a pair of oars and oarlocks. Miriam was dismayed and, glancing at Homer, touched her automatic questioningly. Evans firmly shook his head. To the girl's astonishment, he calmly watched the skipper and his four cronies step into the stolen skiff, shove off and start rowing across the river. Even Moritz showed his disappointment and perplexity by wrinkling his forehead into a frown.

"But they're getting away," whispered Miriam.

Homer smiled. "I think I know where we shall find them. And we have ample time. The current is taking them downstream and the going is hard through the brush on the other side of the river." Beckoning her to follow, and after reaching down to reassure Moritz, he walked briskly along a path and soon they were crossing the bridge just below Luneville. Once across the river, Homer proceeded with caution, slipping noiselessly from tree to tree until they were in sight of the unused blacksmith shop where he had found the boy and the crickets that morning.

"They'll be here before long," Evans said. "We've got to hide in there and see what happens, but don't shoot unless I give the word, no matter what you are obliged to witness. How are the nerves? Quite steady, old girl?"

The tremor in her voice as she answered caused Homer to smile and place his hand on her shoulder. Then he approached a window, glanced in, and tried the door. It was unlocked. He entered, automatic in one hand and his flashlight in the other, then motioned for Miriam and Moritz to follow. The box of crickets was still in place, and after a quick examination of the premises Homer lifted a tarpaulin that had been spread over a pile of junk in one corner. There were wagon spokes and tires, kegs of nails and horseshoes, all badly rusted, plowshares, parts of discarded farm implements, andirons, assorted scraps of metal a blacksmith might have accumulated in his trade, but concealed in the heap was an object that caused Evans to catch his breath sharply and nod with satisfaction.

"Now what, my dear," he asked Miriam, "would a blacksmith be doing with a dentist's chair?"

Miriam, who was keyed up with excitement, gasped: "Dental Jake!"

"Exactly," he said. "Evidently the legends inspired by our uncouth opponent are founded quite firmly on fact. We shall see."

"Oh, Homer," said Miriam. Before her in the darkness she saw the evil face of Jake and his enormous hairy hands, and paled as she seemed to hear the maddening buzz and stutter of a dentist's drill, exploring raw nerves as it ate its way through ivory.

Homer's face was more grave than stern. "I brought you with me because I can depend on you," he said, simply. "Perhaps I should not subject you to such ordeals . . ."

"Oh, yes," she pleaded, clutching his sleeve. "I'll behave! I'll pull myself together! Just tell me what to do."

"Our role, just now, is passive," said Evans. He pointed to a small open loft, also littered with junk, and mounted the rickety ladder. "Come on," he said. "We must hide up here. It's a dangerous place to be caught, but there's no alternative. Come, Moritz."

The Boxer set himself, frowned, then backed up for a running start. His sleek brown body shot upward, his capable front paws clung to the platform while his hind paws clawed for a rung, found it, and he struggled to Evans' side. Miriam followed resolutely. The floor of the loft had wide chinks between the boards, but seemed to be fairly solid. Behind a stack of angle irons and wagon parts there was a small high window. "Ah," said Homer, and with his surprising strength he wrenched it from its frame and replaced it, loosely.

"It's not too much of a drop to the ground, if worst comes to worst," he said. Then he rearranged the junk slightly to afford an adequate barrier in front, and turned off his flashlight. Gently he placed his hand on Moritz's damp muzzle, then let his fingers rest lightly on the back of the dog's neck. In a moment he felt the hair begin to rise.

"They're coming," he whispered, and soon the sound of footsteps came faintly to their ears. A hand rattled the door latch, a match flared outside, and in the light of it, as the door swung open, they could see the ruddy face of Nosepaint and the members of his crew. On the way the bandits had secured some long loaves of bread, a cheese, huge chunks of sausage, and from their tattered pockets protruded several bottles of cognac and wine. One of them lighted a lantern, another started tacking up gunny-sacks to hide the light across the window boards and soon they took seats on kegs and anvils and started wolfing their meal, washing down huge mouthfuls with wine.

They were still eating when other footsteps approached the shack from the direction of the river and a half dozen more men entered, after knocking softly on the door. Three were in stevedore's clothes but the other three wore collars and neckties.

Evans, who was taking in eagerly every detail, saw at once that one of the latter group, a small frightened chap with gray hair and drooping mustaches, had been brought there against his will and was weak with terror. Nosepaint looked at the latter, speculatively, grunted and spat.

"So glad to have you with us," he said, with exaggerated politeness.

The little man would have collapsed with fright had not the others held him up.

"Here! Take a slug of this. It'll buck you up," the skipper said, and poured out a tin cup full of cognac from an unlabeled bottle. The little man hesitated until prodded with a sharpened rat-tail file. Then he gulped, coughed and spluttered as the raw liquor caused his Adam's apple to shuttle up and down, and his windpipe to backfire.

"What do you want with me?" he stammered.

"Search me," said Nosepaint. "We was told to bring you in, and here you are."

"Where's Jake?" asked one of the newcomers.

"Jake's detained, but he'll show up all right," the skipper said. "He's having some stitches taken in his prat."

The bottles were passed around and the fumes of crude tobacco and cheap cognac arose, until the smoke got so thick that Nosepaint ordered one of his crew to light another lantern. Outside there was a faint chugging of a motor.

"Here's Jake," said one of the thugs.

Dental Jake made his entrance a moment later, accompanied by the two men who had met the tug in Rouen. He had under one arm a shoebox, through which holes had been punched, apparently for ventilation.

"We got the guy you wanted," said one of the well-dressed men, and shoved forward the little man, whose knees were buckling.

"I'll give him his workout afterward," Jake said. "He can wait."

Meanwhile a circle had been cleared in the center of the dirt floor and the gangsters were taking seats on kegs or squatting on the ground. One of them got out a broom and remained standing. Jake spread a large white table napkin over the cleared area and pegged the corners down with thirty-penny nails which he drove with his fist, there being no hammer handy. From the shoebox he drew two smaller pasteboard boxes, both peppered with airholes and two ribbons, one black and one red. The ribbons he handed to Nosepaint.

The skipper shuffled the ribbons between the palms of his hands, placed his hands behind his back and faced the shuddering prisoner.

"Which hand will you take?" he asked, and when the little man hesitated someone reached for the rat-tail file.

"This one," blurted the trembling man.

"Red," said Nosepaint, exhibiting the red ribbon. Jake, who was holding out the two small boxes, one in each hand, said: "Red is the left one, mates. Now place your bets."

The members of the murderous-looking crew began fishing out bills of all denominations, large and small, while the Captain made notes in a dog-eared notebook. Evans raised his eyebrows and chuckled silently when he saw what substantial sums were about to change hands in the dingy shed.

"Ready?" asked Jake.

"Which way are you betting?" asked a gangster.

"Black for me," Jake said, and planked down a handful of 1,000-franc bills. He took up the left-hand box and shook its contents out on the napkin and Miriam, watching from the loft, stuffed her handkerchief into her mouth to keep from screaming. For a black-bellied tarantula, two inches or more across, with hideous red spots, landed belly-up on the cloth, waved its hairy legs, caught the linen with its claws and righted itself, squatting tensely in the lantern light. Jake reached for a can of boat paint and with a long-handled brush, smeared the crouching spider's back with red. From the other box he dumped another tarantula of the dread family known as *Lycosa narbonnensis* into the arena. The second landed right side up.

Murmurs of approval went up from the gangsters around the circle, for the spiders seemed exactly of a size and equally vicious and determined. The man with the broom stood ready, should either contestant get too near the off-side lines.

The tarantulas squatted motionless not more than ten seconds, their eight eyes gleaming like sharp quartz crystals, their powerful poison fangs yawning. Then Red made a sally with incredible swiftness and was met by Black just out of her corner. Both spiders recoiled, to size up the other, and Red gave a spring. Even Homer was awed by the spectacle, not only of the loathsome insects but the circle of faces, scarcely human, that glared into the arena. Red and Black soon were tangled into a quivering, clawing mass. They veered and rolled, turned this way and that, then were utterly still.

"Ah," came in a chorus from the dry throats of the gangsters, for Red was on top and was proving the stronger, but Black, the more agile, got a claw in the linen and Red, as if wary of an upset, recoiled.

A stevedore let out a yell, and dodged a horseshoe thrown at him by Dental Jake, for the rule was silence and immobility, since some fighting spiders were distracted by commotion at the ringside. The pair in question, however, were intent on mutual destruction, to the exclusion of all else. For them, it was life or death. They sprang into a clinch again, and once more Red laid Black flat on her back. The tarantulas were belly to belly, leg clutching leg, fangs wide open and ready. But neither dared risk a move to bite. Four pairs of glinting eyes were focused upwards, four pairs glared down. The gangsters, grunting and sweating, shifted on their seats, clenched and unclenched their fists, inhaled and exhaled, muscles straining as they swayed from side to side.

Belly to belly the tarantulas wrestled five seconds more, then Black lunged and closed her powerful jaws, Red shook in frightful convulsions, legs flailing wildly. They rolled over, Black was astride and stabbed her dying antagonist in the back of the neck, stabbed again, again closed her death-dealing jaws, and the fight was over.

Nosepaint, notebook in hand, passed out sheaves of money while the gangsters gloated or mumbled curses, according to their losses or gains. Dental Jake, with a grin, shook the tarantulas back into the shoebox and watched Black dismember and devour the loser, red paint and all. "Nice going, Black," he growled, and turned to Nosepaint to collect his winnings. "That's the first good break I got today. Maybe my luck has changed."

Miriam, in the loft, was almost at the end of her endurance. Try as she might, she had not been able to take her eyes off the ferocious spectacle or to keep from shuddering each time the lewd faces of the gangsters took on new refinements of depravity. When the tarantula fight had reached its horrid climax, and still more revolting anticlimax, she had hoped fervently that the evening's orgy was over and that soon she would be with Homer in the open air. Alas, the session in the blacksmith's shop had only just begun. As Jake was counting his money and Nosepaint was balancing his books, the others passed the bottles from hand to hand and the gurgling noises that ensued caused Moritz, cut off from a view of the proceedings, to snap his ears erect and look at Homer questioningly. Winners drank to felicitate themselves, losers drank for consolation. This time the meek and terrified little man with the handlebar mustaches was not forced to take his turn. He was ignored, as if he were nonexistent. The gangsters studiously avoided looking at him, except for Nosepaint, who approached Dental Jake. Eagerly the members of the gang gathered around the two leaders to listen.

"Well, what about it?" Nosepaint asked, indicating the gang with a sweep of his hand. "Do they stay, or do they beat it?"

Jake, in an expansive mood, said: "Sure. Let 'em stay. But they'll have to keep their traps shut."

Animal sounds of approval issued from all quarters of the smoky shop, the circle was enlarged and one of the well-dressed men of the second contingent to arrive reached into the junk pile for the dentist's chair. An over-sized horseshoe shied playfully by Jake knocked him off his pins, with a gash in his head.

"Keep your shirt on, Camphor," Jake said, to the prostrate dude. "When I'm ready for implements, I'll say so. See? How do we know that this party with the ticklers won't speak his piece without persuasion? Maybe he knows what's good for him, and wants to save us time? Eh, tinker?" The last brief question was addressed to the shuddering guest whose limbs and loose clothing began to flap like a scarecrow's in the wind. The small man's jaw worked up and down, not quite synchronously with his Adam's apple, and after pitiful effort, faint words began to come.

"What do you want with me? I haven't done a thing, except what I was told. Please let me go. It's sure to attract attention, if my shop is closed," the victim said.

Jake grabbed him by the shirt front, sat down on a nail keg (after dumping off its former occupant) and took the helpless little man on his knee, like a ventriloquist's dummy.

"Now look here, tinker," Jake said, in a patronizing way. "I like you. See? I don't want to have to rub you out. All I ask is a little explanation. The Chief was all set to pull off a job at the Salle Gaveau. Am I right?"

"But I did all I could," protested the other, and was

silenced by a smack across the mouth that left his face streaked with red.

"Don't interrupt! The Chief was set to pull off a job, and who knew about it except you? Eh?" Jake turned at random to one of the well-dressed men. "Did you?" he asked the same question of several other gangsters. All replied derisively in the negative. "See?" said Jake to the victim. "You were the only one. And what did our little helpers find at the hall?"

"I didn't say a word. I swear . . ." Another and more forceful slap cut off the little man's words.

Jake continued. "In one of the seats up front we find the Chief of Detectives, in a new soup and fish, with his eight-ball frail. And who was sitting next to her? That fat-head Yank who sent old Barney into stir, and his gun moll right on deck beside him . . . Not only that, but there were bulls at every exit and in doorways all up and down the street. Now, I'll leave it to our buddies here: Do things like that come off by accident?"

A muffled roar filled the shop, until Jake held up his hand.

"That isn't all," went on Jake. "The afternoon before, when a certain party went into your shop, to have words with another party, was there a Dick outside, or wasn't there?"

"Rebec, by God," muttered Evans to himself. "Proprietor of the medal emporium."

Monsieur Rebec tried to speak but could only shake his head and gurgle. Jake watched his victim until the latter's face began to quiver, and he started sobbing. Then he jerked his head toward the junk pile and eager hands drew forth the dentist's chair, while the other gangsters stirred and wet their lips with anticipation.

Under cover of the general confusion, as the chair was being set up and the drill-stand, with its old-fashioned foot pedal, was rigged up beside it, Homer stepped noiselessly to the window in the loft and lifted it from its casing. In his anxiety to catch every word that had been spoken he had not noticed how near collapse was Miriam. Quickly he drew out his memorandum book, tore out a leaf and scribbled with his fountain pen. Lifting Miriam from her feet as if she were a child, he carried her to the window, placed the note in her handbag and, in spite of her unspoken protests, lowered her to within a few feet of the ground. Moritz, he let drop to safety in a similar way.

The cool night air and the necessity for action restored to Miriam her customary poise and without a moment's delay she hurried to the shelter of a thicket, got out the note and her flashlight, and read:

"Shoot several times in the air when I wave handkerchief from loft window. Then make getaway and meet me in lobby of Hotel Serieux. Phone Frémont to guard premises and partners of Siècles Frères, in the Palais Royal, as well as medal shop Aux Citoyens. *Et surtout, la calme.*" (Above all, calm yourself.)

The Boxer, who had followed her with evident misgivings while she had been walking away from Evans and the shop, pricked up his ears and jogged along willingly as she hurried back to her station. He did not bark with approval when she took out her automatic and held it in the alert position, but he looked up at her and made a motion with his paw, somewhat like that a thoroughbred

222

horse might make in trying to behave at the starting gate.

Inside the blacksmith shop, Homer was witnessing a truly dreadful scene, not only because of the cringing half-fainting Rebec, for whose torture the stage was set, but on account of the unholy relish with which the gangsters, with the single exception of Captain Nosepaint, were watching the gruesome preparations. For to Evans, the spectacle awoke echoes all through his historical background. He thought of Torquemada, of the early Christians in Rome, of the dread Chinese mode of execution known as T'sun-dao Chee in which the victim's skin is peeled off bit by bit with a sharp-pointed twig of bamboo.

"The law and ordinance of nature, under which all men are born and, for the most part, live . . ." he quoted from Spinoza, to steady his nerves. "Ah, for the most part. That leaves a ray of hope for the race," he said, and resolved to be lenient with the grisly skipper, when the final showdown came, because he had bolstered Homer's faith in human kind.

The hapless Rebec was lugged to the chair and ropes were passed around his middle by one of the dudes, while a sailor bound his hands behind the back of the chair and tied his feet securely to the footboard. Meanwhile, Jake was pushing the pedal, experimentally, and listening critically to the whine of the drill which he held up to his ear, then tested on a hoof paring he picked up from the floor. A small drink of cognac was poured between the little man's white lips, so that he would not lose consciousness too soon or too often. Then the company took seats and leaned forward.

Jake's ham-like hands had never looked so formidable

as when he advanced with the drill. Frantically, the victim clamped his jaws, squealing horribly through his nose. Jake replaced the drill, clamped his right thumb and forefinger around Rebec's windpipe and pressed until his mouth flew open.

"Gimme a large-sized horseshoe," he growled.

A shoe that had been taken off a full-grown stallion was handed up to him. He hooked the corner of it into Rebec's open mouth, between the jaws, and held it in place with his left hand. Without turning his head, he pawed outward for the drill, like a huge crustacean reaching blindly in the depths of the sea for whatever might swim within range of his murderous claw.

At that point, Nosepaint, who alone among those in the shop, had turned his head the other way, faced about and said:

"Give him one more chance to talk, Jake, as a favor to me."

Dental Jake paused and grinned. He knew that Nosepaint was squeamish, and thought it uproariously funny. "All right, Mother Hubbard," he grunted, and jerked the huge horseshoe from between Rebec's jaws. "Come on, sweetheart," he said. "Speak, or hold your puss until you get your treatment."

Nosepaint came forward and leaned over the chair. "Come on, brother. Tell us what you know! You'll have to break down in the end. The strongest guy Jake ever worked on could only last through three incisors and a molar . . ."

"A molar and a half," corrected Jake.

For the first time, the little man screamed wildly, a piercing, hair-raising sound.

"You see," said Jake, "he won't tell us."

"Maybe he's on the level," protested Nosepaint. "Some guys are. Perhaps he doesn't know anything."

"We can't leave no stone unturned," said Jake. "Now give me elbow room."

He throttled off another scream, replaced the horseshoe, and, pedaling vigorously, took up the drill.

Homer, himself convinced that Rebec had nothing to confess, let his handkerchief flutter from the window. Instantly a fusilade shattered the silence of the night and brought every gangster to his feet. Nosepaint, dousing the lanterns, yelled: "Beat it and scatter." Dental Jake, with an oath, declared that their victim had set a trap for them again and was about to crush Rebec's skull with the horseshoe when, in response to Homer's furious fluttering, Miriam cut loose with another deafening salvo.

"Come on, Jake! They're right on us!" Nosepaint said, dragging his confrere by the sleeve. They were the last to leave the shop, and without wasting a second, Evans jumped down from the loft and cut the ropes that bound the captive to the chair. Slinging the little man, who had fainted, over his shoulder, Homer picked up the shoebox, and balancing it gingerly as the gorged *Lycosa* scuttled from side to side, he hurried out the doorway and set out, through the woods, for Luneville Center and the Hotel Serieux.

"Among their other foul deeds, these cut-throats have made me late for my dinner," he murmured as the lights of the square came into view.

16

Which Brings Tough Luck to Two
Tailors and a Goat

A STUPENDOUS amount of tosh has been written and sung about woman's intuition, but one thing is certain. It operates imperfectly, if at all, during the periods of reverie which follow happy lovers' meetings. For instance, on the afternoon and evening Diluvio was risking death by fire and water, and was gaffed, trussed, sacked, swabbed, stripped and jugged in the bawdy house of Horsecollar Phoebe in Rouen, Beatrice Baxter was as carefree as a magpie in a zoo. True, she had lost a handbag stuffed with hundred-dollar bills and had parted with other valuable considerations. Her legs were bare, she did not speak French, and could not seem to find her way out of the forest. Nevertheless, she tripped along gaily until her feet got sore, then limped without complaining, singing snatches of song and reveling in thoughts which, if dwelt upon, might cause the reader to go out and get himself in trouble.

Long after she had lost track of the miles she saw

approaching on a lonely country road a tall and resolute girl who seemed to be dragging a protesting man in tow. The man was of medium stature, dressed in black, and with his free hand he was swinging a satchel. Beatrice was just about to try to ask the way to Paris, reminding herself that it was pronounced "Paree," when, to her surprise, the man appealed to her, first in French, which meant nothing at all, and then in halting American. With that assured air of one accustomed from birth to giving orders, Miss Baxter asked the big strong girl to halt while the man with the satchel poured forth his woes.

"Please tell her to unhand me," the fellow began. "I, a war veteran and father of a family, am overdue this moment in the stable of the Mayor of St. Germain, where his prize Holstein cow, by Faustus III out of Marguerite, is about to calve. And I have been paid partly in advance. This incredible Amazon, who speaks with a foreign accent I cannot even hazard a guess about, came bursting in while I was at lunch, tore me away from the wine and cheese with an incoherent tale about a wounded dog and an American small-arms expert, and has dragged me through by-paths and brambles for hours. She is mad, madame, and has the strength of a maniac."

Stenka gave her version of the matter in Serbian and only with difficulty was shunted into a sort of French. Her description of the dog she was trying to succor, as translated by the distraught horse doctor, at once intrigued Miss Baxter. Boxers were scarce in those days, even in America, and the only one Beatrice had ever seen in Paris was her late brother's Moritz, by Max out of Leni. If Moritz, of whom Beatrice was fond, was being punctured by rowdies in a Montparnasse hotel, Miss Baxter felt that she ought to take a hand. Assuring the horse doctor that she would pay all fees and refund the Mayor's advance on account of the cow, Beatrice asked him to lead them all to a settlement where she could hire a taxi. And when the vet remarked that a taxi to Paris would cost a fortune, she let it drop that she had only the day before come into five hundred million dollars. The horse doctor, convinced by her words that the whole population of that countryside had gone loco, tore loose from Stenka and, abandoning the tools of his profession, scampered like a rabbit through the woods at such a rate that Stenka could not catch him.

The stalwart chambermaid, thus having lost at one stroke the results of her single-minded efforts of the day, began to bawl and beat her breast, but Miss Baxter succeeded in comforting her and soon Stenka allowed herself to be led to a filling station. The proprietor, who had a Model T Ford that had been left behind by the A.E.F., had once worked as a bookkeeper for the American Express, so he recognized Miss Baxter as an American and, assuming she was fabulously rich, consented to drive them to Montparnasse on a C.O.D. arrangement.

Upon arriving at the Hotel Vavin, Stenka piloted her new protectress to Miriam's room, No. 85, but neither Miriam nor Moritz could be found. Nevertheless, a sight greeted Beatrice's eyes that swept from her mind all thoughts of women or beasts, for lying face upward on the bed was the matchless Guarnerius, "The Sinner without Malice," the ruddy glow of the varnish enhancing the beauty of the grain of the wood. Ecstatically she recognized the sturdy scroll, the angular sound holes, the fine maple bridge on diminutive feet.

"Anton," she cried, stroking reverently the spot that had felt so often the pressure of his chin. "Anton. What miracle has brought me to this place? With my own hands I shall restore to you your incomparable instrument and in that moment I shall know my fate."

Leaving the bewildered Stenka with instructions to wait for news of Moritz, Miss Baxter gathered up the violin and bow and, leaving the Hotel Vavin, hailed a taxi and murmured, "The Plaza Athènée." The chauffeur had had his station in Montparnasse many years, and consequently was not surprised when he noticed that his attractive passenger was sprinkled with hayseed, wore no stockings, and showered baby talk on violins.

Miss Baxter's spirits were dampened momentarily when, on arriving at the Plaza Athènée she found that Grigori was not on duty, for she had hoped to get an immediate report as to Diluvio's whereabouts, if Anton had returned from his excursion down river. Violin in hand, she entered the elevator, not remarking as she crossed the lobby that the clerk was eyeing her with evident misgivings. Sergeant Bonnet, still smarting under the sarcasm of the Chief because he had let the fiddler get away the night before, had been ordered to wait at Miss Baxter's doorway until she returned and to bring her to the prefecture for questioning. When he saw her approaching and noticed what she was carrying, he leaped and whirled like Nijinski. His luck had turned at last. He grasped Beatrice by the arm with one hand

and blew his whistle furiously with the other, while she tried to explain that she had found the Guarnerius in the room of a strange hotel, the name and address of which she had neglected to ascertain, and that her object in taking it had been to return it to its owner, the famous Diluvio.

"Is he known to you, this fiddler?" the Sergeant asked, with a skeptical gleam in his eye.

Beatrice blushed and stammered: "Well . . . Yes and no . . . I really can't explain."

"It is probable that you will have ample time to think of explanations. Several years, if I am not mistaken," Bonnet said, and tightened his grip on her wrist.

The wagon arrived, siren wailing, and Miss Baxter was escorted by two officers in uniform through the gaping crowd in the lobby of the Plaza Athènée and on the sidewalk. Behind her pranced Sergeant Bonnet, holding "The Sinner without Malice" like a tennis racket and directing operations with the bow. He was debating with himself, as he rode beside the crestfallen Beatrice in the Black Maria, whether he should assume an air of injured dignity when he encountered Frémont or pretend that he had forgotten the Chief's unjust recriminations. They were passing the obelisk in the Place de la Concorde when he decided on the latter attitude, and the remainder of the ride he spent in wondering why a woman, unmistakably *chic* although rumpled and without stockings, who had inherited a sum approximating the annual budget of France in an economical year, would stoop to fiddle-snatching. Would such a one hesitate to bump off her brother, by means of poison or in any other way? he asked himself. And by the time they had crossed the

Pont de la Justice his answer was definitely in the negative.

Within a few minutes, Beatrice Baxter was locked securely in the cell to the right of the Goldfish Bowl, in which was confined the Singe, and to the left of the cage in which slumbered Godo the Whack. Chief Frémont, in the office, was inspecting the Guarnerius and trying to ascertain what there was about it that set it off from other violins, to the tune of half a million dollars or twenty million francs. On the desk before him was a transcript of Miriam's message from Luneville, urging him to guard the partners and premises of Siècles Frères, the most conservative and respectable tailors in the Palais Royal. The Chief had not understood the necessity for this bizarre assignment, but had dispatched Sergeant Schlumberger posthaste to carry it out.

The telephone rang and after listening to the noises that spluttered from the receiver, Frémont sprang to his feet and clutched at his hair. "Bonnet!" he cried. "While we have been toying with musical instruments, the brothers Siècles have been murdered. Get Toudoux, who's already in a frenzy, and join me at the sidewalk. Tranquillity, adieu!"

Siècles Frères was a much more commodious establishment than the diminutive medal shop next door, Aux Citoyens. The tailors had two spacious windows in which fabrics of correct design were displayed in a dignified way. There were several dressing rooms, equipped with full-length mirrors, a sort of pulpit for the cash drawer, and a work room in the rear. When the trio from the prefecture were admitted by Schlumberger, they saw, sitting on a stool, his elbows on the cashier's high desk, the senior partner, eyes half open. His brother was leaning over a counter on which a bolt of cheviot was spread, but was ominously still.

Dr. Hyacinthe Toudoux danced up and down with rage and threw his instrument case to the floor, at the risk of smashing the contents.

"Observe," he shouted, indignantly, kicking the standing corpse sharply in the nearest shin. "The same rigidity, no evidence of convulsions, eyes half open! No signs of suffocation or struggle! These mutton-heads have died by the same mysterious poison that has driven me to distraction and interrupted my idyllic home life since that pestiferous Baxter met his long-deferred deserts."

The Chief was peering into the open cash drawer and checking its contents with a neat column of figures on a slip of paper the cashier had left for the partners to verify. "Not a sou is missing. The motive could not have been robbery," he said.

"The motive was to deprive me of my reason, nothing more nor less," said Toudoux. "Cart the bodies to the laboratory, as soon as you have your photographs and fingerprints and the rest of the folderol. Then let us put on suitable clothes, go together to the Minister of Justice, and present him with our resignations. You are a washout at safeguarding the lives of Frenchmen, I am equally useless when it comes to explaining their deaths. Once free of official responsibility, I shall call out all the editors in Paris and run them through, one after another or collectively, as they, being the challenged parties, will have to choose."

Having thus relieved his ruffled feelings, the irate

doctor clamped on his hat, picked up his instrument case, and rushed out into the courtyard for air.

"It's all well and good for Toudoux to prattle about resigning, having married a woman who is worth more than that damnable Italian violin," said Frémont. "But I, if I am made the scapegoat for this wave of crime, will be forced, after years of honorable service, to peddle collar buttons and shoestrings to the end of my days. And now that the Murphy woman, out of spite because I have arrested her arch-criminal light-of-love, has forbidden me to enter her hotel, I must find a larger and more expensive apartment for Hydrangea. I owe too much to Monsieur Evans to reproach him now, but since he has taken to predicting assassinations instead of solving them, he is increasing rather than diminishing the already staggering load borne by the department. However, one must carry on. Sergeant Schlumberger, be so kind as to go next door and fetch the proprietor of the medal shop, Monsieur Rebec. He sleeps on the premises and just possibly may have the decency to be alive."

But in Luneville, Homer Evans was bending over the frail form of Calisthêne Rebec and already he had decided that it would not be possible to arouse the little man from his stupor in order to question him. Miriam was waiting, with Moritz, in an adjacent room of the Hotel Serieux. The proprietor, whose acquaintance Evans had made in the course of the Louvre murder case, had gone to the kitchen himself and provided them with a dinner that made up by its quality for its tardiness. Having seen Evans come in with an unconscious man slung over his shoulder, the hotel man had deduced that something strenuous had been afoot, involving violent exercise and nervous tension. So he had reached into the icebox for a large juicy porterhouse steak, and had garnished it with fried potatoes that were neither brittle nor soggy, also watercress fresh from a near-by stream. The main dish he had followed up promptly with *endives au gratin* of such a delicate flavor that Miriam, for the moment, forgot about dentist's implements or tarantulas and smiled into Homer's mildly quizzical eyes with her customary animation. A fruit cup, flavored with *calvados,* had topped off the meal and had put Evans in just the right frame of mind for the recapitulation of his pressing problems. Nevertheless, he was conscious of an increasing anxiety about Sìecles Frères, and reluctantly left the table to telephone the prefecture. It was with genuine regret and dismay that he received the news that the tailors were no more.

"Dashed thoughtless of me," he said to the Chief. "Had I not been so thoroughly occupied I should have warned you sooner. But tell Toudoux I have a hint to drop about the poison. That may cheer him. No doubt he's in a temper, poor chap."

"At any rate, we've recovered the fabulous violin. It's right here in my office," Frémont said.

"The devil you say," said Homer, astonished. "Would you mind telling me where you found it?"

"We caught the Baxter woman red-handed with it, in the Plaza Athènée," the Chief replied. "She's behind the bars, and soon I shall grill her, not only on account of the fiddle, but her brother's murder. Who else had a motive, and a criminal nature to boot? No doubt she hired the Singe to administer the poison."

"I wish you luck," said Evans, dryly. "As soon as I clean

234

up a few details here, I'll come in and lend a hand. And by the way, don't look farther for Monsieur Rebec, our decorations merchant. I have him here, in the throes of a nervous collapse."

"Alive?" asked the Chief.

"By the narrowest margin," said Evans, and smiled as Frémont's heartfelt sigh of relief fairly shook the receiver.

The proprietor, as Evans returned to his table, asked permission to serve the coffee and brandy, the former being of freshly roasted Colombia blend and the latter from that little region just west of the Armagnac slopes, which produces a small quantity of liqueur known to gourmets as "Le Philosophe Fichu" or "The Philosopher S.O.L." Miriam, aware that the telephone call to Paris had proved disturbing, slipped into her coat, because of the chill she invariably felt when Homer entered a phase of intense concentration.

"I have blundered again," he said, after a pause.

"I'm sure it wasn't your fault," she said, emphatic in his defense.

"The Siècles brothers, most respectable of tailors, with a traditional clientele, have been poisoned . . ."

"Not the same . . ."

"The very same poison that did for Leffingwell Baxter and the hotel manager, Tredwell. The senior partner was propped up at the cashier's desk, the junior was bending over samples. Both had grown rigid in the act of drawing their last breath. Now what does it mean?"

"Why did you ask the Chief to investigate Siècles Frères? Or shouldn't I ask questions?" said Miriam.

"Quite all right," Evans said. "There are not many I

can answer, but that one is not difficult. Leffingwell Baxter and a large Boxer dog" (he patted Moritz's head) "entered the little shop Aux Citoyens with Sergeant Schlumberger close behind them. There was only one front entrance. In fact, the shop is only about three yards wide. How did they get out, unobserved? There is no skylight or hole in the roof, no window in the rear. Now I had a good look along the rue Richelieu, which runs behind the shops on that side of the Palais Royal courtyard, and the only exit within fifty yards is that of Siècles Frères. The suitbox in which Godo the Whack was carrying the stolen Guarnerius was labeled Siècles Frères. That fact is bizarre, therefore significant. The more I thought about the problem, the oftener Siècles Frères came popping into my consciousness. I asked Frémont to take a look, but, alas, I was too late. My hunch was better than I suspected."

"But how did Leffingwell Baxter and Moritz get from the medal shop into the tailors' establishment next door? Schlumberger told us he had examined the wall between them and found nothing except a small-sized rathole, and that had been plugged with cement," said Miriam.

"I shall have a look at that wall myself," Homer said. "It's a pity I didn't rescue poor Rebec before his nervous system cracked. He might tell us a great deal, if he were able . . ."

"You don't think he'll lose his mind?" asked Miriam in horror.

"I think he will recover, but slowly, much too slowly to help us, if this epidemic of wanton murder is to be scotched. Not only are we threatened with a new deadly poison from which no one, however well guarded, can be safe, but that frightful weapon is in the hands of sadistic monsters without a spark of human feeling. Frankly, my dear, I wish you were safe on your father's ranch, where the worst that could happen would be a tumble from a bronco."

Miriam's eyes flashed indignantly. "I'd like to see the bronco that could toss me around, Homer Evans," she said. "Or the man who could send me away when he needs me most . . ." She faltered. "Or do you?"

"No offense," said Homer, lightly, as he touched her hand with his fingers and let them rest there a moment. "To get back to our case, it's evident that Rebec has been in the hands of the faction that is out to depose the Singe and take over the St. Julien Rollers. So, I suspect, were Siècles Frères, incredible as that may seem. Let's start at the beginning, and see if we can develop a theory.

"First Leffingwell Baxter, in the boat train, induces Moritz to spring at Anton Diluvio. Why?"

"I haven't the remotest idea," said Miriam.

"To get a good look at the Guarnerius," Homer explained. "What other motive could he have had?"

"Perhaps he didn't like musicians," said Miriam. "It's hard for me to like them myself, as a general rule."

"In that case he would have waited until Diluvio had one violin case in each hand and his back turned. No. It wasn't Diluvio he was after. The two violin cases on the baggage rack were different in design, and Baxter, unless I am mistaken, had an interest in knowing which one contained 'The Sinner without Malice.' According to Tom Jackson's cablegram, Baxter was the silent partner of the shadiest American dealers in rare violins, Stillwater and Tief, of Boston. Also he has kept this connection dark these many years. Another strange coincidence is that in 1910, when the famous quartette of Stradivarius viols were stolen, Leffingwell Baxter happened to be registered at the Hotel Wilton in the rue Jean-Jacques Rousseau. Sergeant Schlumberger has contributed those facts, for what they are worth. Not conclusive, but intriguing . . . The master mind who has carefully framed the Singe . . ."

"But how?" demanded Miriam. "His fingerprints were all over the place. They are the Singe's fingerprints, are they not?"

"Don't skip ahead. I was saying that the master mind who framed the Singe knows Baxter well enough to play checkers with him, carries suitboxes under his arm, disappears at will and has for his lieutenants such lilies as Dental Jake and Godo. We both had hoped the archfiend might prove to be Barnabé Vieuxchamp, who led the Rollers until he came to grief on account of our good friend, Hugo Weiss, and was sent to Devil's Island."

"Barnabé is dead," said Miriam. "He was bitten by one of those awful creatures I saw fighting tonight, one just like them, I mean." She shuddered.

Homer rose and started pacing the floor, and Moritz, who had been snoozing, opened one eye, sighed deeply, and closed it again. After several minutes Evans spoke, as if to himself.

"According to Toudoux and all other authorities, the tarantula is a much-maligned insect. I'll admit she eats her husband, once he has served nature's purpose, that she lies in wait for other insects and kills them for food, and that she will slaughter others of her kind if they encroach on her game preserves. But who can say that it is not kinder to eat a husband, while he is still under the spell of amatory pleasures, rather than to nag him throughout the years and send him out to rustle the family living? We all, by proxy, lie in ambush for animals, eat their flesh and drink their blood. We hire police to pop off poachers and trespassers. However, aside from any consideration of the Lycosa's morals, her bite is not fatal, even to small animals, and surely not to man. The mild poison she carries would slow up a horsefly long enough for her to stab him in the back of the neck, but for a doctor to declare that a sinner like Barnabé Vieuxchamp would succumb to a spider bite is just too preposterous." Homer stopped pacing and turned to Miriam. "Would you care for a demonstration?" he asked. "I, myself, am not an insectologist and never with my own eyes have I seen the results of a tarantula bite. Now Dr. Toudoux, who is an expert, has offered to put tarantulas in his hat and clamp it on his head."

Miriam turned pale and shuddered. "Please. I beg of you, dear," she said.

"I shall not go that far," Homer continued, "but I noticed in the shed behind this hotel a young goat who seemed to be in perfect health. We have a tarantula handy, and one of the most vigorous extant, of that we may be sure. Will you join me, or do you prefer to get your information at second hand?"

Try as she might, Miriam could not remain behind. She knew that she would scream if she saw the loathsome creature known as Black again but she seemed to be under some kind of spell, so severe was her reaction from the scene she had witnessed in the blacksmith's shop.

Taking up the shoebox containing the *Lycosa,* Homer went out to the barnyard, sharpened his jack-knife on a grindstone, worked up a thin lather with a cake of soap he found near the pump, and entered the small shed occupied by the goat. By the light of a lantern he shaved a small area on the middle of the goat's back, to which operation the goat, although ordinarily intractable, submitted without protest in response to Homer's reassuring words. When all was ready, Evans asked Miriam to hold the lantern closer as he shook the tarantula from the shoebox. The huge black-bellied spider landed right side up on the newly-shaved area, and the goat, annoyed, made a pass with his horns but could not reach the spot. The spider, angered by the hostile gesture, took hold with her powerful jaws. Miriam screamed, half-swooned and dropped the lantern. Homer held her from falling, recovered the light, and leaped back with her, to safety, feeling his blood run cold. For the goat, his head half turned and his agate-green eyes half open, seemed to have been petrified where he stood. There was no doubt that he was dead.

Long after, Miriam, exhausted by the ordeals through which she had passed, had sunk into the deepest slumber, Homer Evans sat tensely by the window and stared at the distant river. At moments, when the pressure inside his skull became unbearable, he would press his hands hard against his forehead, then try to relax again.

17

A Banner Evening in the Old
Disorderly House

HORSECOLLAR PHOEBE'S place in the rue des Cordonniers, Rouen, begins to hit its stride about ten-thirty.
The convivial business men of the city, having sat a
decent interval after dinner with their families and
having read the local and Paris newspapers, begin to
fidget in their chairs. The families are often dull and
the news is usually depressing. The more prudent of the
Rouenais seek solace and economy in sleep, the gayer
contingent gives way to a longing for the strains of the
mechanical piano and the refreshing informality of the
local honkytonks. There the robust Normans meet their
cronies and forget toil and care, and the veterans of the
British Expeditionary Forces, who went native after
1918, relive the old campaigns and sometimes go so far
as to engage in new ones.

Anton Diluvio, in his shorts, was sitting in an upper
room, protected by a blanket from the chill night air and
the mists that drifted inland from the Seine. In the large
brass bed reflected by sets of mirrors, slept Nicole, whose

weariness had overcome her fright not long after dinner was over. The girl's life had been replete with ups and downs, before Homer Evans had got her a job at the Bal Tabarin, and although she winced with terror whenever she reflected that she was in the power of Dental Jake, she did not, because of Diluvio's presence, feel entirely friendless. At intervals, the deep-voiced landlady turned the key in the door and entered. She had been obliged to lock them in, because of Jake's orders, but she was proving most solicitous for their welfare, especially that of Diluvio.

The latter appeared to be almost in a trance, for once the excitement of the fire, the river and his journey in a sack had subsided and he had been fed, his thoughts had flown back to the hold of the *Presque Sans Souci*. Mingled with the fragrance of timothy hay, the elusive perfume (Forvil's "Coral") haunted his confused recollections, causing him to inhale deeply and sigh. Before his face, when he leaned back in his chair, he saw that of his mysterious companion, felt the answering pressure of her lips, heard her words, so softly spoken.

"Could I have been dreaming?" he asked himself, and at once murmured, "No," for on his shoulder was a sensitive spot and the prints of a dainty set of teeth which he stroked tenderly from time to time.

A mood entirely strange to Anton was stealing over him, an indefinable, yet insistent, feeling that a long Odyssey was drawing to a close. The endless succession of women who had drifted in and out of his life had paled before the woman of his destiny, the genuine *femme fatale*. He was aware that Horsecollar Phoebe was giving him the eye, with a shyness quite touching in a woman of her disillusioning profession. He knew that, if he were to get some clothes and save Nicole from Dental Jake, it would be prudent to respond to his hostess's advances.

A few short hours ago, he would have taken on Phoebe, or practically anyone above the age of consent, with his customary boyish enthusiasm that had left a wake of damaged music lovers from the drafty opera houses of Maine to the moon-drenched open-air arenas of California. What held him back? He could not understand.

Horsecollar Phoebe, however, understood all too well, and reluctantly, although graciously, the buxom landlady tossed in her towel. How many thousands of clients had come to her house, seeking solace for the absence of another! Phoebe recognized the far-away stare, the halting gestures—all the symptoms.

"All right, kid," she said, getting off his lap. "Forget it, and let's start all over again. You're in love, am I right? Some female has you where the hair is short, or by God, I'll close up my dump and take in washing for a living."

Anton was so touched by her frankness and perspicacity that he snatched up pencil and paper and wrote, hesitantly at first, but gathering momentum as he progressed, an account of the miracle of the *Presque Sans Souci*.

"Love is just as likely to catch you in a mud scow as a mansion, kid," said Phoebe, tears filling her eyes as she read. "Would you believe that of all the good *hombres* who've been wafted in and out of my checkered career, in Paris, Rouen, Liverpool and San Francisco, I had to fall for a no-account young soda-jerker who couldn't be on the level when he was shooting pool for practice, all by himself?"

"But she's wonderful," scribbled Diluvio, shocked by the implied comparison. "I'm sure she's an angel. I've simply got to find her. You'll help me, won't you?" He looked at Phoebe so appealingly that all her deep maternal instincts were aroused.

"Jake would skin me if I let you go," she said, regretfully. "For the present sit tight, and keep your shirt on, figuratively speaking. He's gone up river, to pull off one of his lousy tricks, no doubt."

Anton reached for the pad and pencil once again. "Will my voice come back?" he wrote, anxiously.

"In a day or two," Phoebe said.

The bell that sounded whenever the front door downstairs swung open, rang long and insistently.

"Let's hope there's a live one in," said Phoebe, and hurried away to receive the new caller, promising to return when the evening rush was over.

Wrapped in his blanket, the violinist alternately sat rapturously in the easy chair and nervously paced the floor, depending on whether he was thinking about Beatrice, or what he was going to say to placate Hattie Ham.

The new customer proved to be Grigori, although no one asked his name. He strode into the dance hall, slapped Phoebe on the shoulder in a comradely way and, after ordering vodka for himself and strawberry extract for the chubby little girl in a lavender bathing suit who had taken a seat at his table, the Russian glanced over the dozen or more patrons present, in the hope of finding a fiddler, an American, or better still, a combination of the two. The only two Anglo-Saxons lounged at a corner table with a half-consumed beer in front of each one, and only one saucer apiece.

"They must be Englishmen," Grigori grunted, and turned away. The girl beside him, in response to his question, told him that she had met a South American only the day before and that, although he had promised to come back, he had not done so. Grigori thanked her, and said he was interested only in North Americans, for the time being. There the matter seemed to rest, and he ordered another vodka, that time a double one.

Long before, the police launch had brought Maître Ronron, the two dancers, Nadia and Yvonne, Bridgette Murphy and Hjalmar Jansen to the quai, and all of them except Hjalmar had set out for Paris. The big Norwegian, according to assignment, had roamed up and down the water front in search of the brick-red tug and had picked up the information that a tug answering to its description had steamed up to the dock at twilight and, after half an hour, had been taken up river again. As to who owned it or where it had come from, no one seemed to know, or at least, was not inclined to tell. Feeling the pangs of hunger, Hjalmar took a recess in a seafood restaurant, where he stowed away a couple of lobsters, a full-grown turbot, six potatoes, a Chateaubriand, rare, and a half pound of cheese, well sloshed with wine, both white and red. Thus refreshed, he started walking toward the rue des Cordonniers, in pursuance, he assured himself, of his orders to search the town for traces of Nicole and Diluvio.

By the time Hjalmar was far enough on his way to be passing the doorway of No. 5, Mathilde Dubonnet, his tearful model, had found it necessary to leave her post at the window and only Hattie Ham was on lookout duty. Hattie, of course, had never seen Hjalmar before, but she caught a glimpse of his jovial honest face as he rolled by, was impressed by his bulk and the set of his shoulders, and felt a twinge of satisfaction when he turned into the doorway of No. 27. The more men of good will there, the better, was her unspoken comment. Anastasia Ivanovna, similarly impressed, began crooning a plaintive Gypsy air.

At the doorway of the dance hall, Hjalmar was welcomed by Horsecollar Phoebe, who had distinct recollections of having seen him in one or more of the seaports she had known.

"Come right in, sailor," she boomed, enjoying the rare sensation of having a man look down into her eyes.

"Drinks for the house," roared Grigori, who had just that moment remembered that he had in his pocket a hundred-dollar bill.

It is strange how kindred souls are drawn to each other in all kinds of environments. Within a few moments, Hjalmar, Grigori and the statuesque Phoebe were seated together, with a sprinkling of unattached girls to add color to the group. On the table before them was a bottle of special vodka in which had been placed a couple of hot red peppers from the Crimea. The mechanical piano, as if aware that a festive occasion was developing, beat out more stirring strains, until the dancers felt new animation and even the Englishmen in the corner, enlivened by the second free beer, began to think they might as well shed their native caution and make a night of it. Passers-by, attracted by the sounds of mirth, drifted in to join the party, and Phoebe, at her best when joy was rampant, had a cordial greeting for each one, and hospitable suggestions for making the evening a memorable occasion.

Grigori sang "The Night Dimitri Was Stretched" in his lusty baritone and Hjalmar countered with "Why Should I Be Poor?" It was at that point that Horsecollar Phoebe, who adored music although she could not sing a note, chanced to remember that the handsome young man upstairs was supposed to be a master of the violin. Just possibly, she remembered Dental Jake and his threats coincidently, for she reached for the bottle and poured a tumbler of vodka, which she drained before dwelling further on the matter.

Just then Hjalmar caught her up with his sinewy right arm and, amid the laughter and applause of the inmates and clients, none of whom had seen Phoebe dance before, swung her out on the floor. The mechanical piano, into which the nearest customer had slipped a coin, was playing an old-fashioned waltz, something about half way between "Over the Waves" and "Why Don't You Work Like Other Men Do." Now Phoebe did not avoid the dance floor, as a rule, because she was not a good dancer, but on account of the difficulty in finding a partner whose face she could see. With Hjalmar, who was amazingly light on his feet for a man who tipped the scales almost to capacity, she whirled, sashayed and pirouetted, eyes sparkling, stately shoulders thrown back, while the swish of her pleated skirt revealed her shapely legs in black silk stockings. Before the waltz was over, Phoebe tossed caution clean overboard and whispered to Hjalmar that there was a No. 1 fiddler topside.

"Bring him down," said Hjalmar, gleefully.

"He's not dressed," Phoebe said.

"He doesn't need clothes to play a violin. He only needs the violin. If you haven't got one, I'll go out to a hock shop and buy one," Hjalmar rejoined.

"I don't know if I ought," murmured Phoebe, but the way she was feeling she was confident that everything would turn out for the best. More than likely Jake would not come back before morning and if he did, well, the big painter and his pal would take care of the situation, temporarily. Primed with music and vodka, the distant scene meant little to Horsecollar Phoebe. "One step enough for me" had long been her motto, so she hustled upstairs, key ring in hand.

At the table, Hjalmar was explaining their hostess's sudden exit to Grigori Hippolitovitch, who, when he heard that the prospective fiddler had no clothes, vouch-safed the information that he was wearing an extra suit, for what purpose he could not then recall, and offered to lend it for the occasion. So a space on the dance floor was cleared while the Russian stripped off his outer coat and trousers, to the accompaniment of delighted giggles from the girls and cheers from their partners. It was only then that both Hjalmar and Grigori began to associate ideas. Both of them had been sent out to find a violinist. Phoebe claimed to have one on the upper floor. The Norwegian confided in Grigori and was pleased to learn that they had identical objects in mind.

"We mustn't give the show away," Hjalmar said. "Don't recognize the guy when Phoebe brings him in."

"That's easy," Grigori said. "I only saw him once, and that was in the dark."

"Go in, kid. Don't be bashful," said Phoebe's hearty voice from the hallway and she returned to the dance hall, holding firmly by the elbows, from behind, Anton Diluvio, naked except for his shorts, and blushing furiously. He was about to yell for help when he caught sight of Hjalmar but a broad wink brought him to his senses. At the same moment he recognized Grigori and, in spite of his embarrassing situation, his heart gave a leap, two leaps, in fact. The first was from joy, to see that Hjalmar had escaped from the flames of the *Presque Sans Souci* and the artillery of the gangsters, the second, on account of Nicole, whose tired trusting face he had seen on the pillow as Phoebe had carried him, protesting, from the room.

Drinks were served to all and sundry and the company was convulsed with laughter as Diluvio, who had been given a preliminary slug of the special vodka, began to get into the spirit of the assembly. With relief he drew on the shirt, pants and coat proffered by Grigori and when he complained that he had no necktie, a local paperhanger unselfishly sacrificed his own, which was long, black and flowing. A violin, borrowed from No. 34 where it had been accepted as security for money due on account of lodging and entertainment, was placed in Diluvio's hands and Hjalmar pounded the table for silence, jarring off four glasses. Phoebe, slapping him resoundingly on the back, assured the big painter that she was going to break them anyway, to feed to a certain party who thought he had her buffaloed. Grigori, who had overheard, suggested the addition of hot applesauce, to give the dish a little flavor. In short, if there were any dismal thoughts in No. 27, they were buried so deep in the subconscious that a psychiatrist, had he been present, would have shot himself, after slinking out of sight.

Anton's first selection was not from the works of Vivaldi, Bach, or even Wieniawski. The paperhanger, it developed, also played the piano and had started off with a popular tune entitled: *"Il n'y a plus des saisons"* (The Weather Can No Longer Be Depended Upon). Diluvio caught the beat without delay. From that time on, the dancing was unrestrained. Volunteers were pressed into service as waiters, and Phoebe, in order to guard against overcrowding, nailed up the front door with eighty penny nails. She had had a key to the place when she had first moved in, but years ago it had got mislaid, she declared.

Before the house was closed to outsiders, however, one of the steady customers, a russet-cheeked ship's chandler who wished to do his share, sent out for two wash boilers full of *chouxcroute garni,* a dish composed of native sausage, Alsatian ham, boiled potatoes, peppercorns and sauerkraut. The entire company fell to with a relish, but none as lustily as Grigori, Hjalmar and Horsecollar Phoebe, unless it might have been Diluvio, who had not fiddled so strenuously in seven years of formal recitals. The excellent food put Phoebe in a sentimental frame of mind and, seconded by the girls, who always felt better after a good cry, she asked Anton to play something sad.

When Diluvio arose, with that detached expression he assumed when about to do his best, every man and woman in the room fell silent, except the two Englishmen, who had reached the second battle of the Somme and disagreed on certain points of major strategy. Hjalmar, with

250

a nod of apology in Anton's direction, tossed them all the way to the kitchen, neglecting to open the swinging doors, and in an instant they were fast asleep.

The paperhanger, *sans* necktie, looked up from his station at the piano, Diluvio inclined his head and tried to whisper: *"Les Plaisirs d'Amour."*

Perhaps the reader is familiar with the old song, which has been passed from one epoch to another, always holding its poignancy and charm. From the words, it is to be inferred that the pleasures of love last only a moment, while the resultant chagrin lingers on through a much longer period of time. But what are words compared with music, the art that transcends the rational and points the way for the the spirit likewise to throw off its bonds? The melody was asserted softly by Diluvio, insidiously mounting until the heartaches of the ages seemed blended into one that was shared by all.

"Oh, God. I shall die," sobbed Phoebe, as she clasped Hjalmar's hand beneath the table.

"Ah, Russia! Ah, poor Anastasia," moaned Grigori, and buried his face in his hands.

Hjalmar had a fleeting recollection that his rent was due, but with his free hand he raised his glass and drained it, not noticing that the vodka had run out and the drink of the evening had become champagne.

To the reader who is not familiar with *Les Plaisirs d'Amour* it should be explained that the piece, like ancient Gaul, is divided into three parts. The first, or introductory passage is nostalgic, but in the second movement the theme seems to get a grip on itself and to reflect that, after all, perhaps the game was worth the candle. The music is exultant, even rapturous, and at that stage

Phoebe felt a tingling of joy and recaptured youth in her veins. For the first time, in the throes of deep emotion, it was not the vapid face of the soda-jerker that occupied her mind, and neither was it the handsome countenance of Diluvio. Hjalmar Jansen was the man. Of that she was sure. No more would she quail before Dental Jake or moon over bygone disappointments. She would take the cash and let the credit go, if Hjalmar did not have a heart of stone, and already she was convinced he had not.

The third part of the selection goes into the minor, in a decidedly reproachful vein, not directed toward the faithless lover, but aimed at cruel fate. The girls wept unrestrainedly, moaning softly the while, and it must not be thought that the men, as callous as they might be at home or in business, did not brush stray teardrops from their cheeks and vow to do better in the future. There is no telling what might have happened had not the outer door crashed into bits, heavy footsteps and growls echoed through the hallway, and into the dance hall lurched Dental Jake, with bloodshot eyes and his hairy arm bared to the elbow.

The girls let out blood-curdling screams, the men, overawed, backed into corners, excepting Diluvio, who stood rooted to the spot, violin in hand, Grigori, who reached for a bottle underneath the table, and Hjalmar Jansen. Vaulting lightly over the prostrate form of a notary public who was taking a nap on the floor, the Norwegian let out a roar, flung back both powerful arms as a warning to the others to keep out of the way, and butted the intruder in the stomach, coming up with a right and a left that caught Jake off his balance and half spun him around. Recovering himself, Dental Jake, insane with rage, kicked Hjalmar's shin with his heavy hobnailed boot and jabbed with forked fingers at his eyes.

"So that's the way you want it," said Hjalmar. The pain in his leg was excruciating. It seemed as if both bones had been broken but the painter stuck out his left, side-stepped, crossed with his right and observed that his opponent was no boxer. Hjalmar could hit him at will, but hitting Dental Jake only seemed to increase his homicidal fury. The gangster, grunting with pain as Jansen pounded on his ribs, picked up a bottle from a near-by table. At that Hjalmar quit boxing and got right down to brass tacks. Within reach was a chair, which he swung as if it were a badminton racket. Jake smashed the bottle, lunged with the jagged remainder and lurched forward as Hjalmar splintered the chair over his head. The broken bottle dropped to the floor, Jansen flung the chair into a corner and got a full Nelson on the gangster's thick neck.

Grigori, who had been dancing around the combatants, like a picador about to negotiate a *quite,* was dragged back to his seat by Horsecollar Phoebe, who was beside herself with glee.

"Let the sailor do it all alone," she begged. "Let that big slob find out what it's like to meet a man who can hand him out a beating. I'm black and blue from the wallops that mug has pinned on me. Ah, my darling! That's the ticket! In the pantry! You've got the system. Jake hasn't any feeling in his head."

For Hjalmar had shifted his grip and, while holding Jake in chancery, he sank a couple of haymakers right into the solar plexus. Then he stepped back and grinned, breathing hard, as the gangster, making feeble and foolish grimaces and motions, sank slowly to the floor, rolled over, twitched, and then lay still.

A few minutes later, Homer Evans, still staring at the river and the sky at Luneville, was aroused from his fierce concentration by a knock on his door. He was wanted on the telephone, the proprietor told him. In the hallway below Homer took up the receiver and heard Hjalmar's voice.

"I've got Jake," the Norwegian said. "Do you want him dead or alive? The shape the guy's in now, I could turn him in either way with no trouble at all. And by the way, don't worry about Nicole and Diluvio. I happened to run into them, too. Whoopee!"

18

A Brief for the Amateur Approach

to Work as Well as Play

THE next morning was cool and cloudy, so although it
may be assumed that the Goddess Aurora did her usual
stuff behind damp and fleecy curtains, her matutinal display, rosy as it might have been, could not be admired
by the hard-working inhabitants of the Norman countryside. For the most part, the early risers didn't seem to
mind. They took the bitter with the sweet, and comforted themselves with the old proverb:

> *"Evening red and morning gray,*
> *Sure sign of a fair day."*

At dawn the rising of the river mists and the good
news Evans received from Hjalmar Jansen seemed to
exercise a clarifying effect on Homer's toiling brain.
Abruptly he arose, slapped his thigh, and with a muffled
exclamation hurried down the stairs. From the kitchen
of the Hotel Serieux he snatched up an out-of-date newspaper and, rummaging in the cupboard, he found and

appropriated several sheets of cellophane and a large pastry container. Between the river bank and the blacksmith's shop he paused, eyes to the ground, and shook his head, reflectively, almost with dismay. For there at his feet and in scattered groups near by was the night's deadly crop of *Amanita verna,* milk white, ovate and bejeweled with dew. Each mushroom was balanced invitingly on its bulbous base, with a neat little collar on its slender stem.

"The Destroying Angel," murmured Homer, as he stooped to pick a number of the dangerous specimens and wrapped them in *L'Action Francaise.*

"Hello, mister," said a voice behind him, which startled him so that he wheeled like a cat.

"Why, good morning, young man," Homer said, recovering quickly. It was the kid whose acquaintance he had made in the same area just the day before. In a trice the boy was cricket hunting, for Homer promptly offered him a fancy price for the mysterious fisherman's supply.

While the kid was thus occupied, Homer explored the woods in the vicinity and at last let out a gasp of satisfaction. In a small clearing patched with wild thyme, where the sun would shine brightly on a pleasant day, he noticed a number of small burrows, spaced several feet apart. Around each burrow was a ring or parapet of pebbles and dry leaves, silked together. Evans cut a branch from a near-by sapling, flattened and sharpened one end and, dislodging one of the parapets, examined it through his powerful reading glass.

"Ingenious," he said, with a sigh, as he worked loose a few fragments of dried cartilage. "I have underrated our antagonist, perhaps."

The other end of his sapling, he whittled to a point, then, kneeling cautiously, he started sapping one of the burrows, one that had a diameter of more than two inches. "Sorry," he whispered, at last, for crouching desperately in a sort of chamber near the foot of the lair was a full-grown black-bellied tarantula. As the outraged spider tried to scuttle away, Homer trapped her with a piece of cellophane and wrapped her, loosely but securely. It was the work of several minutes for him to gather half a dozen large specimens of the dread *Lycosa* and these, each in its cellophane prison, he stored in the pastry box, along with the silk-meshed parapets behind which they had lurked for their prey.

"Kid," he called to the industrious little boy, who already had two pocketfuls of crickets, "I'd give five francs for another pasteboard box, if I should get it within five minutes."

To say that the kid departed would simply imply a dearth of English verbs. "He streaked across the landscape like hot cat****" would be expressive but in questionable taste, although more accurate than "he vanished." At any rate, the kid was back, slightly winded, three minutes before the deadline, carrying a box from which he had dumped the morning delivery of crescent rolls on the doorstep of a certain party who had recently been short with him.

"Gee, mister. Are you a detective?" the kid asked, eyes wide with admiration.

"A meddlesome amateur, worse luck," admitted Homer. He crossed the river, with the kid at his heels, delighted at being permitted to carry the mushrooms and the reading glass. Some distance from the other bank,

Evans found another knoll somewhat dry and exposed to the sun and around it heavy footprints, although it was well back from the pathway.

"So much for the proverbial honor among thieves," he exclaimed, with a rueful smile. There were numerous tarantula lairs in evidence, and Homer, after cautioning the enchanted kid to stand well back, caught six more *Lycosae* and scraped their parapets into Box No. 2. Each of the parapets he scrutinized minutely with the magnifying glass and, in each case, smiled.

"Listen, boy," he said gravely. "You're my assistant. Understand? Until this case is over, you get fifteen francs a week. Here is two weeks' pay in advance."

The kid tried to thank Evans but his voice failed him. Finally he blurted out a question. "Tell me, mister, what do you want me to do?"

"First of all, to say nothing about our meeting this morning or what we have been doing. Second, you must swear, by the detective's secret oath I shall teach you, not to pick mushrooms or hunt spiders in Luneville or anywhere near it until I give the word. We need them all in their places, for evidence," Homer said.

"Sure enough, are these things really evidence?" asked the kid. "I thought evidence was stiffs, or calling cards or mugs who could identify some other mug."

"This case is a peculiar one," Evans said. "You'll read about it soon in all the papers."

The kid was shifting his feet like a cat on fresh snow.

"I'll keep mum! So help me Moses! Now teach me the detective's oath," he begged. Homer inclined his head gravely and, in a low tone, after glancing around them warily, recited certain phrases which the kid repeated solemnly after him. Next, Homer asked the kid to climb a wild apple tree, with low boughs overhanging. Beneath the tree, he spread his large handkerchief and pegged down the corners. From each box he selected a tarantula and dropped them into the arena, face to face.

"Why, Homer Evans, you ought to be ashamed of yourself," said Miriam's incredulous voice, half choked with sobs. "How could you! And in the presence of an innocent little boy."

"Aw, for the love of Mike, go take a powder," was the latter's terse response.

Miriam, who had awakened and was alarmed because Homer was not in his room, had dressed quickly and, with the help of Moritz, had easily followed his trail. And for a moment she had been forced to believe that, in the man she loved and respected above all others, historical or alive, she had uncovered a gnawing secret vice, that of spider-baiting. His arm around her quivering shoulders, Homer quickly reassured her and introduced her to their new assistant as Mademoiselle M., his trigger woman. Then he asked Moritz, who was frowning and eying the struggling tarantulas, to sit down.

The tarantulas had come to grips and were wrestling, body to body, claws unsheathed, hair bristling on their angular legs. Miriam tried her best to turn away, but again she was held by the sheer ferocity of the spectacle. It is one thing to witness an athletic contest and another to follow each stroke of a combat that can only end in death. The Boxer turned his head from side to side, watching, as the battle proceeded, but remained seated, as Evans had requested. The *Lycosa* from the Right Bank, or Luneville side, was first to spring, and succeeded in overturning and pinning the Left Bank entry. Jaws agape, each tarantula measured her opponent's strength. Left Bank threw off Right Bank, got a triple hammerlock compounded with a toe hold, pinned Right Bank to the mat and struck with her jaws.

"A little low," was Evans' comment.

Right Bank was hurt but not out, and by rolling desperately got out of the clinch. Left Bank, confused by her own inaccuracy, hesitated and Right, although obviously the weaker, struck unexpectedly, still farther from the vital spot at the back of the neck than Left had landed.

"Aw, quit stalling," yelled the kid. "Mix it, you punks."

But the kid's admonitions were not heard by the *Lycosa* from the Left Bank. She writhed in horrid convulsions a split second and suddenly died. A moment later there was an ear-shattering explosion and Miriam was sobbing, automatic in hand. If anything remained of the *Lycosae*, either victor or vanquished, it would have taken a more powerful microscope than Evans had with him to have found the largest chunk.

"I will not see that poor creature eaten, just because she lost on a fluke. I won't! I won't I won't!" said Miriam, stamping her feet.

"No matter," said Evans, soothingly. "I've proved what I suspected. All night the simplest solution escaped me, but now this case is drawing to an end, quite luckily, considering the state of your nerves. We will spend July in Normandy, my dear, in search of scraps of information about my freebooting ancestor, the Baron de Vans. Now for Paris and the prefecture!"

"I don't see what you have proven," said Miriam, ashamed of her lack of confidence and control.

"You observed the contest?"

"I couldn't help it," she said.

"Did you notice anything peculiar about it?"

"I thought the other spider deserved to win on points. She had quite a lead, it seemed to me."

"Exactly," said Evans, cryptically, and she knew he was in one of his secretive moods and, with a sigh, desisted from further questioning.

In the kitchen of the Hotel Serieux, the chef had not been idle. He was aware that the previous evening, after he had departed, the proprietor had cooked a meal for Monsieur Evans and he did not want to be outdone. Consequently, he served for breakfast grilled rainbow trout with butter that had been stroked lightly with marjoram and one other herb, and small helpings of new potatoes, matched like pearls, in quail gravy. He was amply rewarded when Homer came to the kitchen and promised to send him the priceless letter, in Brillat-Savarin's own handwriting, dated Philadelphia, June 9, 1802, in which that master expressed the opinion that the American turkey, although excellent in flavor, is a disappointing bird, being just too large for one and not quite big enough for two.

The ride to Paris passed without incident, but in an outer corridor of the prefecture, they found Bridgette Murphy dissolved in tears. Her fighting spirit seemed to be at its lowest ebb.

"The Singe won't speak to me. He has sent me away," she moaned. "He won't do anything to save himself."

"There, there," said Evans, touched by her grief. "You

wouldn't want the Singe to be a rat, according to his standards."

"I'd brain him myself if he showed a yellow streak," cried Bridgette. "But he's sent me away. Told me not to come back. That fiend Frémont wants to cut off his head. Where is he? Lead me to him and I'll tear out his windpipe and lace it through his buttonhole!"

"Let me explain," Evans said. "The Singe is not going to the guillotine. He'll leave here with a clean ticket, I give you my word. And don't you see that he's proved he really loves you? He can't endure your presence, for fear that he'll weaken and squeal. Would you want that, as the price of a few moments' chat, with bars between you, and a couple of flatfeet standing by? Brace up! You must understand that the Singe knows who is out to get him, but he can't speak his name and yell for the police. He's got to play the game, at the risk of his head, all honor to him for it. And I say this, in spite of the work his silence makes for me. While you're bawling like a schoolgirl and upsetting his nerves, I've got to dig up the murderer by the sweat of my brow. Now go home, bathe your eyes and stay sober. Before another day has passed, I promise you results."

Monsieur Rebec, still in a semi-comatose state, had been carried from the automobile to the hospital next door to the prefecture, the huge Hotel Dieu. Homer's collection of poisonous mushrooms, and various insects, both harmless and venomous, had been stowed away in Frémont's safe. Miriam made a quick trip to Montparnasse for a bath and change of clothes, and Moritz hopped into the taxi beside her. But Homer was in no mood for delay. Once he had sent Bridgette on her way, with hope and sorrow struggling in her heart, he made his way to the Goldfish Bowl, nodded to a turnkey, and stepped inside.

"Good morning," said the Singe, in a level emotionless voice. "What now? Has the Chief sent you around to pump me, or is this just a friendly call?"

"I shall not ask questions," Evans said. "As your agent and, I suspect, your distant relative, I wish to make my report."

"My relative! Quit your kidding," the Singe said. "And I have no agents. I work alone."

For answer, Homer pulled some papers from his pocket.

"First, I want to show you the fingerprints you were supposed to have left all over the room in which Leffingwell Baxter was killed," Evans said, handing over a photostat copy of a section of Sergeant Cidre's chart. "Do they look like yours?"

The Singe looked wearily at his capable thumb and grunted.

"They seem to match. So what?"

"I made a set of my own, just for luck. Would you care to have a look at them?" Homer went on.

"As you like," the Singe said, and glanced at the second sheet of paper, at first casually, then with awakened interest. "Strange," he said. "Almost alike. That same whirligig near the center, one large loop, another small one."

"And now for the prize exhibit," said Homer, holding forth a time-stained parchment and unwrapping it with the greatest of care. "I have here the thumb mark of one Claude l'Original, the Baron de Vans, bosom pal of William the Conqueror, in the eleventh century."

"Never heard of him," the Singe said. "I'm shaky on history. Never had time for steady reading. Maybe you could send me a book or two, while these fat-heads are making up their minds. But what has this Baron to do with me? Do I rate a title or something?"

"Examine the thumb mark. It was not made intentionally. I suspect this deed was presented to the late Baron just after meal time. Forks, you know, were not then in vogue. But you will observe the same whirligig, or whorl, and the same loops or deltas, one large, the other small, an unusual pattern. Our ancestor, according to the few records I have been able to find thus far, not only enjoyed the *droit de seigneur,* that is, the right to take his pleasure where he found it, within the limits of his domain, but he exercised that privilege in an open-handed way. The maidens in question, I have reason to believe, were an extraordinarily law-abiding lot and followed not only the letter but the spirit of the statutes. One indirect result is yourself. I also am a descendant. Evans. De Vans. I even have the ancestral name, you see, in an Anglicized form."

"I wouldn't squeal if you were my twin brother," said the Singe. "If you're trying to get around me with this family appeal, save your breath."

"Not at all," Evans said, with the utmost good nature. "I'm offering this in explanation of my interest in your welfare. Now let me talk. That's about all I do, unless someone inveigles me into trying my hand at detective work. You saw a certain party in a train at Rouen, the day you walked to the station to see Miss Leonard and me off for Paris. You were, to say the least, astonished. Flabbergasted, perhaps, is the word. Just previously you had been more mildly surprised at the defiance shown by a party called Godo the Whack. One incident served to explain the other, in a way. Evidently the man in the train had been encouraging Godo. You hopped the train to Paris, unbeknown to me, and, whatever else you did, spent the evening of June 11th in the Hotel Murphy et du Danube Bleu. Quite naturally, only Miss Murphy could swear to that with her hand on the Book."

The Singe faced Homer, livid, but Evans smiled and held up his hand. "Don't worry! I'm not going to drag her into this. It won't be necessary. I've got enough cut out for me, as it is. I've got to explain how you can radio your fingerprints through space and solid walls, and be courting behind the Panthèon and murdering on the Right Bank at one and the same moment. I've got to find the party who gave you such a chill at the station in Rouen, who likewise is the slayer of Leffingwell Baxter, Tredwell, both members of the firm Siècles Frères, and the cause of the untimely demise of two unidentified bruisers who tried to roast you alive. But bear this in mind, esteemed friend and relative. I shall succeed, in the not too distant future. And then I shall retire from detective work for the span of my natural life. Should you care for my friendship, on that basis, drop around at the Dôme or at my apartment in the rue Campagne Pre-mière. And I will try to teach you the secret of good living and modify your passion for pointless exertion. If you find crime amusing, and what intelligent man would not, had he courage, just possibly I can persuade you to in-

dulge your hobby in an amateur way. To place oneself
outside the pale of society in order to ape society's successful men, that is, by carrying on organized activity for
needless profit, is childish, to say the least. You have all
the money you need, you are loved by the woman of your
choice. You have brains, good health; everything, in
short, except friends and leisure and the knack of passing
your time pleasantly. Good morning, coz, and, since you
have little else to worry about, now that I'm on the job,
think over what I have said."

"It's your lower jaw that moves," the Singe said, dryly,
but unable to suppress a smile.

19

Of the Difficulties of Choosing a Suitable

Occupation, If One Wishes

to Make a Change

In his laboratory, separated from the prefecture by
an acre or two of offices in which dim men and disappointed women performed vague rites with documents,
ink, and rubber stamps, Dr. Hyacinthe Toudoux was
pawing through a classified telephone directory, pausing
only to shake his fists reproachfully at the six corpses laid
out on slabs side by side. Left to right, they were labeled: Leffingwell Baxter, Ferdinand Tredwell, Hector
Siècles, Potiphar Siècles, and Montana No. 1 and 2, unidentified. The floor was strewn with broken test-tubes,
beakers and retorts and stained with liquids of various
hues and consistencies.

"Once for all, I am through with public office," the
doctor shouted, tearing out a sheaf of leaves from the
directory and shuffling them furiously as he adjusted his
spectacles. "I was foolish enough in youth and middle
age to cling to the belief that I was fitted by ability and

temperament to conduct scientific research. No longer can I nourish that delusion. Ah, beauteous Eugénie, doomed to share my ignominious failure! What humiliation you will suffer when I resign in disgrace and am forced to enter trade! But what avenue of vulgar commerce is open to a man who has passed the fifty mark, in years, and to boot has been tried and found wanting as protector of the public? *Abattoirs!* Bah! The sight of one more corpse, even that of a mutton or cow, would drive me mad, if in fact I am not already irresponsible."

He thumbed down the column of "A's." *"Abdominal Supports!* Revolting. *Abrasive Wheels.* They set my teeth on edge. *Archery Supplies.* Can I visualize Toudoux, once scion of a distinguished profession, demonstrating bows and arrows in a store window, dressed in knee britches and silk stockings?"

The doctor heaved the heavy book through the window, which luckily was open, and coincidentally was aware of a knock on his door.

"Bring in the bodies! Stack them crosswise, like stovewood, if you please!" roared Dr. Toudoux. "Ah, would that I had a conscience like that quack on Devil's Island who has the temerity to sign a statement to the effect that his most dangerous convict has died from tarantula poisoning. Then, indeed, I could dispose of these cases, and no one would be the wiser, except the immortal half dozen patient men of integrity with whom I have had the colossal conceit in the past to rank myself."

His tirade was brought to a sudden stop when he saw before him Homer Evans, smiling in his most winning manner, and holding under each arm a large pasteboard box.

"Good morning, Doctor," Evans said. "And how is your charming wife?"

Toudoux winced with pain. "I beg of you, do not mention Eugénie, whose esteem of me I am about to shatter. After a night of anguish, in company with these detestable cadavers, all of whom should have been strangled in infancy, I have reached a decision. I shall resign. Science, farewell! Either I must beg, become a dependent of a trusting woman who already has had too much to bear, or find an occupation."

The doctor grabbed up a few loose leaves he had wrenched from the letter "L" section of the telephone book. *"Landlords' Service Bureaus,"* he read, plaintively. "A fitting climax to a lifetime of research. I shall go from house to house, sword in hand, expelling widows and orphans from their hearthstones, for a paltry thirty francs an eviction. *Language Schools.* Were I, like you, a linguist, I might teach a few of my countrymen to understand imperfectly in another idiom what they understand very well in their own language. But, alas, I am ignorant of foreign tongues, both ancient and modern . . ."

"If you will calm yourself, Doctor, I think I may be able to change your mind about resigning. In fact, I am convinced that you are on the brink of the crowning triumph of your distinguished career," Evans said.

"Ah, here I have it. *Lawn Mowers.* No, that's a seasonal occupation," went on Toudoux, unwilling to surrender himself to hope.

"You will be cheered by the Academy of Science, in secret session, of course. In this case, the poison is so deadly and easy to administer that no publicity is possible. Not a word must be allowed to leak out. But what are hymns of praise and the plaudits of the mob compared with the inner satisfaction of having solved a most baffling problem?" Homer continued.

For a moment, Dr. Hyacinthe Toudoux stopped berating himself, his face almost radiant with joy. "You have a clue as to the nature of the poison?" he gasped, but in the same instant he saw Homer open one of his boxes of tarantulas. The doctor slumped into a chair, moaning like a fog horn.

"*Lycosae,*" he whispered. "Black-bellied tarantulas. Among the most harmless of God's creatures. Monsieur Evans, of you I had expected better things. It is one thing for a four-penny prison doctor to prate about spider bites being fatal. But you, my learned friend! You would not mock an already despairing colleague! Give me your tarantulas, and, as I promised, I will put them in my hat and wear it from here to the Sorbonne."

Toudoux reached for his hat and punched it in and out of shape like a *garçon* beating a rug.

"I should not advise you to handle these specimens as if they were harmless," Homer said. "I should strongly suggest that you pull yourself together, watch my demonstration, and listen to what I have to say. We have collaborated before, without friction. Now tell me. Of the various animals you have for experimental purposes, which is the toughest?"

"The turtle," replied Toudoux without hesitation. "A turtle simply will not die. You may boil him in oil, and he will swim out of the pot. He dotes on cholera germs, as seasoning for his meals. Carve out his heart and lay it on the table and it will beat for the better part of a week."

"I should like your hardiest turtle, if you please," Evans said.

The medical examiner pushed flat a cluster of buttons with the palm of his hand and attendants came running in, fearfully. They knew what a temper their employer had developed, since the current investigation had eclipsed all routine work of the laboratory. Within two minutes, a large bull turtle was placed in the center of a white enameled table.

Reaching into the box containing the tarantulas from the Left Bank, across from Luneville, Homer selected a fair-sized specimen and unwrapped the cellophane.

"The turtle will not even blink," said Hyacinthe Toudoux.

The tarantula, placed on the table in front of the turtle, crouched motionless, suspicious of her new surroundings, and for a while the turtle remained snug within his protecting shell. Finally, however, curiosity got the better of the turtle and his head was extended slowly. The *Lycosa*, with startling swiftness, leaped and struck. But the turtle, annoyed, simply snapped off three or four of the tarantula's legs and gulped them down.

"As I predicted," said Dr. Toudoux. He pointed to a shelf above the mantelpiece. "There you will find nine volumes of my works on insect poisons," he said. "The third and fourth volumes deal with the tarantula, and are largely devoted to an effort to combat the public prejudice and superstitious fears that excellent insect has inspired."

"Let's try once more," Evans said, unruffled, taking out a *Lycosa* from the Right Bank group.

This time the turtle did not bother to hide his head

and reconnoiter. He was in no mood to be tickled wantonly by spiders, so he made a pass at the Right Bank tarantula, who sidestepped and leaped on the turtle's neck. Almost too quick for the eye to follow, the spider stabbed and closed her jaws. The turtle never moved again, but Dr. Toudoux began hopping up and down and frothing at the mouth. With a sweep of his arm he gathered all the books from the shelf on which reposed his own works. Those he could tear, before heaving out of the window, he ripped into bits, until the office seemed to be filled with artificial snow. Evans grasped his arms and restrained him.

"Let me explain," said Homer, and in order to quiet his friend took out from his pocket a package of mushrooms.

The sight of the fungi only goaded Toudoux to greater frenzy.

"*Amanita verna*," he croaked and bellowed. "The 'Destroying Angel.' In all the annals of history, no mushroom has caused death, even of a baby, within five hours after it is eaten. You are kind to take so much trouble to console me, but your efforts are useless. My resignation shall go forward this very morning."

"But could not a tarantula modify the properties of the deadly mushroom?" Evans asked.

"A tarantula would starve to death in the largest lecture hall of the Sorbonne if the place were filled with cartloads of *Amanitae vernae* and no other food were available. The tarantula, my misguided friend, is not a vegetarian," said Toudoux.

For answer Evans revealed his collection of crickets

272

and ranged his exhibits side by side on the table, in the following order:

1. The *Amanita verna,* or "destroying Angel."
2. The *Gryllus domesticus,* or European household cricket.
3. The *Lycosa narbonnensis,* or black-bellied taran-tula.
4. The defunct turtle, with head, tail and legs as rigid as sticks.

If the reader recalls Sir Henry Irving, or Lon Chaney, as Dr. Jekyll and Mr. Hyde, he will have some idea of the transformation that shook Dr. Hyacinthe Toudoux. In the act of gasping and shuddering to catch his breath, he started skipping around slabs on which lay the six corpses. When he passed any buttons, he pressed them on the run and sent attendants scurrying for new test tubes, retorts and beakers. For crickets eat mushrooms and spiders eat crickets! The pattern formed instantly in the doctor's mind.

"But how ingenious! I should like to meet the toxi-cologist who had me on the run for forty-eight hours. What has he written, may I ask? To what distinguished societies does he belong? I trust, Monsieur Evans, that the Third Republic would not commit the idiocy of severing such a brain from its necessary body and drop-ping it into a basket. Of course! The poison that silenced this quartet of nitwits has the combined properties of various types, attacking nerves, muscles, glands and various vital organs simultaneously. Death occurs like a shot."

Wringing Homer's hand, the doctor glanced ruefully at the empty shelf on which, a few moments before, had stood *Toudoux on Poisonous Insects*. Then he smiled. "Perhaps it is just as well," he said. "The monograph I shall write for private circulation on this case will eclipse my former works in importance. And again, my inscrutable friend and saviour, I have you to thank for my good fortune! It is needless, I know, to try to persuade you to take the credit. Your modesty is too well known to me. But you must release me from my promise never to divulge to any person what part you play in these investigations. The world I can face, and receive its acclaims which, in justice, are due you. But Eugénie! I cannot enter her presence as an impostor."

"Madame Toudoux will be discreet, I am sure," said Evans, and again the doctor wrung his hand. "However," Homer continued, "Frémont or no one else must be told until I give the word. Not even the Minister of Justice. For while you are completing your tests, I must run to earth the man you admire so much and whose head you would shield from the knife. And he is not, unless I am mistaken, a member of any scientific societies or the author of any works excepting those of darkness. To make my task more difficult, several officials and one physician pronounced him dead last March and certified his burial."

"Not Barnabé Vieuxchamp?" asked the doctor, incredulously. "I knew that the administration of our penal colonies was in stupid hands, but at least I thought the officials could distinguish between the quick and the dead."

"The very same Barnabé," Homer said. "I must resurrect him only to turn him over to the headsman, but somehow I feel that it is distinctly worth while."

"I shall do him the honor, as a scientist, to follow his remains to the cemetery where, if I do not shed tears, at least I shall reflect upon the intellect that has been lost to France. This Barnabé, I feel sure, has never known the purifying influence of a gentle and faithful wife. Alas for him and for the world!"

20

A Stormy Morning at the Prefecture

and the Palais Royal

WHEN Evans entered Frémont's office, as soon as he was able to tear himself away from the grateful Toudoux, he found the Chief in the best of spirits. Before Homer was fairly seated, Frémont held out to him for his perusal a report signed by Schlumberger, which, because of the Chief's excitement, was shimmering like a flounder on a line.

"Read that, Monsieur Evans," he said, and rubbed his hands together briskly. "Ho hee, ho hum!" And as Homer glanced rapidly at the document and the photographs pinned to one corner, the Chief hummed snatches of song from the Blackbirds' Revue. "Two witnesses, and of irreproachable character," he murmured. "Both of them have been wounded, or at least taken sick, in defense of their country. One is the father of five, the other of four. The senior is a photographer specializing in first communions, the other, a salesman of that respectable and indispensable household article, the sewing machine. They will make an excellent impression on the jury, if, indeed, this Singe of yours does not confess and spare the state the expense of a tedious trial.

"You will note that the witnesses were sitting, conversing on serious subjects, in a small restaurant café directly opposite the Hotel Wilton, on the evening of June 11. They saw the Singe enter the hotel at eight-thirty with a suitbox under his arm, accompanied by a tall stranger who fits the description of Leffingwell Baxter. The photographer, who also is an artist, chanced to draw a sketch of the pair on the back of a menu. The resemblance is unmistakable. Clever chap."

"Indeed," said Evans, calmly. "The menu is dated, I suppose?"

"It is, and the *plat du jour* was roast veal, which checks up with the practice of the restaurant," said Frémont. "Furthermore, there is no doubt about the hour. The restaurant clock . . ."

"Was stopped," continued Homer, "and one of the witnesses, noticing it, asked the other for the time."

"Exactly," Frémont said.

"Then all I can suggest is that you arrest the two men and charge them with perjury. But you no longer value my advice, it seems," Homer said.

"I am deeply grateful to you for all you have done for me, but in this case you are letting your romantic regard for the Singe affect your saner judgment," Frémont said.

"Let's talk about Rebec," said Evans, patiently.

"First, let me tell you about the Baxter woman, a modern Borgia if ever there was one. I have grilled her twice, and with what result? She cannot remember where she got the violin, she would have us believe. Found it lying on a bed in a small hotel, the name of which she does not know. And when asked where she met Diluvio, to whom she says she intended to return the instrument, she is dissolved in confusion and refuses to answer. Inadvertently she recognized a photograph of the Singe, admitted having seen him before but she will not say where. She disliked her brother intensely, that she confesses freely. She would not stay in the same hotel with him, because, according to her story, they quarreled constantly. I am holding her for grand larceny, of which she is guilty without a doubt, and soon will link her with the graver crime of fractricide."

"I'll have a talk with her later. Just now I can't get my mind away from Rebec. Would you mind coming to his shop with me, and having a look around?" Homer persisted.

"The shop has been examined by Schlumberger, from ceiling to floor. There is nothing there except ribbons and medals, of little intrinsic value, a few broken fiddles and mandolins, pots of glue, wood-working tools, a cot with appropriate bedclothes, a night table, some technical books and a copy of *La Legende Dorée* which, as you know, contains the lives of the Saints."

"No hidden doors? No skylight? No cellar with underground passage?" asked Evans.

"Every inch of the ceiling, floor and walls has been tested with a mallet," insisted Frémont. "The only rathole had been plugged several months ago with sand and cement. Monsieur Rebec was neat and meticulous, and if you can find out why he was kidnapped and manhandled by gangsters I shall be obliged to you. But I am certain he has no important connection with the murder case in hand."

"Nevertheless, I should like to inspect the premises, and would prefer to have you with me," said Homer. "But first, just one more question. When a criminal dies, what is done with the record of his fingerprints? Or shall I ask Sergeant Cidre?"

"I am in touch with the work of everyone in my department," the Chief said, proudly. "The records of deceased criminals are removed from the fingerprint files and placed in a special section of the archives for a period of five years."

"And has Sergeant Cidre identified the third fingerprint, the one found on Baxter's sleeve?" asked Homer.

"Not yet. But that is of small importance," Frémont said. "Some innocent laundry man . . ."

"Would you care to have me clear up this minor detail?"

"If you wish," said the Chief.

"Ask a clerk to bring us a photostat of fingerprint No. 3, and the records of the late Barnabé Vieuxchamp from the morgue," said Homer.

The Chief pointed to a pile of documents about two feet high, contained in crossed wire baskets, and shrugged his shoulders.

"I can refuse you nothing," he said, "as busy as I am."

A moment later, when Miriam returned to the prefecture from Montparnasse, Chief Frémont was blue in the face and the unsigned documents were as thick on the floor as fallen leaves in a virgin forest. Subordinates were dodging from desk to desk and locking themselves in toilets, to escape the sudden plague of wrathful energy the head of the department was displaying. Sergeant Cidre was on the carpet and refused to budge an inch.

The print on the sleeve could not have been made by a dead man three thousand or more miles distant, and there could be no doubt that the thumb was that of Barnabé. Messenger boys were running to and fro with cables to Devil's Island. Under cover of the confusion, Homer Evans slipped out into the summer morning, leading Miriam by the hand; and with Sergeant Schlumberger, who had been more than glad of a pretext to escape, they made their way to the Palais Royal and entered the shop Aux Citoyens.

With a casual glance at the shelves and showcases of medals and ribbons in the outer room, Evans installed Miriam and the sergeant in worn cane-seated chairs while he examined Rebec's work table, old instruments and the living quarters in the rear. As the minutes passed by, the broad honest face of Sergeant Schlumberger beamed with satisfaction.

"I found nothing to arouse suspicion," the Alsatian said.

"And yet you reported in my presence that the late Leffingwell Baxter and his dog entered this shop by the front door and never came out," Evans said. "That circumstance is unusual and must be explained."

"It has cost me many hours of sleep," the sergeant said. "I had a grandfather who, late in life, saw squads of little soldiers marching in and out under his front door, when it was closed tight, and two uncles . . ."

"Ah, what's this?" exclaimed Evans, selecting a package of glue flakes from several containers in a small cabinet. The package was labeled Lactissimo No. 7 and on it was printed the picture of a smiling cow. In an instant, Homer was smiling more broadly than the trade mark of the glue. The sergeant, bewildered, rose and looked over his shoulder.

"A fiddle maker, quite naturally, has glue all over the place," Schlumberger said.

"Precisely," said Evans. In turn he indicated several glue pots, one after another. "There we have the tenacious Oriental foo-no-ki, made from a seaweed found near the Chinese coast and brought to Italy, most probably, by Marco Polo. It will resist damp climates admirably. In the second pot is a French-Canadian product made from woodchuck leather and capable of withstanding tension up to 3,000 pounds, more than enough to tow the *Ile de France*. That third glue, in sheets, is made of goat's blood and waterproofed with silicate of formaldehyde. Our friend Rebec is no ordinary fiddle patcher but a master of his craft and a student of wood-working, both ancient and modern."

"We still may boast of our craftsmen in France," said Schlumberger, proudly. "But what is wrong with the Lactissimo No. 7, in your hand, the glue that comes, according to the advertising statement, from chuckling cattle?"

"Only this," Evans said. "It is entirely unsuitable for use on violins. Milk glues are quick setting and, if treated with resinous compounds, reach a high degree of strength in a few seconds. But that is not the point. They are soluble in water. If Guarnerius or Stradivarius had used them, their viols would have fallen apart within five years. Now what would Monsieur Rebec want with a quickly soluble glue, and one that would dry before he was half ready for it to set? We have found our starting point, our springboard, as it were, my friend."

In the fireplace was a short pine board one inch thick. Evans split it, lengthwise, across his knee, smeared the edges with Lactissimo, and took out his watch. After five minutes he handed the board to Sergeant Schlumberger.

"Would you mind breaking it apart again?" Evans asked.

The sergeant struck the board sharply on the edge of the bench. To his surprise, it did not come apart. Three times he brought it down, with increasing force, and finally the wood split along another grain and left the glued surfaces intact.

"*Potstausend!*" exclaimed the Alsatian, gruffly.

Evans nodded and turned his attention to a letter file.

"You went through this?" he asked the sergeant.

"Mostly bills for materials," Schlumberger said.

"Ah, yes," Evans said. "Materials." In silence, he thumbed invoices until one of them arrested his attention. Schlumberger, already feeling guilty because of the soluble glue, hurried to Homer's side.

"This invoice is from Stillwater and Tief, musical instrument dealers from Boston who have for a silent partner our late acquaintance, Leffingwell Baxter," said Homer.

"*Parfaitement,*" agreed the sergeant. "That explains why Baxter visited this shop. He came on legitimate business."

"On business, at least," Evans said. "But the invoice lists a considerable quantity, ten pounds, in fact, of Wooflex, the most amazing and expensive of the soft-rubber substitutes."

"Maybe Rebec used it for chin rests," the Alsatian said. "He didn't impress me as extravagant and, besides, a chin rest must be firm. Wooflex may be liquefied, poured into a mold, shaped and surfaced and solidified to any desired degree of hardness or softness," Evans said, thoughtfully. Then he slapped his knee and rose, excitedly. "By the great horn spoon!" he exclaimed, and fell into a reverie.

"You might tell us what has pleased you so," said Miriam.

"Tell me, Sergeant. You searched this place. Did you find any Wooflex here?" Homer asked.

"What the devil does Wooflex look like?" asked the sergeant.

"Like clear solid glass, in the form of a parallelopipedon," explained Evans.

"I had jaundice the year I should have studied solid geometry," said Schlumberger.

"Then let us say, a transparent colorless brick," Homer said.

"No bricks, I swear," the Alsatian said. "I am not a glue expert, and plain rubber, without substitutes, has always been good enough for me. But glass bricks I should have noticed, monsieur. If you find any in this shop, I will either drink them, liquefied, or mold them into any form you name and chew them into bits."

"Shall we have a look at the establishment of Siècles Frères?" Evans asked. "I want, among other things, to clear up your fears about the little soldiers marching in and out beneath closed doors."

"Soluble glue and Wooflex," muttered the ponderous Alsatian, rising to follow Miriam to the tailors' shop next door. "Wooflex and soluble glue. Damnation! Blast these foreign inventions that clutter up our peace-loving

France! Were any of the victims set upon with glue or bashed with invisible brickbats? I am nearer to seeing little soldiers than I was before I embarked on this excursion. My grandfather, poor old gentleman, only saw them in squads. No doubt I shall spend my nights reviewing entire divisions with bands."

"You shall have full credit for what we have found," Evans said. "Frémont had his chance, but he is in the throes of a single obsession, to chop off the head of my talented cousin, the Singe . . . But now, to work."

Evans was standing in the center of the commodious display and sales room of Siècles Frères. With his keen and observant eye, he glanced around the walls and let his gaze rest a moment on a large commercial calendar. The calendar was four feet long and about eighteen inches wide, with a picture of two rather fatuous well-dressed men, according to the notions of the old nobility, somewhat modified by the costumes worn in Paris by the late Edward VII.

"Miriam, my dear. Would you mind taking the sergeant out into the courtyard in front, leaving Moritz with me?" Homer asked.

"If you wish," she said, and took Schlumberger's arm, leading him away in spite of his muttered protests. Homer, with the dog at his heels, went with them and saw them safely seated on a broad bench, the same one the sergeant had occupied while Baxter had performed his disappearing act.

"Now watch me carefully," Evans said. "Don't take your eyes from that front door Aux Citoyens."

With Moritz close behind him, Evans entered the medal shop and was lost to sight in the dim back room.

"He won't get away," the sergeant said, mopping his forehead with a mauve bandanna. But the minutes passed and the Alsatian began to fidget, then to bounce. A quarter of an hour, the sergeant remained, eyes rooted to the doorway according to instructions, then with an oath he rose and started pell mell for the shop.

"Don't hurry away," said a familiar voice, and Miriam nearly jumped out of her shoes.

Behind them was Evans, smiling, and Moritz, who indulged in a single playful bark.

The sergeant's eyes were bulging like spring onions. "Either I am bughouse or I am not," he said. "Perhaps it doesn't matter. It is possible that I shall get used to the little soldiers, that in time I shall prefer them to the irrational sights I witness daily, as a member of the force."

To ease the sergeant's mind, Evans led him into Siècles Frères, took up from behind a screen a device shaped like a blow torch, but filled with boiling water. He unhooked the calendar, sprayed the wall with steam, pushed gently and a panel swung inward. Through the opening could be seen, in the adjoining shop, shelves and counters filled with decorations, both civil and military, of all governments, defunct or extant.

"Your mallet test revealed nothing," said Homer, "because the bond of the glue was as strong, or stronger than the rest of the wall. Now let's have a look in the back rooms of this establishment."

"Here's your Wooflex," said Miriam, pleased to be of service. "There are six bricks of it, under this pile of scraps."

"And here is a package of glue from those feeble-minded cows," Schlumberger said.

Evans was examining the contents of a pigeonhole in an old roll-top desk. "Look at these, Sergeant," he said, holding out what appeared to be some plaster casts of human thumbs. "Do these stir visions of promotion in your mind, and dispel your fears about diminutive soldiers?"

"My reason, such as it is, reposes in your hands, Monsieur Evans," the Alsatian said. "Siècles Frères, as far as I know, did not make gloves, but suits of clothes."

"Please make note of the following," Homer said. "First, I am taking three of these transparent bricks of Wooflex, listed by Stillwater and Tief of Boston at 18,000 francs apiece."

"*Barmhertzige Gott!*" grunted Schlumberger, as he copied down the figures with the stub of a pencil.

"Secondly," continued Evans, "I shall ask you to gather up all the glue in both of these establishments.

"Thirdly, I want the address of the best engraver in Paris.

"And fourthly, will you ask Toudoux to send to my apartment as soon as convenient an impression of the teeth of Hector and Potiphar Siècles . . . Oh, yes. Two more items, if you please. I am about to play a little joke on our well-meaning Chief, to teach him a lesson about jumping at false conclusions, if you care to put it that way. Make an appointment for me with Cecile Sorel, the charming leading lady of the Comédie Française, in her dressing room at the theater. She does not loathe publicity, exactly, so you may hint that a press notice or two may result from our *tête à tête*. Lastly, I want you to consult with Sergeant Cidre and obtain, by hook or crook, a set of legible fingerprints of Monsieur Frémont.

You may not know it, Sergeant, but you are about to announce to the world of criminology and to the public of all civilized lands a most important contribution to the science of identification. Your name and your picture, if you have a supply on hand, will grace the front page of each and every Paris paper and the leading dailies of other capitals as well. No. Don't thank me! It's a pleasure, my dear fellow."

And Evans, in high spirits, led Miriam and Moritz out into the courtyard and away.

21

A Sure Cure for Needless Cruelty

As HOMER was about to enter his apartment in the rue Campagne Première, his concierge informed him that the police of Luneville had been trying to telephone him for more than an hour.

"They do not know, of course, that I have had no chance to bathe or get shaved this morning," he said, in a forgiving tone of voice.

The concierge spluttered. "It's important, the commissaire assured me, or I shouldn't have troubled you," she said, defensively.

"So are cleanliness and comfort," Homer said, gravely, and left the good woman shaking her head and muttering, indulgently. Americans were crazy, she reflected, but she loved them just the same.

Miriam, who had overheard, almost squirmed with curiosity as Homer, after making her comfortable at the piano, went into the bedroom, pressed the button that released the small American flag outside his window, the signal for his barber, Henri Duplessis, whose shop was across the street, and started peeling off his shirt for the bath. Her first impulse was to get Luneville for him, on her own account, and drag him to the phone but she repressed her impatience, sighed, and started with page one of the Czerny School of Velocity. The sound of finger exercises, she knew, would have a soothing effect on Homer's mind. The barber entered, the bath and careful toilet followed, and she was about three-quarters through the volume of musical gymnastics when Evans, refreshed and dressed with just the right degree of care, entered the spacious living room with two long cool Vermouth cassis on a tray. He signaled for her to stop playing and sit with him.

"The ghost of Barnabé Vieuxchamp," he began, "appeared first to the Singe on the railway platform in Rouen. He entered your sensitive mind two days later, very early in the morning, in the Bois de Boulogne. Remember? You asked me, without prompting: 'Are you *sure* Barnabé is on Devil's Island?' Was I sure? By no means. But my inquiry elicited a report that the notorious public enemy No. 36475, had died from a ta-rantula bite in the Charvein penal camp, French Guiana, March 26 ultimo. So let us confine ourselves to the ghost of Barnabé, who is as full of mischief as his principal was when in the flesh. The ghost hobnobs with Bostonians, prods Godo the Whack into dangerous rebellion and swings thugs into line against the Singe. Among them are Dental Jake, Captain Nosepaint, and several lesser lilies, two of which you since have potted standing. The city is overcrowded with men who have received the rosette of the Legion of Honor for less distinguished serv-ices."

"I had to shoot those men," Miriam said, ruefully.

She did not like to be reminded of her impromptu executions.

"Their troubles are over," Evans said. "Our own are only at the three-quarter mark, or entering the home stretch. And what is your slight sally into manslaughter compared with mine? By getting worked up about Diluvio and his violin and sending swarms of police to the Salle Gaveau, I riled the ghost. He assumed, mistakenly, that some one of his men had squealed and set a trap for him. So he killed Baxter and tried to incriminate the Singe, then started mopping-up operations. Poor Rebec was slated for dental treatment, with death to follow. The Siècles brothers were silenced with what Toudoux will call *Amanitalycosine.* Tredwell, innocent bystander, was an accidental victim.

"The ghost has succeeded fairly well, thus far, having slipped up on only two points. He set the fake checker game, with fingerprints, quite clumsily, considering his gift for detail. Frémont prefers to ignore that feature of the case, and that is where the Chief has stubbed his toe. Criminology, while giving ample scope to the healthy imagination, is not a world of make believe. In patching together the pattern of a crime, a few bits may be left out, but no hard fact may be disregarded, if established. The second point not yet achieved in the ghost's relentless program is the death of poor Rebec, now lying half-conscious in the Hotel Dieu. If he recovers, he will talk. Therefore the ghost will see to it that he does not recover."

"But, Homer," said Miriam, deeply troubled. "You are not going to stand aside and see that poor little man lose his life, after what he has suffered?"

"Alas, I seem to have become a chronic brother's keeper," Evans said. "Bonnet, at my suggestion, is lurking in Rebec's ward, with two plain-clothes men. I think we can safely take time for lunch, let us say, at Ciro's. Since this evening we shall, I hope, have a victory celebration and dine in excellent company, we should prepare our systems by eating a substantial lunch. A popular misconception, in the gastronomic field, is that one should fast, in anticipation of a feast. On the contrary, one should eat more than usual. A guest at a festive board who arrives weak with hunger, can never do his part or enjoy the meal. He wolfs the *hors d'oeuvres*, feels immediate pangs of indigestion and finds he cannot swallow the subsequent courses. Ah, no! On the days set aside for first-class dinners, nourishing breakfasts and lunches are decidedly *de rigeur*. I should suggest for us a cold *Boeuf à la mode*, with salad, then *zabaglioni*. After that, stern duty calls."

"But the telephone message from Luneville?" asked Miriam.

"The moment for that has arrived," Homer said, and took up the receiver. Within twenty minutes the connection was established, he heard the commissaire's gruff voice, then that of the kid, his new assistant.

"That you, mister?" said the kid, trying to keep his voice as steady as possible.

"What have you to report?" Evans asked, as gravely as if he were in touch with the head of Scotland Yard. Then he stiffened with sudden interest, and paled a little. "You have done a splendid job," he said. "I shall see that you get credit at the prefecture, a microscope, spy glasses and a BB gun."

"Now for lunch," Homer said, turning to Miriam.

Miriam faced him indignantly. "I won't budge until you tell me every word that boy said, and I hope, instead of addling his mind with detective's jargon, you'll teach him manners . . . just like yours."

"A tall man, whose skin was deeply browned by the sun, was seen in the Right Bank tarantula patch not long after we left Luneville this morning. The boy thought I would be interested, and never was so right," said Homer.

The lunch at Ciro's was well up to standard and Evans ate it leisurely. Miriam was less deliberate. The knowledge that the afternoon would bring to a head the multiple murder cases and the mystery of "The Sinner without Malice" set her nerves vibrating like a Guarnerius giving forth its tone. Still, she did not wish to spoil Homer's mood, and she succeeded in quieting herself finally by dwelling on the prospects of a vacation from Montparnasse, spent in Normandy at Evans' side.

When Homer arose, he asked the pert messenger boy to find him a maroon taxi, in order that the color of the vehicle would not clash with Miriam's costume.

"Drive slowly, if you please," he cautioned the driver. "I have got to figure out between here and the prefecture, how the dead may be raised."

They stopped at the prefecture just long enough to glance through the bars at Dental Jake and Nosepaint, who were sharing a cell just east of Godo the Whack, and twice removed from that of Beatrice Baxter, whose points they were discussing.

Hjalmar Jansen had not accompanied his uncouth prisoner to Paris. In fact, as Homer was looking at Jake,

Hjalmar was breathing deeply of the sea air, far out on the Atlantic, and taking a shot at the sun to get his bearings. For as the Goddess Aurora was touching up the windows of the rue des Cordonniers at Rouen that morning, the big Norwegian had been cornered by Horsecollar Phoebe, in one of the statuesque landlady's most candid and affectionate moods. Jansen had accepted the consequences manfully. But just before Phoebe had fallen into the deepest sleep she had known in years, she had told Hjalmar that she was going to sell her joint, get herself some street clothes, and move to Paris in order to be near him. He had excused himself to think it all over, only to feel Nicole's soft arms steal around his brawny neck from behind, while she sobbed out the information that, as kind and distinguished as Maître Ronron had proved to be, she had not been able to tear Hjalmar's image from her aching heart. And as soon as Nicole had been pacified, Grigori had sought out Hjalmar and let it slip that a furious blonde named Mathilde was in wait across the street, in No. 5.

"In that case, a long sea voyage is indicated," Hjalmar said. "Will you come along? We'll hit for some South American port, amble north and in New York I'll get you a good job with Hugo Weiss." So they had tiptoed together through the rear exit of Horsecollar Phoebe's place and at the quai had signed on with the crew of a tramp steamer called "Le Bolivar" bound for Montevideo.

Having inspected the prefecture, Homer and Miriam made their way to the Hotel Dieu, and after a consultation with the head physician and the interns on duty in Rebec's ward, put on white uniforms and relieved Sergeant Bonnet. They did not have long to wait. A new patient, three beds from the comatose medal merchant, slipped on a tattered bathrobe and walked through the ward, pausing to glance at Rebec. Both Miriam and Homer saw him take from his pocket a crumpled wad of paper and toss it on the pillow. Evans leaped across four cots, to the astonishment of the drowsy patients and, just in time, flicked the deadly tarantula from the collar of Rebec's nightshirt. The new patient made a dash for the window, only to feel the sharp teeth of Moritz take hold firmly in the rear and find himself looking into the muzzle of Miriam's automatic.

"Now that you have seen Devil's Island," said Evans to Barnabé, holding the outlaw's sullen eyes with his own, "I shall offer no objection to your being guillotined. If it is any comfort to you, I can assure you in advance that Dr. Hyacinthe Toudoux will attend the funeral. Now, however, you will walk two paces ahead of Miss Leonard, please, and keep your hands raised above your head. Your playmates, Godo the Whack, Dental Jake and the comparatively worthy Captain Nosepaint, as you may or may not know, are already installed at the prefecture. But I think you will be honored with the tightest cell, known as the Goldfish Bowl, which soon will be vacated by your former friend, the Singe. You were clever in planning your escape from Guiana, and in many other ways, but your Achilles heel, Monsieur Vieuxchamp, is the streak of needless cruelty with which your brain is tainted. For that there is a single cure and the best man to administer it is the executioner."

"Let's go," said Barnabé, without emotion.

22

Peroration on the Brink of an Open Grave

THE six corpses were wheeled from the laboratory of
Dr. Hyacinthe Toudoux and ranged along the west side
of the small stage in the assembly room at the prefecture
and several attendants tried to pry open a window with
some confiscated burglar's tools. In the front row of seats
the medical examiner, Maître François Ronron, the three
show girls, Hattie Ham, Mathilde Dubonnet, Sergeants
Schlumberger, Bonnet and Cidre, the fingerprint expert,
were among those present. The east side of the stage was
occupied by the prisoners, including the Singe, Beatrice
Baxter, Dental Jake, Godo the Whack, Captain Nosepaint and Barnabé Vieuxchamp, the latter of whom was
muttering complaints because Chief Frémont had ordered a window to be opened. Barnabé, since he had had
the fever in French Guiana, had become super-sensitive
to drafts.

At Homer's suggestion, Miriam, with drawn automatic, had taken her place on the revolving piano stool,
from which she could watch each move on the stage and
in the audience.

Of all those who had gathered to hear Evans' elucidation, the one who seemed to relish the prospect least was the Chief of Detectives. Frémont sat glaring first at the Singe, then at Barnabé, pausing only to survey the six marble slabs and their motionless contents.

"I shall be brief," began Homer, when quiet had been attained. "I shall not bore you with too much detail, but our adventure, just now drawing to a close, has been so complex and fascinating that it warrants, I believe, a careful summing up for purposes of the record.

"My own interest in the case was aroused in Rouen, where I witnessed an attempt at cold-blooded murder on the part of our fellow-citizen, the third from the left among the prisoners, who is called Godo the Whack. Godo, in order to defy his superior, M. Peret, known as the Singe, by causing a barrel of applejack to jump the skids, tried to kill two of his pals, one of whom had quarreled with him about a G string for his violin. Since occasional detective work has been forced on me, in spite of my idle inclinations, bizarre events have begun to impress me. I had known Godo the Whack, in connection with the Louvre murder case, and had found him cowardly and uninspired. He was not the type to make a bold gesture. In only one way could I account for his conduct at Rouen. Someone, with resources and considerable power, and an enemy of the Singe, was stirring Godo to mutinous activity and had promised him protection."

Evans turned from Godo to Barnabé. "There are not many professional criminals in France, or elsewhere, who could expect to cross the Singe successfully. The first one who came to my mind, or rather, to Miss Leonard's mind, was Barnabé Vieuxchamp, but he had been sent to Devil's Island and there, according to report, Barnabé had died. Of course, from the moment he was arrested, in connection with the kidnapping of Hugo Weiss two years ago, Barnabé began to plan an escape from French Guiana. With him, convicted on a similar charge, was a former member of the St. Julien Rollers just about his height and build, a man who would take orders from Barnabé and carry them out faithfully. His name was Spike. When Barnabé and Spike were loaded on the prison ship and found themselves among strange officers, they exchanged papers. Barnabé became Spike and Spike, knowing that he would be watched and disciplined every day and night, took over Barnabé's unenviable record and impersonated him.

"It is interesting to note how Barnabé rewards loyal service. In this instance, he murdered Spike in order to make more feasible his own re-entry into France. Once officially dead, Barnabé made his escape through Central America and got into the United States.

"Our talented medical examiner, Dr. Hyacinthe Toudoux, regrets that as brilliant a thinker as Barnabé Vieuxchamp must lose his head. As an example of Barnabé's constructive thinking while a convict, I should tell you that he whiled away the tropical nights and acquired substantial funds by staging tarantula fights. But a straightforward combat, and may the best insect win, was not a sure thing for Barnabé. So he hit upon the idea of feeding poisonous mushrooms to crickets and crickets to tarantulas, distilling in that manner a most deadly poison Dr. Toudoux has named Amanitalycosine. Thus Barnabé fixed the spider fights and mulcted his companions, and finally, by means of his fiendish distillation, did away with Spike.

"Barnabé, once safe in America, went straight to Boston and got in touch with Leffingwell Baxter, who, unknown to the public, had for years been a silent partner in the firm of Stillwater and Tief, dealers in precious musical instruments. Some of the instruments were genuine, others were precious but disguised, still others complete fakes. Baxter, in pre-war years, had employed Barnabé in connection with the theft of the priceless quartette of Stradivarius viols and other jobs of shady character. The theft of the Stradivarii, however, had raised such a furore that Baxter decided to retire from crime and devote himself to the affairs of the Bunker Hill Associates. Barnabé, appearing unexpectedly from French Guiana in a desperate mood, threw Baxter into a panic. Baxter feared exposure and public disgrace in the Athens of America, where he had always been ultra-respectable. Thus Barnabé was able to force him to come to Paris and help engineer the theft of Diluvio's matchless Guarnerius 'The Sinner without Malice.' Of course, Barnabé could have blackmailed Baxter outright and got the cash he needed, but he knew Baxter had half a billion dollars and believed that if the late Leffingwell had a hot Guarnerius on his hands he could be made to disgorge his wealth in stupendous amounts.

"Godo the Whack was chosen to secure the violin from the Salle Gaveau, and was given elaborate instructions. He got into the hall, in spite of the cordon of police, took the Guarnerius and substituted another to gain time for his escape. The substitute is evidently a model made by Guarnerius while he was in prison, and afterward was copied and perfected by the master, resulting in the superb instrument we have before us. In fact, the substitute fiddle might have deceived Diluvio for a while, had not the sounding post been out of adjustment. Godo, it is to be remembered, is a rigger by trade and has learned to climb ropes like a monkey. He got into the hall through a skylight backstage and, in order to throw suspicion on Miss Ham, also to facilitate his escape, he trussed her up and hoisted her into the scenery. Meanwhile, Barnabé had developed one of his ugliest moods, having learned that the Salle Gaveau was swarming with police. Someone, he thought, had squealed. As a matter of fact, it was I who asked Monsieur Frémont to attend the recital and bring the cream of the force with him. Barnabé, however, was convinced his colleagues had tried to double-cross him, so he killed Baxter first, ordered Rebec to be tortured and then murdered, then executed the Siècles brothers.

"You will notice," Evans continued, stepping over to the row of corpses, "that the left eye-tooth of the late Hector Siècles and the corresponding tooth of Potiphar have been filed right down to the gums, the work of Dental Jake. In that way, two respectable tailors were brought into line and became the tools of a relentless gang. Rebec, very likely, was forced to witness the spectacle, or some similar orgy, and submitted without torture. Have I made the pattern clear?"

Frémont rose. "You have convinced us that Barnabé tried to murder Rebec in his bed at the Hotel Dieu, but I can't admit that you have exonerated the Singe. I still have his fingerprints and the two witnesses who saw him enter the Hotel Wilton. Why not send both of these arch-criminals to the guillotine, and let them draw straws for the first turn on the platform?"

"In that case, I myself will resort to blackmail," Evans said, gravely.

"Blackmail?" repeated Frémont. "My life is an open book, except, that is . . . You surely wouldn't agitate Madame Frémont . . . about Hydrangea . . ."

"No, but I shall report to Hydrangea how you have been carrying on with the actress, Cecile Sorel," Evans said. "Hydrangea will take the first boat back to Harlem."

The Chief snorted and blustered. "Never have I spoken to Madame Sorel or approached her, although I have seen her act and admire her excellent diction," Frémont declared.

"I shall prove without a doubt that your intimacy with Madame Sorel has reached scandalous proportions," Evans said. "Will you be so kind as to let Sergeant Cidre take your thumbprints?"

"Most certainly not," said the Chief.

"He has already done so," said Evans, removing a document from his pocket. "Will you admit, after comparing them with your fingers, that the prints are yours?"

"They are mine. I insist that they be destroyed," Frémont said.

"Just a moment, if you please," continued Evans. Then he said to an attendant: "Will you ask Madame Sorel to step in from the anteroom?"

With her characteristic grace and amiable smile, the famous Cecile Sorel posed an instant in the doorway then made her way slowly to the stage. Turning coyly away from the audience, she reached beneath her long draped skirt and took off one of her garters, which had a large silver buckle on which was engraved "Liberté, Egalité, Fraternité."

A murmur of astonishment arose, and Homer held up his hand for silence. "Sergeant Cidre," he said. "Miss Sorel has been generous enough to come here in the interest of justice. There are fingerprints on this garter buckle. Will you develop them, please?"

It was the work of a moment for Cidre to dust the buckle with powder, then a look of astonishment passed over his honest face. Frémont began to bounce, clog and yodel with fury. The tell-tale fingerprints were his own, in every last detail, the same central whorl, the same conspicuous delta. Once his first burst of indignation had subsided, he began to beg and plead, asserting his innocence, while Madame Sorel smiled archly and pretended to be melting with confusion. Maître Ronron chuckled and wagged an admonitory finger. Mathilde Dubonnet, reminded of Hjalmar's infidelity, began tearing her clothes.

"By the way," said Evans, "I still think it would be an excellent idea to indict for perjury your two precious witnesses who saw the Singe at the Hotel Wilton. The photographer who specializes in first communions has a scar from a horseshoe on his left cheek, acquired at a tarantula fight in Luneville staged by Dental Jake. His companion, the sewing-machine peddler, was also present, although he escaped without sustaining wounds . . . They are both in Barnabé's gang. Whenever an alibi is airtight, suspect it, my friend. If clocks stop in restaurants at precisely a convenient moment, it is not difficult to detect the odor of the humble cod."

When at last the Chief sank limply into a chair, Evans asked for quiet again and drew forth from a table drawer a brick of Wooflex, and a handful of casts of human fingers.

"This amazing substance," he explained, "is a rubber substitute just recently devised. It bids fair, in view of the developments in this case, to play havoc with the science of identification. For Wooflex may be liquefied, molded into the exact shape of anyone's hand, and a skillful engraver can copy any fingerprints desired. The Wooflex, while it is being carved, is hard, but afterwards it may be softened until it makes perfect fingerprints which ill-intentioned persons can scatter or plant at will." Homer turned to Frémont, and the Chief, without a word approached the Singe, and unlocked the handcuffs.

"I hope you will accept my apology," the crestfallen Chief began.

"The error was a natural one," the Singe said, graciously, and extended his hand.

While Homer had been speaking, Beatrice Baxter, her wrists in handcuffs, had been staring into space. The revelations of her late brother's chicanery had not seemed to surprise her, nor was she moved by the recital of how Leffingwell had met his death. She was thinking wistfully of Diluvio.

"The Sinner without Malice" was reposing in its open case, on a dark-green velvet background, just to her right, along with the other exhibits. But Diluvio was nowhere to be found. He had disappeared, she had been told, immediately after the fight in the dance hall at Horsecollar Phoebe's, and she feared he had gone to sea with Hjalmar and Grigori. That Evans had convinced the Chief she was innocent of felonious intent in removing the Guarnerius from the Hotel Vavin did not seem to interest her at all, even when Sergeant Schlumberger, grunting sympathetically, unlocked the cuffs and set her free. Imagine her rapture when, as the members of the assembly were beginning to stir in preparation for departure, Anton came rushing in, pale and disheveled.

"I cannot find her," the virtuoso shouted, in despair, his voice still husky from Jake's vile treatment. Then suddenly he saw Beatrice on the stage. As he rushed to her, she rose and sighed rapturously as he enfolded her in his arms. "My angel," he said, and let flow such an affectionate tirade that the reader had better be spared its intimate details. The happy pair were so intent on each other that neither the corpses, the leering thugs or the audience meant anything to them. But Hattie Ham approached gamely and stuck out her hand.

"You win, Miss Baxter," she said, grimly. For Hattie, in searching Horsecollar Phoebe's place for Anton, that same morning, had come across the sheet of paper on which Diluvio had poured out his heart about the miracle aboard the *Presque Sans Souci*. Hattie had been so deeply moved by the simple eloquent prose that she had decided to efface herself and offer no obstacle to Anton's happiness.

The warm welcome the Singe received in the Hotel Murphy et du Danube Bleu went on without interruption for sixty-eight hours, with time out only for the victory banquet over which Homer presided in the evening. There was, on that memorable occasion, a plate on the floor, near the head of the table and during Maître Ronron's speech the contented snores of Moritz, the dog, made a soft accompaniment. Hydrangea, who had not been told of the incident involving Madame Sorel of the Comédie Française, danced a red-hot number and renewed her promise to Frémont to remain eternally in France at his side.

Due to the masterful pleading of Maître Ronron, Dental Jake got one hundred and sixty-eight years at hard labor, but Nosepaint, for whom the genial lawyer asked clemency, got off with only ninety-two, four less than were meted out Godo the Whack.

Within four months Grigori had made his fortune in America and sent for Anastasia Ivanovna, who swooned with joy and was given a royal send-off by the underworld of Rouen.

True to his word, Dr. Hyacinthe Toudoux followed the remains of Barnabé Vieuxchamp to their final resting place in Montparnasse cemetery and, removing his hat, said a few touching words at the freshly dug grave.

"Science mourns not only her distinguished sons but also her most wayward children," the doctor said, as the first thud of earth resounded on the coffin. "Who knows whether or not, some day, Amanitalycosine may not be put to exalted use in the service of humanity? Already, by dissolving it in snake oil, I have hit upon a salve that works wonders with hives. I shall call it Barnabasol. Perverse and unfortunate brother, you have paid the extreme penalty! You died without flinching! If posterity eventually honors your name, accept its homage and my own. Farewell! My tears flow freely, *mon semblable, mon frère!*"

All characters, poisons, hotels or other commercial establishments or goods in the foregoing story are imaginary, and readers are cautioned against trying to get in touch with the persons or to purchase the goods or livestock mentioned.

This applies especially to perfumes which are represented as having an ameliorating effect on the male or female character, and food combinations which tend to increase the staying powers.

The sporting element among the readers is warned not to attempt to stage contests similar to those described in Chapters XV and XVI. But if such fights are promoted, the fans should bet cautiously, as spiders under artificial light are extremely unreliable.

A CATALOG OF SELECTED

DOVER BOOKS

IN ALL FIELDS OF INTEREST

DRAWINGS OF REMBRANDT, edited by Seymour Slive. Updated Lippmann, Hofstede de Groot edition, with definitive scholarly apparatus. All portraits, biblical sketches, landscapes, nudes. Oriental figures, classical studies, together with selection of work by followers. 550 illustrations. Total of 630pp. 9⅛ × 12¼.
21485-0, 21486-9 Pa., Two-vol. set $29.90

GHOST AND HORROR STORIES OF AMBROSE BIERCE, Ambrose Bierce. 24 tales vividly imagined, strangely prophetic, and decades ahead of their time in technical skill: "The Damned Thing," "An Inhabitant of Carcosa," "The Eyes of the Panther," "Moxon's Master," and 20 more. 199pp. 5⅜ × 8½. 20767-6 Pa. $4.95

ETHICAL WRITINGS OF MAIMONIDES, Maimonides. Most significant ethical works of great medieval sage, newly translated for utmost precision, readability. Laws Concerning Character Traits, Eight Chapters, more. 192pp. 5⅜ × 8½.
24522-5 Pa. $5.95

THE EXPLORATION OF THE COLORADO RIVER AND ITS CANYONS, J. W. Powell. Full text of Powell's 1,000-mile expedition down the fabled Colorado in 1869. Superb account of terrain, geology, vegetation, Indians, famine, mutiny, treacherous rapids, mighty canyons, during exploration of last unknown part of continental U.S. 400pp. 5⅜ × 8½. 20094-9 Pa. $7.95

HISTORY OF PHILOSOPHY, Julián Marías. Clearest one-volume history on the market. Every major philosopher and dozens of others, to Existentialism and later. 505pp. 5⅜ × 8½. 21739-6 Pa. $9.95

ALL ABOUT LIGHTNING, Martin A. Uman. Highly readable nontechnical survey of nature and causes of lightning, thunderstorms, ball lightning, St. Elmo's Fire, much more. Illustrated. 192pp. 5⅜ × 8½. 25237-X Pa. $5.95

SAILING ALONE AROUND THE WORLD, Captain Joshua Slocum. First man to sail around the world, alone, in small boat. One of great feats of seamanship told in delightful manner. 67 illustrations. 294pp. 5⅜ × 8½. 20326-3 Pa. $4.95

LETTERS AND NOTES ON THE MANNERS, CUSTOMS AND CONDITIONS OF THE NORTH AMERICAN INDIANS, George Catlin. Classic account of life among Plains Indians: ceremonies, hunt, warfare, etc. 312 plates. 572pp. of text. 6⅛ × 9¼. 22118-0, 22119-9, Pa., Two-vol. set $17.90

THE SECRET LIFE OF SALVADOR DALÍ, Salvador Dalí. Outrageous but fascinating autobiography through Dalí's thirties with scores of drawings and sketches and 80 photographs. A must for lovers of 20th-century art. 432pp. 6½ × 9¼. (Available in U.S. only) 27454-3 Pa. $9.95

THE BOOK OF BEASTS: Being a Translation from a Latin Bestiary of the Twelfth Century, T. H. White. Wonderful catalog of real and fanciful beasts: manticore, griffin, phoenix, amphivius, jaculus, many more. White's witty erudite commentary on scientific, historical aspects enhances fascinating glimpse of medieval mind. Illustrated. 296pp. 5⅜ × 8¼. (Available in U.S. only) 24609-4 Pa. $7.95

FRANK LLOYD WRIGHT: Architecture and Nature with 160 Illustrations, Donald Hoffmann. Profusely illustrated study of influence of nature—especially prairie—on Wright's designs for Fallingwater, Robie House, Guggenheim Museum, other masterpieces. 96pp. 9¼ × 10¾. 25098-9 Pa. $8.95

FRANK LLOYD WRIGHT'S FALLINGWATER, Donald Hoffmann. Wright's famous waterfall house: planning and construction of organic idea. History of site, owners, Wright's personal involvement. Photographs of various stages of building. Preface by Edgar Kaufmann, Jr. 100 illustrations. 112pp. 9¼ × 10.
23671-4 Pa. $8.95

YEARS WITH FRANK LLOYD WRIGHT: Apprentice to Genius, Edgar Tafel. Insightful memoir by a former apprentice presents a revealing portrait of Wright the man, the inspired teacher, the greatest American architect. 372 black-and-white illustrations. Preface. Index. vi + 228pp. 8¼ × 11. 24801-1 Pa. $10.95

THE STORY OF KING ARTHUR AND HIS KNIGHTS, Howard Pyle. Enchanting version of King Arthur fable has delighted generations with imaginative narratives of exciting adventures and unforgettable illustrations by the author. 41 illustrations. xviii + 313pp. 6⅛ × 9¼. 21445-1 Pa. $6.95

THE GODS OF THE EGYPTIANS, E. A. Wallis Budge. Thorough coverage of numerous gods of ancient Egypt by foremost Egyptologist. Information on evolution of cults, rites and gods; the cult of Osiris; the Book of the Dead and its rites; the sacred animals and birds; Heaven and Hell; and more. 956pp. 6⅛ × 9¼.
22055-9, 22056-7 Pa., Two-vol. set $21.90

A THEOLOGICO-POLITICAL TREATISE, Benedict Spinoza. Also contains unfinished *Political Treatise*. Great classic on religious liberty, theory of government on common consent. R. Elwes translation. Total of 421pp. 5⅜ × 8½.
20249-6 Pa. $7.95

INCIDENTS OF TRAVEL IN CENTRAL AMERICA, CHIAPAS, AND YUCATAN, John L. Stephens. Almost single-handed discovery of Maya culture; exploration of ruined cities, monuments, temples; customs of Indians. 115 drawings. 892pp. 5⅜ × 8½. 22404-X, 22405-8 Pa., Two-vol. set $17.90

LOS CAPRICHOS, Francisco Goya. 80 plates of wild, grotesque monsters and caricatures. Prado manuscript included. 183pp. 6⅝ × 9⅝. 22384-1 Pa. $6.95

AUTOBIOGRAPHY: The Story of My Experiments with Truth, Mohandas K. Gandhi. Not hagiography, but Gandhi in his own words. Boyhood, legal studies, purification, the growth of the Satyagraha (nonviolent protest) movement. Critical, inspiring work of the man who freed India. 480pp. 5⅜ × 8½. (Available in U.S. only)
24593-4 Pa. $6.95

ILLUSTRATED DICTIONARY OF HISTORIC ARCHITECTURE, edited by Cyril M. Harris. Extraordinary compendium of clear, concise definitions for over 5,000 important architectural terms complemented by over 2,000 line drawings. Covers full spectrum of architecture from ancient ruins to 20th-century Modernism. Preface. 592pp. 7½ × 9⅝. 24444-X Pa. $15.95

THE NIGHT BEFORE CHRISTMAS, Clement Moore. Full text, and woodcuts from original 1848 book. Also critical, historical material. 19 illustrations. 40pp. 4⅝ × 6. 22797-9 Pa. $2.50

THE LESSON OF JAPANESE ARCHITECTURE: 165 Photographs, Jiro Harada. Memorable gallery of 165 photographs taken in the 1930's of exquisite Japanese homes of the well-to-do and historic buildings. 13 line diagrams. 192pp. 8⅜ × 11¼. 24778-3 Pa. $10.95

THE AUTOBIOGRAPHY OF CHARLES DARWIN AND SELECTED LETTERS, edited by Francis Darwin. The fascinating life of eccentric genius composed of an intimate memoir by Darwin (intended for his children); commentary by his son, Francis; hundreds of fragments from notebooks, journals, papers; and letters to and from Lyell, Hooker, Huxley, Wallace and Henslow. xi + 365pp. 5⅜ × 8. 20479-0 Pa. $6.95

WONDERS OF THE SKY: Observing Rainbows, Comets, Eclipses, the Stars and Other Phenomena, Fred Schaaf. Charming, easy-to-read poetic guide to all manner of celestial events visible to the naked eye. Mock suns, glories, Belt of Venus, more. Illustrated. 299pp. 5¼ × 8¼. 24402-4 Pa. $7.95

BURNHAM'S CELESTIAL HANDBOOK, Robert Burnham, Jr. Thorough guide to the stars beyond our solar system. Exhaustive treatment. Alphabetical by constellation: Andromeda to Cetus in Vol. 1; Chamaeleon to Orion in Vol. 2; and Pavo to Vulpecula in Vol. 3. Hundreds of illustrations. Index in Vol. 3. 2,000pp. 6⅛ × 9¼. 23567-X, 23568-8, 23673-0 Pa., Three-vol. set $41.85

STAR NAMES: Their Lore and Meaning, Richard Hinckley Allen. Fascinating history of names various cultures have given to constellations and literary and folkloristic uses that have been made of stars. Indexes to subjects. Arabic and Greek names. Biblical references. Bibliography. 563pp. 5⅜ × 8½. 21079-0 Pa. $8.95

THIRTY YEARS THAT SHOOK PHYSICS: The Story of Quantum Theory, George Gamow. Lucid, accessible introduction to influential theory of energy and matter. Careful explanations of Dirac's anti-particles, Bohr's model of the atom, much more. 12 plates. Numerous drawings. 240pp. 5⅜ × 8½. 24895-X Pa. $5.95

CHINESE DOMESTIC FURNITURE IN PHOTOGRAPHS AND MEASURED DRAWINGS, Gustav Ecke. A rare volume, now affordably priced for antique collectors, furniture buffs and art historians. Detailed review of styles ranging from early Shang to late Ming. Unabridged republication. 161 black-and-white drawings, photos. Total of 224pp. 8⅜ × 11¼. (Available in U.S. only) 25171-3 Pa. $13.95

VINCENT VAN GOGH: A Biography, Julius Meier-Graefe. Dynamic, penetrating study of artist's life, relationship with brother, Theo, painting techniques, travels, more. Readable, engrossing. 160pp. 5⅜ × 8½. (Available in U.S. only) 25253-1 Pa. $4.95

HOW TO WRITE, Gertrude Stein. Gertrude Stein claimed anyone could understand her unconventional writing—here are clues to help. Fascinating improvisations, language experiments, explanations illuminate Stein's craft and the art of writing. Total of 414pp. 4⅜ × 6⅜. 23144-5 Pa. $6.95

ADVENTURES AT SEA IN THE GREAT AGE OF SAIL: Five Firsthand Narratives, edited by Elliot Snow. Rare true accounts of exploration, whaling, shipwreck, fierce natives, trade, shipboard life, more. 33 illustrations. Introduction. 353pp. 5⅜ × 8½. 25177-2 Pa. $8.95

THE HERBAL OR GENERAL HISTORY OF PLANTS, John Gerard. Classic descriptions of about 2,850 plants—with over 2,700 illustrations—includes Latin and English names, physical descriptions, varieties, time and place of growth, more. 2,706 illustrations. xlv + 1,678pp. 8½ × 12¼. 23147-X Cloth. $75.00

DOROTHY AND THE WIZARD IN OZ, L. Frank Baum. Dorothy and the Wizard visit the center of the Earth, where people are vegetables, glass houses grow and Oz characters reappear. Classic sequel to *Wizard of Oz*. 256pp. 5⅜ × 8. 24714-7 Pa. $5.95

SONGS OF EXPERIENCE: Facsimile Reproduction with 26 Plates in Full Color, William Blake. This facsimile of Blake's original "Illuminated Book" reproduces 26 full-color plates from a rare 1826 edition. Includes "The Tyger," "London," "Holy Thursday," and other immortal poems. 26 color plates. Printed text of poems. 48pp. 5¼ × 7. 24636-1 Pa. $3.95

SONGS OF INNOCENCE, William Blake. The first and most popular of Blake's famous "Illuminated Books," in a facsimile edition reproducing all 31 brightly colored plates. Additional printed text of each poem. 64pp. 5¼ × 7. 22764-2 Pa. $3.95

PRECIOUS STONES, Max Bauer. Classic, thorough study of diamonds, rubies, emeralds, garnets, etc.: physical character, occurrence, properties, use, similar topics. 20 plates, 8 in color. 94 figures. 659pp. 6⅛ × 9¼. 21910-0, 21911-9 Pa., Two-vol. set $15.90

ENCYCLOPEDIA OF VICTORIAN NEEDLEWORK, S. F. A. Caulfeild and Blanche Saward. Full, precise descriptions of stitches, techniques for dozens of needlecrafts—most exhaustive reference of its kind. Over 800 figures. Total of 679pp. 8⅛ × 11. Two volumes. Vol. 1 22800-2 Pa. $11.95
Vol. 2 22801-0 Pa. $11.95

THE MARVELOUS LAND OF OZ, L. Frank Baum. Second Oz book, the Scarecrow and Tin Woodman are back with hero named Tip, Oz magic. 136 illustrations. 287pp. 5⅜ × 8½. 20692-0 Pa. $5.95

WILD FOWL DECOYS, Joel Barber. Basic book on the subject, by foremost authority and collector. Reveals history of decoy making and rigging, place in American culture, different kinds of decoys, how to make them, and how to use them. 140 plates. 156pp. 7⅞ × 10¾. 20011-6 Pa. $8.95

HISTORY OF LACE, Mrs. Bury Palliser. Definitive, profusely illustrated chronicle of lace from earliest times to late 19th century. Laces of Italy, Greece, England, France, Belgium, etc. Landmark of needlework scholarship. 266 illustrations. 672pp. 6⅛ × 9¼. 24742-2 Pa. $14.95

ILLUSTRATED GUIDE TO SHAKER FURNITURE, Robert Meader. All furniture and appurtenances, with much on unknown local styles. 235 photos. 146pp. 9 × 12. 22819-3 Pa. $8.95

WHALE SHIPS AND WHALING: A Pictorial Survey, George Francis Dow. Over 200 vintage engravings, drawings, photographs of barks, brigs, cutters, other vessels. Also harpoons, lances, whaling guns, many other artifacts. Comprehensive text by foremost authority. 207 black-and-white illustrations. 288pp. 6 × 9. 24808-9 Pa. $9.95

THE BERTRAMS, Anthony Trollope. Powerful portrayal of blind self-will and thwarted ambition includes one of Trollope's most heartrending love stories. 497pp. 5⅜ × 8½. 25119-5 Pa. $9.95

ADVENTURES WITH A HAND LENS, Richard Headstrom. Clearly written guide to observing and studying flowers and grasses, fish scales, moth and insect wings, egg cases, buds, feathers, seeds, leaf scars, moss, molds, ferns, common crystals, etc.—all with an ordinary, inexpensive magnifying glass. 209 exact line drawings aid in your discoveries. 220pp. 5⅜ × 8½. 23330-8 Pa. $4.95

RODIN ON ART AND ARTISTS, Auguste Rodin. Great sculptor's candid, wide-ranging comments on meaning of art; great artists; relation of sculpture to poetry, painting, music; philosophy of life, more. 76 superb black-and-white illustrations of Rodin's sculpture, drawings and prints. 119pp. 8⅜ × 11¼. 24487-3 Pa. $7.95

FIFTY CLASSIC FRENCH FILMS, 1912–1982: A Pictorial Record, Anthony Slide. Memorable stills from Grand Illusion, Beauty and the Beast, Hiroshima, Mon Amour, many more. Credits, plot synopses, reviews, etc. 160pp. 8¼ × 11. 25256-6 Pa. $11.95

THE PRINCIPLES OF PSYCHOLOGY, William James. Famous long course complete, unabridged. Stream of thought, time perception, memory, experimental methods; great work decades ahead of its time. 94 figures. 1,391pp. 5⅜ × 8½. 20381-6, 20382-4 Pa., Two-vol. set $23.90

BODIES IN A BOOKSHOP, R. T. Campbell. Challenging mystery of blackmail and murder with ingenious plot and superbly drawn characters. In the best tradition of British suspense fiction. 192pp. 5⅜ × 8½. 24720-1 Pa. $4.95

CALLAS: PORTRAIT OF A PRIMA DONNA, George Jellinek. Renowned commentator on the musical scene chronicles incredible career and life of the most controversial, fascinating, influential operatic personality of our time. 64 black-and-white photographs. 416pp. 5⅜ × 8¼. 25047-4 Pa. $8.95

GEOMETRY, RELATIVITY AND THE FOURTH DIMENSION, Rudolph Rucker. Exposition of fourth dimension, concepts of relativity as Flatland characters continue adventures. Popular, easily followed yet accurate, profound. 141 illustrations. 133pp. 5⅜ × 8½. 23400-2 Pa. $4.95

HOUSEHOLD STORIES BY THE BROTHERS GRIMM, with pictures by Walter Crane. 53 classic stories—Rumpelstiltskin, Rapunzel, Hansel and Gretel, the Fisherman and his Wife, Snow White, Tom Thumb, Sleeping Beauty, Cinderella, and so much more—lavishly illustrated with original 19th century drawings. 114 illustrations. x + 269pp. 5⅜ × 8½. 21080-4 Pa. $4.95

SUNDIALS, Albert Waugh. Far and away the best, most thorough coverage of ideas, mathematics concerned, types, construction, adjusting anywhere. Over 100 illustrations. 230pp. 5⅜ × 8½. 22947-5 Pa. $5.95

PICTURE HISTORY OF THE NORMANDIE: With 190 Illustrations, Frank O. Braynard. Full story of legendary French ocean liner: Art Deco interiors, design innovations, furnishings, celebrities, maiden voyage, tragic fire, much more. Extensive text. 144pp. 8⅞ × 11¾. 25257-4 Pa. $10.95

THE FIRST AMERICAN COOKBOOK: A Facsimile of "American Cookery," 1796, Amelia Simmons. Facsimile of the first American-written cookbook published in the United States contains authentic recipes for colonial favorites—pumpkin pudding, winter squash pudding, spruce beer, Indian slapjacks, and more. Introductory Essay and Glossary of colonial cooking terms. 80pp. 5⅜ × 8½. 24710-4 Pa. $3.50

101 PUZZLES IN THOUGHT AND LOGIC, C. R. Wylie, Jr. Solve murders and robberies, find out which fishermen are liars, how a blind man could possibly identify a color—purely by your own reasoning! 107pp. 5⅜ × 8½. 20367-0 Pa. $2.95

ANCIENT EGYPTIAN MYTHS AND LEGENDS, Lewis Spence. Examines animism, totemism, fetishism, creation myths, deities, alchemy, art and magic, other topics. Over 50 illustrations. 432pp. 5⅜ × 8½. 26525-0 Pa. $8.95

ANTHROPOLOGY AND MODERN LIFE, Franz Boas. Great anthropologist's classic treatise on race and culture. Introduction by Ruth Bunzel. Only inexpensive paperback edition. 255pp. 5⅜ × 8½. 25245-0 Pa. $7.95

THE TALE OF PETER RABBIT, Beatrix Potter. The inimitable Peter's terrifying adventure in Mr. McGregor's garden, with all 27 wonderful, full-color Potter illustrations. 55pp. 4¼ × 5½. (Available in U.S. only) 22827-4 Pa. $1.75

THREE PROPHETIC SCIENCE FICTION NOVELS, H. G. Wells. *When the Sleeper Wakes, A Story of the Days to Come* and *The Time Machine* (full version). 335pp. 5⅜ × 8½. (Available in U.S. only) 20605-X Pa. $8.95

APICIUS COOKERY AND DINING IN IMPERIAL ROME, edited and translated by Joseph Dommers Vehling. Oldest known cookbook in existence offers readers a clear picture of what foods Romans ate, how they prepared them, etc. 49 illustrations. 301pp. 6⅛ × 9¼. 23563-7 Pa. $7.95

SHAKESPEARE LEXICON AND QUOTATION DICTIONARY, Alexander Schmidt. Full definitions, locations, shades of meaning of every word in plays and poems. More than 50,000 exact quotations. 1,485pp. 6½ × 9¼. 22726-X, 22727-8 Pa., Two-vol. set $31.90

THE WORLD'S GREAT SPEECHES, edited by Lewis Copeland and Lawrence W. Lamm. Vast collection of 278 speeches from Greeks to 1970. Powerful and effective models; unique look at history. 842pp. 5⅜ × 8½. 20468-5 Pa. $12.95

THE BLUE FAIRY BOOK, Andrew Lang. The first, most famous collection, with many familiar tales: Little Red Riding Hood, Aladdin and the Wonderful Lamp, Puss in Boots, Sleeping Beauty, Hansel and Gretel, Rumpelstiltskin; 37 in all. 138 illustrations. 390pp. 5⅜ × 8½. 21437-0 Pa. $6.95

THE STORY OF THE CHAMPIONS OF THE ROUND TABLE, Howard Pyle. Sir Launcelot, Sir Tristram and Sir Percival in spirited adventures of love and triumph retold in Pyle's inimitable style. 50 drawings, 31 full-page. xviii + 329pp. 6½ × 9¼. 21883-X Pa. $7.95

THE MYTHS OF THE NORTH AMERICAN INDIANS, Lewis Spence. Myths and legends of the Algonquins, Iroquois, Pawnees and Sioux with comprehensive historical and ethnological commentary. 36 illustrations. 5⅜ × 8½.
25967-6 Pa. $8.95

GREAT DINOSAUR HUNTERS AND THEIR DISCOVERIES, Edwin H. Colbert. Fascinating, lavishly illustrated chronicle of dinosaur research, 1820s to 1960. Achievements of Cope, Marsh, Brown, Buckland, Mantell, Huxley, many others. 384pp. 5¼ × 8¼. 24701-5 Pa. $7.95

THE TASTEMAKERS, Russell Lynes. Informal, illustrated social history of American taste 1850s–1950s. First popularized categories Highbrow, Lowbrow, Middlebrow. 129 illustrations. New (1979) afterword. 384pp. 6 × 9.
23993-4 Pa. $8.95

DOUBLE CROSS PURPOSES, Ronald A. Knox. A treasure hunt in the Scottish Highlands, an old map, unidentified corpse, surprise discoveries keep reader guessing in this cleverly intricate tale of financial skullduggery. 2 black-and-white maps. 320pp. 5⅜ × 8½. (Available in U.S. only) 25032-6 Pa. $6.95

AUTHENTIC VICTORIAN DECORATION AND ORNAMENTATION IN FULL COLOR: 46 Plates from "Studies in Design," Christopher Dresser. Superb full-color lithographs reproduced from rare original portfolio of a major Victorian designer. 48pp. 9¼ × 12¼. 25083-0 Pa. $7.95

PRIMITIVE ART, Franz Boas. Remains the best text ever prepared on subject, thoroughly discussing Indian, African, Asian, Australian, and, especially, Northern American primitive art. Over 950 illustrations show ceramics, masks, totem poles, weapons, textiles, paintings, much more. 376pp. 5⅜ × 8. 20025-6 Pa. $7.95

SIDELIGHTS ON RELATIVITY, Albert Einstein. Unabridged republication of two lectures delivered by the great physicist in 1920–21. *Ether and Relativity* and *Geometry and Experience*. Elegant ideas in nonmathematical form, accessible to intelligent layman. vi + 56pp. 5⅜ × 8½. 24511-X Pa. $3.95

THE WIT AND HUMOR OF OSCAR WILDE, edited by Alvin Redman. More than 1,000 ripostes, paradoxes, wisecracks: Work is the curse of the drinking classes, I can resist everything except temptation, etc. 258pp. 5⅜ × 8½. 20602-5 Pa. $4.95

ADVENTURES WITH A MICROSCOPE, Richard Headstrom. 59 adventures with clothing fibers, protozoa, ferns and lichens, roots and leaves, much more. 142 illustrations. 232pp. 5⅜ × 8½. 23471-1 Pa. $4.95

PLANTS OF THE BIBLE, Harold N. Moldenke and Alma L. Moldenke. Standard reference to all 230 plants mentioned in Scriptures. Latin name, biblical reference, uses, modern identity, much more. Unsurpassed encyclopedic resource for scholars, botanists, nature lovers, students of Bible. Bibliography. Indexes. 123 black-and-white illustrations. 384pp. 6 × 9. 25069-5 Pa. $8.95

FAMOUS AMERICAN WOMEN: A Biographical Dictionary from Colonial Times to the Present, Robert McHenry, ed. From Pocahontas to Rosa Parks, 1,035 distinguished American women documented in separate biographical entries. Accurate, up-to-date data, numerous categories, spans 400 years. Indices. 493pp. 6½ × 9¼. 24523-3 Pa. $10.95

THE FABULOUS INTERIORS OF THE GREAT OCEAN LINERS IN HISTORIC PHOTOGRAPHS, William H. Miller, Jr. Some 200 superb photographs capture exquisite interiors of world's great "floating palaces"—1890s to 1980s: *Titanic, Ile de France, Queen Elizabeth, United States, Europa,* more. Approx. 200 black-and-white photographs. Captions. Text. Introduction. 160pp. 8⅞ × 11¾. 24756-2 Pa. $9.95

THE GREAT LUXURY LINERS, 1927–1954: A Photographic Record, William H. Miller, Jr. Nostalgic tribute to heyday of ocean liners. 186 photos of *Ile de France, Normandie, Leviathan, Queen Elizabeth, United States,* many others. Interior and exterior views. Introduction. Captions. 160pp. 9 × 12. 24056-8 Pa. $12.95

A NATURAL HISTORY OF THE DUCKS, John Charles Phillips. Great landmark of ornithology offers complete detailed coverage of nearly 200 species and subspecies of ducks: gadwall, sheldrake, merganser, pintail, many more. 74 full-color plates, 102 black-and-white. Bibliography. Total of 1,920pp. 8⅜ × 11¼. 25141-1, 25142-X Cloth., Two-vol. set $100.00

THE SEAWEED HANDBOOK: An Illustrated Guide to Seaweeds from North Carolina to Canada, Thomas F. Lee. Concise reference covers 78 species. Scientific and common names, habitat, distribution, more. Finding keys for easy identification. 224pp. 5⅜ × 8½. 25215-9 Pa. $6.95

THE TEN BOOKS OF ARCHITECTURE: The 1755 Leoni Edition, Leon Battista Alberti. Rare classic helped introduce the glories of ancient architecture to the Renaissance. 68 black-and-white plates. 336pp. 8⅜ × 11¼. 25239-6 Pa. $14.95

MISS MACKENZIE, Anthony Trollope. Minor masterpieces by Victorian master unmasks many truths about life in 19th-century England. First inexpensive edition in years. 392pp. 5⅜ × 8½. 25201-9 Pa. $8.95

THE RIME OF THE ANCIENT MARINER, Gustave Doré, Samuel Taylor Coleridge. Dramatic engravings considered by many to be his greatest work. The terrifying space of the open sea, the storms and whirlpools of an unknown ocean, the ice of Antarctica, more—all rendered in a powerful, chilling manner. Full text. 38 plates. 77pp. 9¼ × 12. 22305-1 Pa. $4.95

THE EXPEDITIONS OF ZEBULON MONTGOMERY PIKE, Zebulon Montgomery Pike. Fascinating firsthand accounts (1805–6) of exploration of Mississippi River, Indian wars, capture by Spanish dragoons, much more. 1,088pp. 5⅜ × 8½. 25254-X, 25255-8 Pa., Two-vol. set $25.90

A CONCISE HISTORY OF PHOTOGRAPHY: Third Revised Edition, Helmut Gernsheim. Best one-volume history—camera obscura, photochemistry, daguerreotypes, evolution of cameras, film, more. Also artistic aspects—landscape, portraits, fine art, etc. 281 black-and-white photographs. 26 in color. 176pp. 8⅜ × 11¼.
25128-4 Pa. $14.95

THE DORÉ BIBLE ILLUSTRATIONS, Gustave Doré. 241 detailed plates from the Bible: the Creation scenes, Adam and Eve, Flood, Babylon, battle sequences, life of Jesus, etc. Each plate is accompanied by the verses from the King James version of the Bible. 241pp. 9 × 12. 23004-X Pa. $9.95

WANDERINGS IN WEST AFRICA, Richard F. Burton. Great Victorian scholar/adventurer's invaluable descriptions of African tribal rituals, fetishism, culture, art, much more. Fascinating 19th-century account. 624pp. 5⅜ × 8½. 26890-X Pa. $12.95

HISTORIC HOMES OF THE AMERICAN PRESIDENTS, Second Revised Edition, Irvin Haas. Guide to homes occupied by every president from Washington to Bush. Visiting hours, travel routes, more. 175 photos. 160pp. 8¼ × 11.
26751-2 Pa. $9.95

THE HISTORY OF THE LEWIS AND CLARK EXPEDITION, Meriwether Lewis and William Clark, edited by Elliott Coues. Classic edition of Lewis and Clark's day-by-day journals that later became the basis for U.S. claims to Oregon and the West. Accurate and invaluable geographical, botanical, biological, meteorological and anthropological material. Total of 1,508pp. 5⅜ × 8½.
21268-8, 21269-6, 21270-X Pa., Three-vol. set $29.85

LANGUAGE, TRUTH AND LOGIC, Alfred J. Ayer. Famous, clear introduction to Vienna, Cambridge schools of Logical Positivism. Role of philosophy, elimination of metaphysics, nature of analysis, etc. 160pp. 5⅜ × 8½. (Available in U.S. and Canada only) 20010-8 Pa. $3.95

MATHEMATICS FOR THE NONMATHEMATICIAN, Morris Kline. Detailed, college-level treatment of mathematics in cultural and historical context, with numerous exercises. For liberal arts students. Preface. Recommended Reading Lists. Tables. Index. Numerous black-and-white figures. xvi + 641pp. 5⅜ × 8½.
24823-2 Pa. $11.95

HANDBOOK OF PICTORIAL SYMBOLS, Rudolph Modley. 3,250 signs and symbols, many systems in full; official or heavy commercial use. Arranged by subject. Most in Pictorial Archive series. 143pp. 8⅛ × 11. 23357-X Pa. $7.95

INCIDENTS OF TRAVEL IN YUCATAN, John L. Stephens. Classic (1843) exploration of jungles of Yucatan, looking for evidences of Maya civilization. Travel adventures, Mexican and Indian culture, etc. Total of 669pp. 5⅜ × 8½.
20926-1, 20927-X Pa., Two-vol. set $13.90

DEGAS: An Intimate Portrait, Ambroise Vollard. Charming, anecdotal memoir by famous art dealer of one of the greatest 19th-century French painters. 14 black-and-white illustrations. Introduction by Harold L. Van Doren. 96pp. 5⅜ × 8½.
25131-4 Pa. $4.95

PERSONAL NARRATIVE OF A PILGRIMAGE TO AL-MADINAH AND MECCAH, Richard F. Burton. Great travel classic by remarkably colorful personality. Burton, disguised as a Moroccan, visited sacred shrines of Islam, narrowly escaping death. 47 illustrations. 959pp. 5⅜ × 8½.
21217-3, 21218-1 Pa., Two-vol. set $19.90

PHRASE AND WORD ORIGINS, A. H. Holt. Entertaining, reliable, modern study of more than 1,200 colorful words, phrases, origins and histories. Much unexpected information. 254pp. 5⅜ × 8½.
20758-7 Pa. $5.95

THE RED THUMB MARK, R. Austin Freeman. In this first Dr. Thorndyke case, the great scientific detective draws fascinating conclusions from the nature of a single fingerprint. Exciting story, authentic science. 320pp. 5⅜ × 8½. (Available in U.S. only)
25210-8 Pa. $6.95

AN EGYPTIAN HIEROGLYPHIC DICTIONARY, E. A. Wallis Budge. Monumental work containing about 25,000 words or terms that occur in texts ranging from 3000 B.C. to 600 A.D. Each entry consists of a transliteration of the word, the word in hieroglyphs, and the meaning in English. 1,314pp. 6⅞ × 10.
23615-3, 23616-1 Pa., Two-vol. set $35.90

THE COMPLEAT STRATEGYST: Being a Primer on the Theory of Games of Strategy, J. D. Williams. Highly entertaining classic describes, with many illustrated examples, how to select best strategies in conflict situations. Prefaces. Appendices. xvi + 268pp. 5⅜ × 8½.
25101-2 Pa. $6.95

THE ROAD TO OZ, L. Frank Baum. Dorothy meets the Shaggy Man, little Button-Bright and the Rainbow's beautiful daughter in this delightful trip to the magical Land of Oz. 272pp. 5⅜ × 8.
25208-6 Pa. $5.95

POINT AND LINE TO PLANE, Wassily Kandinsky. Seminal exposition of role of point, line, other elements in nonobjective painting. Essential to understanding 20th-century art. 127 illustrations. 192pp. 6½ × 9¼.
23808-3 Pa. $5.95

LADY ANNA, Anthony Trollope. Moving chronicle of Countess Lovel's bitter struggle to win for herself and daughter Anna their rightful rank and fortune—perhaps at cost of sanity itself. 384pp. 5⅜ × 8½.
24669-8 Pa. $8.95

EGYPTIAN MAGIC, E. A. Wallis Budge. Sums up all that is known about magic in Ancient Egypt: the role of magic in controlling the gods, powerful amulets that warded off evil spirits, scarabs of immortality, use of wax images, formulas and spells, the secret name, much more. 253pp. 5⅜ × 8½.
22681-6 Pa. $4.95

THE DANCE OF SIVA, Ananda Coomaraswamy. Preeminent authority unfolds the vast metaphysic of India: the revelation of her art, conception of the universe, social organization, etc. 27 reproductions of art masterpieces. 192pp. 5⅜ × 8½.
24817-8 Pa. $6.95

CHRISTMAS CUSTOMS AND TRADITIONS, Clement A. Miles. Origin, evolution, significance of religious, secular practices. Caroling, gifts, yule logs, much more. Full, scholarly yet fascinating; non-sectarian. 400pp. 5⅜ × 8½.
23354-5 Pa. $7.95

THE HUMAN FIGURE IN MOTION, Eadweard Muybridge. More than 4,500 stopped-action photos, in action series, showing undraped men, women, children jumping, lying down, throwing, sitting, wrestling, carrying, etc. 390pp. 7⅞ × 10⅝.
20204-6 Cloth. $24.95

THE MAN WHO WAS THURSDAY, Gilbert Keith Chesterton. Witty, fast-paced novel about a club of anarchists in turn-of-the-century London. Brilliant social, religious, philosophical speculations. 128pp. 5⅜ × 8½.
25121-7 Pa. $3.95

A CÉZANNE SKETCHBOOK: Figures, Portraits, Landscapes and Still Lifes, Paul Cézanne. Great artist experiments with tonal effects, light, mass, other qualities in over 100 drawings. A revealing view of developing master painter, precursor of Cubism. 102 black-and-white illustrations. 144pp. 8¾ × 6⅜.
24790-2 Pa. $6.95

AN ENCYCLOPEDIA OF BATTLES: Accounts of Over 1,560 Battles from 1479 B.C. to the Present, David Eggenberger. Presents essential details of every major battle in recorded history, from the first battle of Megiddo in 1479 B.C. to Grenada in 1984. List of Battle Maps. New Appendix covering the years 1967–1984. Index. 99 illustrations. 544pp. 6½ × 9¼.
24913-1 Pa. $14.95

AN ETYMOLOGICAL DICTIONARY OF MODERN ENGLISH, Ernest Weekley. Richest, fullest work, by foremost British lexicographer. Detailed word histories. Inexhaustible. Total of 856pp. 6½ × 9¼.
21873-2, 21874-0 Pa., Two-vol. set $19.90

WEBSTER'S AMERICAN MILITARY BIOGRAPHIES, edited by Robert McHenry. Over 1,000 figures who shaped 3 centuries of American military history. Detailed biographies of Nathan Hale, Douglas MacArthur, Mary Hallaren, others. Chronologies of engagements, more. Introduction. Addenda. 1,033 entries in alphabetical order. xi + 548pp. 6½ × 9¼. (Available in U.S. only)
24758-9 Pa. $13.95

LIFE IN ANCIENT EGYPT, Adolf Erman. Detailed older account, with much not in more recent books: domestic life, religion, magic, medicine, commerce, and whatever else needed for complete picture. Many illustrations. 597pp. 5⅜ × 8½.
22632-8 Pa. $9.95

HISTORIC COSTUME IN PICTURES, Braun & Schneider. Over 1,450 costumed figures shown, covering a wide variety of peoples: kings, emperors, nobles, priests, servants, soldiers, scholars, townsfolk, peasants, merchants, courtiers, cavaliers, and more. 256pp. 8⅜ × 11¼.
23150-X Pa. $9.95

THE NOTEBOOKS OF LEONARDO DA VINCI, edited by J. P. Richter. Extracts from manuscripts reveal great genius; on painting, sculpture, anatomy, sciences, geography, etc. Both Italian and English. 186 ms. pages reproduced, plus 500 additional drawings, including studies for *Last Supper, Sforza* monument, etc. 860pp. 7⅞ × 10¾. (Available in U.S. only) 22572-0, 22573-9 Pa., Two-vol. set $35.90

THE ART NOUVEAU STYLE BOOK OF ALPHONSE MUCHA: All 72 Plates from "Documents Decoratifs" in Original Color, Alphonse Mucha. Rare copyright-free design portfolio by high priest of Art Nouveau. Jewelry, wallpaper, stained glass, furniture, figure studies, plant and animal motifs, etc. Only complete one-volume edition. 80pp. 9⅜ × 12¼. 24044-4 Pa. $9.95

ANIMALS: 1,419 COPYRIGHT-FREE ILLUSTRATIONS OF MAMMALS, BIRDS, FISH, INSECTS, ETC., edited by Jim Harter. Clear wood engravings present, in extremely lifelike poses, over 1,000 species of animals. One of the most extensive pictorial sourcebooks of its kind. Captions. Index. 284pp. 9 × 12. 23766-4 Pa. $9.95

OBELISTS FLY HIGH, C. Daly King. Masterpiece of American detective fiction, long out of print, involves murder on a 1935 transcontinental flight—"a very thrilling story"—NY Times. Unabridged and unaltered republication of the edition published by William Collins Sons & Co. Ltd., London, 1935. 288pp. 5⅜ × 8½. (Available in U.S. only) 25036-9 Pa. $5.95

VICTORIAN AND EDWARDIAN FASHION: A Photographic Survey, Alison Gernsheim. First fashion history completely illustrated by contemporary photographs. Full text plus 235 photos, 1840–1914, in which many celebrities appear. 240pp. 6½ × 9¼. 24205-6 Pa. $8.95

THE ART OF THE FRENCH ILLUSTRATED BOOK, 1700–1914, Gordon N. Ray. Over 630 superb book illustrations by Fragonard, Delacroix, Daumier, Doré, Grandville, Manet, Mucha, Steinlen, Toulouse-Lautrec and many others. Preface. Introduction. 633 halftones. Indices of artists, authors & titles, binders and provenances. Appendices. Bibliography. 608pp. 8⅜ × 11¼. 25086-5 Pa. $24.95

THE WONDERFUL WIZARD OF OZ, L. Frank Baum. Facsimile in full color of America's finest children's classic. 143 illustrations by W. W. Denslow. 267pp. 5⅜ × 8½. 20691-2 Pa. $7.95

FOLLOWING THE EQUATOR: A Journey Around the World, Mark Twain. Great writer's 1897 account of circumnavigating the globe by steamship. Ironic humor, keen observations, vivid and fascinating descriptions of exotic places. 197 illustrations. 720pp. 5⅜ × 8½. 26113-1 Pa. $15.95

THE FRIENDLY STARS, Martha Evans Martin & Donald Howard Menzel. Classic text marshalls the stars together in an engaging, non-technical survey, presenting them as sources of beauty in night sky. 23 illustrations. Foreword. 2 star charts. Index. 147pp. 5⅜ × 8½. 21099-5 Pa. $3.95

FADS AND FALLACIES IN THE NAME OF SCIENCE, Martin Gardner. Fair, witty appraisal of cranks, quacks, and quackeries of science and pseudoscience: hollow earth, Velikovsky, orgone energy, Dianetics, flying saucers, Bridey Murphy, food and medical fads, etc. Revised, expanded In the Name of Science. "A very able and even-tempered presentation."—The New Yorker. 363pp. 5⅜ × 8. 20394-8 Pa. $6.95

ANCIENT EGYPT: ITS CULTURE AND HISTORY, J. E Manchip White. From pre-dynastics through Ptolemies: society, history, political structure, religion, daily life, literature, cultural heritage. 48 plates. 217pp. 5⅜ × 8½. 22548-8 Pa. $5.95

SIR HARRY HOTSPUR OF HUMBLETHWAITE, Anthony Trollope. Incisive, unconventional psychological study of a conflict between a wealthy baronet, his idealistic daughter, and their scapegrace cousin. The 1870 novel in its first inexpensive edition in years. 250pp. 5⅜ × 8½. 24953-0 Pa. $6.95

LASERS AND HOLOGRAPHY, Winston E. Kock. Sound introduction to burgeoning field, expanded (1981) for second edition. Wave patterns, coherence, lasers, diffraction, zone plates, properties of holograms, recent advances. 84 illustrations. 160pp. 5⅜ × 8¼. (Except in United Kingdom) 24041-X Pa. $3.95

INTRODUCTION TO ARTIFICIAL INTELLIGENCE: Second, Enlarged Edition, Philip C. Jackson, Jr. Comprehensive survey of artificial intelligence—the study of how machines (computers) can be made to act intelligently. Includes introductory and advanced material. Extensive notes updating the main text. 132 black-and-white illustrations. 512pp. 5⅜ × 8½. 24864-X Pa. $10.95

HISTORY OF INDIAN AND INDONESIAN ART, Ananda K. Coomaraswamy. Over 400 illustrations illuminate classic study of Indian art from earliest Harappa finds to early 20th century. Provides philosophical, religious and social insights. 304pp. 6⅜ × 9⅜. 25005-9 Pa. $11.95

THE GOLEM, Gustav Meyrink. Most famous supernatural novel in modern European literature, set in Ghetto of Old Prague around 1890. Compelling story of mystical experiences, strange transformations, profound terror. 13 black-and-white illustrations. 224pp. 5⅜ × 8½. (Available in U.S. only) 25025-3 Pa. $6.95

PICTORIAL ENCYCLOPEDIA OF HISTORIC ARCHITECTURAL PLANS, DETAILS AND ELEMENTS: With 1,880 Line Drawings of Arches, Domes, Doorways, Facades, Gables, Windows, etc., John Theodore Haneman. Sourcebook of inspiration for architects, designers, others. Bibliography. Captions. 141pp. 9 × 12. 24605-1 Pa. $8.95

BENCHLEY LOST AND FOUND, Robert Benchley. Finest humor from early 30s, about pet peeves, child psychologists, post office and others. Mostly unavailable elsewhere. 73 illustrations by Peter Arno and others. 183pp. 5⅜ × 8½. 22410-4 Pa. $4.95

ERTÉ GRAPHICS, Erté. Collection of striking color graphics: *Seasons, Alphabet, Numerals, Aces* and *Precious Stones*. 50 plates, including 4 on covers. 48pp. 9⅜× 12¼. 23580-7 Pa. $7.95

THE JOURNAL OF HENRY D. THOREAU, edited by Bradford Torrey, F. H. Allen. Complete reprinting of 14 volumes, 1837–61, over two million words; the sourcebooks for *Walden*, etc. Definitive. All original sketches, plus 75 photographs. 1,804pp. 8½ × 12¼. 20312-3, 20313-1 Cloth., Two-vol. set $130.00

CASTLES: Their Construction and History, Sidney Toy. Traces castle development from ancient roots. Nearly 200 photographs and drawings illustrate moats, keeps, baileys, many other features. Caernarvon, Dover Castles, Hadrian's Wall, Tower of London, dozens more. 256pp. 5⅜ × 8¼. 24898-4 Pa. $7.95

AMERICAN CLIPPER SHIPS: 1833–1858, Octavius T. Howe & Frederick C. Matthews. Fully-illustrated, encyclopedic review of 352 clipper ships from the period of America's greatest maritime supremacy. Introduction. 109 halftones. 5 black-and-white line illustrations. Index. Total of 928pp. 5⅜ × 8½.
25115-2, 25116-0 Pa., Two-vol. set $17.90

TOWARDS A NEW ARCHITECTURE, Le Corbusier. Pioneering manifesto by great architect, near legendary founder of "International School." Technical and aesthetic theories, views on industry, economics, relation of form to function, "mass-production spirit," much more. Profusely illustrated. Unabridged translation of 13th French edition. Introduction by Frederick Etchells. 320pp. 6⅛ × 9¼. (Available in U.S. only)
25023-7 Pa. $8.95

THE BOOK OF KELLS, edited by Blanche Cirker. Inexpensive collection of 32 full-color, full-page plates from the greatest illuminated manuscript of the Middle Ages, painstakingly reproduced from rare facsimile edition. Publisher's Note. Captions. 32pp. 9⅜ × 12¼. (Available in U.S. only)
24345-1 Pa. $5.95

BEST SCIENCE FICTION STORIES OF H. G. WELLS, H. G. Wells. Full novel *The Invisible Man*, plus 17 short stories: "The Crystal Egg," "Aepyornis Island," "The Strange Orchid," etc. 303pp. 5⅜ × 8½. (Available in U.S. only)
21531-8 Pa. $6.95

AMERICAN SAILING SHIPS: Their Plans and History, Charles G. Davis. Photos, construction details of schooners, frigates, clippers, other sailcraft of 18th to early 20th centuries—plus entertaining discourse on design, rigging, nautical lore, much more. 137 black-and-white illustrations. 240pp. 6⅛ × 9¼.
24658-2 Pa. $6.95

ENTERTAINING MATHEMATICAL PUZZLES, Martin Gardner. Selection of author's favorite conundrums involving arithmetic, money, speed, etc., with lively commentary. Complete solutions. 112pp. 5⅜ × 8½.
25211-6 Pa. $3.50

THE WILL TO BELIEVE, HUMAN IMMORTALITY, William James. Two books bound together. Effect of irrational on logical, and arguments for human immortality. 402pp. 5⅜ × 8½.
20291-7 Pa. $8.95

THE HAUNTED MONASTERY and THE CHINESE MAZE MURDERS, Robert Van Gulik. 2 full novels by Van Gulik continue adventures of Judge Dee and his companions. An evil Taoist monastery, seemingly supernatural events; overgrown topiary maze that hides strange crimes. Set in 7th-century China. 27 illustrations. 328pp. 5⅜ × 8½.
23502-5 Pa. $6.95

CELEBRATED CASES OF JUDGE DEE (DEE GOONG AN), translated by Robert Van Gulik. Authentic 18th-century Chinese detective novel; Dee and associates solve three interlocked cases. Led to Van Gulik's own stories with same characters. Extensive introduction. 9 illustrations. 237pp. 5⅜ × 8½.
23337-5 Pa. $5.95

Prices subject to change without notice.

Available at your book dealer or write for free catalog to Dept. GI, Dover Publications, Inc., 31 East 2nd St., Mineola, N.Y. 11501. Dover publishes more than 175 books each year on science, elementary and advanced mathematics, biology, music, art, literary history, social sciences and other areas.